THE RAT TRAP

by

Paddy O'Donovan

*This Rat Trap is dedicated to my brother
Christopher who tragically died in Ireland in
mysterious circumstances in 1963.*

*It would have been impossible to finish this
book without the encouragement and support
from my wonderful wife Marguerite - plus all
the many hours she spent editing the text - and
she disclaims any mistakes!*

*And many thanks to my old friend Roger,
who read several drafts of The Rat Trap, and
made very useful suggestions contributing
with wise and valuable insight*

CONTENTS

The Rat Trap

Dedication

Chapter 1   1

Chapter 2   11

Chapter 3   26

Chapter 4   44

Chapter 5   47

Chapter 6   52

Chapter 7   64

Chapter 8   70

Chapter 9   77

Chapter 10   88

Chapter 11   119

Chapter 12   136

Chapter 13   146

Chapter 14	161
Chapter 15	166
Chapter 16	175
Chapter 17	186
Chapter 18	198
Chapter 19	220
Chapter 20	229
Chapter 21	233
Chapter 22	255
Chapter 23	263
Chapter 24	274
Chapter 25	287
Chapter 26	301
Chapter 27	304
Chapter 28	320
Chapter 29	335
Chapter 30	338
Chapter 31	349
Chapter 32	370
Chapter 33	385
Chapter 34	403
Chapter 35	418
Chapter 36	434
Chapter 37	445

Chapter 38	457
Chapter 39	461
Chapter 40	468
Chapter 41	477
Chapter 42	481
Chapter 43	488
Chapter 44	494
Chapter 45	506
Epilogue	521
Author's notes	524

Preface

The people of England, Wales, Scotland and Ireland have a violent and bloody history. For thousands of years, when not savaging themselves, they suffered overwhelming invasions by foreign forces. First the Celts, then the Romans, the Saxons, the Vikings and finally the Normans. With the Normans came Christianity, which in itself, was a form of invasion, inflicting rigid rules of obedience and eternal damnation for those who shunned its doctrines.

This story, set in Ireland in 1962, is about another invasion, one that if successful would spark a third World war. Using Ireland as its springboard, the aggressor was planning for World domination.

Whilst 'The Rat Trap' is a work of fiction, it is interlaced with numerous facts and happenings at the time. Many of the characters were real people, for example, Peter Fleming, the boffin brother of James Bond's creator Ian Fleming; Sir Richard White, head of the British Secret Intelligence Service MI6; ex-Nazi SS *Obersturmbannführer* Otto Skorzeny, one of Hitler's most trusted commanders; Major General Eric Dorman-Smith, an Irishman, who was the tactical genius behind Rommel's defeat at El

Alamain; and the then president of the Republic of Ireland, Éamon de Valera.

The Irish Republican Army, the IRA, were continuing to wage their war against the partition of Ireland. They vowed not to rest until their country was once again united.

Reichsmarschall Hermann Göring, when asked at the Nuremberg war crimes trials how the Germans had accepted Nazism, he replied: "It was very easy. It has to do with human nature. The only thing we needed to turn people into slaves was fear. Any regime can do the same. Frighten and scare their public and it can make them do anything..."

CHAPTER 1

Donal McKeever's life was pigs. His family had been rearing the same cross breed of pigs on the same farm on the outskirts of Strabane since the late 18th century. He and his wife Una loved the peace and tranquillity of their relatively quiet life. Idyllic, they thought. Their two young sons hadn't been interested in carrying on the family business and had left as soon as they could to seek their fortunes in America. Una was glad because she had high hopes for them. But Donal was sure that pig breeding was in their blood and one day, for sure, at least one of them would be back to carry on the business.

In 1939, Donal himself, like most of the other Strabane lads at the time, had lied about his age and at 16 left to join the Army. He'd been one of the lucky ones to get out of Dunkirk alive, something he never talked about. He'd travelled courtesy of His Majesty's Government and had seen enough of the world, bloodshed and fighting to last a lifetime. The call of the pigs had brought him back. Now, at the age of fifty and fit as a fiddle, retirement couldn't be further from his mind. He and Una looked forward to the many years ahead.

The farm was a stone's throw from the border with Eire just up the Lifford road across the River Foyle. Traditionally, the family herd had always been a cross between the English Tamworth and the almost extinct Irish Greyhound pig, which gave them big bodies and long legs. He was proud of his heritage and that of his lovely 'chorus girls' as he called them.

He was an early riser. Every morning at 6.30 am he'd be up and out to serve his 'girls' their breakfast.   The routine would be like every other day. But this day, Tuesday, February 20th 1962, was a day Donal would remember for the rest of his days. The weather was dry but *baltic* with a fiery dawn made even more colourful by a thick crystal layer of frost. There was snow high on the Sperrin hills, which often heralded a covering later in the day.

He had on his overalls and gumboots, over which he wore his old army moth-eaten greatcoat. Each year Una nagged him to get a new one, but he'd had it so long he felt it had become part of him. He knew each frayed hole.

Its distinctive smell of pigs was like scent to his nostrils and its deep pockets like desk drawers. His left pocket was for paperwork, full of crumpled bits of paper, delivery notes, invoices, and the like. At least, he knew where everything was. His right pocket was big enough for a small bottle of 'medicinal' whiskey and his equally worn old meerschaum pipe, that once belonged to his grandfather, plus a leathery pouch of shag tobacco.

Picking up his portable radio, he stepped out into the bracing morning air and made his way across the farmyard to his large corrugated iron barn. It was the only barn on the farm and so had to house everything he needed. At one end it had a pile of straw bales for bedding, three pens for the mothers and their newly born piglets, and a small enclosed area where he kept medicines, tools, and his gun. At the other end, he kept his Massey Ferguson tractor, trailer, tools, and the locally collected pig swill and cereal feed. As usual, he put the radio on a shelf, tuned to BBC Radio Ulster, and listened to the farming news whilst he mixed the swill with equal parts of cereal in a giant heated vat. The smell again was an acquired taste, but he loved it.

Later in the day, he'd be taking his tractor and

trailer round to the local restaurants and pubs to collect more of their customers' leftovers – Indian, Chinese, his pigs weren't fussy, they'd eat anything. He kept the donors sweet with the occasional fresh pork shoulder or leg joint after he'd taken his girls to Derry's slaughter-house. The thought of the slaughterhouse made him a touch depressed – he'd be off there shortly with the next contingent of young maidens.

Headline news on the radio – 'USA astronaut John Glenn blasted off into space'.

Jesus! he thought, that's nothing more than a bloody great fairground ride. Typical ego chasing American shite again. You'd think their President would have something better to do with all his money.

There had been a disturbance in Enniskillen, County Fermanagh. A couple of young soldiers from Donal's old regiment, The Royal Inniskill-ing Fusiliers, 'The Skins', had been out drinking in the Blakes of the Hollow pub in Church Street and, upon leaving, a gang of local louts, out of their heads on the booze, had targeted them. It was started by the drunks shouting 'Eh ya buffties, we'll beat the feckin bag outta ye! But they had chosen the wrong target to insult. No

self-respecting 'Skin', tolerated being called
a queer. Fusilier Donovan was regimental
middleweight champion and the other just
returned from a training course with No.2 Parachute Regiment in Aldershot.

The three louts ended up in the Enniskillen
County Hospital at Breandrum. The Skins
had been exonerated by witnesses who saw
the whole incident, but they knew they would
still have to account to their Commanding
Officer and his shillelagh.

Serves them feckin yobs right, Donal shouted at
the radio. But that's not news – it happens every
feckin Friday payday night. Mix squaddies with
local lads and there's always a shindig.

The rest of the news was the same daily dreary
drivel. Full of rumour, opinion and expect-
ation... 'the IRA was thinking of giving up its
cross-border guerrilla attacks'. And about time
too, he said to himself. Let's all get on with
some peaceful living for a change.

When the feed was ready, he tipped the first of
many loads into his barrow. Finally, he took
the pouch of tobacco from his pocket, filled
his pipe and lit it. It was all part of his daily

routine to screen the strong fresh aroma of the
pens. Then, feeling at peace with the World, he
wheeled the steaming barrow out of the barn
and along the cobbled path to the first of the
pigsties.

The sties were divided into three groups. The
first group he called the 'Monastery', where
he kept his big 'fellers', the boars; the second
he named the 'Nunnery', where he kept his
pregnant sows; the third, he called the 'Bank',
his piggy bank, where he kept his 'Finish Hogs',
the pigs ready for the one-way trip to Derry's
abattoir. They represented his next source of
income. He often chuckled about the similarity
between pigs and bankers.

As he drew near to the five 'Bank' pens, he could
hear excited grunts and chomping. There were
5 pigs per pen and, unusually, all 25 were wide
awake and thrashing around. T'is the cold air
that must be making them wanting the hot
feed, he thought.

"You're up early this morning, girls," he shouted
above the din. Donal always talked to them as
if they were people. Now their boys had left
home, they were his family. And like the boys,
they too would soon be leaving for what he

liked to call their graduation.

"Who's been tickling your tits this fine mornin then gals," he joked. He had never heard them so excited. The noise was deafening. It sounded as if they were having a giant orgy, but there were no boars in with them and they were too young for sex games anyway.

"What's all the fuss then" he yelled over the squealing, squelching, and excited grunting.

He opened the gate to the first pen and used his barrow to force a way through to the two big feed troughs. Then he saw the reason for the commotion. They were all fighting over chunks of what looked like raw meat, some still on the bone. "What the feck," he exclaimed. "Some fecker's been feeding you lot already. Them tinker shites getting rid of rustling evidence, I'll be bound."

Then to his utter horror, he saw one of the hogs was chomping on what looked like the hand end of a human forearm – then a round football like object that could have been a head. Shaken to the core, he dropped the barrow and struggled to keep his balance. His pipe fell from his mouth, lost in the mire. He felt as though he was going to black-out. He staggered; grabbed

the side of the pen for support; it was all he
could do to stop himself from falling into the
thrashing bodies, knowing that if he did, he'd
quickly become part of their gory meal.

He shut his eyes, hoping it was some terrible
nightmare. But when he opened them and
looked again, it wasn't. It really was part of an
arm but hardly recognisable. The fingers of the
hand had already been chewed away, but it was
an arm for sure. And as his frantic eyes scanned
the floor of the pen, he could see other chunks
of human flesh too. What looked like a foot;
more half-eaten arms and leg parts. Other bits
of bone and offal were scattered amongst the
muck. Now he could see one wide open clear
blue eye in what he'd thought was a football. It
was looking up at him from near the edge of the
trough.

"Jesus holy feckin Mary," he shrieked. He didn't
bother looking in any of the other pens from
which came similar nightmarish noises. He
lurched through to the gate, retching violently
and slamming it behind him. The simple routine of his life was shattered. The sounds of
crunching, munching, and grunting echoed
in his ears. For some moments the shock and
trauma paralysed him. Regaining some com-

posure, he staggered as fast as he could back to the farmhouse and burst into the kitchen. Una, his wife was up, singing away and cooking his daily fry-up breakfast. "You're early mi dear," she said in her usual bright way.

He didn't even look at her. Without a word, he dashed across the kitchen, grabbed the phone and dialed '999'.
The phone rang twice before being answered by a calm well trained operator.

"Fire, police, or ambulance."

"Give me the feckin lot and fast." he gasped. "Somebody's been feeding bits of body to my pigs and if someone doesn't get here feckin quick, they'll have eaten the feckin lot." He collapsed into a chair, just able to give the call handler some more of the gory details and his name and address. He didn't even put the phone down. It hung loosely by his side as he put his head in his hands trying to come to terms with the horror of what he'd seen.

His wife Una saw the shock on his sheet white face. And hearing him tell the police the dreadful details of what he'd discovered, fell in a dead faint on the kitchen floor. The frying pan she held, fell from her hand splattering his bacon and eggs all over her pristine red-tiled floor.

Life would never be the same for the McKeevers.

CHAPTER 2

Two squad cars from the Strabane's Royal Ulster Constabulary station, flashing lights and blaring their sirens, they roared up to the McKeever's farm, just under fifteen minutes after the pig farmer's frantic call. A detective chief inspector, a police sergeant, and six constables. As a long-serving RUC officer of 30 years, 55 year old DCI Bryne Nolan, had dealt with many horrific border murders and shootings. Donal McKeever, still suffering from shock, pointed him to the pig pens, and briefly repeated what he'd said on the phone. "It's a feckin bloodbath up there. Bits of bodies all over the place."

Nolan looked grim. "First things first Mr McKeever, we'll be taking a look at the crime scene to get some idea of what we have here." He called over to his Sergeant and together they walked quickly up the path to the first sty followed by the distraught farmer.

Seeing the bloody carnage for himself, he quickly realised the enormity of the situation.

They were not just dealing with a simple murder or IRA execution. It was as McKeever had said, a massacre, a nightmare and one he, Nolan, would never forget. He told his sergeant to secure the whole area. Then running over to his car, he radioed in to the duty officer at the station. He told him he urgently needed to speak to Danny Doyle, the station chief. Minutes passed then "Doyle."

"Danny, Bryne Nolan here." trying hard to remain calm, he quickly explained the situation, telling him that the incident at McKeever's farm had turned out to be a bloody massacre, a multiple killing, and probably the work of the IRA. "I need more men here Danny boyo, at least half a dozen, if you can round them up - and get our Jayne Flyn to hot foot it down here, her pathology skills are going to be crucial."

"Leave it with me Bryne. Do you want me to alert the major incident team at RUC HQ in Belfast?"

"Good idea Danny, yes please. If they want more details, they can call me on the car radio set." Bryne felt a touch of relief knowing that the pathologist and more men would be on their way. He also knew that as it was a possible terrorist incident, RUC HQ would notify MI6 in London as a matter of course.

Jayne Flyn arrived less than half an hour later, in her Messerschmitt bubble car, still looking half asleep. She had only been in the job of Strabane's pathologist for two months, and at 27, was the youngest pathologist in the whole of Northern Ireland. She smiled broadly as she went over to the DCI. "Morning Bryne, what's so important that you're disturbing my beauty sleep?"

The grim and strained look on DCI's face soon wiped her smile away. He could hardly find the words to tell her why she had been called out. "Agh Jayne my lovely - I'd like to be saying it's a good morning, but for sure it's not - it's a diobolical nightmare we have here. And I know you're qualified and all that , but a young lady like yorself shouldn't have to be seeing such an atrocity. If you like, I'll call David Rork at Altnagelvin Hospital and ask him to come over and you can go back to yor bed"

Jayne wasn't going to have that. Young and not so experienced I may be, she thought, but I'll be damned if I'm going to back off. "Don't you worry Bryne, I may be young, but I've already had my share of brutal and bloody murders, so lead on."

"I doubt you've seen anything like this young lady, so you'd better prepare yourself." Bryn took her arm. "Come and have a look for yourself over in yon pen."

He walked her over to the first pigsty. As they got closer, the excited grunts and squeals grew deafening. She'd told the DCI, she was used to dealing with blood and guts, but when she saw for herself what the pigs were still eating, her professional cool abandoned her. She gagged, frozen to the spot at the sight of the carnage and almost passed out. Bryne Nolan caught her as her body sagged.

She recovered quickly and tho' deeply shaken, went around to the other pens with the arm of the DCI providing welcome support. The boars and pregnant sows appeared not to have been involved. They were, however, restless wondering what all the noise was about, joining in the cacophony in anticipation of what they too might be having for breakfast. Jayne asked the DCI to call the local vet and have them checked out anyway to make sure they weren't involved. In the meantime, she said they had to move fast and get the squealers out of their pens. "Before anything else, we have to stop them munching the evidence," she added.

"Say no more, I'm on the job." Bryne leapt into action. "I'll get McKeever and see how me and the boys can move them into some holding area," with that, he went off in search of the farmer.

Still stunned by the situation, Jayne went back and just stood looking over into the first of the hog pens. This is way beyond my capabilities, she thought, it's a war zone. It's one for State Pathology in Belfast. She turned her back on the grizzly scene and walked up the path to the wide-open kitchen door of the farmhouse. Una was sitting at the table, her eyes wide and her mouth sagging like a zombie. Jayne asked her where the phone was. Una's facial expression didn't change. Unable to speak, she just pointed over to the far side of the room, where it sat on a dresser, the handset still hanging loose off the base where Donal had left it.

Jayne knew the State Pathology team at Forster Green Hospital in Belfast. She'd trained there. She picked up the handset, cleared the line, and asked the operator to connect her. It rang for some time before being answered by a weary somewhat haughty receptionist, "Mortuary."

"Professor Crawford please"

"I'm sorry, but the Professor is engaged with a client, please ring back later."

"Now look here Alice, don't give me that blather, it's Jayne Flynn here. I don't give a shite what he's doing or who he's with. Get him to the damn 'phone." She knew Alice from her time at Forster Green and remembered what a surly old bitch she was. "I have a feckin disaster here in Strabane. Tell the Professor we've got a mass murder on our hands."

Alice huffed but otherwise didn't respond to Jayne. All Jayne heard were clicks on the line as Alice was putting her through. She waited. The stress of the situation mounted and her emotions started to crack. Five minutes and many clicks later, the Professor came on the line.

"Jayne"? he said, obviously put out by being interrupted in the middle of a cadaver. "What's all the panic then?"

"Oh Archie." Her voice straining as she tried to keep her composure. "There's a catastrophe here in Strabane. A terrible massacre. I don't know how many bodies. They're all in pieces -

being eaten by pigs."

"Holy Mother," the Professor gasped, his tone completely changing. Jayne now had his full attention. Difficult to find the words, she outlined the situation as best she could.

Archie Crawford was the chief pathologist in Northern Ireland. At 53, he was already an acknowledged expert in his field. His career spanned working in war zones, famines and disaster areas. A typical professor to look at, his long unkempt white hair; a goatee beard masking his fiery character; and a touch overweight showing he enjoyed his food.

When Jayne had finished telling him the gory details, there was silence. Archie was absorbing the full impact of the situation, considering then deciding what was needed . She thought the line had gone dead - but then he spoke. "Look Jayne, you're about three hours away. Hang on as best you can, I'll be on my way as soon as I've put a team together. From what you've said, we'll need Jack Donovan's forensic skills too. Leave it with me Jayne me darlin."

"Now," he continued, slotting together a mental plan of action, "before we get to you, I want you

to tell the RUC to shoot all the pigs involved.
Then, if you can face it, you need to remove all
their stomachs as quickly as you can before the
remains inside become unidentifiable mush.
Oh, and it'll help a lot if you can make sure we
know which pen each came from. That'll make
it much easier to reassemble body parts."

"We'll want to bring everything back here. A
couple of ambulances should be enough, plus
a truck for the pig guts. Just keep your cool,
Jayne, and we'll be with you as soon as we possibly can. See you later, slan leat."

He put the phone down, visibly shaken by
the conversation with Jayne. Taking a few
moments to collect his thoughts, he called his
secretary into his office. Quickly, he reeled
off a list of instructions. 'I want our forensic
pathologist, Jack Donovan, and four mortuary
assistants in here as quickly as they can make
it. Tell them all we have a national emergency.
Call the transport department and tell them we
need two ambulances and a truck urgently. Tell
Jack to make sure we have plenty of body part
bags and surgical instruments.   Oh - and the
lady I was working on will have to wait. Get one
of the lads to put the dear woman back in the
filing cabinet. We need to be ready to move out
within the hour"

Back at the Strabane farm, Jayne just sat with
the 'phone in her hand, still in a state of near
shock, but relieved that Archie and his team
were going to be on their way. She knew that
for the sake of the victims and Archie's team,
she had to go out again into the horrific murder
scene and pass on Archie Crawford's instructions to the DCI.

As she came out of the farmhouse, she saw
that the police were just about to start clearing
the first of the five pigsties.   "Wait!" she yelled.
"Will you just hang on a jiffy." They all stopped
and stared at her as she ran down the path
towards them. Catching her breath, she told
DCI Nolan that there was a full forensic team
on their way from Belfast. She explained that
it was important to be able to identify which
pen each pig came from. And, as far as possible
could his men be careful not to contaminate the
crime scene as they emptied the pens.
"Ah, you're havin' a laff Jayne," he said, "we'll
do our best, but getting the pigs out with the
sleet lashing down as it is will scupper most of
the forensics anyway." He turned to his men, all
looking pale and drawn. "Right, lads, spruce up!
You heard the lady. We've only got one holding
area in the barn, so we're going to have to mark

each pig to show which sty they came from."

Probably, he thought, the simplest way would be to paint a sty number on them. He asked his sergeant to be in charge of the marking process. 'Quinn, will you get one of your men to go and see if McKeever has a pot of paint and a brush somewhere. If he hasn't, they can whiz down to McNamee's hardware store in town, they've got plenty.

Quinn did as instructed and Nolan told the rest of his team to take a smoke break. As an after-thought, he told his youngest 'goffer' constable, Thomas, to go and see if Mrs. McKeever could rustle up some tea.

When Thomas entered the kitchen, Una was slowly coming out of her stupor. She was pleased to have something to do to take her mind off the unfolding tragedy. She had an old urn she'd planned to use on her stall at the Strabane and District Women's Institute fete. She filled it and poured in two whole packets of Ty-phoo. As the tea brewed, she collected as many cups as she could find. She'd baked four large fruit cakes for the stall, so she gave Thomas two of them too. They took the loaded tray and the urn out to the waiting men.

Whilst they drank their tea and wolfed the

cake, the DCI explained his plan of action. "We're going to empty the pigsties one at a time and run the pigs into McKeever's barn using some of that temporary fencing over there as channeling. Forensics are wanting to find out who or what they've been eatin'. So, it's a tragedy for the porkies, but we are going to have to shoot them all. I've called O'Malley, the vet, and he's bringing his gun to carry out the killing, so at least we don't have that to do."

"Once they're dead," DCI Nolan continued, "they're going to be gutted and their stomachs removed. Dr Flyn and O'Malley are going to be doing that," he said, nodding over to Jayne. "Then, when our reinforcements arrive, we'll get them to take the poor buggers to the far end of the field and start a feckin' great BBQ with the bodies. Over to you Quinn."

"Right fellers, you heard the boss." The sergeant stepped in. "Thomas, Rory, and Blair, you drive the pigs from each of the sties into the barn one at a time – it's going to take some maneuvering and you'll probably need a couple of pitchforks to goad them. I'm sure Mr. McKeever will have 'em somewhere. And remember, they've got a taste for us humans, so make sure they don't bite your arses. You other chaps, come with me. We're going to search the sties once they're empty for what's left of the bodies and bin bag the bits.

O'Malley the vet arrived and together they made a run from the first sty to the barn as best they could, using old fencing and whatever else they could find. One at a time, each pig was driven down the run toward the barn, only pausing for Rory to paint the sty number on its side . Squealing with fear and dread, the pigs seemed to sense their imminent execution,

When Donal McKeever was told what was happening to his ready for market hogs, it only added to his trauma and rage. He was told he would get full compensation, but they were his beloved girls, bred by McKeevers over generations. "Who're the fecking gobshites who've done this? It's not just me livelihood in peril – them pigs are as dear to me as mo páistí - me own children, " he railed.

Jayne Flyn tried to console him. She told him that as far as she could see, only his market hogs were affected and once she and the local vet had finished the gruesome job, she would get the vet to check out the others. McKeever went back to the farmhouse, continuing to turn the air a deep shade of blue with his frustration and anger – he was apoplectic.

Time was of the essence. As each pig was killed, Jayne, helped by the vet, cut open its carcass removing the stomach with the oesophagus.

The extra RUC support arrived. Bryne immediately got them onto the task of moving the dead pigs and starting the funeral pyre. They commandeered Donal McKeever's tractor and trailer to move the bodies to the far end of his field. Soon a pork fat fire raged into the lunchtime gloom of the wintery scene.

Four hours later, just as it had started to snow in earnest, the convoy from the State Pathology Department arrived. Catching sight of Jayne, covered in blood and guts, standing just outside the barn, Archie Crawford stepped out of the lead vehicle and ran over to her.

"Christ almighty, Jayne, it looks like the Battle of the Boyne!" Despite her state, he threw his arms around her. He could feel the stress and exhaustion in her body. "Jesus wept, nobody should be asked to carry out the job you've done Jayne, it's hell on earth."

She soon recovered her composure and showed him the bags of body parts and pig guts, ready to load into the ambulances.

"You've done a beezer of a job here Jayne, but time to back off. You're looking shagged. My chaps can load all the bags into the ambulances. I'm going to go and comb the pens with Jack for evidence and any remains the police may have missed." With that, he allocated members of his team to their tasks.

They worked nonstop through the evening and through the night until the afternoon of the next day. Finally, they reached the point where they all felt the crime scene had nothing more to throw up. As dusk was beginning to fall, the ambulances loaded with their fetid cargo and exhausted personnel, set off for the mortuary in Belfast.

In the furthest field, the fire continued to burn, reaching high into the night sky, lighting up a now blood-smeared snow scene. In and around the farm, the exhausted RUC officers were slowly and methodically cleaning up the crime scene.

Wracked by sheer anger and frustration, Donal McKeever sat with his wife watching out of their kitchen window. "God help mw, if I ever get my hands on them arseshites who did this," he burst out, "I'll be making fecking crackling of them."

CHAPTER 3

Snow slowed the convoy's progress on the journey along the A6 back to Forster Green Hospital. They arrived at 10.50 pm, tired and exhausted. They'd stopped just past the town of Toome on the side of Lough Neagh at the Moneynick café and service station for a pee break and hot drink. Whilst everyone made themselves comfortable, the Professor had used the café's telephone to ring RUC Headquarters and update them on their progress.

He'd spoken to the duty superintendent, who told him that MI6 were sending someone over from London just in case there was any possible IRA connection. The Duty Officer said that he and some of his men would be getting down to meet the convoy at the mortuary. Archie then made another call to the duty pathologist at the Forster Green mortuary to ask him to put out a call for support from The Royal Victoria and other surrounding hospitals for as many pathologists, doctors, and technicians as they could muster. There was a mammoth task ahead.

Now back, and feeling more secure on home ground in his Belfast Mortuary, Archie surveyed the scene. They'd offloaded all the bags from the vehicles and by midnight, each of the four autopsy tables was spread with the bags of human remains. Behind them, bags of pigs' entrails stood in a line leading out into the corridor. The stench was far worse than any other autopsy he had ever known.

The RUC squad car arrived with two constables, a sergeant, and the duty superintendent. The latter, DS Mitchel, left the others in the car and made his way into the building. He stalled in the doorway as the scene in front of him and the fetor hit him. He caught the sleeve of the nearest person and asked for Professor Crawford.

Still shaken up, he went over to Archie and introduced himself. "DS Mitchel sir." He looked around the room. "Dear God, I must say, I've never come across anything so horrific in all my years in the Force."

Archie had to agree. He too was daunted by the mass autopsy ahead of him and his team of volunteers. Explaining to the superintendent how he was going to proceed, he told him he expected to have some results to give him later in the day.

"Well, once you can tell us what we have here," the DS said, "we'll liaise with Strabane and launch a coordinated investigation – I don't envy you your task here."

"Thank you, Superintendent, we all have our jobs to do. If you and your chaps want to watch, be my guest." The DS shook his head and said that he and his men would rather keep out of his way and wait in their car outside. Archie couldn't help but smile to himself. Being a pathologist was not everyone's cup of tea. He turned to the assembled team.

"Look lads and lassies, it's been a monster of a task you've done already, but it's nothing compared to what we have ahead of us. Stick your hand up if you want to call it a day and git off home, I won't be thinking any the worse of you."

"I've called for more helping hands from the Royal and the other hospitals – and I heard that London is going to be sending some security bods over." But nobody raised a hand; they all knew the enormity of the task facing them and there were murmurs of support, all wanting to see the work through and finish what they'd started.

As he was speaking, more people came into the room through the door, passing the line of pigs' guts and loaded pathology tables. The support he'd requested from the surrounding hospitals was arriving.

"Come on in you all and join us," he motioned to the new arrivals, nodding to friends and a few of the familiar faces alike. "You can see the size of the task we're facing."

Then, to his team, he continued. "It's been a shite of a time and y'all covered in blood and muck, enough to frighten the devil himself. So, away to the locker rooms, shower, and change into fresh overalls, it'll make y'all feel better. Then we can make a start."

When they had gone, the Professor went over to the volunteers. Several were senior consultants and even the Head of Pathology from The Royal had rallied to his call. After a few handshakes and greetings to those he knew, he addressed the group. "Thank you one and all for turning out in the middle of the night especially in such awful weather. You can see for yourselves the reason I called for your aid. When the others are back, I'll explain how I plan to tackle the job – but excuse me a mo' while I dash for a quick change myself." And Archie hurriedly left leaving the surprised and stunned newcomers to the silence of the morgue.

It was half-past midnight. Everyone was back in the room, all now in spotless gowns, hats, gloves, and masks. A babel of chatter between those who had been at Strabane and the new arrivals hushed as the Professor called for their attention.

"OK then. The plan is," he paused to make sure he had the full attention of everyone, "the plan is to put this pile of body parts back together in some semblance of their human forms. So, this is how we are going to spread the work. From what I've seen so far, it looks like we have four cadavers here. That's why the bags are spread across the four tables. We'll soon know if I'm right. If it looks as if there are more bodies, we'll just have to wheel in more gurneys." Archie paused again to let his words sink in. "For now, I want teams of four per table to work on their bags and try to reconstruct these poor people. It is a ginormous puzzle to solve; we need to find out what we have; confirm the number of bodies; identify them if we can; work out how they died and whatever else we can determine."

"I'm damn sure all the body parts were mixed up before the gobshites fed them to hogs, so when you find body parts that don't match up with anything on your table, put them on one of the three gurneys over there by the window. That's going to be the body part exchange. "Could you, George, be responsible for managing the exchange gurneys?" he said to his counterpart from the Royal hospital, who'd been the first to respond to his plea for help. "Your eagle eye for detail will be a great help in putting the pieces of flesh and bone with the right bodies"

"Happy to do that, Archie," replied The Royal's eminent pathologist. "I'll need an extra pair of hands if that's OK?"

Archie smiled his thanks. Then to everyone, he held up a full Tesco shopping bag that had been sitting on the desk in front of him. "I've always found sucking mints helps deal with the odours, so here's my personal store of extra strong peppermints for y'all. Help yourselves."

With the teams organised and roles agreed, they immediately set to work. Soon, they became completely engrossed in the challenge that lay ahead of them, mentally and physically anaesthetised to the awful stench that perme-

ated the room. Some five hours later, as the
sky outside was streaking shades of purple,
pink and red with the coming dawn, bodies
were beginning to materialise. Parts of heads,
chewed limbs, and torso bits.

The worst job was emptying the pigs' stomachs.
Archie took this on himself.   It was virtually
impossible to identify any human body parts
from the half-digested minced meat, but he
did find what seemed like two well chewed,
but seemingly identical rings, what looked like
pieces of a watch, bits of jewellery, and part of
an ivory crucifix.

By 9.00 am, exhausted and hardly able to keep
their eyes open, Archie called a halt to the proceedings. He'd arranged for fresh black coffee
and doughnuts to be brought in for everyone.
They had been able to piece together enough of
the butchered corpses to be certain that there
were indeed only four cadavers. Two females,
looking to be aged between twenty and forty;
and two males, one a teenager and the other a
more mature giant of a man. It was impossible
to match the rings with the bodies as fingers
generally had been eaten away. The males had
several tattoos. The giant one had two old gun-
shot wounds in the left shoulder and a scar on
one thigh. He could have been a soldier at some

time in the past. The two females had slim bodies and had probably once been attractive in life. There were indications that they may have been drug addicts and on the game.

There were also signs that they had all been tortured before being shot in the back of their heads. Typical IRA executions thought Archie. The bodies had then been butchered with some blunt axe-like tool.

"Well done everybody. There's nothing much more we can do until our Jack Donovan gets back with the results of his forensics at Strabane. I'll be getting Superintendent Mitchel back in to see what we've been able to assemble so far. It'll be enough for the police to bring in their facial reconstruction specialists.   So, let's just clear up as best we can and put these poor people to bed in the cold room for now."

He was about to dismiss his team when the unmistakable crunch of army boots could be heard coming down the corridor towards the autopsy room. Military Police, distinguished by their red berets, six in all, entered the room in battle denims and armed with Sterling submachine guns. They proceeded to stand guard at the three exits to the room. Following them into the room were two men in civilian dress.

"Professor Crawford?" one of them enquired looking around the room.

Archie, not phased by the appearance of the intruders burst out, "who the hell do you think you are bursting in here like you own the bloody place with your toy soldiers"?

The unwarranted intrusion plus exhaustion, physical and mental, sparked Archie's furious outburst. Without replying, the pair walked over to him, surrounded by the pigs' entrails he had been trawling. "You must be the Professor", one of the men said quietly. "Sorry to disturb the proceedings, old chap. My name's Cunningham,

Major Dick Cunningham. We're the team from London you should have been told to expect. And this is Captain David Slater. We're from Military Intelligence, MI6."

Archie had always had a dislike for anyone or anything to do with the army at the best of times. Such arrogant buggers he thought, they always brought extra trouble and this looked like it wasn't going to be any different. He stood and waved his arms to all the pathology workers in the room and told them to carry on packing up, whilst he dealt with the intruders.

"So, what's all this about then?" Archie asked
aggressively." You'd better have a good story
else you can just fuck off out of here with your
red hat brigade. This is my territory and I don't
like being invaded. I'll be having your identification and authority if you don't mind – you
could be bloody Genghis Khan for all I know."
He didn't usually swear, but the whole situation
was fraught and frenetic. He was getting to the
end of his tether.

The pathologists and other staff carried on
clearing up, but were distracted and kept glancing over to see what was going on between the
Professor and the two civilians.

Archie called over to Superintendent Mitchel,
who had followed the soldiers into the room
and was standing by the doorway to the corridor. "Can you be coming over here, Superintendent? I need you to confirm who these
freaks are?

Dick Cunningham knew that academics and
medical gurus had highly inflated egos and
were always protective towards their domains.
He also could see at a glance the fatigue and

incredibly stressful situation they faced, so he
didn't react to the Professor's hostile manner.

Looking apprehensive, the superintendent
joined them. The Major produced his MI6 ID
Card and quietly said "If you want to verify who
we are, be my guest, and ring the Secretary of
State for War, John Profumo. He'll be at home
having his breakfast." Major Cunningham
passed his card to DS Mitchel as did Captain
Slater. "I'll give you his telephone number if
you like. He's already been briefed on the Strabane situation and I know he would be more
than happy to confirm who we are – mind you,
you might lose a couple of promotion points for
disturbing his kippers."

DS Mitchel looked at both ID cards. "looks fine
to me sir, but it's the armed bunch of MPs you
have with you that confirms you are who you
say you are - I won't be bothering the Minister."

"Well Major Cunningham," growled Archie,
still fuming at the intrusion into his pathology
department. "You may be who you say you are,
but for now, just piss off out of here and let me
and my team get on with the cleaning up – you
are crowding our space and you can come back
when I'm good and ready to talk to you."

"I would piss off, as you say if I thought it didn't have anything to do with us," retorted the Major, in a calm and even voice. "But I'm afraid it does. We lost some of our key undercover agents, two men and two women about ten days ago and we have reason to believe that these corpses may be them."

The Professor and DS Mitchel were completely dumbstruck. They both turned and looked again at the fragmented bodies on the mortuary slabs. There was no question, these were those agents.

"So," continued the Major in the same unemotional voice, "we have already placed a D Notice on this whole sorry state of affairs. That means anyone, and I mean anyone, who is, has been or may be involved in the slightest possible way with this situation will be bound by the Official Secrets Act. They may not disclose anything whatsoever of what they may have seen or witnessed here or at the farm."

Dick Cunningham, ignoring Archie Crawford's smouldering hostility, carried on calmly. "These chaps with me are from Gough Barracks and are here purely for protection and to secure the site. We can't be too careful. It's not that we don't trust you or any of your people here, but this could be a very sensitive issue as far as UK security is concerned. If it turns out that these poor victims are our agents, it's a major disaster and will put our conflict against the IRA back by years."

The Professor was still confused and upset by the sudden unexpected change in direction of the situation. As was his way, he had had everything planned and executed in his usual efficient way. But not anymore.

"Well Cunningham, if you had come a few hours earlier you could have saved a whole lot of people from the horrors of Hades they've had to suffer making sense of this," he said, indicating the tables covered in the bloody human forms and other yet to be identified pieces of flesh and bones.

" We came as soon as we could. I think......"

"So, who's going to be telling them they've been wasting their fecking time" interrupted a fraught Archie.

"I'll do it," 'said the Major. "just introduce me."

The Professor shouted over the rising hum

of conversation around the room, calling for everyone's attention. As they quietened down, he spoke tersely, "There's been a change of plan. These Gentlemen," he couldn't help but stress the word with a sneer, "are from London and have a few words to say."

"Thank you, Professor." Then in a calm yet assertive voice Major Cunningham explained. "We are from the British Security Service, MI6. First of all, I want to thank all of you, who have been involved in this horrific work, both at Strabane and here. You've done an incredible job in reassembling the bodies of these poor victims. It must have been traumatic for you all, particularly those of you who have been working flat out both here and at the farm in Strabane. You all look thoroughly knackered." There was a murmur of assent from his audience.

Cunningham paused. Slowly, he looked around at the once pristine mortuary and dedicated medical professionals in front of him as if to emphasise his words. The scene was more like a slaughterhouse after a busy day, he thought. Then with a grim and serious tone to his voice, he continued. "You will all be aware of the IRA's campaign against the Province. Unfortunately, we believe this to be yet another example of their atrocious activities." Rumblings of voices broke out, causing the Major to raise his voice above the increasing din. "Please, ladies and gentlemen, let me finish." The hum died down. "We have reason to believe that the victims of this hideous killing may be MI6 undercover agents. For this reason, we are, as of now, going to take over the investigation and send you all back home to your beds for some well-earned rest."

"However," he went on, "I have to tell you that as UK undercover agents may be involved, this is a top-level security matter. Thus, the whole situation is being placed under Her Majesty's Official Secrets Act. That means you can say nothing, nothing whatsoever, about what has happened both here and at the McKeevers' farm to anyone outside this room. And that means even those closest to you – your husbands, wives, parents or children"

"On your way out, I would like each one of you to leave your name and address and sign a copy of the Act, which one of my men will have ready for you. And before you go, just to make it crystal clear, you should know that breaking the Official Secrets Act is a very serious offence and could result in your prosecution and probably a lengthy jail sentence." He paused again to let the impact of his words sink in. "Once again, thank you for your dedicated and hellish work."

Amidst an angry buzz of banter, the blood-spattered pathologists and technicians, physically exhausted and somewhat dazed by what they'd heard, slowly made their way out of the mortuary towards the locker rooms. As they passed through the doorway, an MP asked them for their personal details and to sign a copy of the Act. None would ever forget what they had witnessed.

When all the mortuary staff, volunteers and the RUC had departed, Major Cunningham, turned to Archie. "I want to thank you for being so understanding Professor. We'll take our agents with us and make sure they get a suitable burial. We've got a clean-up team waiting outside. When they've finished, there won't be a trace of tonight's happenings."

With that, he called over to an MP corporal near the main entrance and asked him to call in the cleaners. Within less than a minute, more soldiers entered the pathology department, this time dressed in khaki surgical gowns, tie-back cloth caps, masks, green latex gloves, and white wellington boots. They immediately started bagging up the body parts from the slabs and taking them out. Major Cunningham had already told them to load the bags into the

military Bedford 3-ton truck in which he and
Captain Slater had arrived. By the time they
had finished, the rear of the truck was packed to
capacity with the Strabane carnage.

"We'll get out of your hair shortly, but do you
have a telephone I might use." The Major asked.
The Professor's anger was now somewhat de-
flated. Whilst he still felt resentful at having
the situation wrested from his control, he realised that these men from London were only
doing their job. "I'll take you to my office, Major.
There's a direct dial line there and you can have
some privacy."

Dick Cunningham followed Archie to his office
and as he left and closed the door behind him,
Dick dialled one of the few numbers he knew
by heart. The home of MI6's Director of Intelligence, Sir Richard White, otherwise known
as 'C'. After several rings, the phone was answered. "Farnham 3068"

"Major Cunningham here, sir. It looks like
Alpha team has been neutralised. We've collected the evidence and the site here is being
sanitised."

"Say no more – nasty job. Well done Major," 'C'
said. "We'll debrief when you get back." As he
put down the phone, his wife poured him more

coffee. "Trouble at the office, dear?"

"No, nothing, just the usual personnel problem – spies aren't what they used to be." He continued reading The Times with his toast and lime marmalade "It looks like there could be trouble brewing in East Germany. They are introducing conscription into their army. We'll have to keep an eye on that." he mused.

CHAPTER 4

The IRA was quick to broadcast messages by telex to all the major newspapers around the World, claiming responsibility for the Strabane massacre. And they telephoned UK and pro-Irish American press in Boston and New York adding more lurid quotes to the story. They declared that the enemy, meaning the Loyalists and the British, had been dealt a major blow in their fight for a united Ireland, eliminating four of their traitorous undercover agents. They didn't give too much detail about the circum-stances but instead gave the location and tele-phone number of Donal McKeever, the farmer who discovered the bodies.

The BBC was the first to contact the McKeevers. The phone rang and rang, until eventually it was answered by a distraught voice. The reporter asked to speak to Mr. McKeever to verify the story. It was difficult to understand the fraught ramblings interspersed with ob-scenities that replied. However, the farmer affirmed that some Eejit low-life turds had been feeding human feckin flesh to his lovely ladies and now they were dead; murdered by RUC arseshites. Halfway through speaking to him, the line went dead. The security clampdown had been enforced. And before the UK could publish anything of significance, they too were silenced.

'D' notices had no effect outside the UK. South of the Irish border, the Strabane massacre was headline news. Radio Éireann was first to carry the story, then the Dublin Evening News. All giving coverage of the catastrophe. Telefis Eireann, Southern Ireland's television, carried the story too. They'd sent a team up to the border at Lifford Bridge and showed the funeral pyre of Donal McKeever's slaughtered pigs, still blazing across the River Foyle. Their news reporter, Charlie O'Rourke, had only been with the network for a few months. This was his first big story. The camera crew would be stopped if they tried to take their bulky television cameras into Northern Ireland, so he suggested he take a handheld 8mm cine film camera hidden in a shopping bag. He had no problem passing the border police. He walked over the bridge along the A38 past the crackling fire to the track that led down to the farm. There was no police cordon in place as yet and so he wandered through the farm gate. Lights were on in the farmhouse from which he could hear hysterical voices.

Probably the farmer, he thought, worth trying
to get an interview on his way out.

There was an RUC Land Rover parked outside a
large barn, but as far as he could see, no police
in sight. He paused to take the camera out of
the bag, switched it on, and filmed as he walked
the rest of the way down toward the barn. With
the camera to his eye, he continued to film
stealthily through the half-open barn door. It
was obvious what he was seeing. A site of pure
carnage, a scene from hell with a sickly stench
to match. Men in overalls soaked in blood and
excrement were busy with hoses, brooms and
shovels attempting to clean up the site. A pink
mist hung in the air and even after pressure
hosing, the walls and floor of the barn still shed
evidence for the camera. He thought he was
a hard man, but the dreadful scene combined
with the putrid odours of the recent slaughter
were too much. He turned away and threw up.

CHAPTER 5

Argentine's fascist President, Juan Perón, like his close friend Franco in Spain, had always been a supporter of Adolf Hitler. Throughout WW2, the Argentine Central Bank helped the Nazi regime launder money and gold seized from the banks of conquered countries to fund supplies for the regime's war machine.

When Hitler saw that defeat was inevitable, he decided to activate *Betriebsratlinien*, 'Operation Ratlines', a mass evacuation plan for dedicated Nazis from Germany and Austria. *Obersturmbannführer* Otto Skorzeny, one of the Fuhrer's closest and trusted officers, was put in charge and given enormous funds in gold and foreign currencies to ensure its success.

Skorzeny was a giant of a man, who proudly wore a vivid sabre duelling scar down one side of his face. It added to his formidable aura. His charismatic nature and leadership inspired his men and instilled fear in his enemies.

In the early 1930s in Vienna, teenager Skorzeny became an enthusiastic member of the Austrian Nazi party, and shortly before the outbreak of WW2, he enlisted in the German army. Soon afterwards, he was selected to join the elite SS commandos, the *Schutzstaffel*.

He distinguishing himself on the Eastern Front and after leading several daring raids, was made head of the German elite special forces reporting directly to the Fuhrer himself.

The Ratlines exodus was more like a tsunami, with more than 200,000 loyal officers and men estimated to have been liberated. Helping to facilitate its success, the Roman Catholic Church, a type of dictatorship in its own right, gave its full support to Ratlines. Pope Pius XII and his cardinals saw fascism as a God-given way to combat the growing threat of communism in many of the countries where their dominance was fading - South America, Italy, Spain, Portugal, the Philippines, and the Republic of Ireland. Monasteries, nunneries, and even the Vatican were used as staging points for fleeing Nazis, helping cover their tracks with false identity documentation.

Again, the Argentine regime gave their assistance. It provided ships to evacuate the thousands of Third Reich fugitives, men, women, and children from Spanish and Italian ports. Most went to South American countries, of which many already had large German communities – Brazil, Uruguay, Colombia, Venezuela, to name but a few.

The Allies and in particular the United States turned a blind eye. For them, the fewer Nazi minded fanatics in Germany the better. They also saw the threat of communism spreading like wildfire. By the start of the 1950s, the main Ratlines surge had been completed, but routes remained open for residual stragglers and un-repentant war criminals as they were released from prison.

The world believed Adolf Hitler died in his Berlin bunker. But it was a cleverly planned deception to fool his enemies. The truth was the Nazi leader escaped by submarine to one of the German clusters in Colombia. Three years later the deposed Fuhrer was smuggled to a safe residence on the outskirts of Buenos Aires, close to where other top Nazis were hiding. In Skorzeny's mind and those of many others of the conquered Third Reich, the war was not over. To a man, they still believed in the Nazi vision of a global fascist dictatorship. The Phoenix of fascism would rise again.

For Britain, the war had proved a final nail in the coffin of the British Empire. Countries that had been so long under its rule, were demanding their freedom. And with that freedom, the surviving Nazi hierarchy saw opportunity. Whilst the world condemned the much-publicised Nazi atrocities, there was secret admiration for the discipline and relentless efficiency of their military forces.

Having set up the machinery for the Ratlines exodus, Otto Skorzeny used it himself to travel around the globe, visiting countries with fascist dictatorships and those that were emerging from under the thumb of the British Empire. The purpose behind these prolonged visits was to build alliances by offering military training and support in return for harbouring Nazi criminals.

During and after the Spanish civil war, Spain had had a permanent cadre of Nazi military experts training its air, sea, and land forces. It was the first country Skorzeny visited to cement that relationship and advise Franco on the changing needs of Spain's internal and external security.

After Spain, Skorzeny, and his team of ex-Nazi intelligence officers went on to Egypt, where the same team worked closely with President Nasser and his generals. Their job was to advise on military matters and develop the interrogation expertise of their secret police, the dreaded Egyptian Mukhabarat.

In 1956, one of Skorzeny's intelligence sources in Britain discovered that the Prime Minister,

Anthony Eden, had sanctioned Britain's invasion of Egypt and ordered Dick White, in his then-new role as head of MI5, to organise the assassination of Nasser. In the end, the invasion was a military farce and the members of the MI5 death squad were arrested, tortured, and flogged, before a public hanging. The leader, however, John McGlashan, escaped the rope. After 3 months in solitary confinement, suffering constant torture, beatings, and starvation, he was returned to Britain, a wreck, as an example of what would await any other intrusion into the independent state of Egypt. Nasser owed his life to Skorzeny.

CHAPTER 6

Leaving a small cadre of SS 'consultants' in Egypt, Skorzeny moved to Argentina to take up the role of military adviser and security chief to Peron. However, the true purpose behind Skorzeny's time in Argentina was to work with the Fuhrer and his fellow henchmen on a plan to restore the Nazi regime in Europe and ultimately the world - to become the Fourth Reich. Skorzeny and Adolf Hitler, together with a chosen group of ex SS senior military leaders, spent the next two years developing their plan. The group included *Brigadeführer* Kurt Meyer, *General der Fallschirmtruppe* Herman Ramcke, and *Oberführer* Edgar Puaud. Meyer had been one of the Panzer commanders who led the lightning invasion of France in May 1940; Ramcke was a *Fallschirmjäger,* paratroop leader. His units captured Crete and took part in assaults in North Africa, Italy, the Soviet Union, and France; Puaud led the ruthless Charlemagne Waffen SS Brigade. He, like his men, was Vichy French.

The Paraguayan dictator Alfredo Stroessner,

who had already provided a safe haven for a
wolfpack of 12 U-boats and crews, also promised the unlimited use of his Puerto Sajonia
naval base in Asuncion. Brazil was officially
against supporting any Nazi uprising, yet
allowed many ex- SS soldiers take refuge in
its southern German-speaking region of Rio
Grande do Sul. The Fourth Reich planning
group now needed to identify possible bridge-
heads back into Europe. It was agreed that
Spain, whilst being so friendly to the cause,
was under microscopic surveillance by Britain,
France, and the United States of America. Any
large build-up of troops and armaments would
be quickly pounced on. However, Franco had
given safe haven to more then 3000 Third Reich
fugitives. And he'd personally pledged the future use of military bases plus the availability of
aircraft and naval vessels, if and when required.
Franco had not forgotten that his victory in the
Spanish Civil War was wholly due to the support of the Nazi military might.

The group discussed the possibility of another
pact with Russia. Stalin was long dead, but
the idea was soon discounted. Whilst Nikita
Khrushchev might be a more reasonable man to
deal with, no Russian would ever forgive Hitler
for trashing the Molotov–Ribbentrop peace pact
and launching the 1941 Barbarossa invasion

against them. And there weren't many other places friendly to Hitler and the Nazi party - their atrocities had seen to that. Even so, one stood out. The Republic of Ireland.

Eire had been neutral during WW2 and it had allowed hundreds of Ratlines refugees to seek sanctuary there. As far as the Nazi cabal was aware, the government was still anti-British and there was already an active guerrilla force, the IRA, fighting to liberate, as they saw it, the land still occupied by the British. It was agreed that Ireland would make a near-perfect place for rekindling the fire of the Nazi Reich. With the support of their allies in Spain and South America, Ireland could be taken.

An immediate call would be put out through the many networks of Nazi sympathisers across Latin America to recruit a force of ex-Waffen SS and Wehrmacht soldiers, refresh their fighting skills and prepare them as an invasion force. It would be led by *Brigadeführer* Kurt Meyer.

Peron was keen to be involved in the Nazi plans and, much against the wishes of his military commanders, offered seaborne transport to ferry SS troops from the Puerto Belgrano Naval base, South of Buenos Aires, to wherever they were required. He also promised to supply guns, ammunition, armour and transport. His offer was readily accepted.

It was decided that the conquest of the island of Ireland would be known as the 'Shamrock *Blitzkrieg*' and would be implemented in three phases.

Phase one: Skorzeny would establish an Irish headquarters, take command of ex-Nazi Waffen SS soldiers already infiltrated into Ireland via Ratlines, and ingratiate himself with the IRA. He would set up strategically placed military compounds along the border between the Republic of Ireland and Northern Ireland , staff them with his troops and using IRA contacts, source guns, munitions, equipment and transport for the next phase.

Phase two: Skorzeny would signal Meyer in Argentina to launch the main attacking force. It would take them about 7 days to reach Dublin Port at the mouth of the River Liffey. Meanwhile, Skorzeny's *Blitzkrieg* force together with IRA support would attack and take the airports in Belfast and Dublin, and TV and radio stations. They would roam the streets with their Spandau machine guns, ruthlessly exterminating any resistance. A special force would be sent to quickly eliminate the Irish Staff College and Army training base in the Curragh. And in parallel, he would signal Ramcke to launch his airborne forces from Spain.

Phase three: With the added strength of Ramcke's troops, they would attack and neutralise military bases North and South of the border. Then, when Meyer's forces arrived, they could seize control of all other major cities. If the Shamrock *Blitzkrieg* went to plan, victory would be achieved within 10 days.

Otto needed to find a base quickly. So, whilst still in Argentina, he'd telephoned ex-Nazi collaborator Albert Folens, a war crimes fugitive living in Dublin. Folens had a very unpleasant record and was still a wanted man by the Allies. However, he'd built a new life for himself in publishing. He had become the most successful school book publisher in Ireland. Hearing the Nazi Colonel brought back stark memories of his other life which he had long hoped were buried.

Over the phone, Otto wasn't going to tell Folens the reason why he wanted to move to Ireland, so he simply asked him to find a property with land within easy reach of Dublin. Folens was very reluctant to help. However, Otto had expected resistance from the Belgian and wasn't going to take 'no' for an answer. He pointed out to Folens that if it hadn't been for the Ratlines escape route, he would have been executed or at least still serving a life sentence for his wartime collaboration exploits.   He reminded him that when he, like all the other ex-Nazi escapees, was smuggled out of Germany, he was given ample funds to start a new life. In return, he pledged to be ready and willing to support the re-emergence of the Reich.

Nonetheless, Folens still tried to distance himself from his WW2 past. "Otto," he whined. "That was twenty years ago, the world has changed. I have a new life. I'm a respected Irish citizen now. History is history."

But Skorzeny knew Folens for the slimy rat he really was and was already prepared. His voice took on a smooth yet menacing tone. "We all heard about your success Albert. Himmler and your old friends send their congratulations and best wishes."

He heard the book publisher's nervous intake of breath at the mention of Heinrich Himmler, and continued. "It's good to know that our money has been put to good use, Albert." He paused, then with a more threatening tone creeping into his voice, he continued. "Do you think your new-found Irish friends, their government, and all your customers would still think of you as a pillar of their society when they see the delightful photographs I have here

of you in the company of Himmler and Eich-
mann? Remember Albert? Remember?"

"What photos?" Retorted Folens. "What are
you talking about Skorzeny?" His retort feigned
anger, but there was now a tinge of fear in his
voice.

"Well let me remind you, Albert." Skorzeny continued. "The pictures I have here were taken at
one of our prison camps, the one at Amersfoort
near Utrecht. In one picture you and Heinrich
are together. You are holding a gun to the head
of a prisoner. A kneeling British airman. His
uniform is torn, filthy, hardly recognisable.
You are grinning and you all look as if you are
enjoying yourselves. The contrast between you
and your panic-stricken victim is so edifying."

Over the phone, Otto heard Folens swearing to
himself. He continued. "Another of the pictures
shows you all standing over the same airman.
This time he is no more; just a blood-splattered
corpse at your feet - the gun is in your hand.
You are all laughing as if someone has cracked a
joke. Now, do you remember?"

Albert Folens knew he couldn't bluff anymore.
He knew he had no defence. "It was a long time
ago," he muttered sullenly.

Otto told him that having such pictures published in the Irish press would let the Irish people know the truth about the man behind the books used to educate their children. Folens knew it would kill his publishing business stone dead. He would be deported and so there was nothing he could do but acquiesce. In no time he had telexed Otto with a shortlist of suitable properties.

Later when Otto arrived in Ireland, he made Folens take him on a tour of the selected locations. A farm called Martinstown in County Kildare was by far the most suitable as a headquarters for Otto's plans. It was a farm in a secluded location away from main roads but was near the Irish military Staff College and main army training base in the Curragh, plus within easy reach of Dublin and its airport at Collinstown. Perfect thought Otto.

Otto Skorzeny was meticulous in his planning and recording. It wasn't just Folens he had planned to contact. He had a list of virtually every fugitive who had escaped using the Nazi escape routes and particularly, those sent to settle in Ireland. Like Folens, they had sworn that in return for their funded new lives, should they be called into action again, be it in ten, fifteen or even twenty years, they would be ready.

He set about resurrecting as many as he could find. He staffed his new headquarters with the most fanatical and dedicated ex-SS soldiers. Some already in Ireland, some he brought in from South America and Spain. Many had served with Otto before. He'd flown in his old second-in-command, *Sturmbannführer* Harald Mors. It was Mors who had led the crack team of *Fallschirmjäger* paratroopers and *Waffen-SS Kommandos* on the daring raid to rescue Mussolini from his mountain top prison in 1943.

Money being no object, Skorzeny and Mors worked together on the project to convert the once peaceful Martinstown estate into a Nazi headquarters. Using local labour, they oversaw the building of four enormous barns. And then once they had resurrected a core of their own men, they converted them into accommodation for troops and large secure storage warehouses. They equipped a repair workshop, built an underground firing range, and a fully equipped interrogation centre. It didn't take long for Otto to establish contact with the IRA. Their leaders were ecstatic. With his support and military expertise, their dream of a united Ireland would become a very real possibility. It was just like the old saying 'the enemy of my enemy is my friend'.

But for Otto, the IRA was a means to an end,

there to be used and exploited. When the time came, like Himmler's blood purge of the *Sturmabteilung* Brownshirts in 1934, they would be rounded up and exterminated. With their enthusiastic help, he and Mors set about establishing the planned military compounds along the border between the Irish Republic and Northern Ireland. They'd looked in remote and desolate areas for near-derelict farms. He had no difficulty in persuading the poverty-stricken owners to sell - he offered them more money for their properties than they'd ever dreamt of.

At the same time, he'd reminded Galway based German industrialist Günter Wagner, that it was Nazi money that had funded his building equipment manufacturing empire. It was now one of Ireland's largest companies. Payback time had arrived. Wagner's company supplied all the building materials, earthmoving, and welding equipment plus workers to customise and fortify each of the farms. The work aroused some interest with locals, but they were all used to mad foreigners wasting their money on harebrain schemes - only Otto and his men saw the whole picture.

By the end of 1961, Skorzeny had a chain of nine such remote military compounds from Buncrana in the North West to Riverstown near Dundalk on the East coast. Each was staffed by dedicated ex SS soldiers - *engineers, panzergren-adiers and kommandos*. To any casual observer, the compounds still looked like farms, but with refurbished buildings - not that many people wanted to visit the godforsaken places where they were located. Behind their renovated exteriors, the farms hid much. They had become efficient military compounds and because of their rural locations field training exercises went unobserved.

Another key part of the 'Shamrock *Blitzkrieg's* first phase was the building of a secret airstrip. Corkan Island in the middle of the River Foyle was some four miles north of Strabane in Donegal. Otto had bought the whole Island for a song. It was around 110 acres, consisting of low-lying pasture land - perfect for the airstrip. He approached an ex-Luftwaffe pilot living in Limerick, Arno Bachmann. Bachmann had been reluctant to work with Skorzeny. Unlike other recruits, he was no Nazi and hadn't come to Ireland via the Ratlines. He'd been interned in 1942 after his Junkers 88 bomber crash-landed in the bogland of the Mountains of Mourne. He'd been the only survivor. After the war, he'd made Ireland his home but found life hard, scratching a living as an engineer. Bachmann had business ambitions. He wanted to set up a business in Limerick and Skorzeny was offering him a way to do that. The proposal was two million dollars plus costs to build an airstrip and three aircraft hangers on Corkan

Island and, when built, to purchase three war surplus Douglas C-47 Dakotas. He'd never been an enthusiastic Nazi, but he couldn't afford to refuse. He accepted Otto's proposition but kept himself to himself and spent as much time as possible away from the others on Corkan Island.

CHAPTER 7

Skorzeny was pleased with himself. Not only
had he now established his headquarters, but
his farms along the Irish border were progressing well. The arms, ammunition, and equipment levels were nearing fulfillment. He had
also wormed his way into the heart of the IRA.

He was about to sit down to dinner when he
heard the 'phone ring. He ignored it. A few moments later, the door to the dining room opened
and his housekeeper, Frau Binz, entered. *"Oberst
entschuldigen sie, Herr Walsh am Telefon für Sie'*.
It was Liam Walsh on the phone. Liam was the
IRA's Quartermaster General, one of Skorzeny's
vital contacts with the republican movement.

Skorzeny glared at his housekeeper. *"Scheisse!
Du dumme Frau"* he hissed, "we only speak English here you stupid woman, how many more
times must I tell you?" A chastened Frau Binz
cowed her head in an unspoken apology and
left the room, shutting the door behind her.

Otto picked up the extension phone, his flash
of anger vanished as he spoke in a friendly and

personable tone. "Liam, my friend? So sorry for keeping you waiting."

"T'is no problem at all Otto me ol' mucker. I'm just wanting to say thanks for your help with interrogating them agents. It was a hatchet of a feckin job. Sure, it's kicked those arseshite Brits well and truly in the doughnuts."

Otto hated the familiarity and crudity of many so-called officers of the Irish Republican Army. The IRA had received a tip-off about a meeting MI6 agents were having with their London co-ordinator in Belfast's Botanic Gardens. They'd been told the agents would be masquerading as 'down and outs' and would be somewhere in the old run-down Tropical Ravine within the Gardens, a place where few went at night. Their capture was as easy as a walk in the park, hardly any resistance. They were completely taken by surprise.

It would have been icing on the cake, if they had caught their London coordinator, but some-how, he had given them the slip. "Turn on your tele Otto. Telefis Eireann's showin' some fright-enin' pictures of inside the farm in Strabane. Sure, I don't know how they got hold of them, but it looks dreadful enough to scare the living daylights out of anyone. It'll take the feckin Brits years to recover."

"Excellent news, Liam. Did we get any useful intelligence from the prisoners?"

"Oh, we gave them every incentive to blather. Brutal it was. Your chap removed a few finger-nails and chopped off some peripherals, but they still stuck to their tinker cover story. I'll give it to them Brits, they certainly know how to train their people." Skorzeny knew what he meant. He'd had the same problem interrogating resistance fighters in France.

Liam continued. "Sure, they looked like winos; they hollered blue murder; swore blind their in-nocence; but despite them staying stum, there was all the proof we needed - the three code-books hidden in the greenery with a small two-way radio set. And a couple of guns, Berettas they were, and a map with circles and marks all over it - we've yet to find out what they mean. We surprised them and the shites didn't get a chance to resist."

"I agree. they must have been well trained - very few prisoners have resisted the techniques of *Hauptsturmführer* Heim," replied Otto. "I'll go to watch the television now. If nothing more, together we've achieved excellent publicity - publicity that'll strike terror into the hearts of our enemy, Liam."

He was about to put the phone down, and thanked Liam for his call, but Liam hadn't finished.

"Hold on a mo' Colonel. After all your help, me and the boyos thought it was about time we introduced you to an ol' British Army wizard we have workin' with us. You masterminded the feckin Battle of the Bulge - well, our other friend's brilliance was responsible for shaftin' yer ol' mate Rommel at Alamein. With you both aboard, there'll be no stoppin' us. Now, go and watch yer tele Otto and enjoy – the boss said he'd be on the blower soon to fix up a meetin'."

Otto thanked Liam and said he would look forward to hearing more from Finbar Kelly, the IRA's top man. He put the phone down and sat mulling over what Liam had told him. When he'd been told about the capture of the British agents, it had been his idea to make an example of them and have his old wartime friend, Aribert Heim interrogate them.

Aribert had been the commandant at the *Mauthausen* concentration camp in Austria, where he'd earnt the grim name of 'Doctor Death'. He had travelled over specially from his haven on the Spanish Costa Blanca at Otto's request. Otto knew that Aribert had enjoyed the opportunity to practice his sadistic skills again, but obviously, his techniques weren't what they used to be. He'd gone soft thought Otto. Too much good living; no wonder he'd failed to get the prisoners to talk. The publicity was good, but Otto felt disappointed.

"Dorothea, put my dinner in the oven and turn on the television. You can watch it too. It might remind you of your good work at *Ravensbrück*'. He smiled coldly.

As they watched the macabre and bloody scene, Otto's mind was elsewhere. He would look forward to talking again to Kelly, the Chief of Staff of the IRA. He'd met him a few times already and was surprised that such a mild-mannered man was the leader of such a bloodthirsty group. Finbar had told him that he modeled himself on Wolf Tone, an Irish republican and rebel who tried to overthrow English rule in Ireland a few centuries ago. Wolf led a French military force to Ireland during the insurrection of 1798 but failed. This time, he'd said that with Nazi support, they could wipe the bloody floor with the bastard British.

And the 'boyos' Walsh mentioned were the IRA Army Council. But who was the other so-called military genius he talked about? That egocentric *Dummkopf* Montgomery had taken all the credit for reversing Rommel's drive towards Cairo in the Western Desert at Alamein - and he was sure that it wasn't him Liam was talking about. Then he remembered. Before Montgomery came on the Alamein scene, Auchinleck had been the General leading the Allied Army. Auchinleck had stopped Rommel's advance. Was this who he was going to meet? The great Auk? Perhaps, he thought. But on reflection, he also remembered that there had been talk of another senior officer alongside Auchinleck, who Rommel cursed and blamed for his defeat – was this the man? Otto was intrigued.

CHAPTER 8

Dick Cunningham and David Slater had arrived in Northern Ireland in a C130 Lockheed Hercules, one of the giant transport planes used by the RAF. They'd landed at Langford Lodge, a little-known WW2 RAF bomber station on the banks of Lough Neagh. The airfield was no longer used by the RAF for operational work and looked derelict. It was about 40 minutes away from the Forster Green Mortuary. The entrance had two old rusted gates topped by equally rusted barbed wire. Inside the gates, the guard hut had gaping holes where doors and windows had been gutted for use by locals. Bushes and brambles grew either side of the one main concrete runway and up the side of what was once a busy control tower. The only other remaining buildings were three dilapidated Nissen Huts. However, on close inspection, the runway was well maintained and the rusted gates recently oiled. Langford Lodge was regularly used for clandestine visits by British security services to the Province.

The two MI6 officers had stayed at the mortuary until satisfied that every trace of the last 24 hours horror had been removed. The professor stayed too and was more than happy to see the back of them when they departed. He was back in control of his domain.

The Military Police escort went back to Gough Barracks together with the 'clean-up' team leaving Dick and David Slater to take their solitary Bedford truck loaded with its pig and human body parts back to Langford Lodge. They arrived just after midday. They had left the gates open for their return, but now closed and padlocked them before driving down towards the huge C130 standing at the end of the runway positioned ready for take-off.

As Captain Slater drove round to the rear of the plane and up the ramp into the hold, the engines fired up. The truck was dwarfed by the dome like space that surrounded it inside the giant transporter. They hardly had time to secure it with ties, struggle into flight suits and lifejackets and strap themselves into bucket seats before the ramp came up and the plane started down the runway lifting into a steep climb on their way back to RAF Northolt.

Once the plane had levelled out, crossing the Irish coast at Bangor, Dick Cunningham made his way up to the flight deck. The RAF pilot, Squadron Leader Andy McCredie, an experi-

enced C130 pilot, had been with the Special
Forces Aviation Wing for over two years. Many
of his trips were over hostile territories in the
Middle East and so he found it refreshing to
have a simple domestic round trip to Ireland.

Even before Dick had arrived in Ireland, it had
been decided that for maximum security, it
would be best to completely erase all traces of
the undercover agents. Media leaks were inevitable, but without bodies, the fuss would soon
die down. So, the plan was to bury them deep
in the Irish sea with the truck as their sarcoph-
agus. "Andy, when we're well clear of the coast,
I need you to go as low as you can, drop the tail
ramp and circle until I give you the word to
climb."

"No problem Dick, WILCO." He knew better
than to ask for reasons why.

Soon they were over open sea at 10,000ft, 20
miles south of the Isle of Man and 43 miles off
Liverpool. Andy told his co-pilot to descend to
300ft and circle until told otherwise.

The C130 gradually descended to reach the requested altitude. As it levelled off, Andy's voice
came over the intercom. "Low as we can get in
this weather Dick ol' chap. Ramp going down

now – awaiting further instructions"

"Roger that," replied Dick. As the ramp lowered, they could just make out the white-crested waves below - visibility was not good. It looked vile. Strong turbulence shook the giant plane making it difficult for the two passengers to move from their seats and stand up. Adding to that, the tail ramp had let in a whirling dervish gale that raced around the cargo deck. Clipping their safety harnesses onto the sidebars of the plane, they struggled to move around the truck untying the safety straps that secured it. Better their families were kept in ignorance of their hideous demise, thought Dick.

They went to the front of the vehicle and pushed hard with their shoulders. But the truck wouldn't move. It was heavy, too heavy, particularly with its dead weight. No matter how hard they heaved, it just wouldn't budge. There was only one thing for it. Dick got on the intercom again to Andy and told him to slowly climb back to 10,000 feet. They felt the force of the inclining floor of the plane as it angled upwards, but still the truck stayed put.

"Sod it," said Slater, "I forgot to take the bloody handbrake off ."   And before Dick could say anything, he leapt across the gap to the truck, opened the driver's door lunging forward into the cab to release it. It had the desired effect. The truck shot backwards like a bullet and out of the rear of the plane taking the Captain with it. Luckily for him, his safety harness tore him away from the vehicle as it plunged into the abyss.

He'd almost made it out of the driver's cab, but the door caught him a sledgehammer blow sending his body flying like a kite into the open mouth of the C130's rear. His scream echoed around the now empty interior. Horror struck, Dick dived forward grabbing David's lifeline, and with enormous effort, hauled his limp and damaged body back from the tailgate precipice. His left upper body had been badly damaged. His shoulder was a bloody pulp of bone and flesh. His arm hung by threads of tendon and torn muscle. He was losing blood fast and his breathing was almost non-existent. But he was still alive, just.

"Shut the fucking tailgate Andy," screamed Dick over the intercom. "I need help back here. Slater's badly hurt. Bring a first aid kit and warn base that we have a severe casualty onboard."

Dick had only asked David Slater to come on the trip to Ireland at the last minute as a backup in case anything happened to himself. It had been Dick's idea to save a load of unnecessary public attention, paperwork, and bureaucratic enquiries by dumping the bodies into the sea too – as he applied a tourniquet to David's near severed arm, he couldn't help feeling responsibility and guilt for David's injuries. His heart-stopping shriek as he almost followed the truck into the abyss and his terror-stricken face when Dick hauled him back into the safety of the cargo hold would stay with Dick for a very long time. But at least he hadn't joined the mass burial and it was now his job to make sure he survived.

As the rear ramp came up, he and Andy's co-pilot did their best to stem the blood flow and dress David's wounds, Dick forced himself to think of the mission he had been on and the poor innocent victims now entombed at the bottom of the Irish Sea.

As news of the Strabane massacre leaked out, as he was sure it would, he would make sure an official statement was put out to the press. And if possible, posthumous awards for the agents' courage and selfless work, well beyond the call of duty. And it had shown the IRA in their true colours – a bunch of ruthless outlaws, who would sink to untold depths to inflict pain and suffering in pursuit of their goal - to overthrow the legitimate government of Northern Ireland.

CHAPTER 9

As Liam promised, the IRA's top man telephoned Otto Skorzeny within the hour. Finbar Kelly was a much more refined man than Liam. Unlike Liam, who had literally fought his way up from the backstreets of Dublin, Finbar was a quiet well-spoken academic whose passion for completing the 1916 revolution drove him on. Otto congratulated him on the success of capturing the four undercover agents. They discussed the impact it was having in the media, all good for the cause, they agreed. For the proposed meeting, Otto offered the use of his house, but Finbar insisted that they meet near the border with Northern Ireland.

He told Otto that along with the Council, he wanted him to meet a chap called Dorman O'Gowan, the mystery man that Liam had mentioned. Finbar said that he might remember him under his old name, Dorman-Smith, an ex-Major General in the British Army. The venue was to be Dorman O'Gowan's home, Bellamont House in County Cavan.

Indeed, Otto knew of him under his old name. He remembered that Rommel had cursed Dorman-Smith for being behind his Alamein disaster. Rommel had won every battle in North Africa, driving the British from Tunisia to Egypt, like a wolf pack chasing sheep. But Dorman-Smith, Rommel had acknowledged to Otto, was his equal: a tactical guru who had out-smarted him.

The Nazi high command had been jubilant when they found out that this British mili-tary genius was being ignored and even more amazed when he prematurely disappeared from the army. Otto remembered that sources at the time had reported that British senior military officers and politicians couldn't take Dorman-Smith's continual barrage, criticising their out-dated military tactics.

"He told me he'd been sick to death at the way men were treated like pawns in a game of chess, their lives trashed in both World Wars by in-competent air brains, his advice ignored time and again," continued Finbar, "that's why he came back to Ireland. He changed his name to his Irish clan's name of O'Gowan and offered his services to help us with our cause, fighting for a united Ireland. He's not one for titles and we all call him by his nickname 'Chink'."

Finbar went on to say that it was Chink who had told them about the meeting of the British agents in Belfast, and over the past few years had helped many times with other intelligence snippets. He had even offered his estate just outside the town of Cootehill in County Cavan on the Irish border to the IRA for field training in guerrilla warfare and had indeed helped plan several of the successful IRA raids and assassinations in occupied Northern Ireland and on mainland Britain.

Otto was listening, spellbound by what Finbar was telling him. Perhaps this turncoat Britisher could play a part in the Nazi's grand plans. He could do with someone who knew the weaknesses of the British forces and how to strike them most effectively. For now, he would have to wait and see.

Finbar continued. "Chink told us that he meets occasionally with old friends and colleagues, who, he says, are unwitting sources of intelligence for our cause. The British General Horrocks is one of his old mates from as far back as their school days. He even knows the Prime Minister, Harold Macmillan. They were both at the battle of the Somme yer know."

"He sounds like he's a useful person to have

onboard," Otto broke in, "but can we trust him?"

"For sure we can. He's one of us. A pure-blooded Éireannach man of the emerald isle. His roots are as green as the shamrock and centuries-long at that." retorted Finbar. "And I'll be interested to see how you two fine foes from the war get on I will."

Otto thanked Finbar and slowly put the phone down. Always sceptical and untrusting, he was dubious about what Finbar had told him. It would take an awful lot more for him to trust this Chink O'Gowan person, whatever Finbar said. Best to play his cards close to his chest, he thought, at least until he was absolutely sure he could trust him.

Skorzeny arrived in Cootehill, in his chauffeur driven Mercedes 300D limousine. Finbar had given him precise directions. He'd told Skorzeny that the entrance to the Major General's estate was opposite the Garda station in the town, next to the parish church. He'd said it was a short drive up to his residence. Otto was sure they had followed Finbar's instructions but after two kilometres of woodland and an enormous lake, he began to think they had taken a wrong turn.

Then, the forest fell away and he saw Bellamont House perched on rising ground in front of him. He'd felt quite the country squire at his home in County Kildare, but Major General Dorman-O'Gowan's residence was in a different league, more like a stately chateau. They drove up and parked beside a pristine 1926 Rolls Royce Silver Shadow. An aristocrat's chariot, thought Otto, I'm going to enjoy meeting this man who so impressed our Desert Fox. He got out and walked around admiring the car with a touch of envy.

Chink came down the front steps of Bellamont with his son Hugh. Dressed in a brown tweed suit, looking every bit the lord of the manor, he greeted Otto smiling warmly. "Welcome to Bellamont, Colonel Skorzeny. I see you've already met my beloved Betsy," he said indicating the car. "I'll take you for a spin in her later if we have time. But let me introduce my son."

"Hugh this man is perhaps one of the most professional and dedicated soldiers you'll ever have the chance to meet, even though he was our enemy in the last war." Chink didn't add, cruel, ruthless, evil and fanatical to his description of the German visitor. Hugh shook hands with Otto. "My father said you are a living legend, sir."

Otto was flattered and gave Hugh a beaming smile - "Your father exaggerates young man. It is he you should be proud of."

The two old adversaries smiled at each other showing mutual respect, yet inwardly it was wafer thin, both feeling wary and suspicious.

There were still others to arrive for the IRA Council meeting, so Chink suggested that he and the Colonel take a stroll around Bellemont's formal gardens. "Hugh, please go and tell Owen to take Colonel Skorzeny's luggage up to his room. And ask him to usher the Colonel's chauffeur into the kitchen please. I'm sure the man could use some refreshments after the long drive." As Hugh ran back up the steps to carry out his orders, Chink and Otto turned around and walked slowly towards the gardens and down to the lake.

"You have an amazing residence here General. I had no idea you lived in such a palace with such good views." Otto's tone was formal and respectful.

"We are very fortunate, it's been in the family for some time now," Chink replied, "There are over 1000 acres, mainly woodland and with three large lakes, what we call loughs."

"And the house, it is old, yes?"

"Absolutely. It is one of Ireland's best example of 18th century Palladian architecture. It was built three hundred years ago. It looks good, but a financial nightmare to maintain."

They walked in silence for a while, Otto gazing at the scenery around them.

Eventually, Chink broke the silence, trying to sound welcoming and friendly. "I've heard many good things about you, Otto. "I was told you were the brains behind that German counter-attack in the Ardennes. You nearly broke through the American lines. We called it the 'Battle of the Bulge'. Brilliant tactics."

"I accept your compliment, Herr General," Otto replied with the typical formality of a Prussian officer. Yes, but in the end, we lost. I gave the final briefing to *Oberstgruppenführer* Dietrich before he struck with his 6th *Panzer* division from the Ardennes forests. But then praise should really go to your British military theorist, Liddell Hart. We read all of his books at our officer training school, the *SS-Junkerschule* in Bad Tölz. It was our battle planning bible. The concept of *Blitzkrieg*, lightning strikes was his. That's what your old rival *Generalfeldmarschall*

Rommel used when his 7th Panzer division swept through Belgium and France"

"I know Basil Liddell Hart extremely well. He's an old friend of mine. But I'm sure he would be gutted to know that he'd helped the 1940 Nazi *Blitzkrieg*," replied Chink. "He would be even more gutted to know that you and I were going to be working together, one of Hitler's most dedicated officers. But those days are gone. We now have the opportunity to bring all our experience and expertise to bear on helping in this just cause - a united Ireland. I must say, I'm looking forward to it."

"Ah! You are right, General," said Otto, "the past is the past. However, I have to say, Rommel always said that he feared you and Auchinleck. You were, he said, the most professional soldiers he fought against. None of us could ever understand how you just seemed to disappear after the Anzio landing in Italy. In fact, *Feldmarschall* Kesselring thought you had been killed in action."

Chink was embarrassed. He found compliments difficult to swallow. "I don't deserve such an accolade, Otto, I was only doing my job." He paused. My problem was and always has been keeping my big mouth shut. I'm not a politician and when I saw blatant strategic and tactical

errors being made by some of the idiot commanders around me, I couldn't hold my tongue.
I voiced my opinion in no uncertain terms. This
upset a lot of my fellow officers.

Then, at a meeting with Churchill, I was again
unable to contain myself and told him precisely
what I thought of his meddling in military
affairs. Old Winnie believed he could walk on
water, the fool. I was livid with the man and
told him he knew less about mobile military
tactics than a monkey in a zoo. I said he might
have been a great inspiration to the population
at large, but he was a cantankerous opinionated
old busybody. Once I'd started, I just couldn't
stop myself. I went on to castigate him for the
unnecessary loss of tens of thousands of men,
men who had come from all over our Empire to
fight for Britain - Indians, Africans, Australians,
they'd just been used as cannon fodder; so many
lives of young soldiers cut short and families ruined through his meddling. I must be the only
British commander to ever be summarily fired
on active duty."

"If I had dared to say what I thought to Herr
Hitler, I would have been shot on the spot," said
Otto, shaking his head at the thought. "The
nearest I got to that was suggesting to Adolf
at a meeting of senior officers, that we strike

the soft underbelly of your Empire and attack through the Caucasus. We could have swept you aside and driven through Syria, Iraq, and Persia, into Cairo. It would have lost you North Africa and you would never have gained a foothold in Italy. But he listened to cautious Kesselring who hummed and hawed until it was too late."

"So, what happened to you after you left the British Army?" Otto asked

"I gave it all up and came back to my roots here in Ireland. To the freedom you can see around you here. Mind you, I still like to see some of my old chums. Several of them are still serving soldiers. It sometimes gives me useful intelligence. I'm also occasionally called upon to give talks and advise the Irish Army HQ at the Curragh in County Kildare - that must be near to where you live, isn't it Otto?"

"Yes, it's close to Martinstown, but I've never been there and hardly ever see anything of them," he said dismissively. "But it's going to be very interesting for working with you, *mein* General."

"Oh, for God's sake, I left all titles behind a long time ago, just call me Chink, everyone else does, even the President of the Republic of Ireland, Mr. de Valera."

"But Chink is, how you say, the name you people call Chinese persons isn't it? - and you don't have the slant eyes or the yellow skin - so why such a name?"

"It's a long story, but you may have heard of Hemingway - Ernest Hemingway, the American author?" Otto nodded.

"Anyway, Ernie and I met in Italy before the war. We were both regulars at the Grand Hotel Minerva's roof top bar in Florence and got on like a house on fire. He gave me the nick-name Chink because he said I was tall and skinny, and moved just like the Chinkara antelope. I didn't like my first name Eric, such a boring name, and Dorman-O'Gowan's such a mouth full, so I adopted 'Chink'."

Whilst they were strolling in the gardens, the remainder of the IRA war council had arrived. Owen had shown them into the old ballroom which doubled as a conference room. And Otto and Chink, chatting away like old friends, went in to join them.

CHAPTER 10

In 1830, Britain's King William IV commissioned the building of a tunnel from Buckingham Palace to the Houses of Parliament via Downing Street wide and tall enough to allow horse-drawn vehicles to travel along it. Over the years, the tunnel was used by Queen Victoria to visit her government. In 1906, when Edward VII acceded to the throne, he wanted to add a branch of the tunnel to the newly opened Ritz hotel on London's Piccadilly. He sought government funding for the project. Prime Minister Asquith saw the expansion of the tunnel as a threat to government security and only allowed the project to go ahead on the condition that the main tunnel was blocked at the top of The Mall.

Once the tunnel was sealed off, Asquith, whose drinking habits were the subject of considerable gossip, added large secure vaults off both sides of the tunnel under Downing Street to store his wines and collection of ports. And, rather than use the dilapidated stairs, he commissioned the London Hydraulic Power Company to install one of their artesian powered lifts, making access to the tunnel far easier. Slowly but surely over the years, more tunnels and rooms were added by subsequent administrations until a major expansion was ordered by Churchill to house his Cabinet War Rooms.

During the Attlee led Labour Government, the Cabinet War rooms became derelict. Attlee's favourite drink was cocoa and so the wine cellars were abandoned too and the network of tunnels used for Post Office telephone lines and equipment storage. It was on Churchill's return to power in 1951 that the War Rooms were developed and expanded to give birth to the home of Britain's security services. He also reopened the wine vaults to store his vaste collection of single malt whiskeys.

In 1957, when Harold MacMillan took over the reins as Prime Minister of the Conservative Government, the underground facility was quickly expanded to have its own mini- subway trains, linking the centre to the 'In and Out' Club on Piccadilly and 54 Broadway near St James Tube Station. The namcplate outside number 54 was the Minimax Fire Extinguisher Company and it was thought generally to be the headquarters of the counter-espionage MI6. In reality, however, it was nothing more than a gateway into the

hub of the British intelligence services deep
underneath Whitehall.

By 1962, it had become an incredible labyrinth
of tunnels, offices, conference rooms and other
facilities. On five levels, the complex covered
more than 5 acres. It was the closely guarded
nerve centre of British home and overseas
security, MI5 and MI6, otherwise known as SIS,
the Secret Intelligence Service. The whole facility had been nicknamed informally 'Kali' after
the Hindu goddess of many arms. Kali was also
associated with secret societies, sex, violence,
and death. A name everyone thought highly appropriate for Great Britain's security services.

MI5 worked on level one, MI6 on level two.
Level three was a presentation theatre, multiple
meeting and training rooms plus a canteen,
hospital, gym and shop. On level four, there
were several 'safe' flats for personnel protection
and a comprehensive armoury and shooting
range, with an escalator to secure hotel rooms
beneath the nearby Royal Horse Guards Hotel.
And on the lowest level was a sophisticated
containment facility for holding suspects in
cells plus several rooms dedicated to their
interrogation.

The main artery of Kali, an expanded version

of King William's original tunnel, was a 12ft high paved tunnel that ran through level one from Admiralty Arch, beneath Horse Guards Parade and Downing Street to the Houses of Parliament. Whilst it was still big enough to drive a horse and carriage through it, it saw nothing more than pedestrians and a fleet of self-drive electric 'golf' carts Other passageway tentacles of Kali provided more entry and exits located in the Admiralty building at the side of Horse Guards Square, 10 Downing Street, The Treasury, Foreign Office, Home Office, Ministry of Defence, Scotland Yard and the Houses of Parliament. All entrances were guarded by special forces personnel in civilian dress.

There were also discreet access points known only to a few MI5 and MI6 agents at the National Gallery and toilet number three in the gents' lavatories at Charing Cross Tube station.

Mac, as he was known, was a popular Prime Minister. He would always be remembered for saying to the British people 'You've never had it so good', which after the years of post-war hardship, was true.

Unlike most politicians, he'd had a life before Parliament. He had spent time as a regular soldier and fought in the First World War. Wounded three times, most severely in Septem-

ber 1916 during the Battle of the Somme and
although suffering permanent pain and partial
immobility, he never complained. After the
war, Mac had joined the family publishing business and then entered Parliament in the 1924
General Election. During WW2, he was Government Minister for the Middle East, resident in
Algiers. During this time, he flew over to War
Council meetings with Churchill, Auchinleck
and renewed his friendship with Major General
Dorman-Smith in Cairo.

Two weeks after the Strabane massacre, four
men and one woman gathered in Kali's most
secure meeting room located 90ft directly
beneath No10 Downing Street. It was known
as GOLD (Government Office Lower Down).
Churchill had coined its name – he liked acro-
nyms. GOLD had no windows. It had an airlock
entrance and the whole room was encased in a
skin of inch thick lead with independent air and
power supplies.   And on Churchill's insistence,
the original Asquith lift access to the complex
was modernised and expanded to link his private quarters in No 10 down directly into GOLD.

Macmillan felt that the time had come to
accelerate the offensive against the growing
troubles in Northern Ireland. Not with an iron
fist approach, that would turn the Province into

a police state, but one that would bring peace to both sides of the border. It was he who had called the meeting. He knew that there was a very real threat of escalating hostilities and reports of active ex-Nazi collaboration with the IRA were very much on his mind. It was Mac who had handpicked the attendees for this meeting. He wanted a carefully crafted solution to the problem. Those he had invited were not 'hot air' merchants, all peace-seeking blather and no action. They were experienced and dedicated professionals who would give their all if asked.

Heading up the GOLD meeting was the Director-General of MI6, Sir Richard, 'Dick', White, generally known just as "C', the man responsible for counter-espionage. He'd recently replaced Sir Eyre Lloyd, a political appointee, who had let it all go to pot.   White had inherited a live nest of intrigue, deceit, and double agents – the Vassal spy case was still very much alive and MI6 was still looking for the fourth member of the Burgess, McLean, and Philby gang. White had been a Housemaster at Whitgift school in Croydon before being recruited into MI6 in the early 1930s. Being fluent in German, one of his first jobs was working out of the British Embassy in Germany and passing information back to London on the Nazi preparation for the war. And during it, he became a specialist in counter-espionage, working closely with the SAS sometimes even going behind enemy lines to negotiate and bring on-board rebel leaders and partisans in Europe, the Middle East, and Asia.

Also at the meeting was Peter Fleming, ex-Special Operations Executive (SOE) that waged guerrilla warfare behind enemy lines during WW2, Gillian Sattler, espionage consultant, and Colonel Bob Deacon SAS Hereford. And Major Dick Cunningham, who three years previously had been seconded to MI6 from the Royal Artillery. He was much younger than the others, certainly too young to have seen any WW2 action.

"The Prime Minister will be joining us shortly," said Sir Richard. "In the meantime, while we are waiting, let's introduce ourselves. I'm new to this MI6 role. I won't be drawn to criticise my predecessor, but in war and peace, I'm a believer in less talk and more action. I've met you all at some stage in the past and I'm going to leave it to the Mac to tell you why he has called this meeting so let's start with you, Peter."

Peter Fleming had the stamp of an Etonian in his manner and voice. Tall and reasonably slim, his face showed he had lived well, perhaps too well. Aged 55, his eyes were full of life and somewhat mischievous.

"You probably all know of my younger brother, Ian, through his James Bond books and the movie, Casino Royale. During WW2, I headed up a unit of the SOE specialising in military deception. I still run a little workshop for our security services at Hanslope Park, near Newport Pagnell. I don't know what Mac's got in mind. I haven't been told why I've been invited to this meeting, but hopefully, my experience might be of help in some way."

Sir Richard smiled. "All in good time Peter."

Then looking at those around the table, he continued "Peter was very much the role model for Ian's books. If you've read any of them, you would have been reading dressed up biographical reports of Peter's exploits. His SOE number was 007. Thank you, Peter, short and brief." He turned expectantly to Gillian sitting on his right.

"I was brought up in Alsace, France. My father was English and my mother Alsatian. I was at school in Scotland when war broke out and so was unable to go home. I did the next best thing. I lied about my age and joined the Women's Royal Army Corps. With my background, I was soon recruited into the SOE. I knew of you, Peter, but we'd never met."

"My whole family were Anglophiles and hated the Nazis. After pestering my boss, Colonel Buckmaster, who ran the SOE's French section, I was sent into occupied France and spent most of the war back in the Alsace operating a cell in the town where I was born, Altkirch, South of Strasburg. My whole family became SOE operatives."

"My two older brothers joined the Alsatian Nazi Waffen SS and acted as vital sources of information. My father, being English, was viewed with great suspicion by the Nazis. However, with two sons in the SS, he was considered useful to the Reich and was offered the job of writing Nazi propaganda leaflets for distribution during bomber raids. He used to embed coded intelligence messages within these leaflets to our SOE bosses. I think we were the only spy family business."

"Eventually, we were found out. I was away the night the Gestapo took my parents. They were interrogated and sent to Dachau; my brothers were shot and, until I was captured, I fought

with the Lorraine Brigade of the French Resistance. I was lucky to only have 4 months in the
Nazi concentration camp for women at *Ravensbrück* before the Russians liberated us. Now
I'm an adviser working with 'C'. That's me in a
nutshell."

"You are some act to follow Gillian," said Sir
Richard. Then to Dick Cunningham. "Now
Dick, give us your background in a nutshell."

"I'm from a family with a long military history
of serving our country in both the army and
navy. I was educated at Wellington and Sandhurst, commissioned into the Royal Artillery.
I spent a couple of years fighting insurgents in
Malaya and Borneo and then got involved with
MI6. That's me."

"What Dick hasn't mentioned" interjected
'C'," is that he is still the youngest Major in the
British Army, promoted because of his brilliant
record. He spent 6 months undercover living
in a communist terrorist stronghold in Borneo,
for which he received his MC. And that he has
been working with our top undercover agent
in Ireland. He's just got back from Northern
Ireland cleaning up the remains of the Strabane
affair - you probably read about it in the press."

Then 'C' turned his gaze to Bob Deacon. "Colonel Deacon runs SAS Hereford. Now tell us your background, Bob."

"I'm just a simple regular soldier; I've never been a spy. That's not to say I and my chaps haven't operated behind enemy lines - that's what the SAS is all about, carrying on the good work of David Stirling and Paddy Mayne. During my 11 years with the Regiment, I've been part of support operations around the world - countries like Korea, Malaya, Yemen, Afghanistan, and Borneo, helping our allies fight terrorism. Currently, we...."

There was a deafening clanking and whirring sound interrupting Bob Deacon in full flow. It was followed by a noisy clunk and the door of the No.10 lift slid back. The Prime Minister, Harold Macmillan, joined the meeting, followed by the War Office Minister, John Profumo, and Airey Neave MP.

"My apologies for being late, Gentlemen," Mac said as he and his party joined the meeting. "I've called you all here because of the developing situation in Northern Ireland. Airey and I, together with advice from 'C', selected you because you all have distinguished yourselves serving your country - we believe you are the best available expertise in the areas that we think will be particularly relevant."

He paused, walked around the table and sat down. "John is here as Secretary of State for War. He must be in the loop to ensure there are no miscommunications and we end up fighting amongst ourselves. And I've asked Airey to come along because not only is he a full-blooded Irishman, but he was one of the most decorated soldiers in the last war and a Colditz escapologist extraordinaire. Airey's experience and cunning should be a great help. Anyway, he and Peter were close chums at my old school in Windsor."

"So, where are we, 'C' ?"

Richard White told the Prime Minister that everyone had introduced themselves, but he hadn't brought them up to speed with the brewing situation in Ireland.

"Right gentlemen, and of course, you Gillian," continued Macmillan. "You may be wondering why I asked 'C' to invite you to this meeting. Firstly, you are among the very few people in whom I know I can have absolute trust. You may have noticed that I haven't invited anyone from MI5. This is mainly because most of this operation is counter-terrorist and expected to be in the Irish Republic - and, between these leaded walls, there are questions over the integrity of Roger Hollis and his merry men. We can call them in if needs be."

"What I have in mind will call on the experience and specialist skills that you, Peter and Gillian, displayed so admirably during the war. You, Major Cunningham," Mac turned to Dick, "have already been involved in Northern Ireland. I hear Slater was injured on your last outing - how is he?"

"The surgeons have done a great job, sir - he's on the mend."

"Good to hear it," then moving on to Bob Deacon, "and you Bob. You've got an exemplary record for executing successful operations and neutralising threats around the world."

He continued. "Some of Bob Deacon's men and Dick Cunningham have already been involved in what, at this stage, we are calling 'Operation Blarney' and I've asked the Major to give you a full briefing shortly."

"Let's face it, the UK is continually under threat from many quarters. I don't underestimate the security damage that bastard Vassal has done passing our secrets to his paymasters in Russia, and we are continuing to unearth more facts.

And thank goodness we've unearthed George
Blake – he's three floors down from here singing
to your chaps as we speak, isn't he 'C'?"

"Yes Prime Minister. We have everything under
control and expect to make more arrests immi-
nently." 'C' replied.

"Excellent, well done." Macmillan continued.
"I'd like you all to know the reason I was late.
It was because I was on the phone to President
Kennedy, who informed me that Khrushchev
and Guido Castro are attempting to place
nuclear missiles on Cuba - but nothing too
important to prevent me from coming to this
meeting. It all can be considered as no more
than a pinprick compared to what we believe is
erupting in Ireland and the disasterous effect it
could have on Great Britain. We know through
our agent that the IRA has now linked up with
some experienced ex-Nazis and together they
could be an enormous threat to the stability of
not just the United Kingdom, but to Europe and
beyond."

There were raised eyebrows and surprised murmurs from those around the table, particularly
from those who had experience of the Nazis at
close quarters.

Gillian was about to interrupt the PM, but he hushed her, holding up his hand. "Not now Gillian, questions and comments later please. I think you will all have a clearer understanding of the situation then."

Gillian sat back, obviously disturbed by the mere mention of her arch enemies. Mac continued. "Let me make it crystal clear, we have many enemies around the world who would like to see us fall. Reports have already shown that the IRA's misguided sympathisers in North America are pouring funds into their coffers - plus the USSR and their allies are making regular arms shipments into Eire. It all sounds like one of your brother's stories, eh Peter."

"Anyway," Mac continued, "I'm talking too much as my dear wife Lady Dorothy often tells me. But before I ask Dick to give you an update on Operation Blarney, there's one other person I'd have liked at this meeting. He is our top undercover man on the ground in Ireland just South of the border. Because of his vital role, it is imperative that outside this room, his identity remains top secret.

He was a British Army General during the war, who now lives in Ireland. You may know of

Major General Dorman-Smith.

"Well, I'll be damned!" exclaimed Peter Fleming. "I knew him in Egypt in '42. I used to
go clubbing with him in Cairo with his mate
Hemingway and that mad SAS Irishman, Paddy
Mayne. Those were great days." Peter grinned to
himself with the memories

"I didn't know him personally," cut in Airey
Neave, "he was said to be a genius tactician with
a reputation for straight talk and for running
off with other officers' wives. If I remember
correctly, he had a run-in with Churchill. Didn't
he tell him to 'F'-off back to Downing Street
and leave the Desert War to the professionals.
Wasn't that why Churchill gave him the order of
the boot?"

"Bloody unfair if you ask me," Peter muttered
under his breath.

Mac continued, ignoring Peter's remark, "however, the whole row with Winston was a charade, a big cover-up. Churchill may be a shadow
of himself now, but back in 1942, he was not
only an inspired national leader but also an
extraordinarily clear visionary. Despite the dire
situation Britain was in, he saw catastrophic
problems looming in Ireland. The 1916 Lloyd-
George government had made a political nightmare out of negotiations with Éamon de Valera.

I don't like criticising past administrations, but it was an absolute 'pig's ear' of a shambles. You could say that he and his government at the time were responsible for the problems we have today in Ireland. Yet in 1939, even when the Irish Government led by de Valera, had declared neutrality, more than two hundred thousand brave Irishmen had came across the border to fight against the Nazis."

"Yes, who could blame their government being neutral though," broke in Peter again. "We sent in the Black and Tans in 1918 and burnt whole villages during their fight for independence."

"Too right Peter, and because of the perceived worldwide threat of communism, the Catholic Church sympathised with Hitler too," added Airey. "And there isn't a country more solidly Catholic than Eire. I'm a Protestant from the North and if anyone stokes hatred for us, it's that Church."

Mac waited for them to quieten down then continued. He went on to tell the meeting that Winston needed a loyal and trusted man on the ground to keep an eye on the situation in Eire. He saw Chink, with his Irish pedigree, as the ideal person to mastermind a strategy to defeat the IRA once and for all and bring peace to both sides of the border. The challenge had appealed to Chink. And he accepted Churchill's proposal. It was 'job done' in North Africa. He and Auchinleck had stopped Rommel's rampage at Alamein, and they believed any idiot could then chase the so-called Desert Fox out of Africa. So, Chink had suggested the egomaniac Montgomery as an ideal replacement. Monty got the accolades which puffed him up and Chink returned to the UK in apparent disgrace.

The PM continued. "Out of the public eye, Chink worked closely with Churchill at Chartwell. He came up with the idea of being a master spy inside the IRA's organisation. He knew that it would take time to establish his credentials and become an integral part of their structure. That was more than 15 years ago. He changed his name to Dorman- O'Gowan, O'Gowan being the name of his Irish clan, and today, he is a revered member of the IRA Council. He's also advising the Irish Government, the Dáil Éireann, on defence matters." The room was completely captivated by the incredible story Mac was unfolding.

"Chink," he went on, "keeps in touch with 'C' and myself through coded letters, couriered by some mutual friends, plus telephone messages, and, every so often, we get a filmed update.

You are now going to see the latest one of these filmed by Chink and given two weeks ago to his old Uppingham school and army friend General Sir Brian Horrocks over lunch at their London Club, the 'In and Out'. It's well known by his IRA contacts that Chink regularly visits London and meets with Brian. They think he's intelligence gathering for them, but in fact, it's the reverse. He's been passing them pretty useless information and keeping us up to date with their activities and operational plans. Up to now, only six of us, Churchill, Sir Richard, John, Brian Horrocks, myself, and recently, Dick knew what Chink was up to."

"In the years since he went underground, he has got himself close to Charles Haughey, the pro-IRA Irish Government minister. Chink has also built up a chain of restaurants, and other businesses both in Ireland and here in the UK. Well, that's set the scene, so let's hear from the man himself."

With that, Mac pressed a button, the room went dark, there was the whirring noise of a hidden projector and the face of a gaunt bearded man appeared on the screen at the end of the room.

"Hello there Mac. It's been a couple of months since my last film report. Sorry about that. I've been spending time with our old Nazi friend

Otto Skorzeny here at Bellamont. He's a wily old warrior and always alert, but I'm pretty sure I'm gaining his trust. We had a full IRA Council meeting here two weeks ago. The outcome was that I would continue to provide a training base for their men here at Bellamont. Otto said that he had some of his old soldiers working for him who could help. But the Council didn't like the idea. I told Otto that there were already two ex-SAS chaps on the team here at Bellamont in the training role. They're the two of our agents Major Cunningham sent over, Seamus O'Driscoll and Terry Casey. I've met them a couple of times. They haven't a clue we are batting for the same side. They'll probably suggest that they take me out," he said with a wry smile.

"Is that where those buggers disappeared to" murmured Bob Deacon.

"The exposure of our so-called agents in Belfast was brilliantly conducted. Sad for them, but it got me a bag full of brownie points. I said it was Horrocks who told me about them and their meeting place. The planting of the MI6 two-way radios, codebooks, and guns was a masterstroke. It was Otto's people and a few over-enthusiastic IRA fellers, who had them interrogated, tortured and butchered, then fed to the pigs. Otto said terror was an offensive military tool and made good publicity for the IRA cause - striking fear into the hearts of Loyalists and Brits. They were completely taken in by the operation. Well done Cunningham."

"Otto is a professional soldier and ruthless to the core. If he had the slightest doubt about me, he'd slit my throat or arrange for someone else to do it."

"He's asked me down to a meeting at his place, Martinstown Manor in Kildare. Given the Vatican's active role in helping Hitler's henchmen escape at the end of the War and its iron fist hold on the Irish population, Eire makes the perfect destination for the *Obergruppenfuhrer* and his cohorts. I know Otto has been importing some very unsavoury characters. I'm pretty sure that some of them will be at the Martinstown meeting."

Chink added that he needed more intelligence feedback to pass on to his IRA comrades. Targets in the North or even on the mainland they could blow up without endangering people or security.

"And when they strike, exaggerate the facts, lives lost - anything that helps to concrete my street credibility. Just pass the coordinates through dear old Horrocks."

"I have a list of 316 IRA members with their addresses. They're not all active, but at least we know who they are and where to find them. I'll send it over shortly via my House of Lords channel. You'll see that I've underlined the names of a few nasty individuals who could be taken out whenever you like without compromising me."

"Goodbye for now."

With that, the face of Dorman O'Gowan faded from the screen and the lights came on in the GOLD room.

The room was silent. Stunned by the man and what he had to say.

"That's incredible. I can hardly believe it. What a great storyline." gasped Peter Fleming. "My brother could stick his 007 into the script and he'd have another bestseller. If it wasn't for Chink on film, I'd say it was April Fool's Day. And what was all that about the House of Lords?"

"You're right, Peter" 'C' said, ignoring his question. Then looking around the room he continued. "Now you all know that the Strabane massacre was a setup, perhaps you, Dick, could

explain what went on and then an update as to
where we are in the planning of 'Blarney."

Major Cunningham stood up and walked to
the head of the conference room table, where a
blank flip chart stood on an easel at the side of
the screen.

"We set up Strabane to give Chink's credibility a
major boost with the IRA and our Nazi friends,
and by the sound of what Chink said, it worked
a treat. It was grotesque that innocent lives
were lost even though they were the end of the
line drug addicts and winos. However, they
were unwitting heroes in our undercover war.
The Strabane farmer and his wife, all the staff
at the mortuary who had to clean up the mess,
they were all victims too. But the deception
worked As far as the IRA and Skorzeny are
concerned, Chink is now unquestionably a
committed republican and on-side with them
all." He omitted to detail the unceremonial burial at sea.

"Now, Operation 'Blarney." He was about to
continue when Gillian lept to her feet bursting
with anger.

"I can't believe you had those innocent people
killed and put everyone else involved through
a living hell. It's just the sort of thing the Nazis

used to do. She stood up ready to go. "I'm not sure I want any part of this." .

"For God's sake Gillian, sit down," growled 'C' angrily. "Don't tell me you've gone soft after all the blood and guts you spilt with the Resistance. Remember the restaurant in Colmar you blew up just to kill *Feldmarschall* von Schlieffen. How many innocents died then? just hear the Major out."

"Yes, but that was war and we were fighting for survival against a satanic regime," she retorted aggressively and sat down again, still fuming.

"And that's what we are trying to prevent in Ireland – a bloody war and the re-emergence of that same evil regime." He carried on angrily. "Remember the Blitz when thousands of innocent people died in the Luftwaffe bombing. Remember what we did to Dresden too – that was even worse. He turned to Dick. "Tell her why she, in particular, has been asked here, Major"

Gillian was still unhappy. In her opinion, 'C' and his crew had been responsible for a needless bloody exercise.

Dick continued. "OK Gillian, perhaps you'll have a clearer understanding of the situation if I tell you that your old camp commandant from Ravensbrück, Fritz Suhren lives in one of the cottages on Skorzeny's Martinstown estate. And Dorothea Binz, remember her?"

Gillian went white with shock and spluttered. "That whore, she was in charge of a special barrack room bunker set aside for all the pretty women prisoners, used for whatever sexual deviations their Nazi visitors wished. It was hell on earth. And as women were only considered worthless trash, the visitors could satisfy their perverted lust by torturing or even killing them in whatever depraved way they wished. It was a human abattoir. Thank God the Russians got there in time, otherwise, I feared I would have been another of her victims."

Then, after a moment's pause, she exclaimed. "But they're dead. They were both sentenced to hang for war crimes at Nuremberg – I know, I was there."

"That Gillian," continued Dick, "is what everyone thought. But were you there at the hanging?" She shook her head. "Well, it was a circus. Yes, they were convicted, but there were so many in line for the rope that Otto Skorzeny's men were able to bribe the guards, get records falsified, and have them 'disappeared'. We don't know all who escaped, but we do know that probably as many as thirty other very nasty characters got away using the Ratlines escape route. Binz now works as Otto's housekeeper." Gillian sat back speechless with shock.

Dick continued. He was sure that Gillian was now fully on-board. "The situation is not just an eruption of local IRA terrorist activities. If it were, I would agree that our little exercise to give Chink street cred was slightly over the top. The IRA is not only why we are here today. Yes, they are a very real problem, but on their own, they can never succeed. However, the IRA plus ex-Nazi SS soldiers and Otto's financial resources spell big trouble. You heard Chink. He told us that he's met with Skorzeny and that he is going to meet him again at his HQ at Martinstown. After that meeting, we're hoping to have a clearer picture of what Skorzeny is planning. As the Prime Minister and Sir Richard said, all intelligence points to a big escalation of IRA activities boosted by ex-Nazis. And if we don't act now, thousands could die and we could be letting Ireland fall into the hands of another Reich."

"Oh, come on Major, isn't that a bit over the top," Peter cut in.

"I'm afraid I agree with Cunningham," said the PM. "Just hear him out."

Gillian, still shaken by the news that Frau Binz was still alive, had now cooled down and apologised for her outburst. She said she now understood the seriousness of the situation. "But tell me how I fit into this picture – I'm from the Alsace, not Ireland. I could never pass for an Irish Colleen."

"I don't know. You could pass for a Leprechaun, you're small enough" said Peter with a grin." But Major Cunningham," he turned to Dick, "Seriously, isn't all this still being a bit far-fetched. The Krauts were well and truly beaten in the war, Hitler died in his bunker and his henchmen were strung up at Nuremberg. It sounds as if you've been reading too many of my brother's books."

"That's enough of that Peter." 'C' broke in. "You heard Chink. We've got to wait for his next report. And by the way, I was in Berlin at the time of Hitler was supposed to have committed suicide. We were never able to verify that he actually died in his Berlin bunker. It happened in the Russian zone and we only knew what they were prepared to tell us. It took three weeks of negotiation before they allowed us to visit the site. And even then, they wouldn't let anyone from the Western forces see his remains nor any evidence of his death."

'C' looked around at everyone. Nobody had ever doubted that Hitler had committed suicide and he could from the faces of his audience that they too had accepted it as fact. "I was convinced he was dead," the MI6 Chief continued. However, the CIA recently released classified documents that confirmed a sighting of the Fuhrer by an American prisoner of war, Aubrey M. Temples."

"According to those documents, Aubrey had been with the US 82nd Airborne Division. He was no attention seeking wanker. Quite the reverse, he was a tough front line paratrooper with two Purple Hearts to his credit. Unfortunately, he was taken prisoner at the abortive Arnhem fiasco. Luckily for him, he was made to work on a prison farm just outside Nussdorf in Germany. The farm had a grass airstrip used for the transportation of farm produce. On April 30th 1945, a week before the war ended, Temples saw a large black Mercedes flying the Nazi Swastika drive past him and up to a small plane. He was no more than 6ft away from the car and clearly remembers seeing Hitler. Other sightings in Argentina have confirmed our suspicions. That evil bastard is still alive. Perhaps that gives you some idea of the seriousness of the situation we believe we are facing."

Then, looking at Gillian, he added. "I'm afraid you'll just have to be patient, Gillian. You are here for your advice, but there may well be a chance for you to wreak your revenge with interest on the Nazi bastards. This time, we want to make sure they are exterminated. Carry on Major."

"Thank you, sir. Right now, we're concentrating on limiting the supply of arms and explosives reaching Liam Walsh and his merry IRA men."

"We've already stopped several consignments of Russian Kalashnikov rifles, 3-inch mortars, and other weapons. As Chink said, he has achieved a close relationship with most members of the IRA Council and it's through Chink's tip-offs that we have been able to make these offshore seizures. We can't stop them all as doing so would almost certainly compromise him. We are concerned about the ones that are getting through, but we have a fair idea of where most are being stored. As Chink mentioned in his report, the IRA already has secret arms dumps established across the border in Eire and Northern Ireland."

"Apart from Chink, we have far too little intelligence. MI5 has agents on both sides of the border and we may need to bring them aboard Operation Blarney. Either way, we are in the process of inserting an undercover team of MI6 specialists as eyes and ears in the Province. When Chink specifies a target, we tell our men that we have received rumours that suggest a location. They check it out and feedback details through our existing channels. We then pass the coordinates to Bob Deacon's lot to do what's necessary – and 'Bob's your uncle, as they say." he grinned.

"We've already taken out three and have another four on schedule." Colonel Deacon nodded. "And my chaps have strict instructions to carry out assassinations only on my orders, clinically with as little disruption as possible. The last thing we need is for them to target Chink and take him out."

"As of today," continued Dick, "de Valera, the Irish Government and Catholic Church have had an open-door policy for every nasty ex-Nazi who've knocked on their door. We've no idea how many have been allowed in. It could be hundreds or even thousands. That's why we now believe some form of fascist backed IRA coup could be in the offing. Operation Blarney aims to obliterate any chance of this happening and contain the IRA until they fade into being no more than a political irritation.

"We could always send a couple of gunboats to Dublin up the river Liffey," broke in Peter, smiling. "Then again, we tried that forty years ago and it didn't work then – the Irish even wrote a song about it."

Dick Cunningham continued, ignoring the interruption. "If indeed we are right, we've got to wake up the Irish government to the threat and get them to take the necessary action before it's too late.

"Right now, Chink is our main man in the Emerald Isle and we are totally reliant on his feedback."

CHAPTER 11

Chink woke up with a throbbing head cold. He didn't feel like getting out of bed let alone driving to a meeting with Otto and his so-called friends. Eve, his wife, tried to persuade him to ring Skorzeny and arrange another day, but he was determined. Hugh offered to go with him. Having just passed his test, he said he could take over some of the driving. But Chink, was wary of having his family get too close to the Nazis and told him he needed him to stay at Bellamont to look after his mother and help Shaun and Terry exercise the horses.

After a quick family breakfast and several cups of strong coffee, the headache was receding and Chink felt slightly better. Owen McAteer, the butler, was waiting for him in the hall, ready with Chink's hat, coat, and scarf. Owen was a giant of a man from Kerry. He had been a Sergeant in the Parachute Regiment during the war and the lines on his face were like battle scars. He'd lost most of his foot in 1944 during the ill-fated Operation Market Garden attack at Arnhem. Over seven thousand troops died or

were taken prisoner there. Owen counted himself one of the lucky ones. Despite his injury,
he had led his platoon, fighting their way back
through enemy lines and over the Rhine to join
the advancing British relief force. Owen had
been introduced to Chink by Brigadier Simon
Fraser, the Lord Lovat, one of Chink's old army
friends. The ex-para man had been with Lovat
when he'd captured the well-known Pegasus
bridge. Owen, Simon had said, would be ideal
as the butler cum bodyguard that Chink needed.
The only proviso Owen had before accepting
Chink's job offer was that he wanted to bring his
pigeons. Chink had a private chuckle to himself. It was good to know that this giant had a
gentle side.

"I've given Betsy a quick once-over with
a duster sir and brought her round to the
front door for you." Owen said, then looking
more closely at his employer, he realised that
he wasn't his usual self. "Are you sure you
wouldn't like me to come with you sir. It looks
as if you might have a touch of the influenza."

"No, no tank you, Owen, Chink snuffled. "It's
juss a cold and I'm goin to take it easy. Betsy
virtually drives herself. Anyway, I need time to
tink and you are better here to keep a safe eye on
the household."

"Right you are, sir, you can rely on me. But if

you'll excuse me a moment." Owen turned and left Chink standing in the hall wondering what his butler was up to. In less than a minute, Owen was back with a glass containing fizzy liquid . "It's a Beecham's powder with a drop of a tonic my grandmother swore by – it should help keep your cold at bay. And I've taken the liberty sir to put a thermos of coffee on the passenger seat too, just in case you'd be needing to take a break"

Chink took the glass and drained it. Owen fussed around him like his old military batman, taking the glass then helping him on with his coat. Chink thanked him again before going out of Bellamont's main door and down the front steps to Betsy with Owen following like a shadow. Owen had left the engine running and stepped forward to open the drivers door. "Have a safe journey sir." Chink found his mothering overwhelming, but, then again, he thought, it was a good fault. "Tanks Owen, mush appreciated."He smiled to himself.

He didn't have to be at Martinstown house until midday. It was about 100 miles door to door and so he had plenty of time to mull over his tactics for the meeting. One way or another, it was vital to find out what Skorzeny's motivation really was. The weather was fine, sunny and dry and soon Owen's tonic was helping his headache and cold fade into a background sniffle. He felt relaxed and was looking forward to the drive.

He planned to stop off at Tullynally Castle just outside Castlepollard, to see his old friend Frank Pakenham. Like Chink, Frank's family had a long Irish history stretching back over 300 years. He was the 7th Earl of Longford, having inherited the title a year earlier from his brother. Despite a privileged upbringing, educated at Eton and Oxford, Frank was a committed socialist and Irishman. Known commonly as Lord Longford, he regularly attended the House of Lords, was a member of the Labour Shadow cabinet, and a close friend of Hugh Gaitskell, Leader of the Opposition.

Chink and Frank had been close friends since the mid-1930s. At the outbreak of the Second World War Frank had tried to join the army but had suffered a nervous breakdown. So much of their time together was spent in animated discussion about the unfairness of society and the need for change.

He was driving along the R191, just outside Bailieborough, when Chink was overtaken by a pale blue Austin Healey going far too fast. He could see the blond hair of the passenger blowing in the wind. She waved as they sped past. Some bloody idiot trying to impress his cailín, thought Chink.   Some 20 minutes later, as he was approaching the Castletowndelvin turn off to Tullynally Castle, he saw the Austin Healey stopped in a layby with its bonnet up and steam coming from the radiator.

A woman, probably the passenger he'd seen, was desperately waving for him to stop. Chink wasn't feeling like playing the good Samaritan, but he couldn't leave a fellow motorist stranded, particularly with such a pretty blond with her long legs and mini skirt.

He brought Betsy to a halt and backed up into the lay-by in front of the sports coupe, got out and walked back to the broken-down Healey.

"What appears to be the trouble then?"

"Oh, thank you so much sir for stoppin'. Me boyfriend says we've got a burst radiator pipe and he's gone to try and get help. It's been fine since we left Belfast. Then it stopped, just like that it did."

"It's not surprising the speed you were doing. You could have blown a gasket going well over the ton as you were."

"Yer right I know, but we was in a rush to see me parents – me mum's just been told she has the cancer. Then this had to happen," she said, choking back an emotional sob.

Chink gave her a sympathetic smile. "Let me take a look, I'm quite a dab hand with motors." He leant over the engine. Still roasting hot, it was obvious that the radiator was empty. All the pipework seemed OK, then he noticed that its drain tap had been turned on and there were the remains of a pool of water on the ground. Puzzled, Chink leaned further under the hood and reached down to turn off the tap. He was about to stand back up to ask the floozie what the hell was going on, when he heard the crunch of boots behind him. He tensed, but before he had time to react, the car's bonnet crashed down, driving his face hard onto the hot cam box cover, his right eye smashing into the oil filler cap. And at the same time, the bonnet catch hit the top of his spine, like an icepick.

For a split second, he was too shocked to react, stunned by the crippling blow to his back and the intense pain of his scorched face.

He couldn't help screaming out as he struggled to stand, but a full-blown boot in his crotch collapsed his legs and Chink fell back poleaxed onto the gravel. The paralysing blow to his bollocks piled more excruciating agony to his debilitating injuries. He was aware of blood running from his damaged eye, the burns on his face already blistering and he knew he'd damaged his many times broken nose yet again.

He tried to think, but the sheer trauma of the attack overcame his senses – he felt he was passing out. The boot smashed again, this time into his left side. "You shoneen cunt face - get the fuck up will you." The voice sneered the command. Chink was already in so much pain that he hardly felt the blow, but it did bring him back to his senses. It didn't matter who these shites were, he knew they had only just started. Through the fiery and nauseating pain, he attempted to scramble to his feet, but his legs were jelly, hardly able to respond. He just managed to get to his knees.

"Slow now yer bugger." And the stranger whacked the already damaged side of his face with the butt of the pistol he was holding. Another bolt of pain shot through his body and he fell back. "No funny business Mr. Major General Dorman O'fucking Gowan or you'll be eating lead from my friend here. Now get up real slow"

If only he'd taken Owen's offer to come with him. They knew his name. The situation was dire. This wasn't just a simple robbery. It was personal and his attacker hadn't finished by any means. Whilst still suffering and shocked by the assault, Chink recognised the man's accent. Whoever he was, he was from Northern Ireland - Belfast guessed Chink. He needed time to clear his mind and summon up the strength

to retaliate. "How do you know my name?"
He mumbled as he raised himself to his knees.
"Are you high-jacking me? If you want to take
my car, my wallet, go ahead, there's money in
the glove compartment - but for Christ's sake,
please, please don't hit me again."

"Go on, give the Taig another feel of your boot
in his doughnuts Lexie. I love to hear the
snobby shite scream and squirm."

"Bugger that - I've been paid to give our friend
here, the bloody traitor, a nasty road accident,
so let's get on with it.

Chink's mind had suppressed his injuries and
was now working at top speed. He probably
only had minutes to live – it was this Lexie or
Chink. The floozie seemed only to have a cheer-
leader role in the scenario.

He slowly raised himself again onto his knees,
his body bent double, his arms hugging himself.

"Come on you chinless fucking shit, just watch
how you get up." the assailant hissed impatiently. He leant forward to prod Chink with the
pistol.

Chink knew this was probably the moment, the
only chance he was going to get. Out of his one
working eye, he saw the face of the gunman.
Unshaven and pockmarked and arrogant; he
looked almost relaxed with a sneer of a smile.

He thought Chink was beaten and that was his big mistake.

Suddenly, ignoring his excruciating pain, Chink put all his strength into his move, springing up and forward, swinging his right arm, he hit Lexie's wrist holding the gun. At the same time, drove his head with all the force he could muster, butting Lexie in his solar plexus. For a moment, Chink was back in the trenches struggling with the enemy, only survival mattered. They fell back together onto the hard surface of the lay-by, Chink landing face-to-face on top of his assailant. Lexie, winded by the sudden turn of events, had dropped the gun. It was all the time Chink needed. Quick as a flash, he drove two straight fingers into the man's eyes as hard as he could using the eye poke he'd learnt in Japan. Lexie shrieked with pain as his hands came up too late to protect them. Chink grabbed the gun from where it had fallen. As his fingers closed around the handle, the girl stamped hard on his wrist. He hardly noticed; she wasn't going to stop him. He had the gun. Lexie made a half-hearted attempt to grab at Chink, but too late.

Chink shot Lexie's right knee cap out of existence. For a moment, the General had the sweet feeling of revenge. The hired gun was harmless now, a screaming wreck that could start attracting attention – so Chink put him out of his misery striking him sharply the butt of the gun to his temple.

Now, Chink had an unexpected problem. What was he going to do with them. He turned to the girl. "If you want to live longer than the next couple of seconds, you'll do exactly what I tell you to do. Go to the boot of my car, open it. You'll find a box of fishing tackle in there, bring it here."

But she was petrified, hardly able to move.

"I'll count to five and if you don't move yourself, you'll have a taste of your Lexie's gun and you'll never move again. One, two...."

Shivering with fear, she got herself together enough to do as Chink asked. As she went, he painfully lifted Lexie upright, opened the bonnet, and threw him face down over the engine, bringing the cover down sharply onto his back.

"Now see how you like the taste of the sodding cam cover, you turd." To any passerby, it would look as if the man was working on his breakdown. Meanwhile, Chink's mind was racing. How could he use this unexpected situation to his advantage.

The girl found the fishing tackle box and placed it on the ground near Chink. He introduced her to a Mexican quickstep by placing two shots between her feet. It had the desired effect. She jumped back horror-struck then collapsed, crumpling into a heap and wetting herself in the process. "Don't shoot me, Mister, I had nothing to do with all this – please, please" she whimpered.

Betsy's rear was only a matter of feet away from the battle zone. "Lie flat on the ground, face down and, if you move a hair on your head, I'll drill you." She did as he ordered. He opened his fishing tackle box and took out a reel of sea line, tough enough and certainly more than long enough to tie up two bodies. Lexie was stirring, but sufficiently unconscious for Chink to tie him up firmly. Still hurting like mad, but ignoring the pain, he summoned enough strength to heave the unconscious gunman away from the car and down until he was slumped on the ground. Then, holding him under his arms, he dragged him towards his Betsy. Finally lifting him fully upright, he threw him as hard as he could into the boot. The gunman let out an angry groan.

Chink turned to the girl. "Pull yourself together; get up and over here" he barked threateningly. I damn well heard what you said to Lexie about my doughnuts. So, one false move and we'll see how your fanny likes a similar taste of my Crockett & Jones brogues." But she was shaking, beyond any resistance, and came towards him submissively. "Now lean forward into the boot with your face down next to your Lexie."

Using the same fishing line, he bound her hands behind her back and her feet together and heaved her into the boot alongside her man. Despite their protests, he then gagged them both with Lexie's socks. A plan was coming together in his mind. He didn't want Lexie to bleed to death. It wasn't pity, but he needed to find out who sent him, so before he shut Betsy's boot, he used his tie to apply a temporary tourniquet to his assailant's leg.

Chink was shattered. The battle won, he sat on the side of the road, bent double striving to overcome the pain from his face, his back and his groin. He tried to rest his head in his hands, but just touching his face was pure agony. His only consolation was that the perpetrator was in a far worse state locked away in his car. He had to steel himself against his injuries. After what seemed ages, but no more than minutes, he managed to open his one good eye and look around him, at the Healey and the scene of the attack. Slowly his mind kicked into action. The pain was slowly receding and he managed to stand up.

Thank God no broken bones, he thought. He

took a hesitant step, but soon realised walking would be a problem. His testicles saw to that. There was little sign of the struggle, a pool of blood from the gunman's knee, otherwise no incriminating evidence - that was all in the boot of his car. Now, he had to decide what he was going to do with them. What story was he going to tell Frank and more importantly the men he was on his way to meet at Martinstown.

He shuffled around Betsy, opened the driver's door, and perched on the edge of the seat looking back towards the Healey. Anyone passing would just see a broken-down car and probably the Garda wouldn't be called for days, by which time the scene would be washed clean by rain. Agonizingly, he lifted his legs into the car. He sat trying to overcome the pain from his facial injuries, while his hands nursed his throbbing groin. Eventually, he started the engine. He'd decided to tell Frank the plain truth, but not the whole truth.

Frank was weeding the flower beds in front of Tullynally Castle and heard Chink's car as it came up the drive. He went to meet him, beaming with the pleasure of seeing his close friend. But his smile turned to shock as Chink struggled to get out of his car. "Good god, old chap, what on earth has happened to you. You look as if you've done a few rounds with that

Cassius Clay chap."

Without waiting for a reply, He shouted for his wife Elizabeth to come out and help. "Lizzie! It's Chink. He's badly hurt. Come and help me bring him in. Get one of the maids to find some bandages - and hot water – and a bottle of whiskey too.

Despite protestations that he could walk, they half carried him into their drawing room and stretched him out on a chaise-longue. "My word, you're in a bloody mess, Chink," gasped Frank. "I'm going to call the doctor?"

"No no," mouthed Chink through his damaged lips, "I've had worse than this." Then seeing the maid returning with the whiskey and bandages he continued, "Your whiskey is the best medicine Frank, but I could do with an ice pack for my eye." Frank sent the maid off for a bag of ice and poured Chink half a tumbler of neat Jameson's. He gulped it down in one. The initial burning sensation soon anaesthetised the pain of his mouth and spread a healing warmth to his other injuries. Frank refilled his glass. Again, Chink took a large gulp and then started to relate what had happened to him, ending by saying he had his assailants in the boot of his Rolls.

Frank was deeply shocked. "Look Chink, we

should call the Garda. You could have been murdered. It was an attempted assassination." He reached for his phone.

"Frank! hold on. That's the last thing I want. A retired British General is always going to be a target for extremists, IRA or Loyalists. Talking to the Garda will only create publicity. I want to live a quiet life. The less bloody crackpots come after me the better. I'm going to have this chappie in Betsy's boot patched up. He and his lady friend are obviously from the Belfast area and so on my way back to Bellamont I'll take them over the border for the RUC to find. They'll know what to do with them." But in truth Chink was beginning to think of some-thing quite different for Lexie and his so-called girlfriend. But he couldn't tell Frank. He would be horrified.

After about an hour of Lizzie's pampering, Chink felt much better. The ice pack had cooled his damaged eye and the swelling had reduced slightly meaning he could almost see out of it again. Both Frank and Lizzie wanted him to stay longer but Chink had a schedule to meet.

"You've both been so kind and hospitable, but I must get on my way to the Curragh. It's a vital meeting, State security and all that, I can't say more. I'm going to be late as it is, but better late than never." And it was nearly never he thought to himself.

"Let me at least lend you one of my suits and a clean shirt"

"Thank you, Frank, I'm very grateful but no," replied Chink, "I'm sure I can get a change of clothes at Martinstown. The host is about my size – anyway, I'd look like Charlie Chaplin in one of your suits, you're at least 6" shorter than me. But I was going to ask you for a favour."

Chink had previously asked Frank to take letters back to London, using him as an unofficial courier. They were all addressed to Macmillan and Chink said they were letters of political protest. Frank was therefore delighted to help. "I've got another protest for Macmillan. I've written my views on the Conservative party's Commonwealth Immigrants Act that aims to restrict our friends from the Commonwealth entering the UK. Damned hypocrisy if you ask me."

Frank, being very much against the proposed Act, fully supported Chink. In fact, the envelope contained the coded list of IRA members with their names, addresses, and aliases that he'd promised MI6 in his filmed report. Frank, unwittingly, provided a perfect channel of communication. Chink felt bad about deceiving him, but not bad enough not to abuse his naivety and goodwill. "And Frank, on my trip down, I had another couple of thoughts I'd like to make to the PM. Could you let me have a piece of paper and an envelope?"

Frank was only too pleased to oblige, then watched Chink scribble a hurried note to Macmillan, inserted it and his 'protest' envelope into the one Frank had provided. sealed it passed it over.

Chink left the anxious Lizzie and Frank at their castle gate, still fussing and trying to make him stay longer to recuperate.

However, with the pain now dulled by the whiskey, Chink's mind was focusing on how he could play his attempted highway assault to his advantage with the IRA and the Nazis. Just seeing the mess he was in would knock down barriers and get sympathy. Perfect, he mused to himself, the deeper I get into their confidence, the more chance I have of finding out what they are really up to.

CHAPTER 12

Just a couple of miles after leaving the Packen-hams, Chink stopped the car in a layby. Before he faced the Martinstown meeting, he needed to search Lexie for identification plus any material that gave reason for the attack. Luckily, the quality of the Rolls meant that the boot was well insulated for noise and odours. When he opened it up the stench was revolting. The gunman and the girl were semi-conscious and struggling feebly. They'd both pissed and shat themselves and their struggling had spread crap around the interior of the boot. And by striving to release their bonds, the fishing line had cut into their skin causing more bleeding. Chink could hardly catch his breath.

The eyes of the man blazed with hate and even with the gag, verbal abuse flowed in torrents. The girl moaned. Despite all this and with some difficulty, Chink searched Lexie. The gunman's wallet was stuffed with £5 notes, but apart from that and a visiting card, not much else was in it. The card showed his full name. Lexie Mitchell, a good Ulster name, thought Chink.

There was also a cheque book and driving licence with the same name on it and apart from small change in his pockets, the only other thing he had was a photo of Chink.

"So, Lexie ol' chap." You and your Bonnie are going on a little trip with me. I can't say I'm sorry that your little plan failed, but I can tell you for sure, you will deeply regret ever attempting to top me. You may think me a chinless old fart, but I have to tell you, I'm a fucking ruthless one." With that, Chink closed the boot and drove on with the rumbling protests from the boot dwindling into silence.

Chink knew the route to Martinstown House. It was close to the Fórsaí Cosanta, the Irish Army's training base at The Curragh, and their Directorate of Military Intelligence at Piercetown nearby. He'd given many talks on military strategy to officers and cadets at both places. He wondered if Otto's decision to buy Martinstown was influenced by their proximity, or was it just chance.

When he arrived, he was over 40 minutes late for the meeting. The drive up to the house was barred by 12ft high heavy iron gates. As he stopped, a man dressed in a grey chauffeur's uniform appeared from a small shelter hidden by bushes at the side of the entrance. He strode aggressively towards the car as Chink wound

down his window.   The Guard, thought Chink,
looked more like a Rottweiler on two legs, not
the sort of person to meet on a dark night,
As he approached the driver's side of Betsy, he
clicked his heels and bent forward as if to verify
the identity of the occupant.

"Agh! General Dorman-O'Gowan?" His voice
had a guttural Germanic tone tinged with surprise at seeing Chink's battered face. Chink just
nodded. The guard looked more closely at Chink
as if he was mentally comparing him with a
photo he'd seen. "You are having *ein Unfall,* an
accident - yes?"

"Look, just open the damn gates and let me
drive-in." Chink replied tersely ignoring the
question. He was too stressed out to enter into
pointless blather.

"You wait." The guard, went back to his kiosk.
Chink heard him telephone someone, speaking
in German. Moments later, he returned. "Please
to drive up to the house *Herr* General. You will
be met there." Then turning about, he marched
to the gates and with obvious effort slowly
swung each one back for Chink to drive through
raising his arm in a neo-Nazi salute. It was a
long intimidating driveway, heavily wooded on
both sides. Chink had the feeling he was being
watched every step of the way.

Martinstown House was a converted hunting
lodge, built around 1830. For many years it
had been a farm surrounded by lush green Kildare pasture land. There was a large expanse
of lawn in front of the house and several big
outbuildings at the rear. As Chink drove up to
the house, he noticed groups of men wearing
the same style of uniform as the gate guard, but
unlike the guard, they all wore red armbands
and carried what looked like Kalashnikov AK45
rifles. Seeing them, Chink felt an involuntary
shudder run through his body. One of them
broke away from his group and pointed Chink
to a parking area at the side of the house, where
a dozen other cars were parked. Yet another
man in the same style of uniform strutted
towards him from the main entrance of the
house. Definitely military influence here,
thought Chink – and then he realised that the
chauffeur uniform was a near copy of the old
Waffen-SS uniform without any insignia. His
welcomer too was armed, this time with a clas-
sic 9mm German Luger pistol.

The man gave a short Germanic bow as he
clicked his heels together. "General Dorman-
O'Gowan, *mein Herr.* You are being welcome
to Martinstown." He opened the driver's door
for Chink to get out. Even though he wore a
friendly smile, his voice had the same cold,

harsh and haughty tone as the 'guard' on the gate. A tone Chink had heard many times before when interrogating SS prisoners in North Africa. Hardly a feeling of welcome thought Chink. "My name is Richter, I am the chauffeur for Colonel Skorzeny. We met when I drove the Colonel to the IRA meeting at your palace."

Chink vaguely remembered, but he was too weary and in pain to even manage a response - but Bellamont being called a palace amused him. "I am asked to escort you to the meeting," added Richter. "The guards will look after your car."

Richter waited for Chink to swing his legs out of the car and stand. He looked at Chink from head to toe and his eyes widened in surprise at the state Chink was in, but said nothing. Turning, Richter led the way towards the main entrance at the side of the house with Chink waddling as best he could after him. The pseudo-gothic entrance to Martinstown house had double doors, which the chauffeur opened and stepped aside for Chink to enter. He was expected.

As his eyes grew accustomed to the gloom, a ruddy-faced middle-aged woman dressed in a knee-length black dress and pristine white apron appeared from one of the many doors off the large hallway. She must be Otto's ex-Nazi housekeeper, thought Chink, an evil bitch if ever I saw one.

"General Dorman-*Schmidt?*" she enquired in an annoyed tone.

He nodded, not bothering to correct her.

"My name is Frau Binz. Mein Gott, the state you are in. What has been happening, General? You have crash?" Chink ignored her questions. "Frau Binz, please just tell the Colonel that I'm here. I need a private word with him and a wash and brush up before I join the meeting."

"But there is no time. You are late" she replied accusingly. "The meeting is yet waiting for you. Please to follow." Without pausing for a reply, she turned on her heel and started towards the doorway from which he could hear voices.

"Damn it woman." Chink snapped at her back, his patience worn thin by his condition and not helped by her complete lack of empathy. She stopped abruptly, looking round at him, head in the air, her Germanic hackles rising. She was not used to being spoken to in such a manner apart by anyone but her Colonel.

"The bloody meeting can wait until I'm ready. I repeat - I need to talk to the Colonel now - here, in the hall - and be quick about it Frau Binz - *ver-dammt schnelle.*"

She glared at him. Without another word, she

hurried into the meeting room almost colliding with Otto as he rushed into the hall to see what all the noise was about.

"*Scheiss!* " he stopped, horrified by seeing the state Chink was in. "What on earth happened to you my friend, have you been in a fight, yes?"

"You could say that, but you should see my assailants," said Chink with a painful attempt at a smile. He explained about the attempt on his life and how he'd been able to turn the tables on his attackers, who were now locked safely in the boot of his car.

"Frau Binz!" Skorzeny turned to his house-keeper. "What are you waiting there for. Quick woman. Make guest room Arcadia ready for the General immediately- *sofort.*" His tone made her even more indignant, still smarting from the way Chink had spoken to her. But she contained herself, her fury only betrayed by the deepening puce of her already ruddy face. She gave a kurt Germanic bow, turned abruptly and hurried up the stairs.

"Apologies General. Frau Binz is used to being, how you say, queen bee here. I am too soft with her and will make sure she understands that you are my esteemed guest and important ally. But before I show you to your room Chink, I'll have your prisoners taken to a secure place in my outbuildings. The meeting will adjourn until you are ready. Your clothes are completely ruined, *Kaput,* as we say in German. I'll tell Binz to look you out some of my clothes. I'm a bit more around the middle, but apart from that, we are about the same size. In the meantime, I'll ask one of my other guests, a doctor, to come up and give you a check over."

Chink slowly followed Otto up the stairs, trying to make a mental note of the layout. There were five rooms, two rooms on each side of a short corridor and a room at the end, where Frau Binz stood, still glowering sullenly by an open door waiting for him to enter.

"Go to my room Frau Binz, and fetch a suitable change of clothes from my wardrobe for the General here." Then to Chink. "There is no rush, we want you as best repaired as possible before progressing our meeting.   So, we will await you, my friend."

Otto left and a few minutes later, as Chink was about to step into the shower, there was a knock on the door. Without waiting for a reply, a middle-aged distinguished-looking man in a dark suit entered the room carrying a glass of amber liquid.

"Good afternoon General," the visitor said in

impeccable English. "My name is Josef. I am a doctor. Colonel Skorzeny asked me to look you over before the meeting. He also thought a glass of Asbach brandy might help too." Another German thought Chink, and, more than that, he looked vaguely familiar. "You certainly look as if you've been through the hedges as you English say," Josef added .

"Yes, I have had a spot of bother. But you should see the other two doctor." Chink replied with as much of a smile as he could muster. "Oh, and by the way, I may sound English, but I'm actually Irish."

"*Entschuldigung* – I apologise. I'm only a visitor like yourself and the accents are difficult to distinguish. Otto has asked me to look at your captives too, but priority is you."

After a thorough inspection, apart from his broken nose, Josef said that Chink's wounds were superficial and he would recover quickly from the burns to his face. His oversized black and blue testes would also recover with no long-term effects. He said that his nose should be reset as soon as practically possible. "I've seen far worse in my time - far, far worse" he chuckled softly as if revisiting old memories. "I'll leave you now and see you downstairs when you're ready." Doctor Josef left Chink to his shower.

Ten minutes later, when he came out of the shower, a full change of clothes lay on the bed and another glass of amber medicine sat on the side table. It was almost an hour since he'd arrived. He felt miles better apart from his right eye and his testicles, which had swollen to the size of tangerines. Otto's clothes were slightly on the short side for Chink's tall frame, but anything was better than his blood-stained cast-offs. They'd probably been searched by the housekeeper while he was showering, but he never carried anything incriminating. Boosted by the double dose of Asbach, he was ready for the meeting.

CHAPTER 13

He came down the stairs, one step at a time, each one sending agonizing pains through his groin. When he reached the bottom, Frau Binz appeared as if by magic in the hallway.

"Well! at last," she said in a huffy voice. "Please to follow me to the meeting you," she stressed, "have kept for waiting." Chink didn't bother to rise to her rudeness or correct her bad English and limped behind her. She opened the door and stood aside for him to enter.

The room was enormous with bay windows that looked out onto beautifully manicured gardens. It was clear to Chink that it was the manor's main dining room. It was even bigger than Bellamont dining room. A long circular ended mahogany table running down the centre had seating for at least thirty guests. The sun wasn't shining directly into the room, but the brightness outside contrasted with the room's deep red walls. Added to which, a thick haze of cigarette smoke hung over the table making it difficult to see anything more than outlines of figures sitting down either side of it.

As his one-eyed view adjusted to the conditions, he was just able to make out Skorzeny sitting at the far end with his back to the window, and the two top IRA Council members, Finbar Kelly and Liam Walsh on either side of him. The rest were just little more than silhouettes.

Skorzeny stood up and called the meeting to order. The hum of murmuring ceased and heads turned to see the new visitor. "Gentlemen. It is my pleasure to present Major General 'Chink' Dorman-O'Gowan." Everyone stood and broke out into applause. Otto continued, "I have been telling my friends here about your ordeal, your near assassination. We are all greatly impressed with your amazing resilience Chink. Now, please to take a seat up here with your Irish friends." He indicated an empty chair next to Finbar.

For a moment, Chink was quite moved by the reception they'd given him. "Thank you all, but if you don't mind Colonel, sitting is rather painful at the moment. I'll have plenty of time to suffer driving back to Bellamont so for now, if you don't mind, I prefer to stand."

"I quite understand. The doctor was just telling us about your injuries. We are even more saluting you for turning up here, but it's what I would expect of a professional soldier like yourself."

Chink held up a hand in appreciation and tried a smile. "It's I who should be thanking you all for waiting. It would take a lot more than a few scratches to keep me away from such an important meeting like this, gentlemen."

Yes, he thought to himself, but not for the same reasons you all may think. And as his damaged sight became more accustomed to the light, he could now see most of the individuals along each side of the table more clearly, all strangers, apart from the doctor who had checked him over. Yet, several faces looked hauntingly familiar. A picture of Skorzeny shaking hands with Adolf Hitler dominated the room, looking down from over the fireplace, and he could just about make out a Nazi flag leaning against the side of the central bay window.

Still standing, Skorzeny addressed the meeting. "We are here with one single aim. To finalise how we old comrades can help our IRA friends led by Finbar here free Northern Ireland from the hands of the British. I still have extensive funds and *Herr* Folens has promised another two million dollars, so our financial support is virtually bottomless." There was another round of applause as one of the guests half stood in acknowledgement – presumably Folens, Chink surmised.

Finbar broke in. "We are more than grateful

for all your support Colonel. We don't hate the British, do we General," he said looking down the room at Chink. "We just want them to bugger off back to their kennels over the water."

"Right Finbar," Chink replied, "but when it's all over, I'll be the first to extend a hand of friendship. Many of my friends are Irish-Anglo like me and it's not war we want, but the return of our heritage and land. I've spent half my life over there and other parts of their empire, but my heart and my passion are for Ireland and I'll spill my blood for this holy land if necessary." Chink hoped he hadn't overdone the nationalism, but his words brought another round of applause.

"Gentlemen please!" Otto was impatient to get on. "Can we have the chit-chatting later. We must get starting," Then addressing Chink, Skorzeny progressed. "You may recognise some of my old friends and acquaintances, but let me introduce to you anyway. Here on my left, is ex-SS *Schutzstaffel* colleague of mine, Fritz Suhren." Suhren stood and clicked his heels with a bow in true Nazi fashion and gave Chink a warm smile. Chink knew Suhren's evil reputation. He had been the animal in charge of the infamous Ravensbrück concentration camp. Despite his feeling of utter loathing, Chink nodded at him and smiled.

"And next to Fritz is Pieter Menten" Skorzeny moved on.

"Ah yes," said Chink, they exchanged welcoming smiles, "Good to meet you Pieter. I had heard you'd made your home in Waterford. It's great for Ireland to have such a well-known and respected art expert here." Chink knew all about Menten. He was a Dutch art collector who at the outbreak of war had joined the Nazi SS. Responsible for the killing of thousands, he was still wanted for his war crimes in Poland. He had lined his pockets by selling works of art stolen from the Jews.

"And I'm sure you know our Belgian friend, Albert Folens," continued Otto. "Albert was with us during the war. When it ended, Ireland gave him refuge and Albert is now a very successful publisher." The Folens Publishing Company was well known throughout Ireland as the top supplier of children's educational books.

Chink knew Folens alright. Inwardly, he was appalled. He knew the truth about Folens exploits. He was still wanted for his war crimes in Belgium. But he smiled and said how good it was to know that Ireland's children's reading material was in such good hands.

"Then, next to Albert, we have another good old friend of mine, Andrija Artuković." Otto resumed. "Andrija and I served together on several special missions against Tito's partisans in Yugoslavia."

Chink showed no sign of the utter sickness and revulsion he felt. He just kept smiling as warmly as his battered face allowed. He knew of Artuković, 'The Butcher of the Balkans'. An apt name for the fiend he was, considering the many thousands he exterminated during the war. But it got worse.

"Sitting next to Andrija, you may know of Wilhelm Boger. Wilhelm was a senior officer in our old *Geheime Staatspolizei, the* Gestapo. He has recently joined us to help the IRA interrogate their prisoners." Otto had had to act fast to replace to his old friend Aribert Heim after he returned to Spain. And in having done so, he knew that Boger was someone who still had passion for torture and techniques for making prisoners only too willing to talk. Otto gave a cold chuckle. "I thought you might like to see the Interrogation facilities later Chink."

"Wilhelm, perhaps the General would like you to question those *Angreifer bastarde* assailants who attacked him. They deserve some of your treatment. It would be interesting to hear what was behind their attempt - don't you think so General?" Otto looked expectantly at the Chink.

Chink knew Boger all right. He had a well-deserved reputation. He'd been known as 'the tiger of Auschwitz'. "I would be pleased to have a professional find out who was behind the attack - but I want to keep them alive for when I hand them over to the RUC, over the border. So, nothing too rough." Boger nodded. "It would be an honour to find out who was behind the attack on you General." With that, Boger stood, gave a curt bow and left the room.

It's a room full of evil, sadists, and perverts - like being in a snake pit of cobras, Chink shuddered inwardly. He only just managed to mask the horror and revulsion he felt at seeing these people. But there was more to come.

Otto continued. "And of course, you have already met my celebrated ex SS colleague *hauptsturmführer* Josef Mengele."

"So that's why you seemed familiar," said Chink" and gave Mengele his extra wide and charming smile. Mengele, who had been known as 'The Angel of Death' in the Third Reich, was last heard of in Uruguay, at least as far as Chink was aware. He felt a deep cold anger brewing. These were all wanted war criminals, not just ex-Nazis, but evil psychopaths. And in fact, he was sure some had been sentenced to be strung up at the Nuremberg trials - but they were here, alive and kicking in the same room. For now, he had to keep his true feelings hidden and under control. "Your reputation precedes you Herr Doctor - and I'm most grateful to you for fixing me up so well."

Otto continued to introduce others around the table. "Josef is visiting with three old comrade friends of mine from Argentina, Kurt Meyer, Herman Ramcke, and Edgar Puaud. Chink automatically smiled and nodded. But he found it hard to believe that Mengele and these other animals were in Ireland simply to help the IRA. And how was it that they were able to visit and move around Ireland so openly? Who was responsible for allowing them into Ireland? The Irish government's pro-German wartime neutrality was still alive and kicking, he mused. These animals were responsible for killing millions of innocent people. He made a mental note of the names of Otto's so-called 'old friends and comrades. He knew some of their backgrounds already but would ask MI6 for more details when he sent in his next report.

"Hang on a mo there Colonel," interrupted Liam, glancing at Finbar. "It's all very well bringing in your boys brigade, but what's in it for you Nazi fellers here? It's our *feckin* Ireland we are fighting for, not yours."

Otto was already anticipating such a question,
but Liam's rude and insulting tone outraged
him. He answered, "Herr Walsh!" Menace
oozing in the tone of his reply. "My friends and
I need a haven to live out the rest of our lives
in peace, without harassment from lunatic
revenge-seeking Jewish scum and Commun-
ists. Without us, there could never be a united
Ireland. I've agreed with the Irish government,
that in return for our active support, we and
our children will all receive full Irish citizenship. Is that not so Charles?"

The person sitting at the end of the table nearest to Chink with his back to him answered.
"That's right Otto. I have it from the Taoiseach
himself." As he spoke, he turned around and
gave Chink a friendly smile full of concern.
"Sure, you look as if you've been through a
ghastly ordeal, Chink old feller. But it's good it
didn't stop you from making the meeting." It
was Charles Haughey, the Irish Government's
Minister for Justice.

Chink was stunned. He was speechless. It took
him seconds to recover himself. He had no idea
that any Dail minister was involved with the
Nazi plans. He already knew Otto had contacts
in the Dáil Éireann, the Irish government, but
not at Ministerial level, let alone the Minister of

Justice.

"Now there's a surprise Charlie. I hadn't an inkling you would be here involved in these liberation plans.   De Valera never mentioned it and I saw him only last week"

"That's Dev for you. He likes to have his little secrets." Charles Haughey spread a beaming smile round the table. "You know as a government we can't be seen to support any action against the North, support for the IRA, or whatever. But be assured that our government is right behind you all."

Otto was hardly listening to the exchange between Chink and Haughey. Still seething at Liam 's insinuations, he went on addressing the two IRA men. "We are putting our lives on the line alongside yours for a united Ireland. Our help with Strabane should have convinced you of that."

"If you want us walking away, we will." he shrugged dismissively, his apparent anger and apparent hurt showed as he growled. "Our services are always in demand and would be per haps more appreciated elsewhere." He stood, starting to collect the papers in front of him. "We might as well close the meeting now."

"Oh no, oh no, no no" blurted Finbar, taken

aback by Otto's sharp response. As far as the
IRA was concerned, the Nazi financial and
military support was pivotal if the IRA was ever
going to achieve its goal. "Liam 's just a bit edgy
that's all. You, your men, and your money are
a massive help and, Jezus, when we win, we'll
welcome you all with open arms as full-blooded
Irish brothers."

"And what we both did to the bodies of those
Arshite agents was a great example of what
we'll do to any feckin Brit who gets in our feckin
way" added Liam, now seeking to placate Skorzeny's wrath.

"Well, I'm glad we've got that established,
gentlemen." Skorzeny visibly calmed and sat
back down, the tension in the room slowly
subsiding. "I'd hate to stop my engineers at
Portglenone."

Chink was immediately alert. What was that
about Portglenone - and what were Otto's men
doing there? He didn't have to wait long to find
out as Otto continued.

"Your inside man there, novice monk Joseph
Lynskey, did a good job hoodwinking the Ab-
bott at the monastery into letting our men in to
restore their old swimming pool. Once they've
finished their work, he'll know the truth; that
we've built you an underground arsenal to

support the liberation. By then, it will be too late for him to do anything about it. If the authorities knew, they'd be blamed and the entire establishment would be arrested. So, as you say, he'll be forced to be turning the blind eye."

Then turning on Liam, the Nazi Colonel spat out. "And you Walsh, don't you go high horsing with me any more – we have a deal with your government, the Taoiseach, and that's that.

Otto's irritation with the IRA members was slowly subsiding. "Before we get down to some serious business, why don't I get someone to take you to see how Wilhelm and his men are progressing with your prisoners."

Chink was concerned about what was being done to them and at the same time welcomed the chance to take a break from the Nazi meeting. Frau Binz led him from the house towards the interrogation centre, from which muffled cries could be heard.

Otto's Nazi housekeeper opened the door to Boger's workshop and stood back for Chink to enter. He steeled himself for what he was about to see. The scene that greeted him was almost like a hospital operating theatre. Lexie was lying flat on a table illuminated by a bar of lights, similar to those used over a snooker table. Boger was standing over him dressed like a surgeon in the midst of an operation and behind him was another robed man standing beside a tray of instruments. The bastard's revolting theatre nurse, thought Chink. The girl was tied to a chair with wires attached to a number of sensitive parts of her bedraggled body in a dead faint.

"Ah General," Boger greeted him. He put down the saw he had in his hand. "That *hure fraulein* is a waste of our time. She is fainting every time we apply the *Elektrizität* volts. Even buckets of ice-cold water now fail to revive her. But this man, "he said looking at Lexie, "He is a professional, much more interesting. I have tried a little persuasion to make him talk and was about to start some amputation," Besides Lexie's body was a pair of blooded pliers and what looked like fingernails. Even though they had tried to assassinate him, Chink couldn't let the torture carry on. No matter what they had done, Boger's treatment was inhuman and Chink had to stop it. He would rather give them a clean bullet himself than leave them with this Nazi, he decided. "Thank you, Wilhelm, your reputation looks well founded. I'm sorry I can't let you carry on, but I'm about to leave. Wrap them up securely and put them back in the boot of my car. I'm going to have the RUC over the border take care of them." Reluctantly, the ex-

Gestapo torturer agreed and as Chink went back into the house to join the meeting again, Boger and his men started to release the prisoners for return to the boot of Chink's car.

The meeting ended as it was starting to get dark. The weather had changed to a misty drizzle, not the sort of conditions for one eyed man with aching balls to drive in, he thought. Nevertheless, after a slow, tedious and stressful journey, he made it to where he planned to dump Lexi and his partner - on the pavement side of the Fane river bridge on the N53, just inside the Northern Irish border. There was no border post there.

He had thought about ringing the RUC to tell them about where to find the couple, but it would mean a long drawn-out enquiry which was the last thing he wanted. It was a busy road during the day and he was sure someone would stop.. He consoled himself that at least, he had taken them from Boger's clutches and if they lived, they would think twice about attacking him again.

It was midnight when he eventually got back to Bellamont He'd decided to ask Owen to clean out Betsy's boot. He'd spin him some story about having found a couple of road kill deer on the way down to Martinstown. He knew how

much Germans liked game and so had picked
them up and given them to the Colonel.

CHAPTER 14

One week after the meeting at Martinstown House, Lord Longford telephoned 10 Downing Street to say that he had another one of those protest letters from Dorman-O'Gowan for the Prime Minister. The PM was away in Scotland, but his secretary said she would arrange for someone to collect it. She rang the Prime Minister to let him know and he told her to ring MI6 and have them collect it.

Major Cunningham had taken the call. He had a good idea of what the envelope contained. The list of IRA members. He'd dropped what he was doing and hurried over to the House of Lords.

Later, back in MI6 Headquarters, Kali, he went directly to Sir Richard White's office. Outside his office, he was stopped by 'C's Secretary, Rebecca. She was a very attractive blond, tall and slim, but it was her hemline that hijacked the minds of 'C's visitors - a very mini- skirt. He always found himself admiring the recruitment policy of the Secret Intelligence Service's chief.

"I'm sorry Major Cunningham, but Sir Richard asked not to be disturbed, can you come back at say 4.30 pm. He's free for half an hour then."

Still fighting to keep his mind on his mission and not on Rebecca's legs, he told her he had a vitally important message from Ireland. And whatever 'C' was doing, he would want to be disturbed for that.

Rebecca said nothing, gave Dick a hostile huff and petulant stare as if to say 'no bloody way you get past me, Major. But she thought better of it. She turned, knocked on the door of 'C''s office, and went in, shutting it behind her. When she came out, she stood back for Dick to pass her and enter, at the same time giving him a withering look. "Come in - come on in Dick." 'C' called. Major Cunningham entered and the door slammed behind him. The MI6 Chief was sitting at his visitors' table, with a pile of photographs in front of him. "Is she always so aggressive?" Dick asked.

"Oh, I'm sorry about Rebecca," 'C' said. She can be a bit tyrannical. But she's my beautiful Mata Hari guard dog. Her looks stop everyone in their tracks and she can be quite formidable too - as you seem to have found out. Best secretary I've had in all my years in the Service. Her surname is most appropriate - it's 'Bashall'. Anyway, what have you got Dick?"

Dick sat down. "It's the envelope from Chink.

Longford seemed very agitated when he gave it to me," explained the Major as he shut the door. "He said Chink had been badly beaten-up, waylaid - he mentioned something about him taking prisoners and thought Loyalists might have been involved."

'C' looked visibly worried. "Damn it, I've warned him that might happen. There are a lot of hot-head in the North who see him as a traitor. I even offered him another of our men as a chauffeur bodyguard, but he refused. He might think again now. Go on then. Open the envelope."

It contained several sheets listing names and addresses. "It looks like what we were expecting, but there's another envelope inside too addressed to you." The Major handed both over.

Sir Richard scanned the list. "This is going to be very useful. Chink's even marked those he thinks would be good targets for Bob's men."

He opened the other envelope. Inside was a scrawled handwritten note:

I've just stopped at Longford's place on my way down to Martinstown.

Some Loyalist cretins tried to wipe me out. But I turned tables on them and I've got them tied up in the boot of my car. I thought I'd show them to Otto before I hand them over to the RUC. I didn't get out

of it unscathed, but I've had worse on a Saturday
night out in Cairo with Hemingway. It will add to
my standing as a loyal republican.

I will need to brief you chaps after my visit to
Skorzeny. A film report would be completely inad-
equate - we need to discuss the situation. Let's RV
at my fishing hide on Drumlona lough. Major Cun-
ningham knows where it is. Get Horrocks to ring
me at Bellamont. If he asks me for dinner at the
Royal Automobile Club in London, with a date and
time, I'll take that as confirmation of when your
chaps will be coming over. Keep the numbers down,
groups cause suspicion. Don't forget to bring your
fishing gear and wellies too.

Yours ever

Eric

'C' looked at Cunningham. You have to go Dick.
You know Chink and you know the location.
Who else do you want with you?"

"Airey Neave would be a good chap to take
along. If we're talking strategy, he'd be my
first choice. He's also got Irish blood in him,
very adaptable, thinks on his feet and by all
accounts, pretty ferocious when needs be."
Dick thought for a moment, "and perhaps Bob
Deacon."

"Good thinking. Bob would be good. He could
also have a couple of his men shadow you to

cover your backsides. We can't be too careful. If you run into any trouble, well, they'd be there to help sort it. I don't want you ending up as another pig's dinner."

Dick certainly didn't like the idea of being pig feed either.

"Too right sir. March 20th would be good, that's Tuesday next week. Let's say 2100hrs. It's tight but it should give us time to prepare. You know General Horrocks better than I do sir, will you arrange for him to ring Chink and set up the phantom dinner date? Chink should be back from Martinstown by now. And, if you can talk to Airey, I'll have a word with Bob. I know he would like some action away from his boring desk job."

As Dick was leaving, 'C' called him back. "Dick. You are the linchpin for our operations in Ireland, God only knows what would happen if we lost you, so take care and – good luck"

CHAPTER 15

Brian Horrocks rang Chink as planned, and arranged 'dinner' at the RAC . He knew then, when the MI6 team would be at the RV on Drumlona lough. He started to prepare a written report on what he'd learnt at Martinstown to hand over to them, plus he planned to outline his ideas for what forward action should be taken.

It wasn't unusual for Chink to go night fishing for pike on Bellamont's loughs, after all, they were all part of his estate. In all, there were eight loughs all joined by river channels, the nearest one to Bellamont House being Dromore. He often took Hugh fishing, but not for this trip, he thought, he had to be on his own. Fortunately, Eve had taken the lad for a cultural tour of Dublin and wouldn't be back until Thursday, so it wasn't an issue anyway.

It was 1800hrs on the evening of the planned meeting. Outside, the clear blue sky was already tinged with the pinks and golds of a stunning sunset. A delight to see thought Chink, but not so good out on the loughs. A clear sky meant that there would be mist coming up over the water and it would be cold and damp out there. He changed for the weather, putting on a thick woollen vest under a Guernsey sweater and 'long-johns' under a pair of Donegal trousers. On his way out of the house, he went to his study for the Martinstown report he'd written. At the same time, he opened his safe and pocketed his favourite close quarter weapon, a WW2 German Luger pistol, and made sure the magazine was full. After his experience on the way down to Martinstown, he wasn't going anywhere alone without the security of a gun. He put on his old army jeep coat and packed his rods and other fishing gear into the back of his Land Rover. He drove down to the estate boathouse on Dromore, where he kept his UK built 1934 pilot boat, Miranda. It was big for fishing on the loughs but perfect for travelling through the network of rivers that connected them. He and Eve needed Miranda for when they took friends out touring around the waterways. The rendezvous on the banks of Drumlona lough was about 5 miles away. He had plenty of time.

At the same time as he was loading his fishing gear onto Miranda, Dick Cunningham with Airey Neave and Bob Deacon were arriving in Rockorry, a small village on the South side of the border just to the north of Drumlona lough. They used the same airfield Dick and David Slater had used three weeks earlier on their 'undertaking' visit. Bob Deacon's men had arranged rental transport, a Morris Traveller shooting brake with Republican registration plates. They had put an ample supply of fishing gear in the rear, rods, folding seats, and water-proofs. Underneath, out of sight, they had also supplied three 9m Browning handguns, half a dozen stun grenades, one sterling machine gun and a Traumafix military field first aid kit.

It was still light, but the surrounding country-side was low lying and a mist was beginning to form. They were in good time.

"I don't know about you two, I've been on the go since first light," said Dick as they parked in the main street of the village. The local butcher and general stores had shut up shop for the night, there was hardly a soul around, the only sign of life was the local bar, Terry's.

"I could use a pint of Guinness. Let's go into that bar over there. We can talk about fishing, enjoy a glass and confirm our route to the lough on the map."

Airey didn't like the idea, but they had the time and they might get some local intelligence. "OK, but let's be quick and only one pint."

"If you two don't mind, I'd rather stay out here

and keep watch over the kit," muttered Bob, obviously not liking the idea too. "But you two go."

So, Airey and Dick went into Terry's Bar. There were a few local looking men by the bar, admiring the attributes of a pretty barmaid. Otherwise, it was empty. Airey ordered two pints of Guinness and carried them over to where Dick had taken a table as far away as possible from the bar. Dick spread the map out. "Right, let's just check again our position on the map. "We're here," he said pointing. "We'll drive along the R188 here for about a mile. Then opposite this derelict old farm building here, we turn left down this cart track. We go down about 500yds then park up. It's a trudge along the path, marked in green, to the water's edge."

Just then, the barmaid approached. "You fellers be wantin' a bite to go with yor drinks."

"No thanks, we've got some sandwiches in the car." Dick hardly looked at her and turned back to the map.

"Suit yourselves then," she said huffily and returned to her perch behind the bar.

When Dick looked up, he saw her talking to one of the locals and nodding towards where they sat. He assumed she was complaining about his abruptness and thought nothing of it - until shortly afterwards. The man she had been talking to, seemed to make up his mind, left his drink on the bar and hurried out. It could be nothing, but Dick got a sinking feeling in the pit of his stomach. The bloke might have simply gone home for his supper, but there was a chance the disgruntled barmaid had noticed their accents, seen the map, and the boyo slipped off to alert the local Provos. What a prat to suggest coming in here in the first place, Dick thought with regret. Bloody stupid!

He folded up the map. "Airey - we need to get out. I don't like the way that barmaid was having a word with those guys at the bar - they've both been glancing over here and now one has just rushed out - he's even left his drink on the bar. Could be nothing, but we can't take any chances." Airey didn't comment. He'd thought at the time that having a drink was taking too much of a chance in the first place - a crass idea - but then, he hadn't objected and had gone along with it. If there was a problem, he was as much to blame.

As they returned to join Bob in the shooting brake, Dick wondered what might have spooked the man. The loughs were well known for good fishing and attracted enthusiasts from all over the country - that's why he'd brought all the gear. But he then realised that he and Airey were both wearing military issue wellington boots. How fucking imbecilic. Damn and blast, he thought angrily - like wearing big neon signs around our necks saying 'British Army on manoevres'. Shit!

When they got back in the car, Dick told Bob about the possible compromise, and he confirmed that he'd seen someone dash out of the bar and hare off down the street. That endorsed it in Dick's mind. The mission had been jeopardised. He apologised again for his unprofessional slip-up, adding more unnecessary danger to their already risky expedition.

"Maybe we should call the meeting off?" a subdued Dick suggested.

"There's too much at stake for us to do that," Airey argued. "Yes, it was fucking stupid Dick, but I went along with you. Let's not dwell on it, at least we are aware. As you said, it could be absolutely nothing - he could simply have argued with the bar floozie, or suddenly remembered dinner was on the table at home. Best if we think of the worst-case scenario tho' and be prepared. But carry on we must."

In the end, the three agreed and drove out of Rockcorry on their way to the rendezvous. They went slowly and soon found the turning opposite the derelict building and drove down the cart track until it widened. This was the place they'd seen on the map, where they could park. What had been a slight mist was thickening with visibility getting difficult. Finding their route wouldn't be easy, but it would make it tricky for anyone who might be following them too.

They lifted all the fishing gear off the weapons in the back of the Morris. Airey and Dick armed themselves with the Browning automatic pistols, Bob took the Sterling machine gun and stun grenades. They listened for any sound of pursuit, but apart from an owl, all was still. They set off in single file, Dick leading and Bob bringing up the rear.

All seemed to be going as planned. The further they went, the more confident they were that they had overreacted about the bar scenario. They knew there were two of Bob's men out there somewhere hopefully watching their backs anyway.

There was a moon giving some light, but with the mist now denser, they could barely see 5 feet in front. It should have only taken about 20 minutes but they took a couple of wrong turns and nearly started a fire fight when they thought they were being ambushed. It turned out to be a herd of startled Sika deer. Nevertheless, they arrived at the RV only 10 minutes late.

The mist was even thicker over the water. They listened intently and could just hear the faint chugging of an engine. Then through a less dense patch of mist they could make out the bow of a boat. It had to be Chink. Using his torch, Dick gave the prearranged signal, a morse code 'S' - three short flashes. After a tense few seconds, back came the answer, one flash, the agreed response 'T'. The meeting was about to happen.

Suddenly, a bright light from behind them flooded where they were standing. They turned around, blinded. They couldn't see who or what was there. "So now, what the feck have we here. Fecking Brits up to no good, I'll be bound." A bodyless voice announced. "And signaling to yer friends you were - now get yer feckin hands in the air before we drill the lot of you turds. Roisin in Terry's was too feckin right."

" Let's drill the shitty shites." said another voice.

Dick would regret their village stop for the rest of his life. But then came another voice from behind the two Irish locals. An English Cockney accent." "It's you two tossers who should be getting your fucking hands in the air - or you're dead meat, you bogshite micks,

Everyone froze for a very long 2 seconds. A Mexican standoff. Who was going to move first.

Then, one of the Provos turned, dropped on one knee and fired blindly behind him from where he thought the voices originated while the other fired a wild burst in the direction of the trio. It seemed that guns blasted from all directions. Then, it was over. Seconds passed before anyone moved. Bob Deacon was lucky to escape with a flesh wound, but Airey Neave had taken a bullet in his shoulder.

"Apologies sir, Sergeant Rawlings here. We got held up in the fog."

"Thank god you turned up when you did Rawlings, or we'd have been wiped out. You two OK?"

"Not a scratch, sir."

But not so the two IRA men. They were seriously wounded.

"Major Cunningham," Bob called over to where Dick had been standing, but there was no answer. He swept the area with his torch and saw what appeared to be Dick lying still on the edge of the clearing. He went over. It was Dick Cunningham. Or what was left of him. Dick had been standing near Airey. His face and upper body had caught the full force of the IRA's gunfire blasting his body backwards and taking most of his head off. There was nothing anyone could do.

CHAPTER 16

Chink was no more than 30 yards from the rendezvous point. After confirming the MI6 party had arrived, he was about to move in to the shore when the shooting started. It was deafening. Stray bullets sprayed the water around Miranda. Splinters flew when one hit her superstructure, another shattered two windows in the passenger section as it passed through, but luckily Chink escaped unharmed. The firing stopped as suddenly as it started.

He immediately shut off the boat's engine and listened. Through the mist, he could hear raised voices - mixed with groans and whimpering. But as far as he was concerned, it was all unintelligible babble, only catching one or two words. He waited. No more shots. After a few minutes, he decided to take a chance. "What the hell's going on there - what's all that shooting ?" He yelled aggressively. "Whoever you are, you are on my land and I don't take kindly to poachers shooting up the countryside. I'm armed, so don't you be trying anything."

A voice responded. "The shooting is over sir.

We have a fatality, a wounded man, plus a couple of badly shot up blokes who ambushed us."

Hearing the accent, Chink knew it must be Major Cunningham's party. "Just stay where you are," he replied, " I'm coming ashore." He put on his waders, then started Miranda's engine and ran her gently forward into the mud bank side of the lough.

He lowered himself into the shallow water and waded ashore, in one hand a hurricane lamp and the other his Luger He had to be ex- tremely wary as so much rested on him being and remaining undercover. He couldn't take any chances. He could be walking into a trap. Cunningham and his men might have been cap- tured and forced to answer him.

As he came towards the clearing, the light from his lamp lit-up the scene and he could see the results of the fire fight. There was a group of four men, three standing, one sitting looking pretty badly wounded. Groans and moans were coming from two other men lying on the ground behind the group. And on the ground nearest to him was a headless corpse.

"Make one false move and I shoot," Chink shouted over the cries pointing his gun at the group. "Put your weapons on the ground,

slowly now. One false move and I shoot. They
dropped their guns immediately and stood
facing him. He still wasn't sure who everyone
was and it was vital he continued the charade
until he was absolutely certain.

He lifted the lamp high so that he could see
everyone more clearly. He heard a voice calling,
'Chink, Chink, it is you isn't it?' He moved closer
and in doing so recognised the man sitting
holding his shoulder, blood oozing through
his fingers. "Thank God. It is you Chink." The
injured man was his old friend Airey Neave.
Chink went up to him and knelt down. "Christ
Airey, I didn't know you were going to be part of
this malarkey. That shoulder looks butchered.
We'll have to get it patched up pretty damn
quick." Then he looked at the others. "I'm Dorman O'Gowan. Which of you is Cunningham?"

"I'm afraid that's Major Cunningham there sir."
Bob Deacon, pointing at the headless body on
the ground. "I'm Colonel Deacon, SAS, and these
two lads are mine"

"Yes Chink, and if it wasn't for them, I think
we'd all have been wiped out" mumbled Airey
weakly.

"Well, who are those other two over there making all that blather?"

"They're the sods who ambushed us. I think

they're IRA." Bob Deacon led Chink over to
the two groaning bodies lying writhing on the
ground.

"Well, well now, if it isn't Barney and Thomas."
They were part of an IRA squad being trained
on Chink's estate. "Now what have you two
scalawags been up to? It's a fine pickle you've
got yourselves into lads to be sure. Look at the
state of y'all. Are there any of our other lads
around to help, or are you here on your own?"

"Oh, it's thanking the good Lord you arrived yer'
honour" Thomas gasped. "Joseph and Pierce are
out there somewhere in the woods." Between
spasms of coughing and choking, the two IRA
men related their story; of how they had been
alerted by one of the lads who had been drinking in Terry's bar. He'd told them about the
group of military looking Brits. The news of
Chinks ambush had been all around Rockorry
and so, thinking that there might be another
attempt on the General's life, they'd tooled up
and gone out after them. "We split up with the
other two and then found these feckin invaders,
so we did." Barney's words were drowned by
another spasm of bloody coughing.

"Holy shit!" croaked Thomas in bewilderment.
"But you're knowing them lot are you not? Are
they yor friends then? Even through his befud-
dled mind, it had suddenly dawned on him that

he and Barney had stumbled into a clandestine meeting between Chink and some military Brits.

"I should be thanking you for trying to protect me, but you are right Thomas, I do know them. And for you both, it would have been far better if you had stayed with your squad at Bellamont." There was only one action Chink could take. He grimaced as he levelled the gun still in his hand. "I'm sorry, but you've signed your own tickets to paradise." Two head shots quickly followed putting them out of their pain. Chink felt sad having to dispatch them - they had been good loyal men, but he knew that if the slightest hint of the meeting leaked out, his cover would be blown and so would 'Operation Blarney'.

He put his gun back into its holster and rejoined Bob and the others. "Hopefully, that takes care of any witnesses. But now we have no time to lose. Quick. Let's get out of here. The other two IRA men will have been attracted by the shooting and will be here in no time. We are going to have to change our plans. Losing Cunningham was not part of the script.

Chink turned to Bob. "Move Cunningham's body over here and put it near those IRA chaps. Make him look as if that's where he fell. Empty his pockets and get me his identity dog tags. Then put one of your guns in his hand. It needs to look as if it was a shootout with no survivors."

Bob and his men quickly followed Chink's instructions. When Dick and the two Irishmen were rearranged, Bob asked "so what do we do now? We're pretty well buggered."

"You and Airey with your men can come aboard my boat - we'll go down to the next lough, away from any prying eyes. It'll be safe there. Then we can think about what is the best plan of action."

"Right you are sir, but if you don't mind, I want my two chaps to check the area and be a rear-guard in case those other IRA blokes arrive."

"Did you know those two?" he added.

"Oh yes. I knew them alright. They've been training on my Estate. It's a shame, they were a couple of good local fellas."

"Well, once my boys have scoured the woods, they'll return the way they came. They're both living at a friendly B&B in Newtownards over the border."

Chink and Bob helped Airey wade out to Miranda, gently over the side and into the cabin. Once aboard, Chink reversed the boat away from the bank and steered it through the twisting waters connecting the two loughs.

They stopped in the middle of Dromore lough. The mist was even thicker. "We'll be safe to talk quietly here, there's hardly ever anyone out at night here."

In the better light of Miranda's cabin, Bob dressed Airey's shoulder as best he could plus a shot of morphine from the Traumafix kit

"Are you both aware of the part I'm playing in Operation Blarney - and do you know why we were meeting tonight?"

"Damn right to both your questions Chink." affirmed Airey weakly. "Bob and I are part of the MI6 team Cunningham was leading, we were fully briefed."

"You, Bob, are going to have to take responsibility for getting my report back to Dick White at MI6. It's top priority. We don't have time to go into the details here, but at my meeting with the Nazi, Otto Skorzeny, I've learnt about a major combined operations plan by the IRA together with a bunch of scumbag ex-Nazis - it's all in this document. I've underlined the names of those I met and didn't know already. Ask Dick White to find out who they are plus their backgrounds, and let me know." He took the envelope containing his hand written report and handed it to the SAS Colonel.

"We were talking to Dick about something rather nasty brewing. But what happened to your face Chink?" asked Airey, obviously in pain. "It looks as if you've been in a car crash."

"It looks worse than it is. I ran into some trouble on my way to Otto's meeting. I was targeted by a couple of what I believe were contract killers, Loyalists I think, a man and a woman. I know those buggers don't like me, but I never expected an attack on my life. Luckily, they were pretty amateur and I escaped with a few cuts and bruises. But let's not get sidetracked."

Chink went on to tell them about his arrival at Martinstown Farm and the shock of meeting Otto's other guests. - Mengele, etc.... many of whom he had always thought had been executed at Nuremberg.

"That's impossible," Airey perked up in surprise. "I was at the Nuremberg trials myself. They couldn't have survived. Admittedly, I didn't actually see them hang."

"I know, I was gob smacked. So astounded that I found it very difficult not to show the utter horror I felt at the meeting. In my mind, it raised the question - did Hitler top himself in his Berlin bunker? I know Dick White was with MI6 in Berlin at the end of the War and tried to verify the Fuhrer's death, but the bunker was in the

Russian zone and by the time he got there, all evidence had been removed. So, we only have the Russian's word for it."

"God, I never gave it a thought. I just believed he'd committed suicide. But you could well be right. I've never trusted those Ivans." Airey gave a rasping sigh.

"Anyway," continued Chink, "It's all in my report. But now with Dick Cunningham side-lined, I'm going to have to come to London to meet Mac and the rest of those involved in Operation Blarney. In the meantime, I need to get you safely on your way back to London. I presume Bob, you came via Langford Lodge?"

"Yes, we've got a Dakota standing by"

"Right, it should be about 3.00 am by the time we get back to my Land Rover. I'll take you to Langford Lodge myself, it's only just over the hour."

"Thanks Chink" said a hardly audible Airey Neave. "I don't know what we could have done without you. But are you sure it's safe for you to be out on your own?"

"After my brush with those killers, you're right. I'm going to have to be more careful and watch my back from now on." He winced, thinking of how narrowly they had avoided a complete dis-aster at the shoot out on the side of Dromore.

They arrived at Langford Lodge just after 4.15 am. It was in complete darkness, but as Chink drove in, the Land Rover's lights picked out the Dakota C47 at the end of the runway. The pilot, alerted by their approach, came rushing down the steps of the plane, Sterling machine gun at the ready and took cover behind its wheels. Bob jumped out as Chink parked. "Relax Andy, it's us," he shouted across the tarmac,

Andy McCredie came out of his cover and ran over to them. "Christ, where's your car? I thought for a minute that it was some of those IRA terrorists. Can't be too careful. Thank God it's you."

"Bloody good to see you too Andy," said Bob as he and Chink helped Airey out of the Land Rover.

Andy could see they'd not returned unscathed. "Looks like you've had trouble. What's happened to you Mr. Neave - and where's Dick? And who the hell are you?" he said noticing Chink.

Chink looked to Bob to explain.

"Andy, we had a spot of bother. I'm afraid Dick bought it - Airey got caught in crossfire and we wouldn't be back here if it wasn't for this man." He put a hand on Chink's shoulder, "let's just say he's a patriot.

"Well, let's get this bird in the air and you two

back to Northolt. I'll get my co-pilot to take a look at that shoulder Airey, he's a trained medic; the sooner we get you to hospital the better."
He gave Chink a dismissive nod and turning his back, he helped Airey and Bob aboard leaving Chink at the bottom of the steps. Just before disappearing into the interior of the plane, Bob turned to Chink. "I'll go straight to 'C', give him your report and tell him what you've told us - thanks for all your help and for the lift."

"My pleasure Bob. Look after Airey and tell Sir Richard, I'll be in touch through Horrocks about coming over. It's top priority. I'll plan to make it within the next 72 hours - got that?"

"WILCO" Bob shouted over the noise of the starting engines, shutting down any further conversation. The passenger door of the Dakota slammed shut. Chink walked back to his Land Rover and sat for a moment watching the plane pick up full power, speed down the runway and up into the early dawn sky.

CHAPTER 17

Chink arrived back at Bellamont just after 7.00am in time for breakfast. He was giving Owen his fishing tackle to put away when Hugh came down the stairs into the hallway.

"Hi Dad. Good fishing last night?"

Chink threw his arms around his son, squeezing him in a tight embrace. The tension of the night evaporated. For a moment, the relief of being back safely plus the love he felt for his son flooded his emotions. He coughed them away and together they walked into the dining room.

They continued to talk as they sat down. "No luck at all last night I'm afraid. I caught a couple of small perch, but not enough for a cat's breakfast let alone ours. I let 'em go and told them to come back when they were bigger. Sadly, the pike weren't biting either. Did you have a good trip to Dublin with your mother?"

"It was alright Dad," Hugh answered wearily." Boring museums and shops - but dinner at The Brazen Head on Lower Bridge Street was stellar. We got back not much before midnight and I slept like a log. I didn't hear you come back".

"That's because I've only just got in. I fished all night, so I'm probably going to have a catch-up nap after breakfast"

"Are you in all day then?" Hugh asked, "I was wondering if I could take the boat out myself."

"Sorry Hugh, I don't think it's safe for you on your own - only if Owen agrees to go with you." After Chink's attempted assassination, he didn't want his family exposed to a kidnapping or worse. And before anyone went near Miranda, Chink had to repair the gun shot damage and make sure that all the evidence of the night's activities were removed.

At that moment, Owen came in with their breakfast. Chink always had two boiled eggs and four pieces of toast, and Hugh a full Irish fry-up.

"Talk of the devil."

"I beg your pardon sir?"

"I was just saying to Hugh that he could only go fishing if you went with him."

"It would be my pleasure, sir." He placed their food in front of them and paused. "If you will excuse me sir?"

"Yes, Owen, is something wrong?"

"I didn't want to disturb your breakfast, sir, but there's Constable Touhy outside with a couple of our trainee laddies wanting a word with you. Shall I tell them to wait in the hall sir?"

"No, no, whatever it is, it's obviously important Owen. Show them in. Any idea what they want?"

"No sir, but the constable looks very nervous and the boys seem shell shocked."

Owen went to the door into the hall and ushered in the three men. Chink knew them all. "Good morning Constable - mornin' Joseph, mornin' Pierce. Take a seat. Would you like coffee - what brings you all here so early?"

But the constable remained standing. "We won't be taking the coffee, thank you sir. It's not good news I have. There's been some terrible shootin' up on your lough. We've got three corpses over there. These two lads discovered them."

Chink tried hard to look shocked and concerned, trying not to show any sign that he knew exactly what they were talking about.

"Good God. When was this?"

"Well, sir, yor honour" said Pierce, "It was last night. I was havin' a pint in Terry's in the village when a couple of suspicious lookin' blokes come in. Then Joseph here arrives and said there was one of them shooting brake cars outside and another bloke sittin' in it."

"That certainly does sound a touch suspicious, go on," Chink sipped his coffee keeping his eyes on the visitors.

"They were talking posh sir. Brits without a doubt," Pierce added.

"And we were sure they were up to no good at all, what with their waxy jackets and military wellington boots, looking at a map they were too." said Joseph. "So, I told Pierce that I'd go and find a couple more of the lads, tool up and come back to give them a doin' over."

"After Joseph went out, the two visitors folded their map and left. I followed 'em out and saw 'em get into their vehicle. I had my van outside too, so I followed.

Pierce went on to tell Chink how he saw them turn into the track opposite O'Donovan's barn going down to the lough. He then went back into Rockcorry, picked up Joseph, who had hasted back with Barney and Thomas, plus machine pistols for them all. Then, in Pierce's van, they'd given chase, driving down the track where Pierce had last seen them. After about three hundred yards, they'd found the abandoned shooting brake in a gateway on the edge

of woodland. They had decided to split up into
pairs, spread out and find the suspects Pierce
with Joseph, and Barney with Thomas.

"It was then we heard the shoutin' and the
shootin'," Joseph said, shaking with the memory.

Oh bugger, thought Chink. These two were
that nearby. What had they heard - he tried
not to show his alarm, covering it with a mask
of growing anger and concern. "So, what happened then?"

"Aah sir!" Pierce carried on, "The terrible
screamin' was doozy - sure it froze us to the
spot. Then, as soon as we'd recovered from
the shock of it all, we went as fast as we could
towards the noise, but it was slow goin' through
them trees an' all. There was more shots then
silence. It must have been a good twenty
minutes before we found them. The poor fellas
had both been shot dead. It was awful, terrible
to see for sure - blood all over the place."

"But the lads had got one of them bastards -
shot his evil feckin head off," said Joseph.

Chink shuddered inwardly. It could have been
a total bloody disaster if these two had arrived
seconds earlier. Even so, they could have heard
Miranda's engine. To cover that possibility, he
explained he was out fishing on the lough all

night and didn't hear a thing.

"Christ!" he exploded. "Two of our best men lost - but you two, sure you are true heroes of the cause. The big guns at the Somme and El Alamein buggered my hearing. I didn't hear a thing. And the mist deadens noise. Shite, I'd have been there in a flash to help you chaps if I'd known."

As he was speaking, Chink's mind was working at the double. What was his best approach. His attempted assassination could again be useful as a diversion.

"Did you know I was hijacked only the other day, constable?"

"Is that where you got the damage to yor face yor honour. Sure, it looks a nasty mess if you don't mind me sayin'."

"Well, I didn't bother to report it to you. They were some fanatics." The constable was about to interrupt, but Chink didn't wait and continued. "This bunch last night could have been more of those damn loyalist paramilitaries. They seem bent on revenge for my hosting our friends here for a spot of training." He paused, drained his coffee cup, grabbed a piece of toast, quickly buttered it and stood up.

"Right. Let's go and see where it happened. On second thoughts, I'll follow you in my Land

Rover. One of you lads come with me to show me where it all happened. Owen, you'd better come with me too in case there are still some of those damn loyalists lurking about - and get a couple of shotguns out of the gun room too would you."

Owen nodded and went out to carry out Chink's instructions.

"Can I come too Dad?" Hugh said excitedly. Like his father, he was always keen to be part of any action.

"Sorry, old son, there are things I'd rather you didn't see, at least not yet a while. Stay here and guard the fort, I won't be long. And tell your Mother when she comes down that we'll be back soon. I wouldn't want her to be alone with all these shenanigans going on."

Chink played out the charade. He, Owen and Pierce followed the Garda vehicle through forest tracks to Dromore lough. The clearing was all taped off. Figures were busy, clad in white blood-stained overalls. Cunningham and the two IRA men had yet to be removed from the scene. Chink jumped down from his Land Rover and walked quickly towards the gathering in the middle of the clearing - blood and mud churned up together - and bodies twisted in death. Some of the Garda he recognised from the Rockcorry Station and there was the local doctor who worked part time as a pathologist.

"Good God! It looks like a war zone - and on my estate too," Chink barked, trying hard to keep his mask of shock and annoyance in place. "What the hell is all this about."

"We're not quite sure, General," replied a pale faced Sergeant Joseph O'Rourke, Head of Station at Rockcorry. "There's been some sort of a shoot out. Two of our local lads, shot dead they are. And there's that marbhán there" he said pointing towards Dick Cunningham's lifeless remains. "From his dress, I'd say he's probably British military in civies."

"But the mud's been so churned up. There must have been more here than these three corpses. And why on my land?" Chink paused for effect as if putting two and two together. "Do you know, it could have been those damn loyalist bastards again.

"How do you mean sir?" queried the Garda Sergeant.

Chink retold the story of his recent hijacking, suggesting that perhaps this and that incident were related.

"Now I was wonderin' about those injuries to yor face sir. That eye looks terrible sore. We'll keep an extra eye open in the village you can be sure, and let you know if we see any suspicious characters around. And I'll spread the word in Terry's bar too. If you like, we'll put one of our men on patrol up at Bellamont too for you, sir."

"No, no need for that, sergeant. I've got half the IRA running around the grounds - I don't think they'll try anything again in a hurry. But next time I go off to a meeting, I won't go on my own. I'll take Owen here with me and be sure to carry a weapon."

Chink offered Joseph and Pierce a lift back to the training ground at Bellamont, but they were off to Terry's to meet up with family and other friends of the deceased. Chink said he had to get back to deal with urgent estate business, otherwise he would have joined them. He asked the two men to pass on his condolences to the bereaved.

As he and Owen drove along the tracks back to Bellamont, he felt relief that he was not suspected of any involvement. His cover was still intact. Yet he couldn't bury the sense of guilt over the deaths of the two young men. If he hadn't arranged the meeting, they would still be alive. But then again, he thought, Cunningham should never have gone into Terry's; a mistake for which he too had paid with his life.

He consoled himself with the thought that they were just three more casualties in the war fighting for the future of Ireland. At least in talking to O'Rourke, he had been able to make it sound as if the Loyalists were after him yet again. But in truth, he still didn't know for sure who was responsible for his hijacking. Hopefully the Garda would take the easy option and go along with his theory.

Now, he had to make urgent arrangements to meet up with Mac, Richard White and the depleted Operation Blarney committee in London.

When he arrived back at Bellamont, a worried looking Eve and Hugh were in the lounge. Eve had been hardened by the traumas of war. She had spent many sleepless nights in Cairo, beside herself with worry not knowing if she would ever see her husband again - knowing he was up against the formidable Nazi general, Rommel. The same fears came back with his highway incident, and now the shootings on the lough. "Eric what's going on? Hugh told me about the incident over on Dromore; the visit from the Garda; the dead bodies. We came here for a peaceful life, but now that seems gone out of the window. Are we in danger?"

"Eve darling, there's really nothing to worry about. We discussed the potential problems when I started hosting the IRA here. The

British certainly don't like it, but the road side ambush was down to some hot-heads from the North, and the shooting on the lake could just be poachers surprised by our local lads." He hugged her and felt some of the tension leave her body. "Now, tell me how your trip to Dublin went."

She said it had been both disappointing and exhausting.

He gave her an extra squeeze. "Never mind, darling, Hugh said you'd had an enjoyable dinner together anyway."

"That's true, but Dublin's such a one-horse city compared to London. O'Connell Street has a couple of reasonable shops, but it's so boring; nothing compared to London which has so many different restaurants and for shopping, such choice - Harrods, Selfridges, Fortnums, Bond Street - I could do with a week there. But Eric, darling, I really am worried about our safety."

"Nothing to be alarmed about, sweetheart. But, I will take greater care in future. Now, it just so happens I've got to go to London for a few business meetings. I was planning to leave tomorrow afternoon, for an early morning start on Thursday. Why don't you and Hugh pack some bags and come with me? We could stay at

Claridge's and you could take in that new Francis Bacon exhibition at the Tate".

"Oh gawd, not a gallery again," Hugh moaned. "I'd much rather go to the Old Bailey and watch some juicy trials - or perhaps spend a day in the Science Museum."

Chink knew Hugh had a passion for law and the Old Bailey was as safe a place as any for a teenager in London. "Right you are, let's make a deal. You can go to the Old Bailey if you promise not to go swanning off. When you've had enough, get a taxi back to the hotel and stay there until I return. When I've finished my business meetings, I'll pick you up and we can all go to the Science Museum in Kensington. How does that sound?"

CHAPTER 18

Brian Horrocks was always glad to hear from his old friend Eric Dorman-Smith - he never could get used to the change of name to O'Gowan. They had known each other for more than 50 years, first at Uppingham School, followed by The Royal Military College, Sand- hurst, and then fighting on the front line in the first World War. He knew Chink had some confidential business links within the British government, and had asked him to act as an intermediary for the passing of messages. Chink had told him that he was acting as an informal communication channel between the Irish and British leaders, nothing more. Brian was a believer in the old adage, 'need to know', so he asked no questions.

Once again, Chink had phoned him to say he was going to be in the capital on Thursday, and would like to meet him for coffee at 10.30 am in the Palm Court of the Ritz. He also asked Brian to ring the usual telephone number for passing on messages to say lunch would be at 12.30hrs on the same day.

It was Rebecca who was on the other end of the mystery telephone line when Horrocks called. She answered the call and, after hearing the message, simply replied, "Thank you" and replaced the handset.

Rebecca had six direct lines on her desk, each labelled with nicknames for which only she and 'C' knew the real identities. Line No.1 was Donald Duck, No. 2 was Goliath, and so on. Line No.5 was 'Mighty Mouse' and so after Brian's call, she buzzed through to her Boss and gave him 'Mighty Mouse's short message. This was what 'C' had been waiting for, the day and time for the 'Operation Blarney' meeting with Chink. He immediately called Macmillan. They talked about who should be at the next meeting. It was agreed that it was best to keep it to those who'd attended the first meeting, Peter Fleming, Gillian Sattler, Bob Deacon, Profumo, and Airey Neave if he was able to make it after the Irish debacle. 'C' wanted the Director-General of MI5 to be invited too, but Mac and Hollis didn't get on.

The truth was Hollis didn't get on with most of his contemporaries either. Rumours that he was the 4th man in the Philby communist spy ring had been investigated, but despite proven unfounded, Mac was still wary of him and his organisation. They wrangled over the matter

for minutes. 'C' pointed out that to exclude
Hollis from the meeting would only create
more animosity between the Services at a time
when it was vital that everyone worked closely
together.

Eventually, with considerable reluctance,
Macmillan agreed to include him. When Hollis
got his call from the Prime Minister, he seemed
hesitant. He said he was up to his eyes with
work and other meetings on that day anyway.
But the Prime Minister was adamant, he told
the MI5 Chief to cancel whatever he had arranged - no excuse, he would be there.

On Thursday morning, Chink had left Eve
and Hugh still enjoying their breakfast in the
sumptuous atmosphere of Claridge's in London's Mayfair with promises to meet Hugh in
the hotel lobby at 4.30 pm at the latest for their
visit to the museum. Eve had promised to be
back for cocktails at 6.00 pm, which gave Chink
plenty of time for the logistics of getting to the
Kali meeting, returning to the hotel for Hugh,
and fitting in the museum visit.

He went up to their room to collect his well-
worn trilby hat and old British Warm coat, still
marked with the outlines of where his military
badge of rank had been. With a final check to
make sure he had everything he needed in his
large briefcase, he made his way down to the

hotel's foyer and out of the main entrance onto
Brook Street. It was a typical March day, cold
grey skies delivering a fine drizzle pushed along
by a biting easterly wind.

Chink was sure that either the IRA or Skorzeny
would have arranged a tail to report back on his
movements. He certainly would if he had been
in their shoes. He'd thought out an elaborate
plan to throw off any such followers and get to
the meeting unseen. He pulled up his collar
to ward off the weather. It also helped to hide
most of his facial scars and rainbow yellowing
eye. The hotel doorman fought to shield him
from the worst of the weather with a large umbrella and hailed a taxi for him.

His first call was to Flannigan's opposite the
Union Jack Club on Waterloo Road, one of his
several London Irish pub restaurants. He knew
for certain that some of his employees were
IRA sympathisers, so his visit would help to le-
gitimise his travel. Eoin Dalaigh the manager,
was keen to discuss ideas for expanding the
facilities. At any other time, Chink would have
stayed longer, but he had an evasion schedule
planned. After half an hour and two coffees
later he tore himself away and caught another
taxi to City of London Guildhall. From there,
he walked to the Bank Underground station,
took the Central Line to Oxford Circus, changed

onto the Bakerloo Line and resurfaced at Charing Cross, all the time looking for a tail. He
was pretty sure if he'd had one, he'd lost it. So
feeling more at ease, he walked across Trafalgar
Square, up Lower Regent Street to Piccadilly
then along to the Ritz hotel. He was in good
time for his meeting with Brian Horrocks, so he
sat in a chair for guests near the Head Porter's
desk, hiding behind the Daily Telegraph, and
surreptitiously watching the people traffic
through the hotel's Arlington Street entrance.

As far as he could see, nobody was tailing him,
his evasion tactics might have been a complete
waste of time, but he couldn't take that chance.
After 15 minutes, he stood up and walked
through to the hotel's Palm Court and had just
ordered coffee, when Brian arrived, spot on
time.

They chatted away about old times at school
and in the army - something they always did.
Brian said he had been asked by the BBC to
take part in a TV series about the war. And he
was being lunched by the film director David
Lean, after which, he was going to see a pre-
release version of that new film 'Lawrence of
Arabia'. Chink did his best to appear interested
in what Brian was saying, but his mind was on
the meeting in Kali's GOLD. He would have to
make a move soon.

Brian drawled on about how he'd been aide-de-camp to Allenby in 1920 and had spent quite some time with the Arab hero Major Lawrence in Jerusalem. They talked about Lawrence and the potential troubles in the Middle East that caused Britain not to honour its promises to the Arabs. Chink kept looking at his watch, it was time he made a move. Apologising for having to break up the meeting, he picked up his briefcase, said goodbye to his old friend before heading to the gentlemen's toilet. Five minutes later a tall Arab in a full-length kaftan robe, a checkered red and white Kaffiyeh head-dress, plus a khanjar ceremonial dagger and dark glasses, passed by the Palm Court going towards the hotel's Piccadilly exit. Blimey, thought Horrocks, what a coincidence having been talking to Chink about Lawrence. His mind drifted back to his time with Allenby - a lot had happened in 42 years, he reflected.

The doorman outside the Ritz offered to call the Arab a taxi. "Where to yer Highness?" the driver shouted above the din of the Piccadilly traffic. "Number 10 Downing Street," came the guttural foreign response. When they arrived, the taxi driver asked for his three shillings and sixpence fare only to be given a ten-pound note. "Keep change," the Arab told him as he jumped out and strode up to the famous front door of the British Prime Minister as if on a state visit.

The cabbie shouted after him, "Thanks for the tip mate, very generous, I'm sure," grumbling on to himself, "fucking wogs - think they own the sodding world 'cos of their oil."

But the Arab didn't hear him. He was already inside the building. Prince Abu Al Ahmed was expected and immediately taken to the Prime Minister's private office, where, after the door was closed, he was ushered into the lift and down to GOLD deep inside Kali.

Mac knew that the rumble of his lift meant that Chink was arriving, but everyone else was taken aback when an Arab Prince stepped out of the lift. "Let me present Prince Abu Al Ahmed," Mac said, pausing and amused by everyone's surprise, "or otherwise known as Chink." There was laughter at the hoax played on them, but it died to gasps of shock as Chink took off his disguise, revealing his battered features.

"God Almighty Chink, you mentioned your skirmish near Packenham's place but I didn't realise you'd been so knocked about." Chink just smiled, saying it looked far worse than it was, and Mac continued. "Well done on getting here anyway. I knew you would make it and spot on time too." Then to the meeting. "Right, let's get to the meat of the matter. No time to lose."

"Chink, everyone here has read your report and they've assured me their copies have been destroyed as instructed. There's just my copy here." He looked at the attendees around the table, and was answered by nods and murmurs of assent. "So now Chink, please give us a situation report of where we are and what you believe is the way forward."

Chink had scribbled a few notes to make sure he covered everything. "Yes, thank you, Prime Minister. As I stressed in my report, there has always been a constant threat of war between the staunch Protestant North and the Roman Catholic South in Ireland. It's like a volcano. Most of the time it rumbles smokes and splutters, but at the meeting in Martinstown, Finbar Kelly, the IRA Chief of Staff, and Liam Walsh their Quartermaster General outlined the massive volcanic eruption they had in mind. I had some inkling already, but from what they said, it could be the biggest and bloodiest IRA attack since the 1923 Irish War of Independence. Their plan, codenamed 'Big Bang', aims to destroy one of the most prized symbols of our nation and democracy, one that survived Guy Fawkes and the Luftwaffe blitz. They are planning to blow-up Big Ben and the Houses of Parliament."

Chink paused to let his message sink in before continuing.

The pregnant silence was broken by Peter Fleming. "It's a bit early for Guy Fawkes night," he quipped with a smile.

"Oh, for heaven's sake Peter, I've got a good mind to throw the bloody water jug at you," the PM threatened, "this is deadly bloody serious - so don't interrupt unless you've got something useful and pertinent to say."

Peter Fleming looked sheepish and apologised to Chink, promising to keep his humour under control.

"Carry on Chink"

"If this act of terrorism happens, it will cause considerable loss of life. Our Government will be in tatters. Lords and Ladies, MPs, civil servants and many of the public could be amongst the victims. The disruption would paralyse the country for weeks, if not months. And, if we don't stop it, the IRA will have achieved the biggest propaganda coup in their history."

Again, Chink stopped. He looked at everyone. This time, there was complete silence. All eyes were on him, the meeting hung on his every word.

"That's bloody monstrous," exclaimed Airey

Neave, still weak and suffering from his gun-shot wounds. And there were supporting rumblings from the others. "We can't let that happen - Parliament is the life and soul of our nation. To destroy it would be a dagger in the heart of Britain," his voice raised, "we need to...." Macmillan held up his hand for silence. "Believe me, Airey, we all feel the same, but let Chink continue."

"Thank you, Prime Minister. Airey, I share your horror at the potential destruction of Parliament and the global trauma that might cause. However, since I wrote the report you've now all seen, I've mulled long and hard over the situation and I'm pretty damn sure that the attack on our Parliament is intended to divert our attention - a smokescreen to hide the real intentions of the IRA's cohorts, the Nazis. There could be something much, much bigger and far, far more disastrous being planned."

"How do you mean Chink?" asked Profumo. "It would take something earth-shattering to be worse than demolishing our Parliament."

Before Chink could carry on and explain what he meant, Macmillan turned to Roger Hollis. "You've over 40 staff on your payroll North and South of the Irish border Roger. You say you didn't get a sniff of anything untoward on the radar. It's unbelievable that all this is going on without a peep from you or any of your agents."

Hollis looked embarrassed. He didn't take criticism well and his face flushed bright red to show it. "As I told you earlier Prime Minister, there's been absolutely no hint of any disturbances in the offing, certainly not on this scale. I accept that we should have at least caught a whiff of something going on. However, if I may say, sir, if you or Sir Richard here had bothered to include MI5 earlier, not only might we have been able to contribute to the intelligence, but it would have saved a most unfortunate incident" he said looking directly at Chink.

"What the hell do you mean?" snorted Richard White. "We didn't tell you anything because since I left MI5, it's leaked like a bloody sieve - Maclean, Burgess, Philby - and we're worried even more about all the other unearthed Soviet spies in your organisation. Your agents seem more interested in writing their memoirs than doing their day job. And the last thing Churchill, Mac, and I want is for General Dorman-O'Gowan here to be outed. It's taken nearly 20 years of careful planning to get him into a place of trust with the IRA Council and, indeed, with the Irish Government. It's not often one gets an MI6 deep cover agent advising De Valera and his parliament on military matters."

"Look. I had no idea that Chink was working for you." Hollis flared. "As far as I, my organisation and the world at large knew, Churchill booted him out of the army for pure insolence, disobedience, and bloody-mindedness. Everyone knew he'd gone back to Ireland sulking like a spoilt brat with a humongous chip on his shoulder. We've kept an eye on him through one of our agents, one actually in Bellamont. We knew Chink was training IRA personnel. And we also had some knowledge of his status in their organisation."

"One day, I'll tell you all about what Churchill and I agreed," Chink cut in, "but carry on, I'd certainly like to know who you've got spying on me back in Ireland," he added in an icy tone.

Hollis tried to explain. "General, look, I am so, so damn sorry. I wish I could do more than just apologise - and that I sincerely do; but you, MI6, the lot of you, kept us in the dark. We had no idea what was going on south of the border We just hadn't a clue. That abortive roadside attempt to neutralise you was actually carried out by us, MI5."

There were gasps of incredulity around the room. The shockwave created by the admission froze everyone in their seats, but as if oblivious to the bombshell he had dropped, Hollis carried on, his eyes fixed on Chink. "Our main man in Belfast thought it would be a great coup for us and a solid blow against the Provisionals. As it is..."

Chink erupted. He leapt to his feet seething. "You bastard! - you bloody fool." For a moment, he was lost for words, incandescent with rage. You... you... you mean those incompetent amateurs who stopped me in that layby were down to you?"

Hollis visibly shrunk, slumped in his seat, stunned by Chink's verbal assault, his eyes fixed on the table, while the Irish General paused for breath, again trying to contain his fury.

"Look Hollis" he riled, thrusting his face forward, "I got this damn make-over because of your balls up. Is it any wonder the Prime Minister has such a shitty opinion of MI5. I tell you now, if I sent anyone against you, they wouldn't mess up - you'd be history. I agree with 'C', your organisation not only leaks like a bloody sieve, it's just not fit for purpose. And you tried to blame the Loyalists. I've yet to see what MI5 can offer Operation Blarney. In fact, you should get the fuck out of here".

"For God's sake, gentlemen," Mac leapt to his feet and thumped the table. "Cut it out. Cut it out both of you. You are behaving like damn kindergarten toddlers The enemy is out there, not here round the table.   We have to work as a team.   Yes, we made a big mistake in not including you before Roger.   And Chink, I personally take responsibility for your injuries and near-death disaster.   Losing Major Cunningham was bad enough, but to lose you - the devil only knows what we would have done if your team had succeeded Roger."

"But as you've told us Chink, the country is verging on the edge of a major disaster. So, from now on, MI5 and MI6 will, and I repeat WILL work closely together.   Not just on Blarney, but everything else in the interest of our Nation. Let's have no more of the schoolboy petty point-scoring and departmental politics, let's get on with the job in hand."

The Prime Minister waited for his words to sink in.   "As we've lost Major Cunningham, I propose that you, John, as Minister of War, take overall responsibility for the coordination of Operation Blarney.   You, Richard, and you, Roger, bury your bloody hatchet and work together or I'll be looking for replacements."

'C' and Roger Hollis grimaced at Mac's dressing down.   And, without a word, they both reached across the table and solemnly shook hands. Their eyes met still showing distrust and hostility, but there was an overriding determination to make a fresh start and work as one team - at least for Operation Blarney.

Macmillan too was feeling the stress of the
meeting, and his irritation was beginning to
seep through his usual calm. He looked around
the table. "If we go on fighting amongst ourselves, we've no chance of defeating anyone.
Have I made myself clear?" There was silence,
eyes downcast, and heads nodded.

"Now – please continue General".

Chink was still boiling at the MI5 ambushing
cock-up. He was finding it near impossible to
swallow his anger, but Mac was right, everyone
had to work together; a clean slate; forgive and
learn from past mistakes. So be it, he thought.
Yet he certainly wasn't going to tell Hollis that
the attempt on his life had actually had a positive effect - in fact, an enormous boost, enabling
him to get closer to Otto and his Nazi henchmen. Plus, he was now an IRA folklore hero,
worshipped throughout its membership.

 "As I was saying," Chink resumed, speaking as
calmly as he could, only his eyes betrayed his
turbulent feelings. "my gut feel tells me that
Skorzeny and his merry men have something
else in mind, far more ambitious than helping
the IRA 'Big Bang' bombing.   At the meeting,
they talked about a large arsenal funded by Otto
in the grounds of a Monastery in Portglenone."

"Liam Walsh, he's the Quartermaster General of the IRA, later told me that Otto had used his funds to purchase several farms along the South side of the border between Donegal and Mayo in the West to Monaghan and Dundalk in the East. He'd told Liam that he was filling them with ammunition and weapons to support their cause in the North.   Liam said that Otto was manning the farms with ex-Nazi soldiers who had been transported by Ratlines to Ireland - plus British and Irish fascists who had served alongside the SS."

 "From outward appearances, he'd said, the farms looked as if they were being renovated, when in fact, the real work was building workshops to refurbish old Panzer 88mm anti-tank guns and Spandau machine guns, brought into Ireland supposedly for fictitious amateur collectors. They are, so Liam claimed, armour plating Volkswagen Beetles and mounting the Spandaus on Zündapp motorbike sidecars, the same used in their sweep through France in 1940."

He paused again to make sure he had the full attention of everyone around the table. Even Peter was fully concentrating on what he was saying.

"I see why you are alarmed Chink. It gives me the creeps. Are they doing all this just to support the IRA - out of the kindness of their hearts - is capturing Northern Ireland their real aim?" 'C' floated the question.

"There's a lot more behind all this Dick," Chink continued, "When I was at Martinstown and Charles Haughey, Finbar, and Liam had left the meeting, Otto asked me if I would like to see around his farm, whilst they settled a few admin matters. I was sure they wanted me out of the way. He asked Wilhelm Boger, the ex-Auschwitz commandant, to show me around. Boger took me to their interrogation centre. This was where they were working on your two agents, Hollis. He said it was his workshop. It was more like a medieval chamber of horrors and I'm sure they didn't enjoy the experience."

Hollis said nothing. At some time in the future, but not now, he would tell Chink that his MI5 operatives had been so traumatised by their ordeal that they had both been certified and committed to psychiatric institutions for long-term treatment.

Chink went on to describe the rest of the tour which included prison cells and barrack rooms, which he estimated, could house around 300 personnel. He said that he'd seen at least 30 soldiers dressed in uniforms similar to those worn by the Waffen SS in the war without badges. He was also shown a significant store of weapons and munitions.

"There were large crates marked agricultural machinery with Russian writing on them. Boger told me they were in transit to the farms. It appeared that they came into the country under special licence without inspection - Boger beamed as he told me they contained Kalashnikov AK47s."

"Then, after the tour, when I went back with Boger into the conference room, I must have caught them unawares. The frame of the Hitler and Skorzeny picture above the fireplace was hinged back. Behind it was an open safe. They were all in deep discussion standing around a map of Ireland on the table in front of them. Skorzeny quickly folded it up. He mumbled something about 'admin matters', but the embarrassment and concerned glances between the Nazi Colonel and the others spoke volumes".

Chink paused yet again. He had everyone's rapt attention. With his gentle brogue, it was as if he was narrating a mystery thriller. Even stranger than fiction.

"So, what happened then?" The MI6 Chief broke the hush.

Chink took a sip from the glass of water in front of him. Ignoring 'C', he fixed his eyes on the Prime Minister. "Mac. Admin matters be damned; they were plotting something. Picture it - heads down over the map, loud high-pitched voices, hands pointing, Otto commanding - it was a military briefing or I'm a jackass. And that, I'm certainly not. They were planning war".

It took some time for everyone to absorb the situation described by Chink. If he was right, Ireland could be once again on the verge of another civil war.

The Prime Minister broke the silence, firing questions at Chink. "You've convinced me General. How can we verify what they are up to - what time-scale are we talking - how much time have we got?"

"Well Prime Minister, the London bombing is scheduled for July 12, the day the Loyalists celebrate the Battle of the Boyne. If my assessment is right, 'Big Bang' is planned to be nothing more than a diversion to keep me, the IRA, and the governments on both sides of the border focused on the chaos in London. If Skorzeny is preparing for what I think he is, then that would be the most probable time for him to make his move. Therefore, in answer to your question, I would say if 'Big Bang is set for July 12, then they will strike on July 13 or 14."

"You read Rommel's mind when you and

Auchinleck outwitted him at Alamein and stopped the Panzers' advance," Profumo broke in. "You wouldn't remember me then, I was there - one of your many tank commanders" he smiled at the memory "it sounds like you are doing the same here."

"My gut instinct is not often wrong, John, and the truth is, the low life at that meeting weren't interested in helping a bunch of local nationalists - why should they. The more I think about it, 'Big Bang' is nothing much more than hot air; something the Nazis and IRA want leaked out to take our eyes off what's really going on each side of the border. I believe they are preparing a joint attack to unite Ireland. The IRA tried in 1956 with their Operation Harvest. This time, they seem far better prepared and have the backing of the Skorzeny crew And I'm absolutely sure their attack plans are in that safe at Martinstown."

"God help us! what are you suggesting we do?" Airey Neave exclaimed.

Chink was about to respond to him, but Profumo waved him to silence. "It seems to me we have two time-critical objectives. One, we have to deal with the possible threat to Parliament, if indeed there is one - at least we must be prepared. And two, we must plan a quick and discreet raid on Martinstown to see what's in

Skorzeny's safe."

"But what then?" asked Peter Fleming.

"We'll just have to wait and see, Peter. The important thing now is to find out what's in that safe - then we can decide on our response. It's now March 21. If around July 13 is the probable date for their attack, we've got under four months to act."

John Profumo looked at Roger Hollis. "You're responsible for internal UK security, Roger, so focus on a plan to nip their London 'Big Bang' plans in the bud. And you, 'C', put your head together with Chink and the others, get into that safe and find out what this Nazi Colonel and his crew are up to. When you've done that, we'll urgently need to put together an appropriate force to neutralise the bastards."

"Absolutely right, John," said the PM, pleased that he'd put Profumo in overall charge. "and perhaps you Chink will keep us updated with whatever intel you gather."

"Sounds good to me, Prime Minister." Chink nodded in agreement. Then he turned to Hollis, trying to keep his temper under control. "As we are all being so open and civil with each other Roger, perhaps you could now tell me who your MI5 spy is at Bellamont?"

"It's your butler, Chink. Owen has been on our

payroll since he was medically discharged from the army."

CHAPTER 19

"I'm due in the House in about half an hour - can you take over the meeting, John? And why don't you come with me Roger; I'd like to talk more about this 'Big Bang' threat."

"Certainly, Prime Minister," said Profumo. Harold Macmillan and Roger Hollis left GOLD using the lift up to 10 Downing Street.

"I've got to go soon too," said Chink. "I've got family matters to deal with - a lovely wife who spends money like water and a son who I've promised to take to the Science Museum."

"I would have thought that Operation Blarney was a touch more important than family matters." Peter Fleming interjected with a touch of sarcasm. "We need you here with your knowledge and expertise on tap. Surely you can put them off."

Chink had a lot of respect for Peter. He had seen at first hand his brilliant inventiveness when he astonished the 'top brass' in Cairo by creating a simple device for disabling enemy tanks. It had turned out to be vastly helpful in defeating

Rommel at Alamein. So, he didn't rise to the bait. He quietly explained. "Peter, I've been undercover for over 20 years and I don't intend to blow it all now. Making changes to plans, be they family or anything else, can cause alarm bells to ring. I came over on this trip for the family too. Otto knows this and so does the IRA, and you can be sure someone has been detailed to keep an eye on me while I'm here. I always assume I'm being watched. That's why all the elaborate Arab cloak and dagger stuff - which reminds me I must remember to go back via the Ritz to pick up my hat and coat from their cloakroom."

"Gentlemen, the clock's ticking," John Profumo reminded the meeting, "and Gillian, of course, my apologies. We need to focus our minds on finding out whatever is in that Nazi feller Skorzeny's safe."

"What's security like at Martinstown?" Bob Deacon asked Chink.

"Tight, very tight. When I went on my tour with Herr Boger, I saw floodlights and at least two sirens on poles. Boger boasted that they had installed those new-fangled laser walls around the whole property. I would say in military terms, it's a top security compound built with Germanic ingenuity and efficiency. There will be guards on duty round the clock plus many more in their barracks."

"Breaking in sounds just like a walk in the park then," said Bob laconically. "What do you suggest, sir?"

"Someone has to get in and out without being detected. A highly skilled burglar and safe breaker. Someone like that old lag, double agent Eddie Chapman. Is he still on MI6's books 'C'?"

Dick White shook his head. "He was last heard of fleeing the Australian police in Melbourne. It seems his old safe cracking habits die hard."

"Perhaps a Japanese Ninja would fit the bill?" suggested the SAS Colonel lightheartedly.

Profumo, already irritated by Bob Deacon's flippant 'walk in the park' comment, turned on him, "Damn it Colonel, if you've got something useful to say, go-ahead, but stupid comments like that only waste our valuable time. The next thing, you'll be suggesting is we hire that Chinese martial arts chap, Bruce Lee." Then looking around the table, he continued. "Has anyone any serious ideas - and before you say anything, Peter, don't suggest calling in your brother's James Bond."

Peter Fleming had already nettled Chink and now Profumo's annoyance at Bob's suggestion only increased the antagonism creeping into the meeting. But Bob Deacon was not to be put down. He stood up, his manner betrayed the rising anger he felt, and looked at Profumo with cold humorless eyes. "Minister - I'm not wasting your's or anyone else's time. And I didn't come here to crack jokes either. And I resent your saying my comments are stupid. Using a Japanese Ninja is a perfectly serious suggestion. You, sir, are the one wasting time by even mentioning Bruce Lee and 007."

The atmosphere was becoming too tense for comfort and the silence was hostile. Both men fumed at each other. Finally, Profumo burst out. "How dare you! I would remind you, Colonel, that I am the Minister of War and" .... But he got no further. Chink had had enough.

"Christ John, will you get off your high horse and calm down – and you too Bob. Remember what Mac said. The enemy is over the water, not here and we need to work together. My time is limited, so let's just remember why we are here. I, for one, would like to hear what Colonel Deacon has in mind. Bob?"

Bob and Profumo glared at each other. "Well Chink, it was a serious suggestion. I'm pretty sure I have just the man." Everyone looked at him, taken aback. "One of my instructors at Hereford specialises in the Japanese martial arts of Ninjutsu and Kage - sabotage, infiltration, assassination, and guerrilla warfare, all done with extreme stealth."

The SAS man continued. "His name is Katsumi Akanari San and he is a genuine Ninja warrior. He fought in the last war as a member of the infamous Teishin Shudan, the ruthless Jap's commando group."

"Wow," said Peter, "how the hell did you manage to get one of that lot?"

Before Bob could answer, Profumo burst in sharply. "This is ridiculous," He felt he had lost his grip on the meeting, "let's stop all this fantasy poppycock and get back to the problem in hand - no more of this Ninja nonsense do you hear me."

But Chink was having no more of Profumo's pomposity and wanted to hear Bob Deacon out. "John, shut up. Whether it offends you or not, Colonel Deacon might well have the answer. We need an individual, not an army and from my limited knowledge of Ninjas, if there's a way into the Nazi den, then they have the skills. "Carry on Bob - tell us more about this man of yours – and no more interruptions Minister - please."

Bob purposely didn't look at Profumo, who was spluttering incoherently, lost for words. At least, Bob thought, someone was taking him seriously. "Thank you, General. Bear with me. I'll start by telling you how I met Katsumi Akanari San. I was with 22 Squadron SAS in Japan at the time of the surrender. I was driving through Tomonotsu, a port town just outside Fukuyama in the Hiroshima region with a truckload of our lads, when I saw about a dozen American GIs about to gang-rape a woman. To some extent, one could understand their behaviour after the hellish war they'd been through. Rape was commonplace, but this scene was just too terrifying, too inhuman to ignore.

The woman had been stripped naked and tied over what looked like a barrel. The men were behaving like animals. Some even had their trousers round their ankles in drunken anticipation ready for sex, whilst others held what appeared to be a badly beaten man being forced to watch their sickening performance. I stopped the truck, we fired our Sten guns into the air and I told them we'd shoot the lot of them if they didn't back off. Luckily, they weren't armed otherwise it could have ended in an 'OK Corral' shoot-out. They just collected their things and slunk off turning the air blue with murderous threats and verbal abuse. The beaten man turned out to be Katsumi Akanari San - and the woman was his wife. To cut a long story short, Katsumi and I became close friends. I invited him over to the UK with his wife, Kauru, and eventually, with special approval, he joined the Regiment as a Sergeant Instructor."

"Sounds an ideal man, what do you think, Chink?" said Dick White, not bothering to address the Minister.

"Yes, ideal indeed. How soon can we have him, Bob?"

"As soon as needed. Obviously, I'll have to get his agreement, but I'm sure he'd like to see some action. So, subject to that ......"

"I don't like the idea of using foreigners," Profumo butted in, trying to regain some authority over the meeting, but Chink ignored him. "Bob, I'm off back to Bellamont tomorrow with the family. This Akanari chappie won't be known to the IRA, so he and his wife could simply turn up as our visitors. I'll think of a yarn to tell anyone who asks. And by the way, I know how these Japanese are about decorum, bowing and all that. Tell him we are completely informal. No titles please, to him I'm simply Chink."

"And Dick, if you get Brian Horrocks to relay their time of arrival at Dublin Airport, I'll send my man Owen to meet them. Eve and my son Hugh can show the wife around the estate, whilst I brief Akanari on the mission - then it'll be up to him."

Bob reached for the telephone. "I'll just get his approval."

Whilst Bob Deacon was on the 'phone, Peter Fleming leant over the table towards Chink. "You'll need a spy camera and I suggest the Nip could leave behind some of my new discreet eavesdropping devices." He saw immediate interest light up in Chink's eyes. "They have the very latest battery and transistor technology. I sourced them from GEC's research laboratory in Wembley. And as they are voice actuated, they stay live for months. They are no more than the size of a box of matches. What do you think?"

"They sound perfect, Peter. Are they easy to install and how can we listen to them?"

"Oh, dead easy to install and their transmission range is over a mile. You will be able to use our new waterproof CX2010 receiver/recorder. It can be hidden remotely, but you'll need someone to change the tape every week."

"If you can get them to Bob," Chink saw that Bob Deacon was half listening, "then his Ninja can bring them over when he comes."

It was agreed and a delighted Chink stood up to leave. As he did so, Dick White grabbed his arm. "Those names you gave Airey in your note. I got our backroom boys to check them out. They are all heavyweight Nazis." He handed Chink a paper file. In this, you'll find a brief on each one. My secretary's father, Talbot Bashall, worked for the British delegation at the Nuremberg war trials. At the time, Talbot was a translator and got to know some of the prisoners, some of whom you met at Martinstown. Bashall is now working for Roger in Hong Kong."

"Rebecca said she was sure he'd be happy to talk to you about them. You had better just clear it with Roger first."

"Chink thanked 'C'. A chat with Bashall would be very useful, but there was no way he was going to clear anything with Roger Hollis. He was still furious with him after his disclosures.

In the file 'C' had given him, were sheets of closely typed paper, one page for each name. As he scanned their profiles, he realised that Akanari's mission to Martinstown was even more critical.

CHAPTER 20

Katsumi Akanari San was born in Koka City, one of Japan's ancient Ninja strongholds. The martial art of Ninjutsu itself predated Koka by many thousands of years and was thought originally to have come from China. Ninjas were professional specialists in espionage and assassinations. To them, killing was an art form. The secrets of Ninjutsu were passed from father to sons and as far as Katsumi knew, his family had always been dedicated practitioners. It was their way of life.

The Japanese military intelligence service, the Kempeitai, similar to the Nazi Gestapo, used Ninjas. Before the Japanese invasion of Manchuria in 1931, the Kempeitai sent an advance force of Ninjas to spread fear and disorder throughout the country. They blew up buildings aimed at inflicting mass casualties; they destroyed railway lines timed to derail passenger trains; they assassinated government officials and community leaders. Their acts of terror had the desired effect They paralysed the infrastructure of the country and Manchuria was first to fall to the Imperial Japanese military might when they invaded South East Asia. Then only a teenager, Katsumi had been at the heart of that Ninja force.

Katsumi and his wife Kauru had been at such a low ebb when Bob Deacon rescued them from the marauding American GIs. And if it hadn't been for the British SAS Colonel, he and his wife Kauru San would probably have died there and then. They owed him their lives. And thanks to Bob knowing the potential value of Ninjutsu, Katsumi had found a new life in England as part of the elite British special forces. He had been at the SAS Headquarters at Credenhill in Hereford for nearly eleven years. So intense was his instructor work schedule, that he'd hardly seen anything of the UK's towns, cities, or countryside, just the inside of the SAS barracks plus the occasional exercise on Dartmoor and in the Black Hills of Wales.

For that reason alone, he greeted Bob Deacon's invitation to use his skills on an active mission for the British government with overwhelming enthusiasm. The operation involved breaking into a heavily guarded compound, photographing the contents of a safe within its main building, and exiting without a trace. A simple exercise for a Ninja, thought Katsumi, and wondered why one of his SAS students hadn't been

chosen - after all, they had absorbed his lessons
so well.   However, Bob had explained how critical the mission was and that it demanded the
skills of the Ninja Master himself. He went on
to say that it meant travelling to the Republic
of Ireland, where he would receive a detailed
briefing on the location and layout of the target.
After the way Bob had rescued him, Katsumi
would do anything for the British Colonel and
so he readily agreed to the mission. For a long
time. Bob had felt guilty about the Japanese
couple spending so much of their time cooped
up in the SAS compound. Perhaps, he thought,
Katsumi could merge in some holiday time
either side of the job and take Kauru with him.
He suggested the idea to Katsumi, who was
delighted   Bob said she could be looked after
while he completed his assignment, they could
then take time off touring the Irish and English
countryside. Katsumi knew the idea would ap-
peal to his wife and couldn't wait to tell her.

Kauru, like most Japanese wives, had spent her
time in Hereford happily dedicated to looking
after the daily needs of her husband.   But
she hardly saw him. She tried to busy herself
teaching other soldiers' wives Japanese arts
such as Origami and Shodo Calligraphy, but she
missed Japan and the tea party chatter with her
friends. She was lonely and so when Katsumi

told her that she was going on a trip to Ireland,
she was ecstatic.

CHAPTER 21

Brian Horrocks had sent a coded message to Chink letting him know the arrival time of the Japanese visitors. Two days later, the couple set off from the SAS base. The car journey from the Credenhill to London airport took nearly four hours, through Gloucester, the Cotswolds, and then along the A4. When they'd first arrived in the UK, it had been night time and they'd seen nothing of the countryside. This time, they were fascinated by the quaint English villages they passed through and the time passed quickly.

Chink never discussed his work with Eve. She knew he had successful business interests both in Ireland and Britain and that he was a fervent believer in a united Ireland, hence his involvement with the IRA and the Rialtas na hÉireann, the Irish Government, on defence matters. This meant that there were frequent visitors to Bellamont. Old friends from his army days and even members of the Irish government came for the occasional weekend fishing. But she knew nothing about his clandestine work for

MI6 and as far as that was concerned, it was the way he wanted it. Eve had been under enough stress during WW2, hardly seeing him for months on end.

However, she was intrigued when he'd told her that he'd invited two Japanese visitors, Katsumi Akanari San and his wife Kauru, to stay for a few days. He'd revealed the circumstances in which his friend in London had met the couple in Japan at the end of the war. Horror-stricken, she said she couldn't wait to welcome them to Bellamont and show them some Irish hospitality. Although Chink knew Eve would be sympathetic, he wasn't going to tell her the real reason why the visitors were coming to stay, so he made up a cover story.

He'd told her that the visit was part business, part pleasure. Akanari, had become a leading international consultant in military security. In some ways true, thought Chink. He'd gone on to explain to her that the Irish army chiefs were concerned about the effectiveness of security at the military camp and college in the Curragh and he had suggested they use an outside consultant to test it. This had led to them asking him to find someone - so he had hired the Japanese specialist.

Again, he mused, partly true. He stressed the reason for the visit was highly confidential and asked if she could look after Kauru, while her husband carried out his work. They could look around the estate, go fishing in the loughs and perhaps take Kauru to Dublin and show her around the sights of Ireland's capital city. For Eve, although she never said so, life at Bellamont was isolated and hum-drum. Any opportunity to feel the buzz of city life always excited her and said she would be delighted.

Chink felt bad about deceiving Eve, but his story wasn't too far from the truth. Later, his plan was to suggest she and Kauru stayed a couple of days at Dublin's Gresham hotel and Akanari could join them later when he had finished his work. He knew Eve loved The Gresham, Dublin's finest hotel right in the middle of the city and by far the best place in the whole of Ireland for Dublin Bay prawns.

Chink sent Owen with Betsy to meet them at Dublin Airport. Their flight landed at 3.15 pm. When Owen met the flight, it took him no time to spot Katsumi and Kauru, they were the only Orientals amongst the travellers. He introduced himself, took their luggage, and led them out of Arrivals to the car. They both gauped in astonishment at Betsy. They had never been in a Rolls Royce before. The only one they'd ever seen belonged to the Emperor of Japan. However, once they and their luggage were aboard and started on their journey to Bellamont, the excitement of travelling like an emperor soon wore off. The car's quiet and smooth running plus Betsy's luxurious seating, soon lulled them soundly asleep.

Hugh had never seen anyone from Japan before and when his father told him they were expecting a Japanese couple to stay for a few days, he couldn't wait to meet them. He was so excited that he'd spent most of the morning watching for the return of Betsy. When he saw the car coming up the long winding drive towards the front of Bellamont House, he dashed down the stairs shouting to his parents that the visitors were arriving.

The reception committee of three stood watching as Betsy drew up. Owen got out, opened the rear door of the car and the Japanese visitors stepped out. Their jaws dropped. They stared in wonder at the entrance to the house with its 18th-century Romanesque arch and pillars. And for a brief moment, the hosts were taken aback too. Their new arrivals were in Japanese costumes. Katsumi Akanari San was wearing a traditional Happi overcoat with hakama trousers, and Kauru, a Hanten coat over a pale blue kimono. But it wasn't so much their dress that was so surprising, but the diminutive size of their guests, like leprechauns, thought Chink.

He couldn't help feeling a touch disappointed. How could this tiny, slightly built middle-aged man be the dynamic Ninjutsu warrior Bob had described.

Eve had spent most of the morning in the kitchen with Mary the cook. She had decided that they would lay on a typical Irish lunch for their guests. But at lunch, Eve couldn't help feeling slightly disappointed. Katsumi and Kauru seemed to enjoy the prawns and smoked trout starter, but they only toyed with her Irish stew, definitely not a hit she thought. Similarly, the apple-pie dessert met with a polite refusal. However, when with coffee, Chink suggested a glass of Irish whiskey, the Japanese seemed to come alive. Katsumi told Chink that next to Saki, Suntory whiskey was Japan's favourite drink. "I not know the Irish make whiskey," he said.

"Oh, I think you'll find that many centuries ago, our Irish Jesuit missionaries not only took Christianity to Japan, but they set up your original distilleries." Saying that, Chink poured a generous glass of one of the finest Irish single malts, a 30-year-old 'Green Spot'.

"Now, Katsumi San," Chink rose from the table, "Let's leave the ladies and retire to my study. We need to have a quick chat about the business you are here for - and don't worry, I'll bring the bottle."

Hugh had been silent during the meal, struck dumb by the doll-like beauty of Kauru. As the two men started to make their way to Chink's study, he stood up. "Dad, while you and Mr. Aka-nari are discussing business, can I take Mum and Mrs. Kauru out on Miranda."

"Only if you can persuade Owen to go with you. And be back before it gets too dark."

"Oh great, thanks Dad." Hugh rushed out of the room down to the kitchen to find Owen, leaving the two ladies alone chatting at the table.

Chink ushered Katsumi into his study and shut the door behind them. The man from Japan gazed around the room in awe. It was as big as the dining room they had just left. A massive mahogany pedestal desk straddled the room. A large green leather button backed chair stood behind it with three matching guest chairs in front. Bookshelves covered one complete wall and apart from a large window looking onto the front of the house, the remaining wall space was covered in framed photographs, some colour, some black and white. Chink walked over to the desk, put the whiskey bottle down and offered Katsumi a seat.

"You have many memories here, Chink," Katsumi's eyes floated round the room, now fixed on the antelope's head high on the wall above Chink's desk chair. "That beast is why I'm called Chink," the General smiled as they both sat. "I'll tell you a tale about that later and you may be interested in some of the pictures too, but let's focus on your mission before the amber liquid fuzzes our minds"

He explained to Katsumi what he'd told Eve about a fictional security check at the Military College. "Nobody knows the true reason for your visit and we need to keep it that way." A large map lay stretched out across the desk, detailing eight square miles of the Curragh. Top left of the map was the town of Kildare and nearby the Irish National horse breeding centre known as the Stud, marked with a blue circle. In the centre, the Military College and at the bottom a red circle drawn around Martinstown house.

They stood up and poured over the map. "Your drop off point will be here just outside the Stud," Chink pointed to it on the map, "It'll take about two hours to drive there from here and it's about 4 miles to Martinstown house. I've marked a route for you and you should find it easy going over fields. They are mostly pasture for the Stud horses. I've been trying to think of a way to take you down there. I was thinking I would get my butler Owen to take you, but it would mean having to explain the reason why you are here. He's reliable, but the fewer people that know the better."

They continued to discuss ways of taking Katsumi to the drop off point. Chink had thought he might ask Eve to take Katsumi on her way to Dublin, but it would involve more deceit. Eventually, there seemed to be only one option. Chink would take him in the Land Rover. "Everyone drives Land Rovers around the Curragh," explained Chink and it's far less conspicuous than taking you in the Rolls. Now, let's get down to the detail of the mission."

Chink had drawn a rough layout of Martinstown house that showed entry points plus as much detail of the ground floor as he remembered. He had sketched a more detailed diagram of the dining room where he had marked the safe behind the picture of Hitler and Skorzeny. Katsumi confirmed that Bob Deacon had given him a Minox camera and two microphone transmitters, plus the receiver/recorder. Chink suggested one of the transmitters could be hidden under the dining room table and the other somewhere in the hall. He stressed that everything, but everything, in the safe should to be photographed. Chink continued, telling Katsumi about the tight security he'd seen on his previous visit; and about the housekeeper,

Frau Binz, who had been one of the infamous female Nazi camp guards. She was a very nasty piece of work, he warned, and he should be careful not to disturb her. The Ninja smiled, "I will be like gentle breeze. Ninjas leave no trace."

"To help you, I've invited Otto Skorzeny out to an event at the Military College. I'm going to pick him up in Betsy. When you see us leave, that would be the time for you to make your entrance. It should give you three clear hours." Finally, Chink pointed to another point marked on the map, about a mile from Martinstown. "This is where I will pick you up in Betsy after I've dropped the Nazi. I will park until you turn up. If you don't appear I will assume you've failed and been captured. But looking on the bright side, once I've picked you up, we'll go to Dublin and I'll drop you off to join the ladies. Any questions?"

Katsumi shook his head slowly. "No worry, I not fail you. Very clear *Bosu!* It is piece of piss."

Chink was surprised by Katsumi's language, must have caught it from his Hereford colleagues, he thought. He was concerned that the Jap hadn't asked any questions, and had just listened. I bloody hope he's as good as Deacon says, he angst to himself.

"All clear? - are you absolutely sure you understand everything I've said and have the directions in your head?" he asked.

"Ninja has photographic memory. I have map, house layout, and all you say in my head. Not to worry," replied Katsumi. But when you plan to drop me off?"

"The ladies will be leaving on their trip straight after breakfast tomorrow and I thought we would go soon after that."

"Best time for invisible entrance is at dusk, so if trip take time you say, we leave later. If we arrive earlier, no problem. I will spend time observing Nazi camp."

They discussed the pros and cons of when to depart and agreed to delay leaving until after lunch, timing their arrival at the drop off point for around 4.00pm. "That should give you time to reconnoitre the Martinstown estate before it gets too dark." Chink observed, "and find an observation point for the night. After the ladies leave tomorrow morning, I'll show you around the estate. And I must remember to tell cook that we will be in for lunch."

With the briefing finished, Chink showing Katsumi around the gallery of photographs on the walls of the study. They talked about WW2 and in particular the war in the Pacific. Chink knew it had been a murderous campaign. He listened as Katsumi told him about his nightmare experiences after the Japanese surrender at Mingaladon military airport outside Tokyo. "I was there," he told Chink. "When we lose war, I try to commit Seppuku with Kauru you know ritual suicide?" Chink nodded. "But American soldiers seize us and dishonour Kauru. I fight, but after no food for days, I have no strength. If Colonel Bob not arrive, we would not be here." Chink's impression of Katsumi Akanari San was changing. He had never seen such fervour and passion suddenly take over a person's demeanour. Katsumi continued. "The Colonel restore honour. I now live and fight for him, for SAS and the great British Queen. I will not disappoint."

The boating party had returned from the lough when Chink and Katsumi emerged from the study. Eve and Kauru got on so well. They spent time swapping stories about life in Ireland and Japan. Hugh picked up some words and seemed to spend most of his time bowing to everyone and saying *Arigatōgozaimashita,* thank you, and *Kon'nichiwa,* hello, much to everyone's amusement. Kauru was excited about the trip to Dublin. and promised to cook a Japanese meal for everyone when they returned to Bellamont.

Over dinner, the trip to Dublin was discussed. It

was agreed that Chink would ask Owen to run the ladies down there in Betsy, whilst Chink took Katsumi to the Military College in the Land Rover. Katsumi would then join them at The Gresham once he had completed his work. Chink said he had pressing engagements and so, unfortunately, wouldn't be able to join them at the hotel, but Owen could drive down to pick them up when needed.

Katsumi hadn't seen anything of the estate and as they had a morning to fill before leaving, Chink asked Hugh if he would like to show him around before they left. "That would be brilliant Dad. We saw quite a few deer today and loads of other wildlife." Katsumi liked the idea too and so it was agreed that the two would go out as soon as the ladies had left.

The following day after breakfast, Chink and Katsumi watched from the front steps of the house as their wives, chatting away like two old friends, left on their Dublin sightseeing trip. The two men went back inside as Hugh came down the stairs, dressed in a well-worn camouflage jacket, with an old army webbing backpack slung over his shoulder. "*Ohayōgozaimasu*, good morning Mr. Akanari San, are you ready to go," Katsumi returned the greeting bowing low in true Japanese style. "Your son learns Japanese fast" he commented to Chink, then, to Hugh, "I get my coat *Wakamono*, young man, and I come."

The pair of wildlife hunters arrived back in the house just before lunch. They obviously had had a good time and got on well with each other. Hugh told his father that Katsumi had shown him some Japanese stalking techniques and ways to blend into the forest background. Hugh had no idea he was in fact being taught basic Ninjutsu.

Hugh was disappointed to see them depart after lunch, he was hoping he could have more time learning Katsumi's fieldcraft, but they had to go. Katsumi promised to show him more when he returned. Chink and Katsumi left just before 1.30 pm. During the journey Katsumi changed into his one-piece ninja-yoro, a black skin-tight costume, the same one he'd worn since his *Himitsu no gishiki* Ninja cult induction ceremony many years ago in 1932. It took them just under two hours to reach the drop off point outside Kildare town. He checked his backpack, making sure he had the Minox camera and the radio listening bugs plus the adhesive tape he had been given to secure them in place. The largest object in his pack was the receiver/recorder box he had to conceal on the other side of the lane leading into Martinstown House. "*Sayo-*

nara, Chink San," and with that the Ninja slid out of the landrover to begin his mission."

Katsumi followed the route Chink had shown him on the map and within an hour, he'd crossed the Curragh plain, unseen for the whole journey. He had decided not to bring many weapons with him, just five razor-sharp *shuriken* throwing stars. He preferred them to guns as they were silent killers capable of slitting a throat at 20 yards.

Just as Chink had briefed him, the drive up to Martinstown house was flanked by dense undergrowth and trees, perfectly screening the house and outbuildings from the road. He didn't want to carry the bulky receiver/recorder and so placed it as instructed, then crossed the perimeter lane into the Nazi estate. He moved stealthily through the undergrowth, with each step looking for traps or tripwires. Fortunately, there was only one tripwire about a metre in from the lane, which he stepped over. As he moved closer to the house, he searched for somewhere to hide and observe the property during the night. A tree would make an ideal perch. Soon, he found somewhere high up in one of the trees that gave him a panoramic view of the property. Although now dark, there was light issuing from the buildings that enabled him to see guards patrolled around the house and the grounds. They were all armed with what looked like machine pistols and had vicious looking Dobermans straining on their leashes.

Once when a fox ran between the house and the farm buildings, a dozen or more security lights instantly flooded the whole area with light. Guards let the dogs loose, laughing as they caught and tore the fox to bits. Katsumi didn't laugh. He was grateful to the fox.

Chink had told him that when he'd last been at Martinstown, he'd noticed that the main house had a Burgot alarm box above the porch outside the main entrance and control panel on the left just inside. This meant that all windows and doors would probably have sensors and motion detectors in the rooms.

He relished the opportunity to take on all the guards and dogs - he knew he could win. But he had been told that for this mission, it was vital that his visit went undiscovered. A stealthy break-in at night with all the armed guards, dogs, security lights, and alarm system would not be possible, even for a skilled Ninja. Luckily, the plan agreed with Chink was to enter in daylight.

Katsumi sat in his cramped tree perch all night, occasionally practicing the Japanese exercises

Seiza and Agura to ward off cramp and keep his body flexible. Shortly after dawn, the guards changed. As far as he could see, the day guards didn't patrol or carry visible guns. Instead, they went about daily tasks such as gardening, polishing the cars, sweeping the paths, feeding the chickens, and grooming the owner's six horses. All in their grey uniforms. The house and surroundings looked more like the peaceful home of a wealthy landowner. It had obviously been decided that the risk of an intruder during the day was less likely. The Ninja smiled knowingly to himself.

Domestic staff arrived at around 7.00 am. He could hear the housekeeper bawling her orders as she bullied them around the house. Katsumi remembered what Chink had told him about Frau Binz and her atrocious war record. By 2.30 pm, all the maids and cooks had departed and it appeared that only the housekeeper and Otto Skorzeny remained in the house.

Katsumi watched Betsy arrive with Owen driving. It was 3.00 pm. as planned. Chink stepped out from rear of the car to meet the ex-Nazi Colonel, who walked from the house to greet him with a warm embrace.

From his 'crow's nest', Katsumi could hear them talking.

"I am so honoured, Chink, to be asked for this special occasion," he heard the Colonel enthuse, "Though it is close to here, I have only seen the College as I drive past. I'm so looking forward to it, thank you again, my friend."

Katsumi saw them drive off, leaving a woman at the front door of the house watching them go - that must be Frau Binz, he thought.

Unnoticed, Akanari San made his way down from his perch and across to the rear of the building. He listened. No sound. Cautiously, he tried the kitchen door. It was unlocked. He gently opened it. The only sounds he could hear were clumping footsteps a long way off, probably the Binz woman upstairs. Silently, he slipped into the kitchen.

His main objective was to photograph the contents of the safe, but he also had to hide the two transistor radio bugs in the conference room and hallway. There was someone talking. The voice belonged to the footsteps still some way off, he surmised, so he made his way from the kitchen through to the dining room without any problem. He was about to open the safe when he heard the footsteps louder as they came down the staircase.

It was the housekeeper mumbling to herself in a language he couldn't understand. The door into the dining room started to open. Like an eel, the Ninja slid noiselessly under the table and watched the housekeeper's thick milk bottle legs as she walked over to the fireplace. Akanari shifted his position so that he could see her back. "Entschuldigung, mein Fuhrer" she muttered as she drew back the hinged picture of the Colonel with Herr Hitler exposing the safe. He heard the clicks of its combination lock. Dials turned before it swung open with a slight whoosh.

Katsumi's mind raced. Frau Binz coming into the dining room and opening the safe was completely unexpected. Should he seize this opportunity with the safe already open. He could neutralise her and then photograph the safe contents with less chance of being disturbed - or should he wait for her to shut the safe and leave the room before he re-opened it.

He made a decision. In one snake-like movement, he slid from beneath the table, without a sound. She had no time to be surprised. In an instant, he'd clamped one hand over her mouth. Simultaneously, using the index and middle fingers of his other hand, he applied rocklike pressure to the base of her skull just behind the ear. She bucked and twisted, her face turning all shades of red and purple as she fought. She tried to claw at his face and arms, but despite her frantic efforts, his vice-like grip held.   Within seconds, she weakened and within a minute she went limp in his arms. But he continued until he was sure she was dead. It was vital that his visit was undetected and so her death had to appear natural. His assault had left no marks.

He had to act quickly. Leaving her body slumped in a chair in front of the wide-open safe, he went into the hall. As Chink had described it, there was an antique German case clock near the front door, and next to it, was a small table with a telephone. From the hall was the curved oak staircase leading up to the first floor. Perfect, he thought, Frau Binz was going to have a posthumous accident. He wanted the body to bleed and so had to be quick before rigor-mortis set in. Going back into the dining room. Her grotesque corpse was huge and he was small, but he picked it up as if it was a bag of feathers and carried it into the hall, and up the stairs. With a body like hers, he thought dryly, she could have been Sumo wrestler.

Once at the top of the stairs, he turned her to face down the stairs towards the hall. Then, lifting her into a standing position, he hurled her forward with all the force he could muster out into the void of the staircase. Her arms flew out as momentarily her body hung in the air as if trying to fly, then she fell ricocheting and bouncing all the way down. There were sickening cracks and thumps as her body rolled over and over until she lay in a mangled heap on the hall floor at the bottom of the stairwell. Her face was smashed, her arms, legs and her neck twisted at unnatural angles and blood was starting to seep from every orifice. What a tragic accident, he smiled mischievously.

He had no time to admire his handy work, there was a job to do. He shot down the stairs, skipped silently over the crumpled body of the late Frau Binz, and into the dining room. He took out the Minox camera that Bob had given him, and within 20 minutes had photographed the entire contents of the safe, including Swiss bank statements, a list of properties, a sealed container the size of a shoebox, an address book, detailed maps of parts of Ireland and a document entitled '*das vierte Reich*', the fourth empire.

He copied as many pages as his 50-frame film could take. Having completed the task, he put everything back into the safe meticulously making sure the same order was maintained. After a final check, he closed the safe's door and put the picture that had been used to hide it back in place. His last task was to place the tiny speech activated transmitters, as instructed.

He used the Sellotape he'd been given to fix one to the underside of the dining room table and, returning to the hall, stuck the other under the telephone table. He gave one last look at Frau Binz's mangled body. He had been told about her past and so felt no pity - in fact, he felt sad, she had met a better end than she deserved.

He scanned the hall and the dining room again to ensure his visit would be undetected, then retraced his steps through to the kitchen out into the woods without seeing or hearing any of the guards. He retreated through the trees and across the boundary lane to where he had hidden the battery-powered receiver/recorder. He turned it on as instructed. He could hear the ticking of the clock in the hall of the house. Satisfied it was working properly, he put it back deep into the vegetation.

Three hours later as dusk descended, Otto returned with Chink in Betsy. He insisted that Chink came in for a drink before setting off back to Bellamont. Chink was only too happy - he wanted to a quick look inside to make sure there was no hint of the Ninja's visit. Otto opened the front door and entered into the dimly lit hallway with Chink following behind. Normally Frau Binz would have heard the car and would be in the hall to greet him, he thought. He called out for her, but no answer. It was then he noticed something at the bottom of the flight of stairs. He reached for the light switch. And as the light came on, they both saw the broken and crumpled body of his housekeeper.

"*Scheiße, vas Zum Teufel!*" he cried. Momentarily transfixed by shock, he rushed forward and knelt down beside her body, hoping that she might still be alive. He felt for a pulse, but by the way her head, body, legs, and arms were twisted plus the spread of congealed blood, he knew she was long gone. He stood back stunned.

Chink was just as shaken as Otto, but for another reason. He was rooted to the spot. It was plain to see that the Ninja's visit had gone terribly wrong. Far from being undetected, it looked like a catastrophic disaster. What now, he thought as he put his arm around the ex-Nazi Colonel's shoulders to console him.

CHAPTER 22

Chink stayed with Otto Skorzeny as he slowly came to terms with the shock of losing his long-serving housekeeper and close companion. He'd suggested calling in the local Garda, but that was the last thing Otto wanted. He didn't want them sniffing around his property with their inquisitive questions. They sat in the dining room with a bottle of Bushmills dulling the shock of Frau Binz's death.

"Why - why Dorothea, why my Dorothea? She was the nearest thing to having love in my life." Otto blurted. Her death had obviously knocked him for six.

"She must have slipped and fallen down the stairs," Chink suggested gently.

"Yes, you are right - what else? The steep steps - I told her to be careful." His eyes downcast. Then, clutching his glass, he knocked back the contents and pushed it towards Chink for a re-fill. "Yes, that's what must have happened." He hesitated again. "But just in case, I will get Josef to take a look at her body to make sure it really was an accident."

"What, do you suspect one of your guards?"

"One never knows. She and I had a very close relationship. We shared many years of history, but even tho' she was nearly 70 years old, she had a libido of a teenager - the memory made him smile through his sadness and tears welled in his eyes.

Chink realised that the man he thought had the skin of a rhinoceros, was human after all. "Would you like me to stay?" he offered.

"That's very kind of you my good friend, but no. I will manage somehow. I'll call the Doktor now and sit here keeping my Dorothea company until he arrives," he emptied his glass again, this time refilling it himself from the near-empty bottle.

It was fully dark as Chink got back into Betsy. He reminded Owen they were picking up Aka-nari at the junction where the road from Martinstown joined the R448. Owen drove down the Martinstown drive and onto the main road to Kildare town. Chink's mind was in turmoil. The threat of Otto and his merry men finding that his housekeeper's death wasn't an accident or discovering that his safe had been interfered with were strong possibilities. If so in either case, the shite would hit the fan. The invitation to the Irish Military Staff College would be seen as a ploy to get Skorzeny out of the way, and he, Chink, would be the prime suspect.

And had that slant-eyed bloody Nip had a chance to photograph the contents of the safe? he fretted, barely able to contain his growing anger and frustration.

Reaching the junction, Owen drew to a stop and gave three short flashes with his headlights as the prearranged signal Chink had told him to use so that Akanari would recognise it was them.   As Betsy came to a halt, the nearside rear door wrenched open and the Ninja jumped in.

No sooner had he sat down, when Chink launched into a verbal attack. "You cretin! You fucking idiot! Were you out of your mind? Killing the sodding housekeeper wasn't part of your damn brief." He shouted.

Akanari, shocked by the unexpected outburst, said nothing. This annoyed Chink even more. "You were supposed to be going in undetected, open the bloody safe undetected, photograph the contents, and leave undetected. But no, what did you do? you screwed up, and because of that, all our plans are probably blown to smithereens together with my cover." He was beside himself.

Akanari turned his head and looked at Chink. If

eyes could kill, Chink was a dead man. Akanari was a warrior and nobody, but nobody talked to him like that; nobody called him an idiot. His honour and that of his family was deeply insulted. He was on the brink of physically responding to Chink's outburst. Hardly able to hold back, he replied icily in a voice that sounded like a viper's hiss. "I am Ninja. You insult me. You have no trust." He fought to control his emotions. "I complete mission; I was unseen; I leave no trace of visit." Then after another long pause, as he grappled with his anger, he continued. "I photograph contents of safe; I set up surveillance devices; I did what you ask - see, here is film."

He thrust the film at Chink, who took it, taken aback by the Japanese's aggressive response. "Now look here, I didn't mean to insult your ancestral heritage," still frustrated at the thought Operation Blarney might have been compromised, "Killing the sodding housekeeper wasn't part of the plan. Just explain to me how she ended up dead. If they think it was foul play, all hell's going to break loose. I was...."

But Katsumi Akanari had heard enough. "Baka gaijin, stupid foreigner!" he growled back venomously, "You not give me time to say situation. You listen now." Chink was startled into silence. "When you left with German,

I slide into house and hide in big room with safe. Woman entered. I watch her open safe and start taking out files. You say you want all information photographed, so, I make decision. I stop her from taking any away, broke her thick neck, Ninja style. I very careful not to leave marks on body. I heave corpse to top of stairs and throw her down to bottom. It look like accident; it look like she slip and fell."

"Yes, I saw the body. A bloody mess. But Skorzeny has now asked his doctor to check the body."

" I am sure he too think accident," replied the Ninja with a cold, hard smile - I know my business."

"Well let's hope so." Chink put the film away in his pocket. He realised he had gone way over the top with his tirade, not helped by the tensions of his outing with Skorzeny. "Look Katsumi, I overreacted. The last few hours haven't been easy, it's been like walking on eggshells, nerve-racking to say the least. There's so much hanging on finding out what the real Nazi plans are and I'm petrified that my cover might be blown. I can see now you had no option. We'll just have to wait and see."

They drove on to Dublin in silence. The important thing now was to deliver Katsumi Akanari

San to The Gresham. After their wrangling,
the atmosphere cooled and Akanari fell sound
asleep, but Chink remained wide awake. His
mind going over and over the scenarios of what
the fall-out might be from the Ninja's visit.
Looking on the bright side, he thought, we have
the contents of the safe on film and when we
see what's on it, we'll know what Skorzeny is up
to. I never liked that bloody woman Binz anyway, she got what she deserved.

They came into the centre of Dublin and Owen
parked in the semi gloom of Liam Brugha
Street, at the side of The Gresham, taking particular care not to be seen.

"Wakey, wakey Katsumi. Sorry to wake you -
we've arrived at your hotel." The Ninja woke,
jolting upright in his seat, looking startled and
defensive. Then he remembered he was safe in
the General's Rolls Royce. "Sorry to wake you,
old chap, we've arrived. Chink said. "The main
entrance to your hotel is around the corner on
O'Connell Street. Go to the reception desk and
they'll tell you which room your wife is booked
into."

Owen went round to the nearside rear door and
opened it for Katsumi. As he was about to get
out, Chink caught his arm. "Look, Katsumi,
I apologise again for my rant and rudeness. I
don't know what got into me - it must have

been the stress." Chink held out his hand. "You did the right thing; I can see that now. We have the film, that's what matters. Thank you for everything and I hope you and your wife can now enjoy our wonderful city - and I look forward to seeing you both back at Bellamont".

For a moment, Katsumi just looked at Chink and his extended hand, his face showing no emotion. But then it cracked into a smile and he grasped Chink's hand. "Your apology accepted, General San. I enjoy excitement and challenge. *Oyasumi, okyakusama,* good night sir." With a broad grin on his face, the Ninja got out of the car, bowed in true Japanese style, and slipped around the corner into O'Connell Street and into the reception of the hotel.

On the way back to Bellamont, the weather couldn't have been worse. Thunder, lightning, stair-rod rain, and even hail, but with Owen driving, Chink allowed his mind to focus on what to do next. Before anything else, it was vital that the film was developed. The question was, how was he going to do that? If he sent it to London, it would delay finding out what it contained by at least another precious 24 hours. There was nobody he could trust locally to process it. He laughed to himself at the thought. Then another idea struck him. Of course. It was blindingly obvious. Why hadn't he thought of it before. Hugh!

Photography was one of his son's hobbies.
Hugh had sacrificed part of his bedroom space
and built his own darkroom. It looked a complete shambles, more like a Bedouin's tent with
a permanent acrid smell of photo developer, but
it worked well. There were some of his wildlife
pictures in the lounge and dining room as well
as in the hall. And, because of his interest, Eve
and Chink had bought him a very sophisticated
picture enlarger. Still, it was vital that there
were no mistakes, and processing a Minox film
was a specialist job. Was it right to put the responsibility of developing the film onto Hugh's
shoulders? But time was of the essence, there
was no alternative.

CHAPTER 23

It was just past ten o'clock in the evening, when Chink walked up the steps and entered Bellamont's hallway. He was consumed with worry. Had Katsumi's visit been detected? Had his cover been blown? And had the camera worked - did the film capture the right images? His mind was a whirl of 'what ifs'. The more he thought about it, the more stressed he felt, almost to the point of throwing up.

The weather was so bad that he was soaked in just the short distance between the car and his front door. But he ignored the rain, the priority was to see what was on the Minox film. He was about to call out to Hugh when the phone rang. He picked it up.

"Guten Abend mein General."

He recognised Skorzeny's voice. He blanched. Instantly, beads of sweat broke out and ran down his face. The fears of the Ninja's visit being discovered were overwhelming. He tried hard not to give anything away as he answered. "Ah! Otto. I was just thinking about you and the frightful shock of seeing Frau Binz in such a state when we arrived back. Any news? Do you know what happened yet?" His questions hung in the air, he'd tried hard to sound concerned and sympathetic.

"Agh! Chink my friend. I still can't believe it. Finding poor Dorothea dead like that. Terrible, it was terrible - You were a great comfort." There was no aggression in Skorzeny's voice, only sadness and tiredness. "I rang to say thank you for staying with me while I got over the shock"

Chink's relief was physical. The build-up of anxieties over the past twelve hours flushed away. He could relax.

"Did Josef take a look at her body?" Chink asked.

"Yes, I called him straight away. He confirmed what I thought. She must have tripped at the top of the stairs and been unable to stop herself falling. She'd a broken neck, shoulder, several ribs, and many other fractures. Josef said she would have died instantly so that at least is a comfort for me."

Chink's emotions were being tested. Minutes ago, he was tense with fear of discovery, Now the euphoria he felt was equally overwhelming. Yet he needed to show sympathy and friendship. "Otto, I'm so sorry for your loss. You and

Dorothea must have been very close. What are you going to do now? She was obviously such a good companion and housekeeper."

"I will bury myself in helping you and your IRA friends make their attack a magnificent success." Chink was astonished that a cold-hearted Nazi like Skorzeny felt such anguish.

They talked further about the visit to the Military Staff College at the Curragh for which Skorzeny thanked him profusely and they arranged to have another telephone chat the following day.

When Chink came off the phone, the enormous sense of relief was replaced by a feeling of guilt for the way he had verbally attacked the Ninja. He would make amends. Meanwhile, the priority was to find out what was on the film.

"Hugh" he called out. "Hugh - I'm home." No reply. He must have gone out thought Chink. "Hugh where the hell are you?" he bawled. Then a faint response came from upstairs. He must be in his bedroom, thought think. He ran up the stairs and was about to go into Hugh's room when the door opened

"Hi Dad, have you just got back? I was working in my darkroom and only just heard you. Look, I took some photos on the lough and was just enlarging a shot of a red-breasted goose. I've never seen one before - I think it's rare, don't you?"

"Do you know, I think you're right - I've never seen one either. If it's the one I'm thinking of, they're native to Siberia. Anyway, it's funny you are working in your darkroom because I wanted to talk to you about developing a film and making some prints."

Hugh's look of interest turned to surprise when Chink took the film from his pocket and handed it over.

"Wow, I've never seen one of these before, but I've read a lot about spy cameras. Is the film from a Minolta or a Minox film?"

Before Chink could say anything, his son continued.

"Developing and printing one of these is tricky without the right equipment. It wouldn't take long. I need to tape one end of the film to the bottom of a larger 120 film spool so that film is at an angle to the base of the reel. Then wind it round and put it in the developer. I'll have a go if you like Dad. I've read all about how to do it in the Amateur Photographer, but I can't guarantee it'll work."

No, thought Chink, it's too vital to take a chance. "Hugh, you certainly know your photography. I'm grateful for the offer to try, but I can't chance the contents being damaged."

"OK Pops, let me know if you change your mind - now I must get back to my goose - I don't want it to be overcooked." And with that, grinning at his own joke, Hugh disappeared into his 'Bedouin' darkroom.

Speed was of the essence, thought Chink. The critical factor was to get the film developed as quickly as possible and then assess the contents. He could fly to London again, but too many trips might be seen as suspicious. He could give the film back to the Akanari San to take to London, but that would add another few days' delay. Would it be worth the risk of getting Hugh to try to develop the film here and now. There were many options.

Then he hit on a possible solution - he would ask Owen. Chink hadn't told Owen that he knew he was an MI5 agent, and MI5 would most certainly have photographic facilities in Belfast. That, he thought, could be the solution. He would tackle Owen.

He knew where to find him. He would be in what Owen termed his 'guard room', in other words, the kitchen. Chink went downstairs and as he'd thought, Owen was sitting at the kitchen table with a part drunk pint of Guinness

in his ham-sized hand. On the table was a loaf
of bread, a chunk of Cheddar cheese and chut-
ney from which he'd made himself a 'doorstep'
sandwich. "I'm sorry to interrupt your supper
Owen, but there's something we need to sort
out and then something I need your help with."

Owen looked up at Chink in surprise. It was the
first time he'd ever seen his boss down in his
'guard room'. He finished his mouthful, swal-
lowing quickly. "How can I be helping you, sir?"

"Firstly, let's get one thing out of the way - I
know you are an MI5 plant." Owen's face went
sheet white. His eyes showed a strange mix of
fear and aggression, but he said nothing. Chink
saw his eyes moving towards the large carving
knife he'd used to cut the loaf. Was he about to
attack? Chink thought. But he remained sitting,
waiting for Chink to continue. "Look, you've
nothing to worry about. You weren't to know,
but we are both on the same team. I met your
boss Hollis the other day and until I met him,
Hollis himself had no idea I was working for
MI6. Your friends in Belfast even tried to assassinate me."

"I had an idea they would try something like
that, that's why I suggested I came with you."
Owen relaxed slightly.

"Yes, I should have let you drive, but it all

turned out for the good. Anyway, when Hollis found out I was MI6, he immediately informed me about you. In any event, I just want to say that you're a brilliant butler and as far as I'm concerned, an even better agent. I had no idea whatsoever."

"I just had to report back oh your movements, sir, glean whatever information I could about your contacts, people you've been meeting, and what's been going on here at Bellamont. I would never have hurt a hair on your head or the family even if I'd been ordered to. Working here for you has been the best job in my whole life - only," Owen looked crestfallen. "Does this mean I'm fired?"

"No, no, certainly not. We can talk about all that later and I'll fill you in on what's been going on here and at Martinstown." Chink replied. "Right now, I have a critical need. When we picked up that Japanese chap, he gave me a film." Chink placed the tiny cassette on the table in front of his butler. "It's very critical that we get it developed as quickly as possible. Do you know if your MI5 section leader over the border has access to photographic development facilities?"

"I would imagine so, sir, I've never had reason to ask."

"Well, can you find out and if he has, take the film to him - like now - you can take Betsy. Get him to develop it, and rush the prints to MI6 HQ."

"That will take hours Sir. May I suggest a much faster way of getting it there. We could use one of my pigeons."

"Pigeons?" Chink couldn't believe his ears. "You are joking Owen, aren't you? We used them in the trenches in France during WW1, that was nearly 50 years ago. Let's be serious.

Owen chuckled. "Oh, I am being perfectly serious. Why do you think I asked you if you minded if I kept my racing pigeons here sir? They play a key part in my communications. You may or may not know about the Special Courier Service at Hanslope Park, just outside London. They have a pigeon section there."

Chink knew the 17th-century manor house in Buckinghamshire. It was the joint research centre for the security services, and Peter Fleming was based there. But the pigeon section was news to him.

"That's how I've been sending situation reports to MI5" continued Owen, "and that film would be perfect for pigeon post."

"But hang on, Pigeons fly to their roosts. How come yours go over there?"

"You know I travel around Ireland and even over to the mainland to pigeon fancier events with my birds. Each time, I meet up with an SCS agent who gives me a couple of Hanslope Park birds and I give him a couple of mine. Simple really and very secure."

Chink reflected on the wider issue of petty politics and bickering between MI6 and MI5 causing lack of interaction and communication with each other. If only I'd known, Owen and I could have teamed up months ago and his pigeons could have given us all a faster and less cloak and dagger way of keeping in touch. And we wouldn't have needed that meeting on the lough; Cunningham would still be alive. I wouldn't have been assaulted. But - we are where we are. It's water under the bridge. "Christ Owen, your pigeon service would have saved us all an awful lot of time and bother if I'd known about it earlier." Chink sighed.

Owen just nodded his head. He opened a drawer in the kitchen table and took out what looked like a small pepper pot. "These canisters were designed to take Minox films. I've used them to send films of IRA training exercises here back to MI5." He picked up the film from the table and slipped it into the pod. "And if you want to send a note with it, there's just enough room for a piece of rice paper. Do you want to go ahead.?"

"Well, I can't think of anything better. Are you sure it will work - is it secure enough?"

"A pigeon makes a good lunch for a hawk or buzzard, that's why I always send them at night when the raptors sleep," Owen replied. "I've never lost a report yet and it will be there by early morning if we send it now."

Nothing was without risk, but for speed and security, Chink decided that this was by far the best solution on offer. "Nobody at SCS knows me and so you'd better write the note. Just make sure whoever receives the film notifies MI6 immediately." Owen wrote 'most urgent – please pass to MI6, signed ARNHEM, his MI5 code name.

Ignoring the rain, Owen grabbed a torch and with Chink, dashed over to where he kept his pigeons at the side of the wood store, about 15 yards from the kitchen. With the film already in the carrier pod, Owen opened the door to the coup. For a moment, Chink was fascinated by the neatness of the interior and the way all the birds were lined up on their roost, chuntering angrily at being disturbed. They both stepped inside and in the light of the torch, Owen selected one of the three MI5 homing birds perching amongst the others.

"This one's called Mercury after the Roman god of communications, she's one of the fastest and most reliable birds I've ever used."

He picked her up, holding her with one hand and with the other, clipped the pod to her leg. He gave her one last stroke then, holding her gently in both hands, he went outside the coup and launched her into the stormy night air. He shone the torch into the sky and they both watched anxiously as Mercury circled around as if trying to sense her navigational coordinates. Then suddenly she was gone, disappearing into the night sky.

"I hope for God's sake and for peace in Ireland she makes it," Chink muttered to himself. "The fate of Ireland and the lives of many innocent people could well be depending on that one small bird."

CHAPTER 24

When Roger Hollis left the GOLD meeting, he was determined to make amends to Chink for his near assassination. His men had slipped up. No, he thought, no, it was entirely his fault and he had to take the blame. It was a complete cock-up. But how the hell could he have known that Dorman-Smith was working for MI6 - a deep cover plant. It had been public knowledge and all over the press that he'd been fired by Churchill. MI5 files recorded that he'd changed his name to Dorman-O'Gowan, gone back to Ireland, and had started training the IRA. Such an obvious target to take out that Hollis had personally sanctioned the assassination attempt - a feather in the cap for MI5, he'd thought at the time. 'C', the bastard, was ultimately responsible for the attack on Chink. He should have been open and told Hollis about his assets in Eire.

Whilst he'd agreed at the meeting to work closely with 'C', they had a mutual hate for each other. And it would always be so, Hollis told himself. Intrigue, lies, suspicion and cynicism

were all part of the spy game. Trust wasn't.
He'd make sure MI5 only disclosed matters relating to Operation Blarney. Right now, he had
two Blarney matters to deal with. The first, as
agreed at the GOLD meeting, was to make sure
the IRA 'Big Bang' plot, if it existed, was nipped
in the bud. He and Dick White had to work
together on that. The second matter for MI5
was to find out what was going on at that Portglenone Cistercian monastery.

Hollis rang 'C', trying hard to sound friendly
and cooperative. "Dick, I thought I'd let you
know that I'm going to bring in our London IRA
moles to see what they know about 'Big Bang'.
I thought a private dining room at Rules in
Covent Garden would be a good central venue."

"So why are you telling me - just do it", replied a
gruff 'C'.

"Well, I thought you or one of your chaps might
like to come along." Hollis was taken aback by
'C's openly cool reaction. "I'm going to ask the
Met to send along John Bone, their head of anti-
terrorism," Hollis continued, "and maybe invite
a member of the SAS Royal Engineers bomb
squad too."

Remembering his pledge to be more in concert
with MI5, Dick White warmed. "You are quite
right, Roger. I'm sorry if I sounded reticent,

my mind was away with the leprechauns in Ireland. Let me know when you have arranged it and I'll try to come along. If I can't, one of my chaps will definitely be there."

"That's excellent. Now, regarding that possible arms dump in the Cistercian Monastery in Portglenone your man O'Gowan briefed us on, I've got the seed of a plan vis-a-vis how we can find out what's going on there too."

"It's a shame it took the Prime Minister to bring us to our senses. Let's hope we can keep up this new spirit of cooperation." Said 'C' ruefully. "What do you have in mind?"

Roger knew Dick White had the same reservations about cooperation between their security services he himself had. "For the sake of Operation Blarney, we need to be joined at the hip," replied Roger, "and be as one organisation. There should be no secrets between us. I will keep you fully informed about what we are doing and I trust you'll do the same." Hollis found himself actually believing what he was saying. Good God. He was surprising himself!

"Of course," affirmed the boss of MI6, inwardly being as wary as the MI5 man.

"Well, I plan to insert a man into the Monastery to evaluate the true situation there. And if it turns out to be the arms and explosives dump

we think it is, we, and I mean MI5 and MI6 together, need to take whatever action necessary
to neutralise it."

"Agreed" confirmed Dick White.

"For several years now, unknown to anyone
else in MI5," continued Roger Hollis, "I've personally run a mole within the Catholic Church.
His remit within the Church takes him all
over Europe. He keeps me informed about any
ecumenical plans that might be seen as supporting terrorist activities. He's also been able
to infiltrate the 'Ban the Bomb' movement, the
Campaign for Nuclear Disarmament, to such
an extent that he is now a member of their
Council. His reports have kept us on top of their
activities."

"That's incredible Roger, absolutely astonishing. I had no idea." From the way Roger Hollis
had described the person, Dick White knew immediately who Hollis was referring to, and was
impressed. "That man is a moral figurehead in
CND. How on earth did you turn him?"

"It's a long story Dick, one I'll tell you over
dinner sometime," Hollis smiled, White wasn't
the only one with deep-cover agents. "Anyway,
I plan to use him to place an agent into the Irish
Monastery, perhaps as a novice monk. I've
already put tentacles out looking for the right

man. He should have a military background, some cloak and dagger experience plus a knowledge of explosives. Someone who can pass for a monk, assess the threat, and advise on the action we should take."

"You and I should have been working more closely a long time ago - and I apologise again Roger for my reluctance to share information. We are both paranoid about security breaches, what with the Portland spy ring, Vassal and Philby and his cronies. We still don't know who Philby's fourth man is or anyone else who might be in that bloody network. I have to admit I had growing concerns that you might be involved in it too"

The mask of bon-ami almost slipped from Hollis as he felt a flush of anger at the admission his loyalty was ever doubted.

"Et tu brute," Hollis countered, "I had you under investigation too. We were suspicious of your friendship with Maclean and Philby." For a moment, there was silence as both men struggled to keep their animosities at bay.

Then Roger Hollis continued. "Let's put all that behind us now Dick. You're welcome to come to the Rules dinner and meet my Holy Roman spy. If you or one of your flock can't make it, I'll keep you in the picture."

"Thank you, Roger, I'd appreciate it. While you are on the phone, there's another matter I need to talk to you about. It's better if l come down to your office. We have a very sensitive situation that could blow Operation Blarney out of the water and send our brave Irish General to the dogs."

"I'll be in for the next half hour, so I'll have coffee ready." Hollis smiled as he put the phone down. He called his deputy, Stuart Fellows, into his office. "Stuart, I've got Dick White coming down in about half an hour."

"That's a first then," Fellows looked surprised.

Ignoring his deputy, the MI5 boss continued. "When he's here, I don't want to be disturbed. In the meantime, I've got an urgent job for you."

Hollis went on to explain that MI6 had received intelligence from Ireland that the IRA were planning a major bombing in central London and he needed Stuart to arrange a meeting with their Provo undercover agents. He told him to place the usual coded ad in the personal column of the Manchester Guardian, scheduling a meeting for three days' time in a private room at Rules restaurant in Covent Garden. "Book the room and confirm when the ad is going in so I can tell MI6. And I want to know as soon as it's all fixed up. Get hold of me wherever I am."

Stuart Fellows said he would get straight on with placing the ad. As he was leaving, Hollis called after him. "And Stuart, your way out, ask one of the canteen girls to bring up a tray of coffee for two."

Hollis had a plan for his other task hatching in his mind. How to infiltrate a man into the Portglenone Monastery. MI5's deep cover agent in the Catholic Church was top secret. So top secret that his real identity had only been known by Hollis. Now he had had to share that secret with the Prime Minister and Dick White. The fact that this agent was also MI5's man inside CND was a huge bonus. He picked up his phone and dialled the direct number of Joseph Simpson, the Metropolitan Police Commissioner at Scotland Yard. It rang for a while before the Commissioner answered - "Simpson"

"Good morning Joe, Hollis here."

"Ah, Mr Hollis sir, how can I help." Joe Simpson was a formal man. He knew Hollis never rang just to pass the time of day.

"We are getting some worrying security vibes from our contacts within CND. There are too many left-wing extremists in that organisation and feedback says they have plans afoot for major demonstrations and riots. We want to nip them in the bud. And so, I'd like you to pick up those 'Ban the Bomb' buggers - Fenner Brockway, Canon Collins, and Bertrand Russell for questioning."

The Commissioner never challenged requests from MI5. "That's no problem. Where do you want us to take them?"

"Put them in a Black Maria and take them down to the security centre at Fort Monckton, near Portsmouth. Our chaps there will give them a thorough interrogation. We want to get into their thick skulls that, as a matter of national security, we will take whatever action is necessary to stop their fanatical rebel-rousing over nuclear weapons. And I want to make sure they understand that they will be held person-ally responsible for any damage to property, injuries, or loss of life. I spoke to the Home Sec-retary and he is looking into charging them all with terrorism, even treason. Oh, and Joe," he added as if an afterthought, "bring in that CND troublemaking priest, Father Leo Emery. He could do with a reality shake-up too."

Joe Simpson hid his surprise at Roger Hollis's request in a pause. "So, err, when would you like this done sir?"

"As soon as you possibly can please, Joe."

As he put the phone down, the tea lady with the tray of coffee and Dick White nearly collided in his office doorway. The flustered woman put the tray down on Roger's desk muttering apologies and hastily left the room.

"It's not often you come down into my parlour, Dick" grinned Hollis. "I assumed you'd like a cup of coffee."

"Thanks. Roger, I certainly would - so long as it's not drugged." They both laughed nervously.

"To be serious for a moment, Roger, what I have to tell you mustn't go any further. I haven't even told the Prime Minister. Only I and the agent involved know. I've agonised about telling you, but I can't see I have an option. First, tell me when was your office last swept for bugs? "

"Like your office Dick, twice a day," Roger Hollis replied gruffly. He could have taken umbridge at the question, but thought that what Dick White had to tell him must be earth shattering. He sat forward in his chair expectantly. "I've got an update for you too, but this sounds intriguing."

"Intriguing! huh. It's catastrophic. A human time-bomb." The MI6 Chief burst out. "Our Minister of War, John Profumo. He has been compromised"

"What! What do you mean - compromised?" Dick White had Roger Hollis on the edge of his chair.

Trying to remain calm, 'C' began to explain. "As a matter of routine, we have been watching a certain Captain Yevgeny Ivanov, the cultural attaché at the Soviet Embassy. We know he's a spy, just like our chaps are in Russia, so watching him was purely routine. He had a few contacts that were on our books, none posed any threats as far as we knew. Nevertheless, we always put watchers on such contacts to make sure we know what they're doing and to be sure we're not breeding any more dangerous spies in our midst - like that fellow you've just arrested, John Vassal. Like most of these Russian spies, Ivanov is a randy bisexual bugger, so we started to watch his girlfriends too."

"Damn it Dick, you and I certainly need to work more closely together. "Roger Hollis interrupted. "We might have a case of our watchers watching your watchers watching our watchers," he hesitated for a moment, "we've been watching Ivanov too. We know he's a Major in the KGB. We've had him on a rein for some time, but nothing of much importance has been reported by my chaps. Anyway, without being too bureaucratic, UK security is MI5's patch, not MI6's. But carry on".

"Yes, I know and you're right. My apologies again. We need better coordination, but we only started watching Ivanov in our role as counter-espionage. We planned to turn him as we've done with some of the other foreign spies we've got working for us."

"Nonetheless, getting back to Profumo." 'C' lent forward in his seat." There's a girl called Christine Keeler. She's a model and one of those topless showgirls at the Windmill. She works part-time in a massage parlour run by her pimp, Stephen Ward. Ward, as it turns out is one of Ivanov's boyfriends. As you probably know Roger, several of our MPs visit these massage parlours to 'relax', as they put it. It just so happened that Profumo started frequenting Ward's establishment and like a fly in a spider's web, fell head over heels for the stunning Miss Keeler."

Roger Hollis was lost for words. His operatives hadn't reported any of what he was hearing. "Christ all mighty!" he gasped, "I had no idea. Not the faintest whiff anything like that was going on. I'll have to have some serious discussions with my agent who's on minister watch. But go on, Dick."

"You might find your chap has been seduced too" suggested 'C', "anyway, we've had someone tailing our Minister for War round the clock. He's had several rendezvous with Miss Keeler, some included Stephen Ward and some were overnight liaisons in discreet hotels. Now you can see why we can't trust our Minister. We've got to cut him out of the loop. He's the human timebomb right at the heart of our government.

"I can hardly believe what you are saying. This is disastrous. If any of this gets out, it would bring down the Government. So, what do you think we should do about it?"

"Oh, Profumo is basically a decent enough chap and I don't want the balloon to go up. At this stage, you and I say nothing, just keep our cards close to our chests. We certainly don't want to tell Mac. If he knew, being the man he is, he would do the honourable thing and fall on his political sword - that is after Profumo tells Parliament what a stupid arse he's been and resigns."

"Surely, we can't just leave it like that," replied Hollis. "He already knows too much. We need to know how much he has told that bitch - and then there's Chink. Any indiscreet mention of his name might filter back to Skorzeny and that would seal his fate. He would let that bastard Boger give him a very slow and painful death."

Dick White thought for a moment. "We'll confront him. Tell him that we know about his affair with Keeler and threaten him with exposure if he doesn't finish it. We'll still need to interrogate him to find out what he might have said."

They agreed that that was the only approach. 'C' would ask Profumo for an urgent meeting, then he and Hollis would go and tackle him face to face.

CHAPTER 25

True to his word, the Met commissioner actioned the MI5 Chief's request and had all four CND targets, Canon Collins, Fenner Brockway, Bertrand Russell and the priest Leo Emery, rounded up and arrested. Despite their vehement protests, they were blindfolded, handcuffed, bundled into a windowless police van and taken down to Fort Monckton, where they were to be interrogated.

After a disorientating bumpy drive that lasted over an hour, they were half carried, half dragged into the interrogation centre in Fort Monckton's basement. Still shouting angry protests, the four had their blindfolds removed before being hustled into separate cells. For a while, they all continued to vent their outrage, but soon realised it was pointless. They had no idea where they were and, apart from them, the place seemed deserted.

After about another hour, the silence was broken by the sound of heavy footsteps crunching down the concrete passageway. The protesting started up again with renewed vigour   The first to be taken for interrogation was Fenner Brockway. He was blindfolded again, put into a wheelchair, and pushed towards the interrogation suite.

When his blindfold was removed, he could see nothing, just dazzling lights all around him. Disembodied voices came from beyond the lights. They bombarded him with all the usual questions around his membership of CND - where did they get their money - what plans were there for demonstrations - who were their foreign supporters? They told him they knew he was an active communist, a KGB agent. Did the Russians give funds to CND? A series of other personal questions about his political views and those of his wife Edith. Brockway was a seasoned left-wing fanatic and had been hardened to interrogations. He'd served time in prison during the First World War for being a conscientious objector and again so in the Second World War. He refused any refreshments and didn't answer any of the questions fired at him. Instead, he gave them a tirade about his wrongful arrest. After a belligerent 50 minutes or so, he was taken back to his cell.

The same routine followed for Russell, then Collins - same questions, same aggressive responses. Finally, it was Leo Emery's turn. The warders entered his cell and blindfolded him again. Taking no notice of his struggling and blasphemous rantings, he was forcibly strapped into the same wheelchair used to transport the others and taken towards the interrogation rooms. As he passed the cells of his compatriots, they joined his protesting with supportive angry, and abusive shouting.

Once through the two soundproofed doors, he relaxed, quietened down, and even smiled.

He was wheeled past the interrogation room, where the others had been questioned, and into what could only have been described as a carbon copy of a medieval torture chamber. In the centre was a concrete slab, stained with dried blood, with well-worn straps positioned to tie down a body. Next to it was a trolley on which was a grey box with two large dials and several electrodes running from it. Each one had a clip to secure it to parts of a victim's body. Chains hung from the ceiling and bloodstains splattered the walls. "There you are, your reverend," said the ex RSM with a sneer as he removed his blindfold, "The others got off lightly, but it looks like you're in for some special treatment from our spooky lads."

Not waiting for an answer, he and the other guards left him alone and returned to their guard room. There, the RSM picked up the internal phone and dialled. "The priest's in the

'Chamber of 'Orrors as instructed, sir."

"Thank you, Sergeant Major. I'll call you when we've finished with him."

Hollis and the others, who'd flown down from Kali by helicopter, took the staircase down to Fort Monckton's basement interrogation centre. They opened the heavy soundproofed door of the MI5 'Chamber of Horrors' to find a grinning Leo Emery. "Good God, Roger", he grinned. "I can't seriously believe your interrogation methods are this crude."

Hollis smiled. "Oh, come on Leo, you know it's all for show. Good to see you again. This facility is part of our Agent Development Programme, ADP for short, for training MI5 and MI6 agents. They get the full treatment here. Sleep deprivation, waterboarding, high voltage genital stimulation. Real and true to life torture. You name it, they get it. You'd be amazed how after 72 hours with no sleep, a couple of sessions of near-drowning, and a touch of electrical therapy, most forget it's part of the training and crack wide open, pleading to leave. Probably less than half pass this stage of ADP. With some of them, they disintegrate even before we get to the shocking part."

"But let me introduce Sir Richard White, Head of MI6, Peter Fleming, brother of 'you know who'. Peter runs our spooks specialist support and weapons department at Hanslope Park in Buckinghamshire. As in that 007, film Goldfinger, he is our 'Q'. And Bob Deacon is in charge of our elite SAS Regiment."

Leo shook hands with everyone. There were no seats in the room and so Roger, 'C' and Peter sat in a row on the concrete torture block and Bob stood alongside Leo in his wheelchair.

"Leo, I must apologise for the way in which we brought you in, but we have a national emergency - nothing related to CND, but we thought we'd shake up the pacifist roots of your 'ban the bomb' colleagues anyway. We urgently need your help on another very pressing matter."

"Oh, I found being arrested and coming here quite exhilarating. You certainly put the fear of God into the others. So, what can I do to help?"

They briefed Leo on the situation in Northern Ireland, the possible Irish Republican Army 'Big Bang' terrorist attack on The Houses of Parliament, the build-up of a Nazi force in Eire, and, without mentioning Chink by name, they told him that MI6 had a deep cover agent within the IRA. The agent had found out that there was a team of ex-Nazi *Vermarcht* Engineers who under the guise of renovating an old swimming pool for the monks at a certain Cistercian Monastery in Portglenone, had built a large underground bunker for munitions storage.

"The agent confirmed," said Dick White, "that the bunker is now being stocked with boxes of various explosives, plus a stash of weapons."

"That sounds totally unbelievable - a theme for a fictional thriller. If I didn't know better, I'd say you've all been smoking the weed like half our CND lot. However, to be fair, the Church is one of the biggest organisations in the world and where there's good, there's always evil skulking around. I've heard of the Monastery, but I've never been there. How I can help?"

"We need to get one of our men inside the monastery and we need your help to do that." Hollis went on to explain that although MI5 had agents in Northern Ireland, they were mostly protestant unionists and wouldn't go near a Catholic Church, let alone a monastery. "With our man inside, we will be able to verify the intelligence and if needs be, take immediate action.

"You've certainly got my interest, gentlemen. So, what exactly is it you want me to do?" Leo Emery, now looked deadly serious.

"We believe that the munitions are planned for use in a major IRA attack in Belfast," said Hollis. "Our operative is well versed in weapons and

explosives. We want you to give him an intensive course on how to pass as a devout Catholic
with a vocation to be a monk."

"And find a way to infiltrate him into the Portglenone monastery," added 'C'. Then we'll take
it from there."

"I can certainly give it a go, but tell me more."

"Well Leo, it's a long story, but we'll try to be
brief."   Roger Hollis and Dick White filled in the
background of Ratlines and how a certain Austrian Archbishop Hudal had been a key player
in helping arrange the exfiltration of Nazis out
of Germany at the end of the War. Even the
Vatican was involved, they told him.

"Now I do remember something about that.
I've never heard of Hudal, but I certainly heard
rumours about the Church helping Nazis escape from post-war Germany. The Pope sent a
papal letter to every Catholic church around the
world denouncing it all."

"I can confirm it certainly wasn't propaganda
- it is the truth," 'C' continued. "Another Austrian, an ex-Nazi SS Colonel called Otto Skorzeny, teamed up with Hudal and together were
responsible for thousands escaping to sympathetic countries around the world - mainly
where the Catholic Church is dominant.

"Anyway" Roger interjected, "one of those being

helped to escape was an Irishman, Joe Lynskey. Lynskey, a dedicated IRA terrorist, had
fought with the SS thinking he was helping a
republican cause. In the process of escaping,
he, Hudal and Skorzeny became good friends.
Skorzeny now lives in the south of Ireland and,
without going into too much needless detail, he
and Lynskey came up with the plan for an arms
dump at the monastery." Roger said he was
sure the Abbot and his monks were entirely innocent. He was convinced that when Lynskey
had offered to turn an old swimming pool at the
monastery into a storage warehouse for farm
equipment, all at no cost, they praised the Lord
for bestowing such kindness through one of his
brethren.

"They obviously thought that the Monastery
was the last place we'd look for IRA activity,"
Dick White carried on, "and they were right.
Fortunately, our man inside the IRA found out
about it and raised the alert."

Father Emery looked at everyone. There was
sadness in his voice when he spoke. "With
the world as it is, you may find it quaint that
I still have a deep faith in my Church and God
Almighty. But I'm a realist as Roger knows. I
agreed to join MI5 because it's compatible with
that faith. It is a force for good. I find it so
distressing to hear stories of such blatant cor-

ruption, but it's the same in every organisation - even in your organisations, gentlemen."

They all looked at each other. Even with the tightest recruitment process and ongoing vetting and security, they knew what the priest was saying was true. Dick White threw a glance at Hollis - he knew he too was thinking about Profumo and his mistress; her KGB control; Vassal, Burgess, and all the others they'd exposed within MI5 and MI6. In many ways, 'C' reflected, the fact that we are constantly investigating each other is a very good thing.

The silence was broken by Bob Deacon. He said he had the perfect man to go undercover in the Monastery. He was an Army Royal Engineer, a demolition expert seconded to the SAS. He was currently working behind enemy lines in Northern Borneo. His name was Chris Lavelle, Captain Chris Lavelle. In spite of being one of the youngest Captains in the British Army, he'd already received a string of commendations and a chest full of medals for exceptional bravery. "Chris speaks almost perfect German. His grandfather was one of the Lavelles from Tuam in County Galway.

Bob was about to continue when there was an urgent knock on the door. Without waiting for an answer, Stuart Fellows, Hollis's right-hand man, burst into the room. "My apologies, gentlemen," he said, "Mr. Hollis sir, you told me to let you know immediately anything came in from Ireland. Special Courier Services have just sent us a Muirhead secure fax to say that one of their winged couriers had arrived from 'ARN-HEM' with a Minox film in its pod." Everyone but Leo Emery knew what he was talking about. They looked at each other. It had to be the film taken by Bob Deacon's Ninja warrior, Akanari San. "Apologies for the interruption Leo, but this could be particularly relevant". 'C' said.

What could Arnhem in the Netherlands have to do with what they were discussing, puzzled Leo Emery? He was completely nonplussed. But without taking time to explain, Hollis turned to Peter. "Can you have a word with your SCS chaps and get them to send the film down here on one of a feathered flight. It should be here within 2 hours. We'll prioritize its processing and then have copies of its contents put onto overhead projector slides for us all to see."

Peter Fleming nodded, "consider it done" and he went to the 'phone on the wall at the back of the chamber, and direct dialled Julian Partridge, Head of SCS, instructing him to send one of Fort Monckton's homing pigeons down with the film from ARNHEM.

"Thank you, Peter." Then seeing the puzzled frustration on Leo Emery's face, Hollis explained that ARNHEM was the code name for one of his MI5's agents in Ireland. And 'the feathered flight' was a courier homing pigeon. "We've found them a fast and extremely secure means of communication with most of our agents in the field. We believe this film contains vital pictures relating to what we are discussing – I can't say more."

But 'C' didn't want to leave it there. He wanted to emphasise the importance of the situation to Leo Emery and continued where Roger Hollis left off, "We believe those pictures are photographs of the Nazi's war plan for Ireland. It may prove to be a damp squib, but if it is what we think it is, we'll have captured their operational blueprint for attacking and conquering the whole of Ireland."

Leo Emery was stunned. He looked at Peter Fleming. "It sounds so much like one of your brother's books – wow - it makes my work with CND rather parochial."

They talked more about the Nazi threat in Ireland and how, in particular, Leo Emery could help infiltrate Captain Lavelle into Portglenone. One way or another, they all knew that the monastic arms dump had to be neutralised whatever the Minox film contained.

"You've told me how you want me to help and

I'll work out a way of getting your man into the monastery. As soon as you have your 007 aboard, tell him to come to Westminster Cathedral. I hear confessions there most days between 4.00 pm and 6.00 pm. He can see the weekly duty roster at the side of the main entrance, which will show him in which confessional I'm serving. Tell him to identify himself by saying 'Golden Eagle'. I will reply 'Irish mist' then I'll arrange to meet him elsewhere, probably in my flat around the corner in Mount Street. We will then work out a plan of action. In the meantime, I should leave you all to your gala film show and get back to my CND friends. I must say, I don't fancy the trip back to London, they'll be ranting and raving the whole way back."

Everyone agreed. Hollis stood up and went to call the Sergeant Major.

"Just a moment, Roger," Leo raised a hand. "Before you bring him in, you chaps need to rough me up a bit - I don't want to go back in pristine condition - it won't be good for my image - a couple of hard slaps and a black eye should do the trick."

It was a long uncomfortable drive back to London in the back of the police van. Once in the van, they'd had their blindfolds removed. In the dimly lit interior, they could see the dishevelled and blood-stained clothing plus bruising on Emery's face. They realised they'd got off lightly. But, whilst commiserating with him, it was not a time for individual sympathy. They had all been kidnapped and abused at the hands of what they assumed were the security services. They were seething. Everyone agreed that a joint open letter to the Prime Minister, copied to the Guardian newspaper would be the least of their actions - perhaps, suggested Canon Collins, a protest in Parliament Square. They could take a photo of Leo's face and put it on placards. Meanwhile, the priest emitted groans and moans for effect. Bob Deacon had given him a very effective makeover. His left eye was almost closed and the smacking had puffed his lips and made his nose bleed. But his mind was on other things - a plan was forming in his mind.

Just under three hours later, back at Fort Monckton, 'C', Hollis and the rest of the group were seated in one of the Security Service's training rooms. In front of them was a projector about to show the contents of Akanari's film. The first two slides, taken from the Ninja's treetop perch, showed the layout of the outbuildings and a partial view of Martinstown house. The next slide showed Skorzeny's meeting room with all its Nazi regalia. From then on, the slides were full of text and diagrams all in German. 'C', who had spent several years in pre-war Germany, was the only one able to understand what was being displayed. "I don't know how much you understood gentlemen, but this is the real McCoy. Peter Fleming had the gist of what they had viewed from his time behind enemy lines with the Special Operations Executive (SOE). "Absolutely bloody amazing."

To Bob Deacon and Roger Hollis, it seemed little more than gibberish. They waited for 'C' to enlighten them.

"It's what we've all been praying for. Thanks to your Japanese warrior, Bob, it looks as if we actually have Otto and his Nazi cohorts' detailed plan to overthrow the governments of Eire and Northern Ireland and establish a fourth Reich across the whole of the Emerald Isle. I'll take these slides back to Kali now, review and summarise them. We urgently need to assemble again once I've done that. Say three days' time in London. We also need our tactical maestro, Chink, to come over too. Can we use one of your feathered friends to send an urgent message to him, Roger?"

"No problem" replied Hollis. "And," looking meaningfully at 'C', we need to finish our business with Mr. Profumo."

CHAPTER 26

It was Thursday afternoon, April 24, two days after the Fort Monckton meeting. MI6's Chief was ready to brief everyone on the contents of the film sent over by Chink. The meeting was scheduled for 2300hrs in Kali's GOLD room. Chink had already been sent notification of the meeting via agent 'ARNHEM', calling him to the briefing. The note suggested that he booked a room at the 'In and Out' Club on Piccadilly, London, on the premise of having yet another dinner with Brian Horrocks. After which, he could use the Security Services tunnel transport into Kali. If he was being followed, the 'tail' would assume he was tucked up in bed at the Club.

Earlier that same day, 'C' and Hollis had met with Profumo and told him they knew of his affair with Christine Keeler. He was mortified. He swore that he had no idea she was also the mistress of a KGB agent but seemed totally unrepentant about his affair. Both security chiefs were astonished by his attitude. They looked at each other quizzically. How could they break through this old Harrovian school brazen bravado?

Hollis broke the silence and asked if the Minister had said anything to Miss Keeler about Operation Blarney. Profumo retorted vehemently, denying any such impropriety.   He insisted she never asked questions and he never offered any details of his work. "Too busy screwing, I suppose" murmured 'C'.

Profumo shot up from his chair, his face flushed with anger. "How dare you talk to me like that White. That is outrageous. I am a Right Honourable Minister of Her Majesty's Government. I will not toler....." But Dick White cut him short. "Sit down and shut the fuck up John, you pompous ass. I'll tell you how I dare." Even Roger Hollis looked surprised by 'C's language. The MI6 chief continued." You are a damn traitor. A traitor not just to your colleagues, your friends, your wife Valerie, and your children but to every man, woman, and child in this country. You should think about how many servicemen and women might have died through your unintentional and irresponsible pillow talk."

They told him if he didn't do as they demanded, their next stop would be Downing Street to tell the PM about his betrayal. And if that happened, the political shit would hit the proverbial fan. The message went home. Profumo slumped in his chair, all arrogance gone. The reality of the situation hit home. He was a broken man. "So, what do you two want me to do?"

"You will go and see the Prime Minister immediately," replied 'C'. You will tell him that Operation Blarney is just one of many threats to our country around the world. The pressing need is for your ministry to modernise our forces to ensure they are ready and equipped for whatever may be thrown at us. You will say to him that you believe it would make more operational sense and remove a level of management if Roger and I reported directly to him concerning all operations in Ireland."

"And if he doesn't accept?" Profumo's voice was little more than a croak.

"Resign" they barked.

CHAPTER 27

Chink took the afternoon Aer Lingus flight
from Dublin and a taxi from London's Airport
to the In and Out Club on Piccadilly. He was
early for his dinner with Horrocks and the
arranged meeting with MI6. He had plenty of
time before dinner, set for 7.30 pm, so he decided to change and go for a quick run around
Green Park opposite the Club. It was a chance
to see if he was being followed. He jogged out
of the Club, down through the Piccadilly ped-
estrian underpass and briskly up the steps into
the park. Stopping at the top, he surveyed the
people around him. There was no obvious tail;
there were runners, walkers, lovers and touts,
but nobody looked particularly suspicious. He
then ran as fast as he could across the park
down to the Mall, then up to The Wellington
Arch at Hyde Park Corner. He slumped onto a
bench, not just catching his breath, but keeping
an eagle eye open to see if he indeed did have a
follower. It was impossible to tell, there were
still too many people around. A couple of the
runners he'd seen earlier passed him, smiling as
if to say 'Run out of puff, grandpa?' - he acknow-

ledged them with a grin.

A middle-aged man approached him impec-
cably dressed in a three-piece pinstripe suit
sporting a military tie and carrying an unfurled
umbrella. Obviously ex-army, thought Chink.

"Excuse me, aren't you Major General Dorman-
Smith?"

"Er, yes" he replied hesitantly.

"My name's Thomas, Elwyn Thomas. I served
under you as a Major in the 8th Royal Tank
Regiment at Alamein. You wouldn't remember
me, but I will never forget the way you and General Auchinleck led us against Rommel's drive
across North Africa. I've always said that you
turned the tide of the war."

"Well thank you, Major." Those were desperate
times." Chink didn't want to get drawn into a
long conversation, but those were brave men at
Alamein and he couldn't just cut him short. "I
remember the 8th, a fine and brave bunch. You
had minesweeping Matilda tanks if I remember correctly. You chaps cleared a wide path
through the mines for our main force to attack."
They chatted on about the war for a while, but
Chink was suspicious - was it a chance meeting,
or was Elwyn Thomas tailing him - perhaps
he was working for Skorzeny. Better to be safe
than sorry, he thought. "You'll have to excuse

me, Major, I've got to get showered and changed
for dinner at my Club, funnily enough, with
someone else who served in Africa." They
shook hands. Major Thomas gave him a dog-
eared business card, and with promises to be in
touch, Chink ran off back to the 'In and Out'.

The wine cellar of the Club was the envy of London's West End, but that and the dinner were
not foremost in Chink's mind. As he sat at the
reception waiting for Horrocks, he puzzled over
the appearance of the Alamein Major. Could he
have been following Chink and then cooked up
some 'cock and bull' story as a cover? He took
out Major Thomas' business card. It showed he
worked for Global Life Assurance. Chink knew
that many ex-forces personnel had ended up
selling insurance. Jobs weren't easy to find and
the 'commission only' offers of insurance companies gave some possible hope of an income.
Even so, he'd give Thomas's details to Dick
White and have him checked out just in case.

Chink and Brian had an enjoyable dinner,
accompanied by a bottle of the Club claret.
They talked generally about their families,
raking over their school days at Uppingham
again, the threats to NATO, the Cold War and
the nuclear arms race. After a couple of hours,
Chink feigned tiredness and cut the dinner
short saying he had a busy business schedule

the next day and needed his sleep. He genuinely felt sorry to rush off. He enjoyed his time with Brian, but both knew that their lunches and dinners were little more than charades as cover for Chink's frequent trips over to England. In case they were being watched, Chink made a show of saying goodnight, and went up to his room. He had taken the usual security precautions just in case he'd had an unwelcome visitor during his absence. He checked his briefcase. It was still locked, but anyway, there was nothing in it that would blow his cover. He had a particular way of laying out his toiletries in the bathroom. Again, everything was in order - except, yes, the label on his 'Old Spice' deodorant had been turned around. It could have been a maid who turned down his bed covers and nosed around the bathroom - or it could have been someone checking him out. Perhaps he was being too sensitive, but it was vital that he kept his guard up. He was in good time and so he took another shower to freshen up before the long night he knew was ahead of him.

The theatregoers were making their way home as Chink left his room and took the lift down into the basement of the Club. He knocked on the door market 'Security'. An extremely large plain-clothed security guard opened the door. He was expected. He gave the guard the agreed password 'March Hare'. Without a word in response, the guard passed him through to a further door, which turned out to be yet another lift. He entered and descended deeper to the tunnel train into Kali. He could hear the rumble of the Piccadilly line above him as he stepped out of the lift. In front of him was the train, more like a driverless sedan on rails. As soon as he was seated, the doors shut and it started moving.

The trip was less than a mile and took about 5 minutes. He passed through security screening again at the Kali end. After which, one of the armed guards escorted him to join the others. Peter Fleming, Bob Deacon, Roger Hollis and a recovering Airey Neave were seated around the table of the GOLD top security conference room. Richard White was perched on a high stool next to an overhead projector. Chink was glad to see Gillian there too. He had thought up an idea of how to use her capabilities.

"Perfect timing Chink," said 'C', "I was just going over a few points with the others, but now you are here, we can begin."

"First, as a point of order, Roger and I met with John Profumo regarding his role. He felt that due to his heavy workload on military matters, he couldn't give the time Operation Blarney required, and so asked the Prime Minister to be excused. Roger and I are now reporting directly to Mac."

There were murmurs of surprise around the table.

"I hate to say it 'C', but that's the best news I've heard today," Chink said, Profumo was behaving like pompous arse at our last meeting, and his departure from this committee will make life a whole lot easier."

"Damn right - I couldn't agree more," added Bob Deacon. "The man's an idiot."

"OK, OK, that's enough, let's not trash the man; after all, he is an elected politician and we have to respect that. Now, we can't waste precious time, we need to focus on why we are here." Dick White looked grim as he continued.

"The situation is even more serious than I had possibly expected. I've produced 6 copies of my situation report based on the film. This is a briefing aid and I want all copies back at the end of the meeting. Nothing written leaves this room. You're all going to have to rely on your memories."

Dick White paused to let his message sink in. "But first let me say, Roger and I have agreed that Operation Blarney is dead. What we thought was an IRA round up and put down is, in fact, far, far more deadly and serious. It is war."

"In a nutshell, Colonel Otto Skorzeny is set to lead a Nazi takeover of Ireland, North and South. According to the captured documents, there are around a thousand ex WW2 Waffen SS troops spread along the border. They may be somewhat rusty, but they are fanatics. The documents show that some of the lunatic ex *Britisches Freikorp,* the so-called British SS Legion of St George and French collaborators from the SS Charlemagne Brigade are included, but the majority appear to be German. Most are located in farms purchased by Skorzeny, but crack *Kommandos* from his old SS unit are stationed at Martinstown. And it confirms that there are at least twenty ex SS Engineers already in Northern Ireland at a Portglenone Monastery, posing as workmen as we discussed before." 'C' paused again to let the facts sink in.

"Remember Otto's reputation. His planning is meticulous. Without the documents that Bob's Ninja managed to copy, we'd only have suspicions and, looking across at Chink, gut feel. We are indebted to Akanari, Bob."

"Well, I for one was highly sceptical, Bob." Chink looked at the SAS Colonel. "But you were right. It was a job for a Ninja and Akanari San did a fantastic job."

There were similar accolades from everyone round the table. 'C' held up a hand for silence. "Now we have their plans, we will not only win this confrontation, but Roger and I have agreed that our new mission is to finally destroy Nazism in our Islands."

"They escaped at the end of the War using their Ratlines escape route. This time they won't escape - so, the new name for our Irish mission is Operation Rat Trap. A trap to catch the Nazi rats and any of the IRA who side with them."

There were chuckles and heads nodded in agreement around the table. 'C' then switched on the projector and placed the first slide from the pile in front of him.

On the screen was a map of Ireland. 'C' sat down and Roger Hollis took his place. "Thank you, Dick. I'm now going to go over the current situation as we see it."

"I'm sure you all recognise this slide, a map of the Emerald Isle. It's the front page of the enemy's plan and you can see the border and the swastikas placed along it. They represent Otto's farms, or as he refers to them, his *Militärbasis* and the green shamrock emblems are Irish army bases."

Roger then pointed out the Cistercian Monastery at Portglenone in County Antrim and

finally Martinstown, Otto's den as he put it.
"I'm sure it's not a coincidence that this is
merely 8 miles from the Curragh in County Kildare where the Irish army's main base, training
centre and military college, is located."

There were other emblems on the map, but
these he said would be explained later. "You'll
note that each of the farms has against it the
number of troops stationed there. And this
one," he pointed to the farm just outside Strabane. "note the aircraft emblem. Corkan Island
is a large island in the middle of the River Foyle,
just a few miles upstream from the infamous
pig farm massacre. In the Nazi plan, it is re-
ferred to as the *Luftangriffsbasis,* which means
air attack base."

"They've levelled a grass runway on the island
and their document says they will have three
operational Douglas D3 Dakotas in RAF livery
and an old German two-seater reconnaissance
spotter plane, a Fieseler Fi 156 *Storch,* there."

'C' stood up again and joined Hollis, putting
another slide onto the overhead projector.
It showed the same locations, but this time
there were sweeping arrows from each of the
locations. "I've added these arrows to indicate
the direction of their planned attack. Troops
from the Derry farm here and the Donegal

farm here," he used his pencil to indicate on
the screen, "will travel to Corkan Island and
be used to make three simultaneous airborne
attacks. Two will be to neutralise the Inniskill-
ing Fusiliers' base at St Lucia Barracks, Omagh,
and here, at the Thiepval Barracks at Lisburn
in County Antrim.   The third attack will be to
seize the BBC television centre in Belfast. That,
they hope, would remove our first line of military response and give them vital time to start
making broadcasts announcing the takeover of
Northern Ireland by the IRA."

"Strict simultaneity is key to Otto's plans. As
his airborne troops make their attacks, Otto's
men from the Portglenone Monastery, dressed
in British Army uniforms, are scheduled to
take over Northern Ireland's main airport at
Aldergrove."

"And," Hollis cut in, "at precisely the same time
as the air attacks and the Aldergrove coup,
the IRA is set to blow up the five main bridges
crossing the River Lagan in Belfast. East Bridge,
Queens Bridge, the railway bridge, the Albert
Bridge and the Ormeau Road Bridge."

"That's really going for the jugular," Peter Fleming cut in. "If they manage that, they will blow
the heart out of Belfast."

"But what about their expertise?" added Airey

Neave. "They are going to need an expert demolition team and tons of explosives placed
with precision to blow those bridges. Where on
earth are they going to get all that from?"

"Well, according to the plan," 'C' explained,
"Nazis engineers have already built a 6ft high
wall around an old swimming pool at the Monastery and roofed it. Inside, they have been
accumulating a store of ammonium nitrate.
As you all probably know, this chemical, when
exposed to intense heat, will explode with
immense force. By the end of April, they will
have over 7 tons stored there. The IRA have the
detonators. Does that answer your question
Airey?"

"Yes, but how are they going to get all that
placed under the bridges in Belfast without anyone seeing?" queried Airey.

"Hollis pointed on the map, "Carrickfergus here,
has a harbour about 12 miles east of Belfast and
35 miles from the Monastery. Our friend Skorzeny has funded the purchase of 6 fishing boats,
which will be berthed there. Two nights before
their 'Shamrock *Blitzkrieg*', a convoy of trucks
will take the ammonium nitrate to the Carrickfergus harbour where it will be loaded onto
the boats. Then, during the night before their
Blitzkrieg, they will be sailed up the River Lagan
and positioned under the bridges They are set

to be detonated at rush hour on Thursday, July 12 to cause maximum damage and optimise disruption. It's as you predicted Chink."

Chink said nothing. He merely acknowledged Hollis with a faint smile and nod of his head. He wanted to hear everything the Hollis-White duo had to say before making any comment.

"That part of their plan should be easy to scupper anyway," said Bob Deacon, "We'll just sink the buggers."

"Not so easy Bob, if we show our hand too early, we could scare them all off. We'll let them place the boats in position, set the fuses and depart, then we'll need your men to get aboard and defuse the bombs."

"That's bloody suicidal." Bob reacted angrily. Surely, there's a better way?"

"Let's come back to that later, Bob. If there's a better way, then obviously we'll take it, but right now, we need to move on. We will come back to specifics, but I want you all to see the whole picture," 'C' was becoming impatient. "We've only got three more hours before our Eric here has to be back in his bed at the club and there's a lot more to cover."

Hollis and White went on with their double act. They explained how Otto's SS troopers at Martinstown would make a dawn raid on the Irish

Military Headquarters at the Curragh, whilst
at the same time, his men from the Dundalk
and Ballybay farms would split into groups.
One would surround the Irish Parliament, the
second would take over the TV and radio station, Telefís Éireann in Dublin. There would
then be a special announcement, saying that
British armed services had attacked vital Irish
military installations in an attempt to reunite
Ireland under the British flag. Announcements
would be made that the Taoiseach and the Irish
Government, the Dáil Éirean, had been moved
to a safe and secure place and, in the meantime,
people should not venture onto the streets until
safe to do so. And the third group will round up
and arrest the Irish President, Éamon de Valera,
the Taoiseach and the whole of his Cabinet."

"Surely, they can't believe that such a cock-
eyed plan would possibly work," Airey Neave
broke in. "They may take over the TV and radio
stations, but people listen and watch the BBC.
They'll quickly realise the whole thing was a
hoax".

Chink broke his silence. "Airey, you of all people
should know what the SS were like in the war.
They are soulless fanatics - evil personified,
driven by their abominable Aryan ideology - if
you are not one of them, you are sub-human.
Remember what they did to Poland. The

massacres in the streets of Warsaw, the mass executions - they thought nothing of rounding up people and machine-gunning them in their thousands. They believe utterly in the paralysing effect of terror. They'll roam the streets of Dublin, shooting at will, killing anyone who dares to show a face."

"I, for one, will do everything in my power to screw their plans before they get anywhere near the streets of Dublin, you can be sure." He added forcefully.

The discussion went on for another two hours. It would be impossible for any British forces to be involved south of the border and so it was agreed that Chink would meet with the new Irish Army chief, Lieutenant General Sean MacEoin to brief him on the situation and the Nazi threat. Chink said that he knew MacEoin and had met him several times in his role as a defence advisor to the Dáil Éireann. He was sure MacEoin was a man of impeccable integrity.

Chink also told the meeting that after the demise of Otto's housekeeper, Otto had asked Chink if he knew anyone who could do the job. Chink's immediate thought had been to see if Gillian was prepared to go into the Nazi nest at Martinstown. He said she could easily pass for an ex-concentration camp guard, an *Aufseherin*.

She had plenty of experience inside the barbed wire. With her German Alsacienne accent, she could pass as having worked at Natzweiler-Struthof extermination camp in the Vosges mountains.

"Gillian on the inside will be able to feed us any changes to their plans." Chink looked directly at her; his face full of concern. "Nobody will think the worse of you if you say no Gillian. You, more than any of us, know from first-hand experience what evil bastards the Nazis are. It could be extremely dangerous."

Gillian erupted, leapt up, hands angrily on her hips. "Look! I'm not just here for bloody decoration." She shocked everyone with her out of character explosion.

"I was beginning to wonder why the hell I was here."

The opportunity to play an active role against the Nazi scum who had erased her family, gave her a rush of adrenalin; she broke out into a cold sweat; her eyes flaming. "This is just the opportunity I need; a chance to get involved. It's what I was hoping for. I'll play any part in this Operation, *Fick die Gefahr - fuck* the danger, so long as we annihilate *die Nazi-Scheiße,* the Nazi shites. Get me in there."

Everyone applauded her passion and determination and agreed with Chink's idea. Bob Deacon suggested she could do with a weapons training and unarmed combat refresher at the SAS HQ in Hereford. And Chink said he would rack his brains to find a way for Gillian to make her entrance into the Nazi headquarters.

CHAPTER 28

The meeting was coming to an end. It was nearly 4.00 am and everyone was feeling tired and edgy. Bob Deacon was made responsible for preventing the destruction of the Belfast bridges over the River Lagan, but it was re-emphasised that no aggressive action prior to the boat bombs being placed in situ was vital. And Airey Neave was to brief the Army's Chief of the General Staff, Field Marshal Sir Richard Hull, and the Prime Minister of Northern Ireland, Sir Basil Brooke, on the growing threat to Ireland

"It looks as if all that CND interrogation charade was a complete waste of time then," Peter Fleming was tired and starting to feel tetchy. "I'm sure Leo Emery had better things to do. I certainly did."

"Not so, Peter, just calm down." It's essential we get Bob's man into the Portglenone Monastery. You have sent for him haven't you, Bob?" The SAS Colonel confirmed and said he would be arriving in the next 72 hours.

'C' continued, looking directly at Peter Fleming.

"Captain Lavelle's task will be to doctor the bomb detonators in such a way that they are deactivated, yet still look live. And he needs to do it before Otto's Shamrock Blitzkrieg is erupts. If he can do it, the Belfast bridges will be safe and your men Bob will be saved from a perilous mission."

Peter apologised. "I must say, I'm usually in bed at this hour. So, apart from the briefings and getting Gillian inserted into the rats' nest, where do we go from here?"

"I think we're all getting tired," said 'C' suppressing a yawn, "I don't think continuing is going to be that productive, so let's get some brandy, coffee, and bacon sandwiches, then call it a night."

There was weary agreement around the table. Hollis called the kitchen to place their order. Meanwhile, 'C' wanted to explore the possible support Hanslope Park could provide for Operation Rat Trap. He asked Peter if there were any devices that could provide secure communications between everyone. "We can't go on meeting like this," he said, "it's a continuing risk for Chink and costly on everyone's time."

"Funny you should ask, Dick. I was checking out a couple of interesting devices before I came down here. They might be just the thing you need," replied Peter. "The first device is a mobile telephone scrambler. Current scramblers, as you know, work only on specially adapted phones, like the one in your office, Dick. Our new device, the MTS, means you can have secure telephone conversations between any two ordinary phones wherever they may be."

He went to the GOLD phone and took out of his pocket what looked like a packet of twenty Dunhill cigarettes. As if by magic, the top burst open, and two flimsy rubber cups sprang out, each connected to the packet by a thin wire. He then proceeded to show how one cup slipped over the mouthpiece of the phone, and the other over the earpiece. "Inside the rest of the packet is some of the latest miniaturised transistor technology that does the scrambling and unscrambling of telephone conversations. It also has an additional facility that makes the call untraceable, even in public phone boxes.

"That's going to be so useful," Chink enthused. "Damn sight faster than pigeon. Does that mean I can use it from Bellamont?"

"Absolutely," said Peter. "You can use it from anywhere. There's no way anyone can listen in to a call unless they are in the room with you. They'd just hear garbage. And that's what call recipients hear until they fit one on the phone at their end."

"And if you like the MTS Chink, you are going to love this." With that, Peter bent down and picked up his briefcase, placed it on the table and opened it. "May I introduce you all to the complete agent support kit, we call it the 'CASK'."

He had everyone's wrapped attention. "As you can see, it looks like an ordinary briefcase, with a couple of folders inside. However, under them is probably the most advanced multi-purpose communications devices existing today."

He removed the folders to display an array of buttons, a telephone dialler plus a pop-up microphone and built- in speaker. "Top left here on the console," he pointed, "are four buttons, red, white, blue and yellow; each one switches on a particular mode of operation."

"The red button enables fixed frequency two-way radio communications with another CASK briefcase within a 2-mile radius."

"The blue button sets the CASK in spy mode." In spy mode, the CASK becomes a listening post. Left in one location, it automatically transmits sounds, voices etc., to the CASK owner wherever he or she is, up to the same 2-mile radius."

Peter reached into his pocket and produced what looked like a cigar. "This looks like a cigar

- yes? Well, its actually a short wave radio re-
ceiver - the spy simply sticks it in his ear and he
can hear his CASK."

"That's ridiculous," Hollis huffed, "You can't
just walk around with a cigar in your ear. Spies
are meant to be inconspicuous." There was
laughter around the table at the idea.

When everyone had quietened down, Peter continued. "Sorry Roger, please excuse my weird
sense of humour. You're quite right, he doesn't
have to stick the cigar in his ear, he sticks it in
his mouth like a real Havana. Not many people
have heard of 'bone conduction', but believe
me, you can actually hear through your mouth.
With the cigar clenched between his teeth, an
agent can hear clearly"

"I see where you are coming from Peter, a very
useful facility." said Chink. " I only wish I'd had
a CASK at my last Martinstown meeting, when
I went out to inspect the interrogation centre,
I could have listened to what Skorzeny and his
scumbags were discussing. So what about the
white button then?"

"Ah well now, that's the anti-snooping mode.
Diametrically opposite to the blue button func-
tion. When it's pressed, the CASK generates
what's called 'white-noise', an invisible sound
proof dome-like shield, about 10ft wide and tall

around it. People inside the dome can have private conversations without any chance of being overheard."

"You mean that with one of these briefcase CASKS here, we wouldn't need to be couped-up in this lead balloon?asked 'C'

"Yes, theoretically you're right" Peter replied.

"Very interesting...." 'C' could see how Peter's magic briefcase was going to revolutionise the security services. "And the yellow button, what does that do?"

Oh yes well, nothing special. Press it and the CASK becomes a hands-free scrambler telephone that can talk to any other phone with an MTS attached."

"And is it rugged; tough enough to take into a war-zone," Bob Deacon asked.

"I haven't tried a steamroller yet Bob, but it survived a 30ft drop onto concrete and being run over by a car - so I would say yes." Peter replied.

"But before I forget," he continued, there are two other vital features - one is a concealed quick access button on the side of the CASK here." He turned the case, so that everyone could see the button, then pressed it - the handgrip of a Walther PPK pistol shot out from the side ready for use.

His audience were spellbound - completely bowled over by Peter and his spy briefcase.

"And finally," Peter said, " the other feature is this small round orange flip cover next to the yellow button. Under it is a self destruct switch. Lift the cover, flick the switch and you have 30 second to run before it blows itself up."

"Oh Peter! Absolutely fantastic; stunning; genuinely brilliant; unbelievable," 'C' could hardly find the words to express his amazement at what Peter had unveiled. "CASK is an agent's dream. How soon can we have a dozen?"

"I have five MTS here for you now and one extra for the PM." He handed the devices around the table. Dunhill agreed to our using their branding to make them look as ordinary as possible and when they are in your pockets, they'll hardly be seen at all."

"Again, fantastic, but what about the briefcase device?"

There lies a bit of a problem" replied Peter, "we only have two working models ready for use at the moment. They are being produced for us by one of our security approved manufacturers, International Aeradio in Feltham, by London Airport. Let me know how many you want and I'll tell their MD we need them yesterday."

"Tell him we'll treble the price if he can supply

them in a week," pledged 'C' eagerly. "And could Chink take this one here back with him to Bellamont?"

"Absolutely fine," Peter replied," I'll just have to explain how to operate it in more detail and…"

"That's a great idea, but I can't chance being seen with an additional piece of luggage," Chink broke in, "I'm pretty sure I have a permanent tail following me. They are trained to report back anything out of the ordinary. Why don't you have it taken to Harrods in Knightsbridge and put into the Business Travel Department for my collection. If you can get it there this morning, I'll go and 'buy' it before catching my afternoon flight back to Dublin.

"I'll certainly do that" assured Peter.

"When I get there, I'll look at a few other cases, then surreptitiously ask for the one you've left."

At that moment, there was a knock at the door and an attractive young blonde waitress brought in the coffee, sandwiches, and a large bottle of Napoleon brandy. She wasn't the usual old Cockney dragon, Mrs. Sherwood. At last thought 'C', our personnel department is improving in their staff selection.

"Would you like brandy glasses, sir?" she asked nervously.

He nodded in response and she went out and brought back half a dozen Irish Waterford crystal balloons.   How appropriate, thought Chink. Eyes couldn't help but follow her as she served the coffee and when she leant over to place the bacon sandwiches in the middle of the table the table, eyes bulged. A pretty and well-developed young lady and she knew it.

After their short break, the heads of Britain's security services called the lift that would take them directly up to 10 Downing Street to brief the Prime Minister. He always got up at 5.00 am, so they wouldn't have too long to wait. After they'd left, Bob Deacon, Airey, and Gillian went ahead of Peter Fleming and Chink, discussing the refresher training she would need at the Hereford SAS camp.

"I need to get back to my bed at the Club, but why don't we stop off at the all-night cafe on this floor and talk about what other special devices you might have up your sleeve," suggested Chink.

Peter agreed and they went and took a table in the empty cafe. They talked about the weapon research and development being carried out at Hanslope Park. Peter amazed Chink with some of the astonishing devices in their portfolio. Exploding cockroaches; a micro gun that looked like a wristwatch; stun grenades made to look like golf balls; machine gun umbrellas; a fountain pen that shot poisoned needles; cigarette packet smoke bombs; and a location beacon that fitted into an agent's rear passage. Chink blinked at the thought but said nothing.

They went on in deep discussion and Chink was in the middle of giving Peter a long shopping list of his requirements, when they heard raised voices emanating from the kitchen. Shortly afterwards, the young waitress, who had served them in the GOLD room, stomped out, red-faced. Minutes later, Mrs. Sherwood came to their table, red-faced, flustered, and looking even more dragon-like. "Evenin' Mr. Flemin sir, I'm goin' orf now. Ja wan anyfin' before I go?"

They asked for two more coffees and the rest of the GOLD bottle of brandy.

"It sounded as if you were having a bit of a problem in the kitchen. Anything to do with your new staff?" Peter asked tactfully.

"Oh, ja mean tha f'ing tart. Gime bloody lip she did. Only star-ed yesterday. An there she were, tellin me 'ow to do my job. We've ad a lota staff off wiv the f'ing flu, so we ad te get someone in quick like. She's too bloody 'igh an' migh'y, so I tol er te take er f'ing arse off and when she come tomorrow, she betta watch 'er attitude. Jus can't get decen' staff these days."

They both thought a young lass like that was excellent for male morale, plus anyone with any spirit would find it hard to work with Mrs. Sherwood. She fetched the brandy from the GOLD room and after depositing it with them huffed her way back to her kitchen den.

They both left shortly afterwards, Peter Fleming took another of Kali's exits, toilet number three in the gents at Charing Cross Tube station. There, by keying in the appropriate code in the security keypad, he swung back the secret door behind the cistern and toilet bowl and out through the closet door saying 'out of order, not in use'. As he went to go out, another Kali security guard, posing as a lavatory attendant, acknowledged him.

"Not exactly what you signed on for is it?" Peter said with a smile.

"Oh, it's not so bad, sir. We take it in four-hour shifts" the guard replied, glad to have someone to talk to. "At least I'll never be caught short when I'm working here. It's the cleaning bit we all have to do that's a pain in the arse. Mind you, I have a bit of fun with those blokes who want to share a cubicle."

They said goodnight and Peter caught a taxi to King's Cross to hop on the early mainline 'milk' train back to his Hanslope Park spooks support department.

As Chink returned to the 'In and Out' Club on the tunnel train, his mind returned to the Major who had approached him in Green Park. He'd given Dick White Elwyn Thomas's visiting card to check him out and would just have to wait for the response.

After two hours sleep, Chink went down to breakfast in the Club dining room. It was 8.00 am. He had just been served with a plate of bacon and scrambled eggs, when he noticed Major Thomas enter and sit at the far end of the room. Their eyes met and both raised a hand in acknowledgment. There was something not quite right with that ex-major, thought Chink, but he couldn't put his finger on it.

He went to Harrods as arranged, casually looked around the luggage department at the same time keeping a surreptitious eye open for a possible tail. Seeing no one, he asked for the special briefcase that Peter had sent there for him.

He caught his flight to Dublin on schedule and was back at Bellamont in time to sit down to dinner with Eve and Hugh.

As Owen served Chink, he handed him a note. "The flying courier service has just delivered this for you, sir. Sounds important."

The note simply said, 'Urgent ring me' 'C'.

He excused himself from the table and went to his study and shut the door firmly behind him. This'll be a good test, he thought. Then taking the Dunhill packaged scrambler out of his pocket, he fitted it to his phone as Peter had demonstrated, and dialled 'C's number. The phone was answered by a noise like a bath tap gushing full tilt. Then, when 'C' put on his Dunhill scrambler at the other end, the ruckus shut off. "Hello, hello Dick, how do you hear me."

"Loud and clear Chink. I'll keep it brief, but you need to know that one of the slides I showed you on the overhead projector is missing. It may have got mislaid, but if there's the slightest possible chance that it's got into the wrong hands, you could be in serious danger."

Chink thought for a moment, then it came to him. "That young waitress. She was the only one to come into the meeting. She was a great distraction. If it has been lifted, she's very likely the one who took it while we were admiring her knickers. Dick, if she doesn't come back tomorrow, she's guilty. If she does come back, take her straight down to the interrogation centre and give her the third degree."

Dick White promised to do exactly that and said he would ring Chink back in the morning.

Chink put his phone down and removed the scrambler. As he put it in his pocket, he realised that if it was the young girl, she had only got one of the OHP slides. But it would be enough to alert Skorzeny to the fact that his plans had been compromised. She wouldn't have known him or anyone else in the GOLD room from Adam. So, he was pretty sure his cover was still safe - for the moment.

There was one way he could find out. He could send someone down to retrieve the latest tape from the voice-activated wireless recorder in the undergrowth outside Martinstown. He pulled the cord of the servant's call bell system in the kitchen, summoning Owen to the study.

There was a knock at the door and Owen entered. "Owen, I urgently need someone to go down to Martinstown and retrieve the voice-activated tape from the recorder our Ninja chap planted. Could we ask one of those ex-SAS fellers training the IRA recruits, Seamus O'Driscoll or Terry Casey to go? Roger Hollis told me they were working for MI5 too. It's better if you ask one of them - the fewer people know I'm batting for the same side the better."

"I don't think that's a problem sir. Seamus is a motor bike fanatic. He's got one of those BSA 500cc bikes and is always tinkering with it," Owen said, he'd jump at any opportunity give it a spin. "I'll make sure he understands the importance of the job and emphasise the need for speed and to make sure he's not seen. I'll go and round him up now"

Chink had copied the hand drawn map Akanari had made of where the recorder was located onto a road map of the Curragh area and reproduced Akanari's notes on how to recognise its hiding place. "Here's the map plus our Japanese friends instructions for Seamus to find the recorder. He probably knows how to get to the Curragh, but tell him it's almost a straight road down if he takes the R191." Chink also gave Owen a step by step guide explaining how to take out and replace the tape.

"When I find him, I'll make sure he fully understands what he has to do. If there are any issue, I'll come back to you sir. Otherwise, he should be back here with the tape in no more than a couple of hours." With that, Owen left the room in search of Seamus.

CHAPTER 29

The phone rang and rang, but no answer. Minutes later, it rang again. This time, Otto Skorzeny heard it. He came down the staircase into the hall. "Skorzeny" he answered abruptly. He listened intently to the caller. The news from London was potentially disastrous. His undercover agent, Axel, had discovered that the British security services had somehow found out about his *Blitzkrieg* planning. "Exactly how and what have you detected?" Skorzeny asked.

Axel explained that his contact within the security services headquarters had been in touch. When she was clearing up after a late-night meeting there, she found a piece of cellophane on the floor. She had given it to Axel. It was an overhead projector slide of a map of Ireland. As Axel described what was on it, Skorzeny realised he was hearing a precise description of the map at the front of his strategy document for Shamrock. "*Vielen Dank* Axel, thank you. If you or your *fraulein* discover any further information, call me immediately. You can tell her she will be amply rewarded."

Otto crashed the phone down. Cold fury
gripped him. He stood up, slamming his fist
down on the telephone table. How could those
Verdammt Scheiss Britishers have a copy of that
map? he snarled. The only people who had seen
the map were his most trusted allies in Spain
and Argentina, or one of those who sat around
his dining room table when he revealed the
Shamrock *Blitzkrieg* to them. It couldn't be that
Irish Minister, Charles Haughey or his *dummkopf* IRA friends. They had left the meeting
before he went through the plan with his fellow
Nazis.

Otto sat at his large dining room table with
his head in his hands, concentrating, trying to
work out in his mind the maze of events over
the past weeks that might cast some light on
where the leak could have sprung from. It was
at times like this that he missed Dorothea. Her
analytical mind and clear thinking were just
some of her many assets he missed. His mind
strayed, thinking of the many good years he had
spent with her.

He had a sudden thought. Mengele confirmed
that her death was an accident. Perhaps it
wasn't. Had someone somehow managed to
evade the guards and get into Martinstown?
If they had, could his Dorothea have been tortured and forced to open the safe? Then she was

killed and her murder made to look like an accident? He dismissed the idea. The Herr Doktor would have noticed signs of torture.

He stood and faced the picture of the Fuhrer, raising his arm in the Nazi salute. "Mein Fuhrer," he barked, "we shall not fail you. The *Blitzkrieg* will triumph. We shall bring forward our plans, seize the initiative, and strike with lightning speed. *Sieg Heil*! hail Victory." He could almost hear the voice of his Fuhrer urging him on.

CHAPTER 30

On the day following the GOLD meeting, Dick
White had contacted the Ministry of Defence
and requested the secondment of the Royal Engineers' Captain Christopher Lavelle as a matter
of urgency.

In 1955, after two years at The Royal Military
Academy Sandhurst, Chris had been commissioned into the Royal Engineers. He'd spent
six months at their training depot in Chatham,
where he specialised in demolition technolo-
gies. He took to the art of destruction like a
duck to water. And after another six months
of intensive training with the SAS in Hereford,
he'd spent much of his time in hot spots around
the world, more often than not working undercover to achieve specific objectives dictated by
the British Government and its Allies.

One particular operation he had been assigned
to was in East Germany. Chris had been based
with The British Army of the Rhine, BAOR, in
West Germany and spoke almost perfect German. And because of his dedication and track

record for successfully accomplishing missions, he was picked for the task of eliminating one of the Third Reich's remaining mass killers, one Vincenz Müller, who lived openly in East Germany, under the protection of the regime.

During the Second World War, Müller had been in charge of the 14th Ukrainian SS Grenadier Division made up mostly of military volunteers from the country's Galicia region. Between 1941 and 1944, Müller, had overseen the murder of more than a million Ukrainian Jews.

After months on the run from the Allied forces, he escaped to East Germany where he was recruited to mastermind the creation of East Germany's armed forces. The request for his judicial elimination had come from the West German Government who, apart from his Nuremberg war crimes commission death sentence in absentia, feared Müller was behind the escalating tensions between the East and West.

In May 1961, after two months living undercover in East Berlin, Chris Lavelle notched up another successful mission, when Müller 'accidentally' fell from the balcony of his flat.

Chris' returned to his military base in West Germany, only to be told his specialist services were required with the SAS behind enemy lines

in Northern Borneo. He was just beginning
to acclimatise to the tough jungle conditions
behind enemy lines, when he received a message to say he was needed for yet another vital
undercover job - no details, just that he was
being picked up by helicopter from his jungle
hideout and would be taken directly to the Paya
Lebar Military Air Base in Singapore. It was a
life he had become used to.

It was 11.30 pm when he was met off the
helicopter by an RAF pilot in full flying gear,
"Evening sir, I'm Archie Wiltshire. I'm the pilot
of that de Havilland Comet over there on the
runway. I've been ordered to whisk you off to
RAF Brize Norton in the UK."

Chris, recovering from two sleepless nights
on patrol and the hectic helicopter dash was
almost out on his feet, but he managed to shake
hands with Archie and ask him how long the
trip was going to take. "Usually," Archie replied,
"it takes 23 hours to fly to the UK with one
stop over en route, but you must be sombody
special. This particular Comet belongs to the
British security services. It has extra large
fuel tanks built into the fuselage more than
doubling its range - so the trip will be non stop
and should take no more than 15 hours, ETA
0800hrs local time there."

They boarded the plan and Archie showed Chris into the accommodation section. "Sit where you like sir, you are the only passenger. There's a drinks cabinet in the corner and toilet facilities are just past where we boarded." Chris thanked him and chose a forward facing window seat. The pilot told him there was a change of clothes and a few other odds and sods in the locker above his head. "Enjoy the flight. I'll wiz back to my cockpit and get this bird on its way. If you need anything, there's a call button..." But Chris wasn't listening, he had already fallen fast asleep.

When a spate of turbulence woke him, he'd been asleep for nearly 8 hours. A good time to change, he thought. Opening the locker, he not only found a complete set of clothing, but also shaving equipment, shampoo and hair brush, deodorant and a sachet of soap. He couldn't wait to get out of his filthy active service greens and wash off the caked jungle grime accumulated over days.

Using the cramped toilet facilities, he washed, shaved off his two-week old stubble and generally cleaned up as best he could, after which he dressed in the clothes. The black corduroy trousers were the right length, if slightly loose around the waist; the maroon shirt neck size was spot-on; the thick blue Guernsey sweater size was perfect; he wasn't too sure about the bright yellow socks and the brown suede shoes; someone had certainly checked his vital statistics, he thought, but their colour sense was questionable.

Feeling more human, he opened the drinks cabinet. He just wanted water, but that was the one drink it didn't offer, so he settled for a bottle of pale ale. It had the desired soporific effect and he went straight back to sleep.

It would have been a lonely flight had he not been so wacked. Apart from being woken up once more, by the co-pilot with a cup of tea laced with brandy and a thick bacon sandwich, he slept for the rest of the journey, only to wake again as the wheels of the Comet hit the runway. When they came to a standstill, another member of the crew came to collect him. He handing Chris a duffle coat. "Bit of a temperature drop here sir, the Wing Commander thought you might need this," he said.

Archie was right. The contrast in temperature between Northern Borneo and Brize Norton hit him as soon as the aircraft's door opened, and brought on an involuntary shiver. Instead of the humid warmth and star lit skies of the jungle he'd left behind, grey cloud and damp drizzle greeted him.

As he descended the steps from the Comet, a black Rover P5 car drew up. A Military Police corporal stepped out, opened the rear door, stood stiffly to attention and saluted, waiting for Chris to get in. As he was in civilian clothes, Chris acknowledged the formal welcome with a nod and a smile . The car had smoked glass windows and so the interior was dark and gloomy but he could see that there was already one other occupant.

Colonel Bob Deacon had come to meet him. Chris knew Bob from his time in Hereford. Dick White had thought it would be a good idea to spend the journey time into London giving Chris a general overview of the situation in Ireland. And who better to do that than someone he knew. Chris hadn't seen Bob since his training at the SAS base. And he realised that whatever the reason behind his extraction from the jungle, if Bob was involved, it would be challenging. Bob had also spent time in North Borneo and initially they talked about the war there, plus a catch up on mutual SAS friends and their activities around the world.

As the car sped sped along the A40 towards London, the general chatter dried up. They both looked out at the passing countryside. The

silence was pregnant with Chris waiting for Bob
to give him some idea of why he had been sent
for. Finally, he could hold back no longer. "So
Bob, what's all this about? Nobody's told me a
damn thing. Where are we going? come on,
spill the beans.

"The reason you're here is because we've got
problems in Ireland and there's a specific undercover assignment over there tailormade for
you," Bob explained. "I really shouldn't tell you
anything more than that, you are going to be
briefed later." He paused, than added, "but off
the record, it involves a monastery and an arms
dump that has to be neutralised quietly and
without too much fuss and public attention. I
suggested you for the job, so I was asked to meet
you off the plane and drop you off at the In and
Out Club on Piccadilly. There's a room already
booked for you there"

When they arrived outside the Club, the two
friends shook hands and said their farewells.
Bob wished him the best of luck with his assignment. " MI6 will be in contact shortly, but
until then, check-in, relax and enjoy the Club
facilities.

Chris went in through the pillared entrance
of the In and Out. As Bob had said, his accommodation had already been reserved. He gave

his name to the reception clerk behind the desk. After finding his name in the register, he handed Chris the key to his room.

"Best room in the Club sir." said the clerk. "Enjoy your stay. Would you like help with your baggage and someone to show you to your room," Chris shook his head.

He thanked the man and said he would find his own way. He didn't bother to tell him he had no luggage, nothing apart from the clothes he stood in, and no cash to leave a tip.

Despite still being exhausted, Chris was gagging for a proper shower. Something he hadn't had for what seemed like months. He'd done his best to clean up in the tiny toilet facilities on the aircraft, yet despite his efforts he was well aware of pervading jungle odour. Once cleaned up and refreshed, he thought he might nip round to his tailor, Gieves in Bond Street, buy a suitcase and some decent clothes to wear. It was 3.00 pm local time and so he had a couple of hours before they closed.

The room he had been given was actually a suite. As the receptionist had said, it was the Club's best. Rather different from nature's accommodation, he thought. The bathroom not only had a shower but a really large, deep,

inviting bath. Not wanting to wait for the bath
to fill, he stripped off and for the next twenty
minutes just enjoyed the hot water washing
over him. Refreshed and feeling relaxed, he put
on one of the Club's towelling gowns and went
back into the bedroom. It was then he noticed
a small parcel on the bedside table with an envelope attached.

I even get presents; Chris smiled to himself. He
opened the envelope and took out a neat, handwritten letter on a single sheet of foolscap.

*Welcome back to England Captain Lavelle. I
apologise for taking you away from your assignment in Borneo, but we have an urgent mission
for you closer to home. It's a mission that will test
your skills and, when successful, will contribute to
saving many lives in both the short and long term.
Bob Deacon will already have briefed you on the
general background, but I asked him specifically
not to brief you on the actual mission we have in
mind for you.*

*In the parcel, you will find a device called a mobile
acoustic scrambler. Instructions for using it are
enclosed. Please ring me on my direct line tomorrow at 7.00 am on Whitehall 4306 and use the
scrambler. Then I will explain why we have a particular need for your talents.*

Also in the parcel, you'll find five hundred pounds cash for incidental expenses.
Sincerely

Sir Richard White   Director General MI6 Secret Intelligence Service

PS. This letter is written on rice paper. Please eat or flush it down the toilet.

Chris memorised the number, ate the paper and grinned. Having not eaten since the bacon sandwich on the plane, he was starving and a piece of rice paper didn't do anything to quell the gnawing in his stomach. So, he decided that after seeing what was in the parcel, he'd call room service and order something substantial.

This is all a bit melodramatic, he thought. However, he knew Sir Richard's reputation, and whilst Chris had never met him, he'd always thought MI6 was behind his mission into East German. And he'd heard many stories about the MI6 Chief's exploits before and during WW2, some almost beyond belief.

Inside the parcel, there were 25 crisp £20 notes plus the box mentioned in the MI6 chief's note. He put the money in his pocket. The box looked like a packet of Dunhill cigarettes. He carefully

opened it to find another sheet of rice paper
with instructions on how to use the device. Following the instructions, he practiced attaching
it to the room telephone a couple of times, then
put it back in its box, replaced the sleeve, and
ate the paper.

CHAPTER 31

Chink sat with Owen in his study beside the Grundig tape recorder. Seamus O'Driscoll had no problem retrieving the tape from the hidden recording device. He'd managed the round trip to Martinstown House in 2hrs 20mins. The recorder had been well hidden and he'd told Owen it had taken him some time to find it, but following the instructions, he'd changed the tape reels and put the box back where he'd found it.

They listened to the stop/start of the voice-activated audiotape. The recordings were mostly domestic run of the mill conversations, ordering food and wine supplies and administrative calls to the Nazi farms. Skorzeny wasn't used to having to cope with such issues and was obviously missing his friend and housekeeper, Frau Binz. He sounded stressed.

As the hidden microphone transmitter was under the telephone table in the hallway of Otto's Manor, there were also recordings of conversations with visitors as they arrived and departed, but these were of no real value. Some of

the calls were obviously long distance, mostly
in German, but with some Spanish and English
too.   The quality of the line and the faintness of
the callers' voices made conversations almost
impossible to comprehend. They were near the
end of the tape and beginning to think that,
so far, there was nothing of particular value
when they heard Otto's phone ring. It was
someone called Axel. They listened intently as
Axel told Otto about his contact in the British
Intelligence headquarters. And whoever it was,
they had given Axel a copy of a map of Ireland.
As Axel described the details of the map, Otto
swore and cursed, He had realised the slide was
a copy from his Shamrock *Blitzkrieg* plan. They
heard Otto curtly thank his agent, then a loud
crash as he slammed the phone down and the
recording stopped.

"Christ!" Chink gasped, "That's really screwed
up everything. Our plans to counter their
Shamrock *Blitzkrieg* are 'kaput'. I'm going to
have to play that last bit of the tape over the
phone to Dick White and Roger Hollis."

"With respect sir, you can't risk that. You don't
know who might be listening – the IRA or even
the Nazis might have a tap on your phone. The
tape's too heavy for a pigeon, but you could
write a message and I'll have it on its way over

to MI5 in no time."

"I didn't tell you, Owen. The wonders of technology. Your feathered friends can take life easy from now on. When I was in London on my last trip, I was given a special device that fits onto an ordinary phone. It scrambles the conversation. The person being called hears nothing other than a sound like a vacuum cleaner unless they have a similar device at their end. It means I am able to have secure telephone calls to anyone with a similar device."

Owen knew about phones with built in scramblers, but this was the first time he had heard of a scrambler that could be fitted to any phone. He was mystified and at the same time fascinated, as he watched Chink place his briefcase next to the Grundig recorder, open it up, take out the dummy files, and link two rubber cups to the hearing and mouthpiece of the hand set of his telephone.

He wanted to remain, but reluctantly, he stood up to go. He felt that, as his butler, Chink would want him to leave. "I'll be in the kitchen of you need me, sir"

"NO, no, Owen, for God's sake stay. You're a great butler, but the Lord Lovat said you were a brilliant Staff Sergeant too and that's what I

need you as now. Keep up your role with the
family, but in this study, we are a team. This is
a critical situation and if we are going to beat
these Nazi bastards, it's vital that you know
everything. So, please just sit down again."

Owen sat down again and Chink continued.
"There's a microphone built into the case and
a loudspeaker too. It will enable us to play the
tape to 'C' and Hollis and you can hear their
comments too. The rubber cups I attached to
the phone do the scrambling. It's ultra-secure.
If you wind the tape back to the start of that last
recording, I'll get London on the phone".

Owen did as he was asked. and Chink dialled
'C's direct line and switched on the scrambler.
'C', answered the phone on the second ring. He
heard the mush of the scrambler and quickly
fitted the acoustic scrambler at his end.

"Hello Dick, Chink here. We've got a change of
situation."

"Go on then, tell me what's happened"

"We've retrieved a tape from the recorder Bob's
Ninja, Akanari, planted. I need to play it to
you and Hollis. And by the way, I've got Owen
McAteer, my butler here at Bellamont with me
- remember Hollis telling us at our GOLD meet-

ing, that Owen here is an MI5 agent, otherwise known as 'ARNHEM'.

"Yes. yes. Hold on then, I'll get Roger in here ASAP." 'C' went to his office door and asked Rebecca to tell Roger Hollis he had Chink on the phone and urgently needed him to come up to his office.

Roger Hollis came as soon as he could. "What's the panic?"

"Just take a seat, Roger. Chink is with your agent ARNHEM and he's about to play a tape from our listening device at Martinstown over the phone."

"OK Chink, Roger's here now, so let's get on with it and hear what you've got." With the phone to his ear, 'C' stood up and lent across his desk so that he and Hollis could both hear with their heads, cheek to jowl.

They listened intently to the recording of Otto talking to his agent in London. When it had finished, they both looked at each other. "Shit, that's really buggered everything up," Hollis muttered as he sat back. But 'C' wasn't fazed by what he had heard.

Chink and his butler sat at the other end of the

phone line waiting for some reaction, but the silence spoke volumes. Then 'C' spoke in a calm and measured tone.

"Well, well. So Otto now knows we know something of his plans. However, he doesn't know we know he knows and he doesn't know how much we know. He said he's going to have to bring forward his Shamrock *Blitzkrieg*. Right. We'll just have to change timescale and beat him to the punch. And, we also need to find that two-faced skunk, who leaked our information."

"Yes. Find out who it is, but don't arrest them. We can use them to feed Otto with false plans," replied Chink. "From what we heard, we know it was a 'she' and I'm ninety percent sure it's one of the kitchen staff. However," he continued, "as a matter of urgency, like tomorrow first thing, I'm going to pay a visit to my friend Sean MacEoin, the Irish Army chief. The quicker we make them aware of Otto's diabolical plans the better."

"OK, let's talk tomorrow night, same time" 'C' replied. "You got anything to add, Roger?"

Hollis nodded. "Yes. Chink. I just want to say that you'll need to be careful when you explain to MacEoin how you found out about Otto's

Shamrock *Blitzkrieg*. I know you are an experienced well-seasoned warrior and I'm not trying to tell my grandmother to suck eggs, but one slip and you could blow your undercover role with us."

Chink chuckled. "That's not a problem Roger. As 'C' knows, I'm a member of DJ2, the Irish equivalent of MI6 otherwise known as the *Stiúrthóireacht na Faisnéis*. You might think that in some ways I'm a double agent."

Hollis was speechless. He glared angrily at 'C'. "What fuck else don't I know?" he spluttered.

"Roger, cool it will you," Dick White, returned his glare, his hostility to Hollis aroused yet again. "You bloody well know we all operate on a need-to-know basis. And you didn't need to know that Chink was a valued member of the Irish DJ2. It's through his inside contacts in the Irish Army intelligence service and the Irish government that makes him such an invaluable agent for us. He has proven time and again which side he is really on."

Chink didn't respond. He simply said he would update them after his meeting with MacEoin. He couldn't help but smile at the bickering between the security chiefs and wished both pleasant dreams. The phone call ended with

two abrupt 'good-night's from the London
end.   But Chink knew there would be no sweet
dreams for him. He would have a sleepless
night thinking about his meeting with the head
of the Irish Army - and how together they could
nip Otto's Shamrock leaf in the bud.

"That was an eye opener," Owen couldn't
contain his astonishment at the revelation of
Chink's dual role.   "Double agent or not sir, I
can't say I give a stuff. I've never enjoyed myself
so much, here with you and the family." He rose
from his chair as if to go, "MI5, MI6 or DJ2, it's
all bollocks to me sir. My loyalties are here at
Bellamont. Goodnight sir."

"Look Owen, don't go. I need you here." The
butler sat down again feeling somewhat out of
place. Chink continued. "Thank you. I appreciate your honesty and allegiance. For my part,
you are and always will be a friend and very
much part of the family. Before you go and say
goodnight to your pigeons, we need to spend
some time talking about the overall situation
and how we get London and Dublin to work together to win this war."

Chink took out two glasses and another bottle
of his favourite whiskey and half-filled each
glass. He then unrolled a large map of Ireland
across his desk.

It was passed 11.30 pm when they finished. Owen left to shut up his flock, but Chink stayed at his desk. He knew that every second counted. He needed to fix the meeting with Sean MacEoin at his army HQ in Dublin as quickly as possible. He picked up his telephone handset, removed the rubber cups of audio scrambler, and dialled MacEoin's home number.

Sean had gone to bed early and was not best pleased with being woken up. But when he heard it was Chink, he knew the call had to be important. Chink apologised for the late call, but he said that he needed to see the General urgently. It wasn't a matter that could be discussed on the phone. They arranged to meet in the General's office at Cathal Brugha Barracks in Dublin. He had a full diary, but he said he would postpone whatever he was doing as soon as Chink arrived there.

Chink had breakfast as usual with Hugh and Eve. He said he had to go to an urgent meeting in Dublin, but hoped he would be back in time for tea. Eve couldn't get enough of Arnotts, the department store on Liffey Street. She'd enjoyed her last trip to Dublin with Mrs. Akanari and said she would like to come with him and this time bring Hugh too. She said she was sick and tired of Hugh's long, unkempt hair

and could take him to the new barber's shop
on Grafton Street. Then, perhaps they could
all meet up for lunch at one of the Arnotts'
restaurants.

"What a great idea. I'm not too sure how long
my meeting is going to last, but if I'm going to
be late, I'll send Owen to find you and let you
know what time I'll be finished."

Chink also had to go and see Pat O'Neil who
was in charge of the funeral undertaking side
of Chink's business interests in Ireland. He
thought he might do that after lunch so giving
Eve even more shopping time.

"I need to get off as soon as possible. It's going
to be good having you both with me. Owen and
I will drop you off at Arnotts on the way to my
meeting.

Within 40 minutes, they were in Betsy and on
the road to Dublin. Chink had been awake for
most of the night, a plan of action for a revised
Operation Rat Trap forming in his mind. He
had already decided how he would approach
the meeting with Sean MacEoin.

Eve said she wanted to talk to Arnotts' interior
design department and ask them to come to
Bellamont, take an overall view of the house

and see what refreshing ideas they could come up with. She regarded the decor throughout the house as so 'thirties. She was constantly saying how much it needed brightening up.

Who was Chink to argue? He felt guilty at spending so much time working, overseeing his retail and restaurant chains, and advising the Dublin Government on defence matters. Added to which, he had his trips to London for his lunches with Brian Horrocks. Eve could never understand why he saw so much of Horrocks. Combining his trips with family, made life so much more enjoyable and less stressful. And if Arnotts gave Bellamont a makeover, it would keep Eve happy and busy for months. Despite the excited chatter between Eve and Hugh, Chink dropped off and slept most of the way, only waking as Betsy pulled up outside Arnotts.

They said their goodbyes and arranged to meet in the department store's Kitchen restaurant at 1.30 pm. Eve's last words were 'and don't be late darling'. Chink didn't want to let her down, but the odds were he would.

Fifteen minutes later, they arrived at the entrance to Cathal Brugha Barracks on Military Road. The pock-marked pillars on either side of the entrance told the story of the Irish fight for independence. They had shiny new signs with the name of the establishment. Up until a few years earlier, it had been known as Portobello barracks, the original British name since it was built in 1810. The new name was in memory of one of Ireland's best known IRA folk heroes, Cathal Brugha. After the 1916 uprising, Cathal became Minister of Defence in the first independent Irish parliament. However, he died in 1922 in a battle between the IRA and the Irish National army at the siege of Dublin's Four Courts building.

General MacEoin's secretary had already advised the Cathal Brugha Military Police guard at the gate to expect Major General Dorman-O'Gowan and to notify her as soon as he arrived. The Police Provost Sergeant recognised Chink from previous visits and his driver, but out of courtesy asked Owen if they would like an escort to the General's office. Owen thanked the Provost Sergeant, and said it would not be necessary. The Sergeant saluted and waved Betsy through before going back into the guardhouse to ring through to MacEoin's secretary. As Betsy drew up, Sean MacEoin appeared from his office building greeting Chink with a beaming smile. "Great to see you Chink. Sure, I've been so busy with our reorganisation that it seems months since we last met up."

Chink didn't get out of Betsy. Instead, he opened the door. "Sean, so good of you to make the time. If you don't mind, I'd rather not come into your office - join me in here. You may think I'm over cautious, but what I need to tell you is as top of top secrets as it gets. I don't want the slightest possibility of what I'm going to say leaking out and I know my car's not bugged. And you've met my chauffeur, butler and right-hand man, Owen. Needless to say, he has my full trust. He has top security clearance and for continuity, I would like him to listen in too."

Puzzled, but knowing Chink of old, the General complied promptly and stepped in sitting down beside Chink in the Rolls' plush interior. They shook hands greeting each other as old friends do. "So, what's all this cloak and dagger malarkey mi ol' friend"

Chink faced him. Sean could see from his grave expression that what he was about to hear was explosive. "Ireland is on the brink of an unbelievably vicious assault," Chink spoke in a quiet yet forceful tone. "Through my web of contacts, I have discovered that there is a Nazi plot to take over the whole of Ireland, North, and South. And we've less than a month to stop it."

"Is this some April Fool prank you're having on me, Chink - are you serious?" Sean MacEoin sat back and looked at Chink in a way that said he thought his friend had gone completely barmy – off his head.

Chink put his hand on Sean's arm. "Look, Sean, just hear me out. You know that MI6 looks upon me as a friendly ally and they know I work with you and your colleagues. Well, through them I've learned that in a series of simultaneous lightning attacks, a large force of ex-Nazi SS stormtroopers are planning to neutralise the Irish army; take over radio and TV stations north and south of the Border; blow up five bridges over River Lagan in Belfast and shut down Dublin. And they plan to take over the airports too. They told me that it's all being planned by Otto Skorzeny from his HQ at Martinstown in County Kildare.

"Oh, come on now. Sure, I know Otto myself," the Irish General broke with scepticism written all over his face. "The Colonel's the perfect gentleman and a member of my Club too, the Turf Club at The Curragh in Kildare. We're even thinking of asking him to join the board of the club."

"Well, after I've told you what I know, you may

certainly want to reconsider that. Let me explain." Chink then went on to tell Sean MacEoin the whole story from the pig farm carnage to the stealing of the Nazi plans from Otto's Martinstown residence. Sean said nothing. He now realised that Chink was deadly serious and his bon ami evaporated. He listened intently. Chink continued. He went on to tell Sean about the 2000 ex-SS soldiers spread around Martinstown and the farms Otto had bought with Nazi gold.

"Excuse me, Chink, how the feck did we manage to let 2000 ex-SS shites into our land?" exclaimed Sean.

"It's been a carefully planned infiltration over many years starting in 1945 at the end of WW2. I'm sure you know, Sean, that the Vatican played a big part in forwarding Nazi refugees to Catholic countries all over the world. Well, as a good Catholic country, Ireland came under the same hat. Because of our neutrality during the war, and being virtually run by the Church, we seem to have turned a blind eye to their origins and crimes and simply opened our doors."

"Now I come to think of it, our security services have told us about some pretty unsavoury characters, but they have been good boys, no trouble at all. And in many ways, they've been big contributors to the progress of Irish economic growth. D'you know that Belgian, Albert Folens. They told me he'd been in the Gestapo and SS during the war. But Albert's a really nice feller, I've met him a few times socially. He's done Ireland's schools a grand job with his textbook publishing business, you know. But go on Chink, I've a feelin' there's a lot more I don't know."

"I'm glad you know Folens. I want to talk to you about him, but I'll come to him later."

Chink continued, telling Sean about Skorzeny's farms and where they were. He told him that they'd built an airstrip at the farm on Corkan Island on the River Foyle and had three operational Dakotas parked there. Chink was desperate to convince MacEoin of the impending danger. He told him about the arms and ammunition dumps and the assault vehicles being prepared. Finally, to emphasise the urgency, Chink explained that Otto had found out that MI6 had managed to get a copy of his Shamrock *Blitzkrieg* document. So that there was every possibility that the scumbag was going to change his plan of attack and bring everything forward as quickly as possible.

Sean MacEoin took a deep breath. "Well, well, that's a shockin' story you're telling me. You're a fine man to be sure and a great help to our

military defence plannin'. I'm no doubtin'
Thomas, I believe every word you're saying, but
I'm sure you'll understand, I'll need concrete
evidence to set the wheels in motion and take
action. Otherwise, the powers that be will think
it's a load of the old blarney."

"I knew you'd say that." Chink responded.
"Why don't you send a couple of Air Corp planes
on a photo-reconnaissance mission to check
out Martinstown and the farms, especially the
one on Corkan Island? That should give you the
concrete you need. And if you do that, you'd
better add a few other target locations just in
case we have any Nazi sympathisers around
here - you never know."

"That's certainly something we can do. Right
now, I'll keep what you're tellin' me to myself.
What else would help the cynics around me?"

"I can give you a recording of Otto on the 'phone
being told that MI6 had discovered his Shamrock *Blitzkrieg* plans. That should do the trick."

"It would certainly reinforce the concrete ol'
chap, but how in the name of Jesus did you
come by that?"

"That's a long story, which I'll tell you later over
a bottle." Chink took out a copy of the original

tape from his pocket and handed it to Sean. "The only thing I ask is that you destroy this once you've listened to it."

MacEoin took the tape, still baffled at how Chink had managed to get such an explosive piece of evidence.

"And," continued Chink, "you could arrange for one of your senior officers at the Military Staff College to pay a surprise courtesy call on the Colonel at Martinstown. They are, after all, Otto's neighbours in the Curragh. They could see the uniforms the staff are wearing, see the high security surrounding the place for themselves."

"That sounds like a good plan and enough for me to convince the President. I'll have a word with Nick Nolan, he runs the Air Corp. He will send a couple of our de Havilland vampire jets over the farms to take the photos and I'll go myself to pay a quick visit to see Otto in his lair."

"Fine Sean, but remember, the Nazi *Blitzkrieg* could be launched anytime from now on. To-night, tomorrow, this week, or next. We have very, very little time," warned Chink.

It was agreed that General MacEoin would expedite the photo-reconnaissance as a matter of extreme urgency. And he would cancel his meetings for the next day and visit Martinstown unannounced.

"When I have the aerial photos and after my visit to see Otto, I'll come straight up to your place."

"When you do, I'll arrange for a call to the head of MI6. He'll confirm all I've said and then together we can decide on how we can unite Britain and Eire to fight this common enemy."

"You've certainly got your feet under the table with the MI6," mused the Irish General.

"Oh, now look here, Sean, is that a touch of the doubts I'm hearing about my loyalties? You know which side I'm on. I'm an Irishman. And it's a united Ireland I'm fighting for, and that will only happen if we have a close and friendly relationship with the British over the water. de Valera, and I'm sure, you too, have the same passion. When I last saw Dev, he told me of his plan for Eire and the North to come together and become part of the British Commonwealth. It makes such good sense, but there are many hardliners, both sides of the border, who would rather die than support him."

Chink went on to explain the British Operation

Rat Trap in detail. He emphasised that MI6 and the British Army would take care of all matters north of the border and he had been told to assure the Irish Government that Britain would also support the Irish defence forces in any way they wished. However, from Chink's point of view, he realised that there were still raw nerves regarding the Anglo-Irish relationship and any British troops setting foot in the South would be viewed by many as a step far too far.

They discussed the role of the Catholic Church. They both knew how it still ruled Eire with a rod of iron and were actively supportive of the IRA, but MacEoin was surprised to hear about the way the monastery in Portglenone was being used. Chink told him that MI6 was preparing to smuggle in a British SAS trained spy as a novice monk to neutralise that threat.

"Somehow, the Church has to be brought on side too. They want nothing more than to bring Northern Ireland under their rigid ecclesiastic rule. If they believe that Skorzeny is simply supporting our IRA friends to reunite our country, they could seriously complicate your Rat Trap." stressed Sean.

That's a fair point," acknowledged Chink. "But I may just have a solution to that."

The meeting ended. Chink felt sure he had Sean MacEoin on-side and would just have to wait for his call once he had the results from the aerial reconnaissance. And as soon as he returned to Bellamont, he would ring 'C' and update him on his meeting with Sean. Meanwhile, he had the lunch appointment with his family at Arnott's Kitchen restaurant to keep.

CHAPTER 32

After breakfast in the Club restaurant, Captain Lavelle returned to his suite, and took out the acoustic scrambler he'd received in the package on his arrival. Remembering the instructions he'd read and eaten the previous day, he pulled out the two wafer-thin rubber conical diaphragms from their metal case. Weird, he thought. He couldn't help but smile. They reminded him of contraceptive Dutch caps, one pink and the other blue. Each had a wire running from it back into the small case. Remembering the rice paper notes, it had said only attach them to the phone once the call has connected. So he placed the device beside his bedside phone.

It was one minute to 7.00am. He picked up the phone and asked the switchboard operator for the number given in Dick White's note. As the phone rang, he reflected on the previous evening. He'd thoroughly enjoyed spending over half of the expense money he'd been given on clothes and a British Warm overcoat at Gieves in Bond Street followed by a feast at the Ritz.

Now the serious stuff starts, he thought.

There was a distinct click and he could hear a noise like the whine of a radio tuning in, so he connected the pink diaphragm to the ear piece end of the phone and the blue 'cap' to the other end - the noise immediately disappeared and a voice came on the line.

"White."
"Captain Lavelle, sir. I got your note."

"Morning Captain. I'm not going to say too much on the phone. Bob Deacon told me he'd explained we have some problems in Ireland. We are going to mount an operation to resolve those problems and you have a specific part to play. But before I go into any detail, you have the option to withdraw and not be involved. And if you do, I guarantee it won't affect your career prospects."

"Look sir, it may sound a touch hackneyed, but I joined the army not just to serve my country, but for the thrill of action." Chris replied. "Career prospects don't motivate me. Colonel Deacon emphasised the importance of the job, but he didn't give me any details of the actual task you had in mind for me - sir."

"Glad to hear that Captain. And don't call me

'Sir', just 'C' will do." Dick White continued.
"The task we have for you involves going undercover in Northern Ireland; in a monastery. We
know you were brought up as a Roman Catholic
and so you will be familiar with your next step.
It is to go to confession at Westminster Cathedral at 1600hrs this afternoon.

There are five confessional booths, take the
third one on the right. Say 'Golden Eagle'. If you
don't get the response 'Irish mist', you know
you are in the wrong booth and some priest will
think you're bonkers - our agent may have been
delayed. If that's the case, try again on the hour
until you get the right response. If by the end of
the confessions, you haven't been able to make
contact, ring me again. Clear?"

"Absolutely 'C'."

"Right. You and I, Chris, won't need to talk
again until after the operation is concluded. It's
code name is 'Rat Trap'. And your mission is
vital to its success. We know it's a tough call,
but Bob says it's right up your street - so good
luck."

"Thank you, sir," Chris replied, forgetting the
informality, but 'C' had already put his phone
down. Chris still was baffled regarding his actual task. A difficult assignment; going under-

cover into a monastery - that was all he knew - what else?

With time on his hands before going to the confessional in Westminster Cathedral, Chris spent an hour on the phone with family. His parents first, then his brother Tim, who had left the Army and started a career in computing, followed by his sister, Angela, married to a police inspector in Birmingham. With each call, he explained that he was briefly passing through the UK and regrettably didn't have time to see any of them, but when he returned, he would take some leave. When he finally put the phone down, he felt a rush of emotion as he realised that it might be the last time he spoke to any of them. He felt gutted too, that he was unable to speak to his younger brother Jonathon, away at boarding school and not allowed calls during the day.

With time to spare, he decided to visit some of his old haunts in Soho. It had been over 5 years since he had been there and so many of the coffee bars had either closed or changed hands. The only place where the owner remembered him was The Sphinx, a Greek Taverna in Beak Street, just off Golden Square. Simon greeted him with open arms. They sat and demolished a bottle of retsina with some of Chris' favourite kleftiko.

Chris hadn't been involved with the army's war against EOKA, the Greek Cypriot terrorists in Cyprus, but they discussed the morality of it and other British colonies wanting their independence from the old Empire. They both agreed that if the majority of the population in any country wanted self-rule, they should be given it, violence on either side never worked. They could have gone on talking for hours, but Chris remembered his appointment in the confessional at Westminster Cathedral.

It was five minutes before the appointed time when he arrived at the Cathedral. The striped brick and stone pattern of the building reminded him of the ornate artistic and architectural style of Byzantine buildings. Thoroughly out of place he thought amongst the grey boring office blocks and department stores of Victoria Street. He stood in front of its massive Italian oak doors, remembering the stories told to him by nuns at school. Stories that at the time made him wet himself, about how sinners who had forsaken the Church, were consumed by the fires of Hell as they tried to walk through the doors of God's house. So unfair to fill children's heads full of such tosh, he pondered.

He entered the building and as his eyes grew

accustomed to the gloom, he saw the line of confessional booths on the right-hand side - each one like a large wooden cupboard with two openings covered by dark red curtains. One side was for the priest and the other for the kneeling penitent with their soles exposed under the curtain, like fish out to dry he thought. He walked nearer. There was a list on the nearest pillar showing who was on duty, and he saw that Father Leo Emery was in the third one along. He knelt in the nearest pew for over an hour until the stream of penitents waiting to offload their sins had dwindled to a trickle. Then, as the third booth became vacant, he made his move and entered.

There was silence, then the sound of a shutter opening. Who should speak first? From his childhood, Chris remembered he should say 'Bless me Father'. This he did and added

"My name is Golden Eagle."

Silence again. Had he chosen the wrong confessional?

But a voice came back. "Well, well. The Eagle has landed. And I'm lost in the 'Irish Mist'." The response Chris was expecting.

"No time for niceties," the voice continued in a business- like manner. "I have been told to have you initiated in the ways of a monk. Later this evening, I'm going to arrange for you to see the Abbot of a Benedictine monastery in West London. I'll tell him that you and I have spent many hours discussing your call to the priesthood. I'll emphasise that you had seen and taken part in many horrors during your time as a soldier and were consumed by guilt and sought forgiveness. You now wanted to spend the rest of your entire life soley serving God. You should then ring him".

"That's a great story," said Chris in a suitably quiet voice. "So, give me his contact details. When should I call?"

Leo Emery passed a slip of paper under the curtain between him and Chris. On it was the name and telephone number he needed. Leo continued, "Call any time from tomorrow morning on. Move out of your Club, find somewhere else to stay; buy the largest set of rosary beads on your way out from here; ring around your friends and tell them of your conversion - spread the word. Just remember, from now on, you are going to be a novice monk. 'C' told me that you have and will always have a 'good shepherd' watching your back, so there's no need to contact MI6 again. I don't know who, but someone at '6' will contact you again shortly. Their password will be 'Dublin Bay prawns'."

"If I move out of the Club, how will they know

how to find me?"

"Don't worry, they'll know."

Chris was an experienced soldier, top of his trade and with some experience of the world of spooks. As with every mission he'd been on, he started to feel his adrenalin rising.   Yet, whilst half of him relished every new challenge, the other half felt like Daniel in the lion's den - vulnerable and defenceless.   'C' had said that many lives depended on his success. That was his real motivation.

"Finally," the priest continued, "go and do what you have to do. May God go with you - and good luck."

Chris bought his rosary beads and left the Cathedral. He made his way back to the Club and told the receptionist that he would be checking out in the morning. Sitting on the bed in his luxury suite, he mulled over the task in front of him. Everything on the surface seemed simple. He had to role-play a monk, get into a Portglenone monastery. What then? the devil was in the detail he'd yet to hear. Then again, it was easier than spending days in the Borneo jungle being eaten by leeches, being bitten all over; constantly on the lookout for enemy patrols - kill or be killed 24hrs 7 days a week.

For the next few days, he needed somewhere to

stay. His younger brother Tim and family lived
in Kingston upon Thames, perhaps he could
park himself there, he thought.

Tim was delighted with the idea. He hadn't
seen Chris for three years and in the meantime,
he had married and had two children who
had never seen their uncle. But after two days
of the young toddlers crawling all over him,
constantly needing their uncle's attention, he
couldn't wait for the contact promised by the
priest. Then, on the evening of the second day
as they were just about to sit down to a family
dinner, it came in a most unexpected way.

A loud knock at the door interrupting the
family's shepherd's pie. Tim went to answer the
door. There were muffled voices; eventually
Tim, returned looking angry and perplexed
followed by two policemen and a man in plain
clothes. The latter looked around the room, his
eyes focused on Chris. "Captain Lavelle sir. My
name is Jones. I'm a customs officer and I have
a warrant for your arrest." He held up an official
looking document and handed it to Chris.

"This is a load of garbage." Tim turned on the
customs man aggressively. "How many times
have I got to tell you. He's my brother, only
just returned from serving his country in the
bloody Borneo jungle. This is ridiculous - there
must be some mistake."

"No mistake I assure you sir," said Jones in an officious tone. "We've been keeping tabs on Captain Lavelle since he arrived back in the country. And I'm sorry to interrupt your family dinner, sir, but this is a very serious matter. It says here on the charge sheet that he has been involved in the mass importation of counterfeit Dublin bay prawns from Singapore." Then looking at Chris he said, "We don't want any trouble Captain, I hope you're going to come quietly."

"Preposterous! rubbish!" Tim's voice raised in outrage, sparking the children bawling", but the mention of Dublin bay prawns was all Chris needed. Although for the sake of the family, he needed to continue the charade,this was the contact he'd been expecting. He stood up, suppressing a smile, filling his face of indignation. "I can assure you, officer, or whoever you are. I haven't a bloody clue what you're talking about. I'm actually here to spend time with my brother and his family before saying farewell and entering a monastic life. Could you at least wait outside until I finish my dinner. Give me 15 minutes."

"Oh yes. And have you scarper over the back fence. We can't have that now, can we? You can have your fifteen minutes, but we're staying right here so I can keep an eye on you."

Chris told Tim and his wife that he was sure

there had been some mistake and he would call them once he had sorted things out. The children stopped their crying, and with Tim still simmering with anger, they finished their meal in shocked silence. Then, having quickly packed his case under the watchful eye of one of the police officers, he embraced his brother and sister-in-law, bent down, gave both of the bewildered tots, little Jamie and Stephen, a bear hug, and followed the customs officer out to a Metropolitan Police van parked outside.

The family watched in bewilderment as one policeman opened the rear door of the van. There was nothing to be seen, just a dark void, into which Chris was pushed. He noticed the feeling of carpet under his feet and as the door shut, a light came on. He was able to make out two sofas, one on each side of the van's rear interior and a small cabinet against a partition cutting off the front seats. Lounging on one of the sofas was a middle-aged man in a blazer and flannels sporting a cravat.

"Sorry to break up your visit old chap," the stranger said, greeting Chris with a smile, " Do take a seat." Chris was slightly dazed as the man continued.

"My name is Peter Fleming. I'm part of the Operation Rat Trap team. I run the special tricks department of MI6 and that's where we are going now. 'C' asked me to brief you on the detail of your mission and arm you with some useful gadgets before you enter into the 'lion's den', so to speak."

Chris, feeling slightly bemused, sat down on the edge of the sofa opposite Peter Fleming. "I got the 'Dublin Bay prawns' bit, but why all the theatricals? Was it really necessary to scare the wits out of my brother and family like that?"

"You're back in the theatrical world of spooks, Captain Lavelle. It's all one big act from now on. And we want to make sure you are fully prepared before the curtain goes up on the performance. And anyway, you can ring and tell your brother it was all a fearful mistake when we arrive at my den."

It was a two-hour drive to Hanslope Park, where Peter Fleming had his special weapons and spy gadget workshop. Peter opened the cabinet against the partition and took out a bottle of 1926 Tariquet Bas Armagnac XO. he opened it and poured two generous glasses. He passed one to Chris. "I was told you had a taste for a good Armagnac, so I brought a bottle of the best to pass the journey."

Chris sipped the amber liquid. He knew it was exceptional. It smelt like warm toast and tangerine peel combined and he felt himself relax as its warmth spread through his body. They talked about Peter's background, his brother Ian's books and their secret work during the war. They discussed religion and how a schism of the Catholic Church had perverted the Christian cause by spreading ex-Nazis throughout Catholic countries of the world. There was much more that Peter would have liked to tell Chris about the rest of Operation Rat Trap, but he held back. The less he knew the better just in case he was caught and interrogated.

"We've arranged for someone to brief you on the Portglenone monastery tomorrow morning and what we need you to do. We've taken some aerial photographs of the place that will help speed up your orientation for when you arrive. Plus, I will give you the gift of a bible, specially prepared by my boffins. More about all that tomorrow. Before that, let me top up your glass and tell me about your life as Tarzan in the Borneo jungle. When have you got to be at Ealing monastery?"

"The priest at Westminster Cathedral said he was going to call the Abbot, tell him about my dramatic convertion to the faith and to expect my call. So, I was going to call tomorrow morning and arrange it all."

"Excellent. We'll fit that into the schedule, but get your feet up now and relax. Once we arrive at the Park, we're going to need you to be bright and perky."

Chris finished his drink. One thing he'd learnt in the jungle was how to snatch a quick kip. He lay back on the sofa and, helped by the Armagnac, quickly fell into a deep sleep.

The next day, Chris called the Abbot at the Benedictine monastery. Father Emery had already paved the way for his call and the Abbot was delighted to welcome him to Ealing Abbey to clarify what entering a monastic life entailed. It was arranged for two days later. He now had over 24 hours for MI6 to explain the details of his mission. He was to enrol as a postulant Cistercian monk at Our Lady of Bethlehem on the outskirts of a town called Portglenone.

He was shown a map of the grounds and told to memorise it. His target was a storage facility. It had originally been an old swimming pool supposedly being renovated by outside volunteers, who happened to be IRA plus some ex-SS Nazis from across the Irish border. Unbeknown to the monks, it is currently being used to store a large amount of explosives, weapons and ammunition. After his experiences in East Germany, Chris wanted to know more about ex Nazi involvement, but was told the less he knew the better. His part in Operation Rat Trap was to find the fuses for the explosives in the converted swimming pool and make them in-operable. And if he was unable to do that, blow the whole place to smithereens.

When his briefing had finished, Peter gave him the specially modified bible. It looked like any other well used bible. However, when Peter showed him its hidden tricks, he realised he wasn't going into Our Lady of Bethlehem unarmed.

CHAPTER 33

True to his word, after his meeting with Chink, General MacEoin cleared the decks of his routine work. Aerial reconnaissance of the Nazi farms and Otto Skorzeny's Martinstown property was top priority. Sean knew that there were daily training flights from the Air Corps Casement airfield at Baldonne, South of Dublin, so Sean telephoned the Commandant there. He explained that as a matter of extreme urgency, he needed aerial photos of several locations, the map coordinates of which he would send him immediately by fax. It was 1.15pm. As luck would have it, there was a flight of three Vampire jets scheduled for 2.30pm. The Commandant said they all had photographic equipment as standard and as soon as he had the information, he would see to it that the flights were rerouted and pilots briefed.

He tried repeatedly to ring Chink, but he was obviously still on his way back from Dublin with Eve and Hugh. On his third attempt, the cook answered and he asked her to tell the General to call him in his office as soon as he arrived back.

It was early evening, no more than 8 hours after Chink's visit, that he returned Sean's call. "Sean, I've only just got back with the family – sorry to miss your calls."

Sean was aware of the security risks of talking over an open line, anyone might listen in including operators at local exchanges, and so he chose his words carefully and cut to the quick. "I have those rat nest pictures."

Chink knew Sean MacEoin was a fast mover, but he hadn't expected him to get results so soon after their meeting.   From the tone of Sean's voice, Chink knew that the aerial reconnaissance had confirmed what Chink had told him, and he immediately understood that Sean was being careful with what he said on a public phone line.   He answered in the same vein. "So, you can see the problem with all the rats then?"

"I certainly can, Chink," Sean replied, "and we are going to have to take some decisive steps to trap the little buggers in their nests before they break out and cause a deadly plague".

"What do you have in mind then?"

"I'll be ringing a friend of mine, who has the health of the Nation as his top priority. Thanks again Chink for alerting me to the outbreak – I'm sure I'll be calling you later." With that, Sean put the phone down. Chink would now have to wait for that call.

For Sean, his only course of action was to ring the President of Ireland himself. He had Eamon de Valera's direct line number, which made it more secure than the public network, but could he risk calling? What he had to tell the President was dynamite. For minutes, he debated with himself on how to proceed. Finally, he took the risk and made the call. The phone rang and rang.

Sean thought he must have dialled the wrong number, when a bleary voice answered, "Dev."

"Sir, t'is General MacEoin here."

"Ah General, sure you caught me having a shut-eye. It's a tad late for a social call, what can I be doin' for you."

"Sir, I'm sorry to disturb you, but I wouldn't be ringing at this late hour if I didn't think it was of vital importance."

Sean told the President about Chink's visit to see him earlier in the day to tell him he had found out that ex-Nazis were building fully armed fortresses along the Irish border and that Otto Skorzeny was involved.

Chink had been told this was all to support the IRA in their war against the North, but he'd recently found out there was far more to it - a possible Nazi takeover of the whole of Ireland. Sean went on to say that after the meeting with

Chink, he had ordered the Air Corp to conduct aerial reconnaissance of the farms and Otto Skorzeny's Martinstown estate. The photographic results plainly showed that Chink's information was one hundred per cent correct.

de Valera was stunned. During the war, he had made sure Eire remained a neutral country. In fact, he'd had a soft spot for Hitler until all the Nazi atrocities had been exposed. And after the war, he was still all for letting bygones be bygones and in partnership with the Church, had let many ex-German soldiers and war criminals settle in the country. Now, he thought, it sounds as if my chickens are coming home to roost. I'm going to be regretting all that.

Sean MacEoin thought for a moment that de Valera had put the phone down. Then the President spoke. "Sean, I'm going to be straight down the line with you. I've had an ear into what's goin' on at Martinstown and at the farms. I asked Charlie Haughey to keep an eye on that man Skorzeny and he has been keeping me in the picture. But I have to admit, I've been turning a blind eye because Charlie said they were only supporting the IRA boyos. Nothing too aggressive - I was assured. Just training like Chink told us he was doin' at Bellamont."

He paused to gather his thoughts. "Good God,

you're so right to call me. From what you're saying, we have a national catastrophe on our hands. Is there any chance we can get Chink down here? And I mean as soon as possible - right now."

The General looked at the phone piece in his hand. He was astounded. He didn't know what to say. The President of his country had known about the Nazi activities and yet there'd been no feedback to him, Sean, the Chief of the Defence Staff. If nothing else, Dev had made a bloody fool of him. What else was de Valera not telling him? He was furious, but now was not the time to throw his toys in the air. "We'll be with you as soon as we can Mr. President."

Sean called Chink back. "I've talked to Dev, and he would like you to meet us at his place as soon as you can make it."

"I'm on my way." Chink replied.

The official residence and family home of the President of the Republic of Ireland is 'Áras an UachtaráinIt' in Dublin's Phoenix Park. With some 95 rooms and stately architecture, it was said to have inspired the building of the White House in Washington DC. He'd left within minutes of Sean's call, just giving himself enough time to leave a note for Eve and make a quick scrambler call to 'C' to update him on the developing situation. He'd also asked Owen to drive so he could update him on the developing situation as they drove. This time, he'd made sure they were both armed; a pair of Sterling submachine guns and the Beretta he had taken from Lexie Mitchel. He'd also hastily packed a quick change of clothes - there was no knowing how long he would be away. It took them little under 3 hours to drive down.

The three men sat at one end of the dining table in Éamon de Valera's private suite. de Valera had just finished reading the summary of Otto Skorzeny's Shamrock *Blitzkrieg* plan, the one that Chink had left with Sean. He looked at Sean and Chink, his knuckles white and he clenched the plan. "God help us, we certainly have a devil of a situation here gentlemen. Sure, I'm......"

Chink held up a hand. Speaking in almost a whisper, he asked, "Éamon, before you say another word - when was this room last checked for hidden listening devices?"

de Valera looked nonplussed. "Never as far as I know. Why?"
Without answering, Chink picked up his briefcase and placed it on the table in front of him and opened it. In the lid was the little row of buttons and dials that Peter Fleming had demonstrated at the GOLD meeting in London. He pressed one of the buttons, sat back, and now

spoke in full voice. "You can never be too careful. This is a magic box of tricks given to me by MI6. One of its many functions is to block any microphones and listening devices that may be hidden nearby.   It does this by generating what are called white sound wave harmonics that build an acoustic wall around us here at the table, an audio barrier. You can't hear anything, but I assure you, now nobody outside this room can either. Our discussion is now totally secure."

de Valera looked astonished.   He'd always thought a shut door was sufficient to have a secure conversation.

"I see I have a lot to learn" he paused.   I was just going to say what a bloody idiot I've been. Holding out the hand of forgiving friendship to the defeated Germans, then to have it all thrown back in my face - I'm bitterly disappointed, let down by my own stupidity. I've been blind not to recognise the feckin threat these Nazis represent.   I believed they were bringing much-needed industry and engineering know-how to our country. I've never trusted the Brits, but if we are going to beat these Nazi buggers, it seems we're going to have to for now."

"Dev, you are absolutely right, what's past is past, so don't be flogging yourself." Chink put his arm around the President. "Hey ol' friend, we'll show Otto Skorzeny and his merry men what tough nuts we Irish can be. We have to eliminate them before they eliminate us, simple as that."

Chink told the President that, whilst the Nazi's original plan showed that they were going to launch their lightning strike on July 12, Skorzeny had found out through one of their spies that it had somehow been leaked. Chink said he was convinced that they would try to seize the initiative and strike as soon as possible. "It could be at any time, but I believe they aren't quite ready." Chink paused, there was no time for prevarication, the urgency of the situation demanded swift and decisive action. "Dev," he continued, "the threat is to the whole of our Ireland, North and South. And so, we are going to have to work hand and glove with the British. My box of tricks here has a few other unique functions. One allows us to have a secure two-way phone conversation. And with your permission, I would like to call the head of MI6 and have him take part in this meeting."

de Valera couldn't stop a sharp intake of breath - he grimaced at the mention of involving the British. At the time of Eire's fight for independence, he had been persecuted, suffered physical interrogation, and spent months in an English prison. He still had nightmares. It had left him with an enormous anti-British chip on his shoulders. But it wasn't just his personal experiences. He couldn't forgive the hundreds of years of oppression by the British landowners, the potato famine, the 'Black and Tans', the burning of villages by their army and many other atrocities committed during Ireland's fight for independence. He never thought the day would come when he would rely on their support.

It was a bitter pill to swallow but reluctantly he knew Chink was right. He and his countrymen had to work with the British sassenachs but that didn't mean he could or would ever forgive them the bloody past.   For some moments he was silent as he wrestled with his emotions. "OK.   Go ahead then, let's do it."   He went over to a drinks cabinet on top of which was a telephone. Luckily, it had a long lead and he brought it over and placed it in front of Chink. Sean and the President watched in amazement as Chink picked up the handset and fitted it with the rubber cups of the audio scrambler. The President's private line was STD, a system that allowed the caller to dial calls without operator assistance. He dialled Dick White's home telephone number. It rang for some time before being answered, initially, by a rushing sound similar to a high-pressure hose, then "White" a terse answer as the head of MI6 came on the line.

"Dick, apologies for disturbing you, Chink here. I'm ringing from the residence of the President of the Republic of Ireland. Éamon de Valera himself and General Sean MacEoin are both here with me."

Dick White had obviously been sleeping and woken by the call. But he was instantly alert. "Good morning, gentlemen." His voice came loud and clear through the speaker in the briefcase. de Valera and the Irish General, still astonished by the technology, both mumbled a greeting. Chink told 'C' that both the President and General had read the Shamrock *Blitzkrieg* plan summary and were up to speed with the situation.

"Well, gentlemen, let me first say that Prime Minister Macmillan and the Chief of the Imperial General Staff, Sir Richard Hull, have been fully briefed," 'C' Said. "They have given me total authority to make whatever decisions are deemed necessary and provide whatever resources are required to support the decisions we two countries make here at this meeting. As well as the Nazis' plan, I trust Chink will have told you about 'Operation Rat Trap', he continued. "Let me just say that I have full confidence in him and back his decisions to the hilt." de Valera looked at Chink and couldn't help wondering which side he was really on. Who was he working for? - Britain or Ireland, but he kept his thoughts to himself. He would raise that question later. Right now, whichever side he was on really didn't matter. This was an immediate problem - winning this fight and exterminating the Nazi bastards was of paramount importance. The meeting went on discussing the overall situation on both sides of the border.

It was getting light when, finally, they seemed to have come up with a plan of action. The first priority was to find some way of finding out when Skorzeny was planning to make his move. Chink had already told Dev and Sean about the listening devices hidden in Martinstown, but had explained they only recorded conversations that could be played back later.

"What we need is someone in there at Martinstown" Chink said, "perhaps this is where Gillian Sattler could be useful." The Irishmen looked puzzled so Chink explained. He told them that Skorzeny's housekeeper had died. He didn't go into the gruesome details of how, but said Otto was desperate to find a loyal replacement. With the right introduction, Gillian, he said, would be ideal for the job and could give us eyes and ears inside the Nazi HQ. She was originally from the Alsace and spoke Haut-Rhin Deutsch. And she'd spent time during the war as a British saboteur behind the German lines.

He told them how eventually she was taken prisoner and knew first-hand the hellish insides of the Natweiler, Ravensbrück and Sachsenhausen concentration camps. She could easily pass as an ex-camp guard, which in Otto's book would be qualification enough.

"Could we use Charlie Haughey to introduce her, Dev?" Chink asked. "Brilliant idea!" Dick White exclaimed. However, the Irish President didn't like the idea of using his minister. He thought that after the leaking of the Nazi's plans, Haughey's credibility might be wearing thin with Skorzeny, and he said so.

Then Chink hit on an alternative. "Éamon, you'll be knowing about that Belgian renegade Albert Folens. Wasn't it yourself who sanctioned his refuge after he escaped from prison in Belgium for his war crimes?"

Éamon de Valera gave a quizzical nod as Chink went on to explain. "Well, Folens and Skorzeny are great buddies. Thinking about it, I'm sure he's part of this Nazi plot. Since he's arrived here and with your amnesty, he's built a very successful publishing business". Chink didn't say that it was Nazi money that had funded him. "He's the biggest supplier of school books in Ireland is he not?"

"He is that. So, what! What are you getting at?" de Valera was showing some irritation. "Are you suggesting I've a finger in Folens' till? Is that what you're getting at Mr. Dorman-O'Gowan?" "The thought never entered my mind Mr. President," answered Chink calmly, "but the fact that he owes his success to you, plus now you now know of his skulduggery with Skorzeny, you could twist his arm and persuade him to introduce Gillian to Martinstown."

"I can see where you're coming from Chink." 'C's voice came over the speakerphone. "Are you suggesting we have enough leverage to force Folens to swap sides and work for us?"

"Exactly right Dick," Chink responded, "but only Éamon here can put the screws on our Belgian friend." Then looking de Valera directly in the eye and he continued. "It's down to you Éamon. On one hand, you tell Folens to show his allegiance to Ireland and do what we ask of him or, on the other hand, you will nationalise his business and pass him and his family over to the Belgian authorities. I'm sure they're still aching to get their hands on him and if he goes back there, he'll never again see the light of day."

"Do you think the offer's enough to turn him Chink?" said de Valera.

"I do that, but you could sweeten the pill by offering him Irish Citizenship plus the Irish Presidential Distinguished Service Award for services to education," answered Chink. Dev liked the idea. His irritation had subsided. He said he wouldn't waste any time and would call Folens in for a friendly cup of tea and a chat that very morning.

"I'll enjoy that for sure. I'll get himself to toe the line. If not, the Garda will arrest him on the spot and put him on the next plane to Brussels." It was agreed that after the President had his meeting with Folens and the outcome was positive, Folens would sell the idea of the new housekeeper to Otto. Only once the SS Obergruppenfuhrer had accepted the idea would Gillian be brought up to date and fully briefed. She would then fly to Basel to spend a few days in the Alsace getting used to speaking German with the Alsacienne dialect. Once she felt ready, she would take a Lufthansa flight from Frankfurt direct to Dublin. As she needed to avoid being seen in the company of any British or Irish officials, she would be met at Dublin Airport by Folens himself and taken by him to Martinstown. The meeting went on to agree how Operation Rat Trap would be executed. All matters over the border in the North would be the responsibility of the British forces. They would prevent the destruction of Belfast's bridges and guard the TV station and airport against any attack. However, to do this, the Nazi airborne troops at the Corkan Island farm had to be prevented from taking off. And to do this, it was agreed that a joint exercise of Irish and British paratroopers would attack the Island, destroy the aircraft and neutralise the SS troops there.

Sean MacEoin had been silent for most of the meeting, but now he spoke. "A joint attack on Corkan Island will eliminate the airborne threat to Belfast. However, surely the solution to this whole bloody exercise is much simpler." Everyone looked at him in surprise. "Think of the Nazi threat as a snake," continued Sean. "They are poised for a deadly strike, but if we cut off the head, the snake shakes around a bit, but death is assured. If we destroy the Martinstown Headquarters before they have a chance to react and deploy their crack mobile troops onto the streets of Dublin, the other farms will be relatively easy to mop up. They'll probably surrender en masse once they know that we have captured Martinstown and their leader, Skorzeny." Everyone nodded agreement with Sean, and so, although de Valera was reluctant, it was also agreed that Sean and Britain's Army Chief of Staff would liaise on specifics.

"Well gentlemen, that about wraps it up." said the President. "I realise time is of the essence, but how long is it going to be before we are ready to squash these vermin? Can we get our joint forces ready to strike within say three weeks?"

"OK, Iet's make it three then," interrupted Sean,

but another thought just struck me. Why don't you, Chink, talk to the IRA Council about the Nazi plans. Right now, they are all blindly going along believing that their friend Skorzeny's preparations are solely to support their cause. Show them the Shamrock *Blitzkrieg* masterplan. Then they'll know the real purpose of the Nazis and see that once victorious, Finbar Kelly and his fellow freedom fighters would be first in line for mass extermination - just like the Brown-shirts were liquidated in the 1934, the Nazi Night of the Long Knives."

"Why on earth didn't I think of that?" Chink was amazed and so was 'C'. "The thought never crossed my mind - you're smart as a whip, Sean. I think you'd agree Dick, we wouldn't want them as part of our operational forces, but with their cooperation, our job will be so much easier."

de Valera went over to the drinks cabinet again, this time he bringing out a large bottle of Bushmills and three glasses. He filled the glasses, gave one to Sean, the other to Chink and raised his own. "I'm sorry you can't be joining us Mr. White, but gentlemen, I'd like to raise a glass and drink to the success of our Rat Trap. May God be with us." They stood and drank. At the other end of the telephone line, Dick White re-filled his whiskey glass with his favourite 10-year-old Springbank malt, stood and joined in the toast.

"Just a moment - before we go, I've had another thought." Chink explained the situation at the Portglenone monastery in County Antrim to de Valera. He told them that MI5 had identified a large arms and explosives cache within the grounds there. According to the Nazi plan, it was going to be used to blow up all the main road and rail bridges in Belfast. And, he said, there were SS soldiers posing as building labourers there.

"The reason I'm telling you this is because getting the IRA to cooperate is one thing, but we need the Roman Catholic Church to cooperate too. I went to the Cootehill primary school with John McQuaid, the current top dog in the Irish Church - Archbishop Primate for the whole of Ireland and a good friend.

If you all agree, I'll have a chat with him and explain the problem we have with the Monastery. He doesn't need to know anything more than there's an IRA arms dump there plus some very unsavoury characters posing as monks. I'll explain that we have an agent going in to deal with the dump and that there may well be some local ructions. We don't need the men of the cloth to get in the way." The President, Sean and 'C' agreed.

"And just one more thing Mr. White," de Valera

jumped in, "would it be possible for my General McKeown here and myself to have a couple of these magic briefcases like Chink's got here? It would mean our on-going chats would be safe and secure."

"That's an excellent idea Éamon. We're expecting a delivery this week and I'll make sure two are sent over by courier. I'll make it a top priority."

CHAPTER 34

Otto Skorzeny was jubilant. Thanks to Albert
Folens, he had now been able to replace his
housekeeper. In introducing her, Folens had
felt like a traitor. The *Obergruppenfuhrer*, for all
his mad fascist ideas, had given him the funds
to start up his book empire and it only needed
one of those photographs he'd told Albert about
to reach the press and he'd be ruined. He was
desperate to keep his business, lifestyle, and his
family. But he was between a rock and a hard
place. If he didn't do what de Valera asked, he
would end up in a Belgian jail - for life, or worse.
The thought of losing everything freaked him
out. He had no option, but to go along with the
President's demand and lie through his teeth.

In the meantime, Gillian had been briefed on
her mission by Dick White and Airey Neave at
MI6 headquarters. She was to play the role of an
ex-camp guard, Hertha Bothe. Fraulein Bothe
was notorious. She had been a supervisor at the
infamous Natzweiler death camp in the Vosges
mountains. She was one of the few regime
guards to be awarded the Nazi War Merit Cross

for her services. And as part of her new identity, Gillian was given a well-weathered Merit
Cross to take with her. As luck would have it,
Bothe was from Gillian's native Alsace and so
her Alsacienne Germanic dialect fitted in with
her roleplay.

Her frustrations at not playing an active part
in Operation Blarney, then Operation Rat Trap
had been replaced by the thrill and excitement
of now being involved at the sharp end. She
knew her involvement was thwart with danger,
her chances of getting away with the deception
were pretty minimal - just like every mission
she'd made into Nazi-occupied Europe during
the war.

Peter Fleming was also at Gillian's briefing. He
had with him some unfinished knitting on
two substantial wooden needles stuck into a
ball of wool. "You can't carry a gun Gillian, so
I designed this knitting to be something even
more useful. The wool is impregnated with the
explosive trinitrotoluene, TNT, and at its centre
is an ounce of a new explosive called Semtex. It
has an 18-second fuse." He explained how the
fuse was triggered by grasping both needles
and pulling them simultaneously out of the
wool. "And if you ever have to do that, run like
hell," he said, "it's blast will kill anyone within a

10 yd radius." Peter explained that each of the knitting needles was armed with a tiny metal dart treated with 'Curare', the killer poison used by South American Indians and showed her the tiny exit hole at the sharp end of each needle. He explained how to ready a needle for shooting a dart, she simply had to twist the knob end, he said. Then to fire a dart, she simply had to press the knob down.

"It's perfectly safe to pull one needle out and then the other if needed, without detonating the bomb." continued Peter. Let me demonstrate. Now watch carefully. The MI6 boffin stood up, took the ball of wool with the two knitting needles stuck into it. He moved closer to Gillian so that she could see exactly what he was doing. He pulled one knitting needle out, twisted the knob end, pointed the needle towards the door to the room and pressed the knob. There was a faint 'ping' as the dart hit the wood.

"Easy as that!" Peter said with a smile, "and now this is how to detonate the bomb." He inserted the needle back into the wool, and then pulled both out together. There was pandemonium as everyone but Peter dived for cover under the conference room table, believing their eccentric boffin had finally gone doolally. He laughed as the ball of wool fizzed like a firework then exploded into a cloud of pink dust. "Oh! sorry chaps, I forgot to tell you this was a demonstration model".

When Folens phoned Otto, he'd told him that he had contacted some of his old wartime friends in Belgium and Germany and told them that a senior ex-Nazi SS Colonel needed a housekeeper, *ein Haushälterin*. He said his friends had come up with several suggestions, but only one had seemed to fit the role of a housekeeper and cook. Folens was getting used to spinning his fabricated story, and in fact, in some weird way, he was enjoying it. He went on to give Otto details of an ex-SS camp supervisor, *ein Aufseher-innen*, called Hertha Bothe. Bothe, he said, had been convicted of so-called war crimes, along with many other camp guards. She'd served her time in the infamous Landsberg am Lech prison in Bavaria and had only recently been released. What he didn't tell Otto was that she had been murdered by a Natzweiler camp survivor shortly after her release. Her death had never been publicised.

As Fritz Suhren had been a concentration camp commandant for most of the war at Auschwitz, Buchenwald, and several other notorious camps, Otto had asked him if he'd ever heard of her. Fritz said he'd never been to the Natzweiler camp, but he had a vague memory of someone with that name associated with putting down an inmates' revolt single-handed. That sealed it for Skorzeny, and he'd immediately taken up the opportunity

It took a few days for Gillian, now Fraulein Bothe, to arrive in Ireland. She had been told that she was being met by one of Skorzeny's friends. She had no idea who, but the person would be holding up a board with her under-cover name on it. It worked like clockwork. As she came off the plane into the Arrivals at Dub-lin airport, she saw Hertha Bothe's name held up by a smartly dressed man in a business suit and tie. He greeted her coolly just to establish her name. He didn't even offer to help carry her luggage; his only words were 'follow me'. When they reached his car, he again showed his disdain by simply telling her to 'get in'. Once they were on their way, she tried to make conversation by asking how long the journey to Martinstown would take, 'one hour' was his terse reply. After that, they hardly spoke to each other during the whole journey.

She noticed the tight security at the gate of Martinstown and on the drive up to the front of the house, she spotted people milling about,

most in grey uniforms. When they arrived
at the front of the house, her escort got out
telling her curtly to wait in the car. He had
started to walk towards the front door, when
it opened and a tall well-built man came out.
The two men talked together and then walked
towards Gillian. When they came closer, she
saw the man's face was disfigured by an ugly
scar running down one side of this face. She
realised she was being welcomed by the Colonel
himself. Skorzeny opened the front passenger
door of the car for her to alight. "Welcome to
Martinstown, Fraulein Bothe, I have been looking forward to having you here." They shook
hands in a typically formal Germanic way.   He
picked up her case without asking and with a
slight bow, pointed towards the house for her
to go in. She turned to thank the man who had
brought her, but he was already back in the car
ready to drive away. At least Skorzeny has better manners than that creep, she thought.

Otto was puzzled by her having so little
luggage. She explained that she had such
little time to buy civilian clothes after she was
released and had only what the prison authorities had issued her with. He took her up the
staircase to the room of his late housekeeper
and told her about Dorothea's tragic accident.
Gillian feigned sympathy for her new em-

ployer's loss. He asked her if she minded having the same room, she said it was not a problem, anything was better than the prison cell she had left.

"Fortunately fraulein, you are about the same size as Frau Binz, you can see if any of her clothes are to your liking." The same height and slimmer, Otto reflected, and certainly better looking and seemingly with a less abrasive manner. Refreshingly better, he smiled to himself. He told her he would like her to wear the black dress and white apron from Frau Binz's wardrobe during the day but for other times she could help herself to anything else that fitted her.

Fraulein Bothe had only been at Martinstown for a few days, but the difference was marked. Her cooking was creative, far better than Frau Binz. Otto liked traditional German food, but not every day. No more sauerkraut, no more schweinshaxe, no more schnitzel. Fraulein Bothe 's menu choices were varied: traditional Alsacienne choucroute garnie, spaghetti carbonara, chicken curry and even French vol-au-vent. And her general housekeeping was far better than Binz. No wonder he was pleased.

Now Otto had other things to think about. How had the British penetrated his security and found out about the Shamrock *Blitzkrieg*? He was certain that it must have been around the time of the fatal accident of Frau Binz. Was there a spy at Martinstown? he asked himself. Or was it that 'hail fellow well met' ex British Army Dorman-O'Gowan? Either way, the first phase of the plan had been compromised. He needed to revise the timetable and whole plan of attack, but at the same time, he needed to ensure the amended plan stayed secret. Also, how much did they know? It would appear from his London spy that only the Irish side of the Shamrock *Blitzkrieg* was on the overhead projector slide found by the agent. And from what the woman had overheard in the canteen, nothing was mentioned about Argentina or Spain, just Ireland. From the reports he'd received from his farms, they still had some work to do finishing the modifications to the VW Beetles and the BMW motorbikes and sidecars. There were also boxes of uniforms to be delivered to each farm Overall, it looked as if they could be ready for action by mid May, a clear month earlier than originally planned.

He decided that he would prepare an amended blueprint for the Shamrock *Blitzkrieg*. To make sure absolute secrecy was maintained, he wouldn't include that pompous *dummkopf*, Charles Haughey or the IRA. And much as he would have liked the tactical genius of Dorman-O'Gowan alongside him, he couldn't risk the faintest possible chance of a security breach. He told Fraulein Bothe that he had an urgent job to do and expected to work through the night. He asked her for a large pot of coffee and some snacks to keep him going. But she said that coffee went cold and stale very quickly and he needed fresh food too. She would stay up as long as was needed, all night if necessary, to support him.

At 4.00 am, the final details of the plan were coming together. He had drunk at least two litres of coffee and was now lacing it with Asbach brandy. He liked the idea of attacking the Belfast bridges and taking over the TV and radio stations there. There was no reason why those plans for North of the border should be changed, apart from the timescale. In their ignorance, he was sure he could rely on the IRA support there. In the South, the attack and seizure of Dublin would have to be radically changed. It was vital that his forces seized the initiative and struck where least expected. He would give each farm specific targets in Dublin. One to take over the radio and TV station, one to seize the central Garda station on Pierce Street, and one to occupy the Oireachtas, the Irish Parliament. That left one mobile section from the Dundalk farm to roam the streets, spraying chlorine gas and machine gunning anyone who showed their faces. Terror was the main weapon. His specialist *Ingenieur* group from Martinstown would split into two sections. One section to destroy road and rail bridges over the River Liffey, leaving only the Grattan and O'Connell Street bridges for the attacking forces to use. Overall, there were some 14 bridges to destroy. His men would have to start laying the explosives from 11.00 pm the day before the uprising day, *das Aufstandstag.* They would have to work hard to ensure all would be destroyed simultaneously at 0600hrs on the day of the attack. At precisely the same time, the other section would seize Dublin airport. A key part of both operations was that the SS troops would all be wearing Irish Ranger uniforms - a neat way to confuse the enemy, a trick Otto had learnt when his SS *Kommandos* infiltrated the Allied lines at the Battle of the Bulge.

In order to ensure absolute secrecy, details of the second phase of the planned *Blitzkrieg* had not been discussed at his general meeting in Martinstown, only with his close and totally reliable Nazi team. It had been prepared in detail three years earlier when he was at the military base loaned by Franco in Zaragoza,

Spain. Only some minor changes were needed plus the timescale would have to change - the frustration of his war-hardened Waffen SS *Kommandos* would soon disappear as they unleashed their ruthless blood lust. Whilst they were accomplishing their objectives, Otto would go with two of his most trusted men and capture the Irish President. At the same time as his troops launched their *Blitzkrieg*, Ramcke's airborne force would be on its way from Spain using old but reliable German Junkers that Hitler had gifted to Franco during the Spanish Civil War, and Douglas C-54 transport planes from the Spanish Air Force. Timing was vital. They could only land once Dublin airport had been taken by Otto's men. Meyer's invasion force from Argentina would launch once Operation Shamrock had secured Dublin. It would take them seven days to reach Ireland. and so Otto's and Ramcke troops would have to hold out until they arrived. With Belfast and the rest of Northern Ireland in chaos and with control of Dublin, the main invasion troops would move fast to take Cork and other strategic places including Limerick and Galway.

First, he would brief Josef Mengele, Friedrich Boger and Fritz Suren on the new attack mo-

dality.   Then, he would make a flying visit to
Spain to finalise arrangements with *General der
Fallschirmtruppe* Ramcke and *Oberführer* Puaud.

He couldn't help but smile.   He had the plan
clear in his mind.   This time, he wasn't going to
spend hours discussing and documenting the
details for them to leak out to the opposition.

Otto had bought a large 8' x 5' foot map of Eire
at Eason's 'book shop on Dublin's O'Connell
Street and a large pinboard on which to mount
it.   Having sketched his plan on paper, the next
job was to transcribe it onto the map. He would
then photograph it and take the picture with
him when he went to brief his war council in
Spain.   Then, with perhaps a few modifications,
he would brief the *Untersturmführers* officers at
the farms.   He was confident that they and their
stormtroopers would carry out their orders
with the same selfless and ruthless zeal for
which they were feared.   They were all battle-
hardened and itching to go.

He mounted the map onto the pinboard and
was just starting to mark the assault forces
and their moves on it when Gillian came in.
"*Herr Oberst*, I mean Colonel.   You can't work all
night without having a break."   But he was too
engrossed in his work to even acknowledge her
and didn't look up.   He went on annotating the

forces and linking them with red ribbon to their targets. She quickly memorised as much as she could from what she saw and in particular the heading in bold letters at the top of the map 'Shamrock Bitzkrieg - 0500hrs Sunday, May 20. "Colonel, you really should stop for something to eat. I have made you some Frühstück. Eggs, cold meats, and bread rolls."

Normally, Skorzeny would have been on his guard. What he was doing was top secret, very much for his eyes only. But he was tired and suffering from too much caffeine and the effects of half a bottle of brandy. Very reluctantly, he stopped and turned to her. "Fraulein Bothe, Hertha. I must finish before my flight to Spain tomorrow. When I get back, I will explain to you what it is about to be happening. But for now, thank you for all the coffee and now breakfast. You look after me well."

"It is my pleasure to serve, Colonel," she said humbly and turned to leave, but Otto called her back. "Hertha, join me in a toast," he said, reaching out for the Asbach. He poured two generous glasses. "To our Shamrock *Blitzkrieg* - Heil Hitler!

The next day, when Otto had left for Spain, Gillian waited until there was nobody around in the house, then quickly picking up the tele-

phone, she asked the operator for the number
she had memorised when being briefed by Peter
Fleming. She'd been told only to use it in a
dire emergency or if she had vital information
to pass on. And, if she called, she needed to
give the password phrase - 'Singapore noodles
with spicy squid'. She thought it weird at the
time, but when the call was answered by a high
pitched female Asian voice saying "Ching-ming
stir fries - please to give order" - she realised it
was Peter's typical sense of humour.

"Singapore noodles with spicy squid," she
said, and couldn't help smiling to herself. Mi-
raculously, the voice descended an octave and
became very English. It was Peter himself. "My
dear, what goes?" She told him she had very
little time but the Nazi Shamrock *Blitzkrieg*
had been rushed forward to May 20, Sunday
at dawn. She also told him what she'd seen on
Skorzeny's map, that airborne troops from Zaragoza in Spain would be involved plus seaborne
forces from South America. She didn't know
the numbers, but they would be large. Suddenly, Gillian heard someone coming through
the kitchen.

She quickly put the phone down. It was *Sturmbannführer* Harald Mors, Skorzeny's second
in command. Always, distrustful, he looked at

her suspiciously and asked who she was talking to. Off the cuff, she told him she was trying to get through to Herr Folens to thank him for introducing her to the Colonel. He still looked suspicious, but then it was an inherent quality of a good Nazi, she thought. She just hoped that she had given Peter sufficient information.

CHAPTER 35

Like many religions since the beginning of
time, the Roman Catholic church had for centuries sought to expand its 'empire' by building
churches and abbeys, all aimed at converting
heathen sinners and heretics to worship God.
Nothing was more true than with the Ordo
Cisterciensis, the thousand-year-old Cistercian order of monks. Our Lady of Bethlehem
in Portglenone was a very good example of
the empire-building. The Abbey had been
established in 1948 by 14 Cistercian monks
from the Mount Melleray Abbey in County
Waterford. Mount Melleray Abbey itself had
been established 100 years earlier by monks
from the Abbaye du Mont-Saint-Michel in Nor-
mandy. Cistercian monks, otherwise known
as Trappists, were bound by the strict rules
of Saint Benedict. One was a vow of absolute
poverty and so it was always thought a mystery
how they could afford the purchase of the dilapidated Portglenone Manor House in its 300
acres of overgrown arable farmland.

In fact, the funds to buy the estate had come
from donations from other monasteries, dona-

tions around the world including South America and the Vatican. There were street protests stirred up by staunch Protestant elements in the local community. They were against being invaded by the 'Taigs', as they called Roman Catholics, from over the Border. However, in spite of all the opposition, the Portglenone town council approved the sale. They said that it was for the good of the area and the new monastic community would need food and materials from local suppliers.

Since 1948, Our Lady of Bethlehem had grown from the original founders to just under 70 monks and novices. In just 14 years, it had created a working dairy farm and was in the process of building their place of worship and accommodation for even more monks.

Father Emery had written to the Abbot explaining that Christopher Lavelle was ex-military and had suffered severe mental problems because of the murderous killing and brutality he'd seen and taken part in. He'd come to realise that the way of life in the British Army was evil to the core. The letter went on to say that he'd left the army and joined the Campaign for Nuclear Disarmament, where he'd met Father Emery at one of CND's Hyde Park gatherings. Chris was a poor damaged soul.

The letter, crafted by Roger Hollis and Father Leo Emery, didn't try to hide Chris's army past. Chink had told them that the IRA had spies and sympathisers amongst the monks in the Abbey community and he would have to be constantly on guard. They would certainly be suspicious of any new arrival from the mainland, particularly an ex-soldier. By being upfront, Chris wouldn't have to play a fictional role, just bend the truth. The letter had gone on to say that Chris was a qualified structural engineer whose grandfather was one of the Lavelles from Tuam in County Galway, descendants of the Irish clan, *Ó Maol Fábhail.* Now, he wanted nothing more than to get back to the land of his fathers and seek God's forgiveness for what he saw as his life of sin and seek the solace of monastic life.

The reply by return of post wrote that they would welcome him with love and caring into their community. They would arrange to meet him at Ballymena train station if he let them know the expected time of his arrival.

Chris had travelled by train to Liverpool, then ferry to Belfast. He was taking the train to Ballymena and rang the monastery to tell them his time of arrival. Everything worked like clockwork and he was met by the Monastery's Novice Master, Father Jerome. Father Jerome

had been very friendly and welcoming during
their walk to the Monastery. He'd told Chris
that he'd read the letter Father Emery sent to
the Abbot and was distressed to hear about the
traumatic time he'd spent in the British Army.
He wanted Chris to know that he was welcome
to make a new life in the monastic community
of Our Lady of Bethlehem. It would be his family. He stressed that God loved repentant sinners and Chris would earn his place in heaven,
simply praising the Lord Almighty through his
abundant skills. As his Novice Master, Father
Jerome had explained that the monastery
followed the strict Trappist rule of silence,
but Chris could talk to him at any time. As a
'closed' order, life was uncomplicated. Trappist
monks praised God through hard and physical
work, meditation, and prayer.   And he'd also
told Chris what to expect on his arrival. He
would be given a simple white robe, the dress
of a pre-novitiate. Apart from his bible, his lay
clothes and all his possessions would be taken
and stored in case he decided to go back to life
outside. He would then meet the Abbot for
a short ceremony to welcome and bless him
into the community, after which, he would be
shown to his dormitory.

The first three days, he thought, were very
similar to when he'd arrived for officer training

at the Royal Military Academy of Sandhurst.
No time to think, the regime was brutally
strict. Father Jerome turned out to be more like
a drill sergeant, herding the 6 new postulant
monks from one place to another and his brief
meeting when he was introduced to the Abbot,
reminded him of meeting his Sandhurst College Commander. 'Drill Sergeant'. Jerome's role
as Novice Master necessitated speaking. He
frequently scolded any postulants who broke
the rule of silence, or failed to keep to the rigid
timetable. Already, Chris had been rebuked for
talking. He was gently told that if he continued
to break the vow of silence, he would be seeing
the Abbot again and a more severe penance
would be meted out. He was glad his stay was
temporary.

For six days a week, the routine was the same.
Reveille at 3.30 am followed by morning
prayers, then straight to work, no breakfast.
The long-drawn-out mornings were the tough-
est part of the day. Lunch was the first meal of
the day. Some monks worked in the vegetable
garden and orchards, some tended the monastery's dairy herd of one bull, 6 calves and
62 cows. Others were engaged on the various
building projects. There seemed to be an air of
peace and happiness throughout the Monastery
as everyone went about their tasks seemingly

living in a parallel tranquil and mystical universe.   At the end of the working day, supper, more prayers, then bed at 8.00 pm. It was a relief from the leaches, snakes and fetid heat of the jungle, but monastic life was no panacea. It was hard graft and he was glad it wasn't his vocational choice. The vegetarian diet was something else Chris found difficult, apart from the beer. Father Jerome had mentioned that the Monastery had its own in-house brewery and used an ancient Cistercian recipe with figs, raisins and coffee to add a unique flavour. Unfortunately, they were only allowed beer with their meals, otherwise they drank water.

Father Jerome explained, work was prayer, doing one's best in praise of God. "Everyone has complete choice of work," he'd told Chris, "But your specialist construction skills could be greatly beneficial and we would be so grateful if you would be part of our abbey building team." Chris didn't tell him that his actual specialist skills were completely the opposite, destruction

"I will do God's will," Chris said, knowing in his own mind that he aimed to be out of the place as soon as he had accomplished his mission. "But while I'm allowed to speak, Father, I noticed what looked like construction work going on near the river. Is that something I can help with?"

"Oh, that's nothing to do with us, just outside
contractors working on an old swimming pool
built before we came here," the monk had replied. "One of our ex-novices, Joe Lynskey, may
God bless his soul, felt the life of a monk wasn't
for him. He left us some ten months ago and
returned over the border. And as a gift to the
abbey, he and some of his republican friends
offered to convert the pool into a storage place
and workshop for repairing our tools and agricultural equipment. About 10 of the workers
live in tents on the side of the River Bann and
others come and go with tools and materials.
We have very little to do with them. Joe has said
it would ready for us to use by the end of June."

Father Jerome's explanation fitted with the
briefing Chris had been given by Peter Fleming
and it soon became very clear that the monks
had no idea what Lynskey was up to, nor did
they know of his new vocation serving the IRA.

After a week of getting used to the rigid daily
routine of the monastery, Chris decided it was
time to reconnoitre the so-called construction
work at the swimming pool. It could only be
done at night. For him, being undetected on his
way to the site posed no problem - he'd learnt
the hard way on patrol behind enemy lines in

the Sarawak jungle. However, for safety's sake, he decided to start out two hours after lights out, giving the inhabitants time to sink into deep sleep. He needed to be back in his bed an hour before the monastery woke up at 3.30 am. That gave him over 4 hours.

Monks slept in dormitories fully dressed in their daily robes. The six new pre-postulants, and a Novice to oversee them, all slept together. Again, just like army barrack-rooms. It wasn't easy for Chris to get out without waking them, but being new to the hard routine meant everyone slept soundly. With utmost stealth, Chris slipped out of his bed. He took the bible Peter had given him, so if he was challenged, he could say that he couldn't sleep and just needed to meditate amongst God's creatures outside. A thin excuse, but at least it was one. He bunched up his bedding so that a casual observer, would think he was still there asleep. He crept warily down the stairs from the sleeping quarters, into the main hall, passing through the refectory into the large vaulted kitchen and out of the rear door. So far, so good, he thought, no problems.

It was a bright moonlit night. Trees, shrubs and monastery outbuildings created the shadows and pools of darkness for him to use as he

moved towards the area of the swimming pool
on the side of the River Bann, little more than
300 yards from the abbey. During the day,
he'd seen the windowless barn-like structure
Lynskey's gang had built covering the pool.
Now, he saw light coming from a large 10ft high
doorway. He was some 50 yards away when
he started to hear activity and voices. He could
make out a truck and men off-loading what
looked like heavy boxes and barrels. Another
15 yards. Now, the voices were more distinct.
They weren't speaking English or Irish. They
were some of the Germans he'd been told about.
It fitted the briefing he'd been given by MI6. The
barrels must be the explosives, and the boxes
ammunition and guns, he thought. He waited
and watched. Eventually, the off-loading finished. The driver and some of the men got into
the vehicle and drove off, leaving others standing in the doorway.

He could hear them chatting away. Then one,
obviously their leader, announced - "OK! *Trup-
pen, es ist Zeit zu schlafen*" - time for bed. And
they turned off the lights inside the building
and slid the doors closed. There was some discussion, which he couldn't understand, then
they headed towards the tents some distance
away, leaving one person outside the building
as guard. Chris hadn't reckoned on there being

a guard. What he'd heard probably related to the guard roster, he thought. Now, all he could hear was the rippling water of the river and the occasional animal noises - barn owls screeching; the high-pitched bark of a fox. The guard started patrolling the perimeter of the building. Monks have no watches, so Chris counted the seconds away. He reckoned it took the man about 300 seconds, five minutes, to complete his route, just enough time out of sight for Chris to slip in unnoticed, but he waited. He wanted to be sure of the timing. After the guard completed five circuits, he decided, to make his move.

The sliding doors weren't locked. Whoever was in charge might have thought being in a monastery a guard was enough, or it was simply a security blunder. Either way, his luck was holding. He gently pushed one of the door panels and it silently glided open along well-greased rollers. He entered and slid the door shut behind him. It was pitch black inside. This was the first opportunity he'd had to use Peter Fleming's gift, the 'modified' bible. It had passed the scrutiny of 'Drill Sergeant' Father Jerome. It had all the pages of a regular bible and the cover was black leather with a large gold-leafed cross on the front. However, cleverly built into the spine, was an ultra-thin and

powerful pencil torch. It was just one of the unusual attributes the bible had.

With the torch, he could make out a ramp
leading down into the defunct empty pool.
He followed the torch light until he was at the
bottom of the ramp. All around the sides of the
pool were racks on which boxes were stacked.
He went closer and swept the beam of his torch
along them. They were made from strips of
wood and by shining his torch through the gaps
between them, he could make out the contents
- some had rifles, some had ammunition belts.
This was confirmation of the intelligence he'd
received.

Then he noticed a door that had been built into
the side of the pool immediately at the bottom
of the ramp. This again was easy to open and
inside he found a cavern of equal size to the
pool into which the barrels had been rolled.
He didn't have to go in to know what was in
the barrels. The bleach like odour of acetone
peroxide crystals, the high explosive, was over-
powering. He counted 14 barrels in all.

He could improvise a fuse, using one of the
other attributes of his 007's bible, and blow the
lot up. That would cause one God Almighty
eruption, he grinned to himself.

In the early 1900s, swimming pools didn't have the luxury of clean filtered water supplies. When he and Peter Fleming had looked at the old plans of the monastery at Hanslope Park back in England, they'd seen that it had been ingeniously built so that the top of the pool was just below the water level of the river. A pipe from the bottom of the pool had then been used to fill and empty its contents into the river. From the plans, he'd seen that there was a pump house, a small lean-to cabin, at ground level at the far end of the pool. He went back up the ramp, it was still there. The door was rusty and it creaked noisily as he opened it. He paused to see if the sound had disturbed the slumbering men outside. Inside the cabin, the pipes and the pump looked to be still intact. It would be so simple to turn the stopcock wheel and flood the whole armoury, he thought. It would look like a natural disaster, he could then slip back to his bed, mission accomplished. In the morning, he would tell Father Jerome that monastic life wasn't for him. By the end of the week, he could be on his way back to Malaya and active service – or the security services might have another job for him.

The large 2ft diameter stopcock wheel and the rest of the pumping equipment were some 80 years old and completely rusted. He tried to turn it but it wouldn't budge. Jammed solid and time was running on. He could go back to the dormitory and return the following night and have another go, but the urgency of the mission had been stressed and if he could do the job now, so much the better. Without a watch or any means of telling the time, he had to act quickly and execute his plan before the monastery reveille. He left the pump house and went down the ramp to the bottom of the pool again. In their hurry to convert the building onto an IRA munitions dump, the workers had left the floor as it was. Apart from the door into the explosives area and the ramp, every square inch of floor space was filled with racking. He needed to know that the original water pipe used to fill and drain the pool was still there and not blocked up. He painstakingly searched the deep end, gently moving boxes looking for where he'd seen it on the plans. Precious minutes later, he found it, still with its original grating, rusted and covered in leaves and other debris from the building work that had been carried out. If he could somehow open up the stopcock and let the river water in - job done, simple and easy.

He went back up the ramp and into the pump house. If he could heat the valve mechanism,

perhaps it would loosen up and turn. This
was another job for his bible. Peter had shown
him that beneath its paper covering, the inside
of the holy book's front and back covers were
made from compacted string impregnated with
saltpeter, into which was twisted magnesium
wire. Both ends had self-igniting caps he could
strike against a hard surface to light - just like
match heads. He ripped the covers off exposing
the strings. He pulled them out. Soon he had a
length of fuse some three yards long. He wound
it around the base of the stopcock valve. He
paused, waiting to hear the guard's footsteps
fade away on another tour of the building,
then struck one end against the wall. The fuse
string lit on first strike. He could feel the heat
as it burnt. The light from the magnesium was
blinding and he tried to avert his eyes, but he
had a job to do. When he felt the heat might
have eased the valve, he seized the wheel and
heaved with all his might. There was some give.
He tried again - this time, it moved slightly,
but not enough. Once more he heaved at the
wheel. This time it moved. First slowly, then it
gave way completely and turned. But nothing
happened. He'd expected to hear the sound of
the rushing water echoing around the building
structure. What a bummer, he thought, I'll
have to go to plan 'B' and blow the sodding lot.
But as he went to the top of the ramp, he heard a

noise from below. At first a faint hissing. Then, growing louder and louder, water gushed out of the drain pipe into the bottom of the pool at such force that it collapsed some of the shelving above it. Even though he'd shut the sliding door when he entered the building, the noise could well have disturbed the sleeping workers.

Chris enjoyed a moment of satisfaction having completed his mission successfully. It was time for him to return to his bed in the monastery. He slowly retreated and was about to open the door, when it slid back on its own. He was face to face with the guard, who must have heard the noise of the filling pool and was about to investigate. The guard's face froze in surprise seeing the disheveled figure dressed in a filthy white robe. Luckily, Chris' jungle experiences had honed his reactions to be lightning fast. Kill or be killed. Acting by pure instinct, his right arm shot out and he caught the guard with a lethal straight four finger blow to his larynx , cutting off his air supply. The guard died instantly, his look of surprise now a death mask.

Chris listened. Apart from the sound of water flowing into the pool, all was quiet. He dragged the guard's body to the top of the ramp and, with a shove, rolled it down into the rising

water. He went back to the door and listened.
Hearing nothing, he opened it and stepped out
into the night air.   That's when he heard the
familiar clicks of safety catches being released.
He'd walked into an armed reception committee. - no chance of escape.

CHAPTER 36

Finbar Kelly, the IRA Chief, was beside himself seething with anger when he rang Chink. "General Sir! I'm just after having a call from Lynskey at the monastery. He's telling me that our feckin' arms and explosives dump there has been 'bagged up'- useless the lot. The whole place is swimming with water."

"Good God, Finbar! How in hell's name has that happened?" Chink feigned shock at the news.

"We can't be blowin' up those feckin Belfast bridges now, can we," ignoring Chink, Finbar ranted on, "it'll take forever to rescue the weapons and forever again to make them serviceable. It's screwed our plans to kick those feckin protestant arses back into the sea."

"Yes, I understand Finbar, but just calm down for a moment and tell me what's actually happened." Inwardly, he was thinking - fantastic - well done that man from Borneo. "You said the place was heavily guarded," he continued. "Was it an Army raid? How many men have we lost?"

"Sure, there were armed guards and we've always been prepared for a raid by the 'pigs', but some shit of a feller dressed like a monk from the monastery slipped through the lads. He somehow opened up the old water inlet valve to the pool and flooded the lot," the distraught IRA boss babbled on. "All bloody ruined".

Chink's relief at having the arms dump destroyed turned to alarm as Finbar went on to say that they had captured the bastard who had done the deed. He told Chink that Lynskey had gone to the monastery to see if they were missing one of their postulants. They confirmed that indeed one was missing, they thought he had found monastic life wasn't for him and had slipped out during the night. After talking to the Abbot, Joe discovered that the postulant in question was an ex British Army engineer.

"Is he alive? Has he said anything? What are you going to do now?" Chink fired a string of questions at Finbar.

"Oh, he's alive alright, but not the talking sort. We roughed him up, but all the shite said, as calm as anything would you believe, was 'any chance of a cup of tea?' So, we're sending him down to see our German friend Mr. Skorzeny. Otto didn't squeeze a word out of them agents in Strabane, but for sure, his men have some devilish techniques when it comes to making their victims sing." Chink could hear the bitterness of revenge in Finbar's voice.

The last thing Chink and the intelligence services wanted was for their man to fall into Nazi hands He tried to persuade Finbar to bring the prisoner to Bellamont, but he couldn't intervene. He shuddered at the thought of what and who, the British officer was going to be confronted by when he arrived at Martinstown. Chink couldn't risk giving the whole game away, but perhaps it was time for Finbar and his fellow IRA Council members to know about the truth behind Skorzeny's plans.

"Look Finbar, I was going to ring you anyway. I need you down here urgently. I have found out some serious top-secret information through my contacts.   I can't say anything on the phone. Portglenone is a disaster, but nothing compared to what I've uncovered. Just get down here and make sure Lynskey comes too."

Finbar was taken aback. What could be worse than the destruction of their main armoury. Whatever it was, he knew that if Chink said something was urgent, it was bloody urgent. He promised Chink he would contact his fellow Council members and arrange for as many of them who could make it, to meet up at Bellamont that evening. When Finbar put the phone down, he was left puzzled. He was certain that Chink was a true-blooded Irishman, dedicated to the cause, but he had a feeling that the General wasn't that surprised about the Portglenone disaster - had he an inkling it was going to happen. Nonetheless, without delay, he got straight on the phone to ring around the Council members and muster as many as he could for the meeting.

Meanwhile, Chink made a secure call to 'C' in London. He told him about the successful destruction of the arms dump and that he was about to have a meeting with the IRA Council to let them see the Nazi Shamrock *Blitzkrieg* plans. He said he was sure that by the end of that meeting they would be on-side. However, he broke the tragic news about the capture of Captain Lavelle, who was now being taken across the border to Otto Skorzeny's headquarters.

Chink and 'C' racked their brains to think of some way they might rescue the Royal Engineer Captain, but there was no way without blowing everything sky high and incurring the loss of many lives. They both knew that Chris' briefing at Hatfield House by Peter Fleming had been on a need-to-know basis and nothing about the

joint British and Irish plans to annihilate the
imminent Nazi menace had been included.   Yet
it was utterly distressing for them both to know
that after serving his country so selflessly, such
a brave young soldier was to be condemned to
Skorzeny's henchmen's'sickening interrogation
skills. There was nothing they could do without jeopardising Operation Rat Trap.

On the evening of the same day Chris was taken
down to Martinstown, there was a full IRA
Council meeting at Bellamont House. Chink
revealed the full plans of the Nazi Shamrock
Blitzkrieg. He was frank and as open as he could
be without giving away his work with MI6. He
told them that the Irish Army was preparing
a plan to destroy the Nazi threat and that, because the whole of Ireland was involved, British
troops would also be involved. That was a bitter
pill to swallow. Nonetheless, after two hours of
heated discussion and being told that the Irish
President, de Valera himself, was behind the
plan, everyone reluctantly agreed to give their
full support to Operation Rat Trap. But Finbar
and the rest of the Council made it perfectly
clear that as soon as it was over, they would be
continuing their fight for a united Ireland - and
Chink agreed.

Dick White was working late. He'd had another

call from Chink to report that the IRA Council were now on side. Chink told him that as soon as Finbar was told by Skorzeny when he planned to launch his Shamrock *Blitzkrieg*, Finbar would notify Chink, who would then alert Sean MacEoin. Then, when Chink told them that the Irish army was about to launch the Irish end of Operation Rat Trap, the IRA would stand their lads down. Northern Ireland would be safe and one major hurdle out of the way.

He called his secretary into his office. "Rebecca, I need a top-secret 'eyes only' memo to go to the PM with copies to Roger, Field Marshal Sir Richard Hull, and the Prime Minister of Northern Ireland, Sir Basil Brooke, oh, and Airey Neave." She took out her shorthand pad and waited for 'C' to start.

'Portglenone threat neutralised. No need to tell them the details, thought 'C'. *IRA has agreed to stand down. Irish army and our paratroops ready to launch Rat Trap. Solution needed for Spanish end. Critical we stop the Nazi Armada from supporting Shamrock Blitzkrieg'.*

"And get that off as soon as you can, Rebecca - use secure Telex, it's faster than courier."

As Rebecca stood up to leave the room, she turned. "Sir, may I make a suggestion?"

"Yes, go ahead," said 'C', without bothering to look up from his desk.

"I don't know if you know that my Dad knows Field Marshal Kesselring."

"Uhm..Yes," he was only half-listening.

She went on, "Kesselring was the ex-Nazi head of the Luftwaffe. Dad translated for him during the war trials in ......"

"Yes, yes, I know all that, Rebecca - it's detailed in your security vetting," 'C' cut-in impatiently, still not fully paying attention to what she had to say. But Rebecca persisted, she wasn't going to be put off.

"Well sir! Dad told me that the Field Marshal had led the German Luftwaffe support for Franco in the Spanish Civil War. And he said Kesselring had had a close relationship with Franco. The Generalissimo said that the Stuka dive bombing and machine gun strafing of the Republican forces had won him the war. I just thought…"

'C's head shot up. His secretary had now sparked his full attention now. "Bloody hell Rebecca - go on, go on. You just thought what?"

Rebecca, pleased that 'C' had caught on to her

line of thought, continued. She said her father often talked about the Field Marshal. He'd said that 'Smiling Albert' , as Kesselring was known, was a professional soldier, and hated the Nazi cult. Perhaps 'C' could talk to her father and see if Kesselring might contact the Generalissimo on behalf of Britain and Ireland. 'C' was stunned. This could be the answer, right under his nose. But would Kesselring be prepared to be their intermediary with Franco? Could he be trusted? Would Franco play ball? Kesselring would need to put pressure on the Spanish dictator and tell him that if he didn't quash the Spanish part of Skorzeny's Shamrock Blitzkrieg, Britain would spark another civil war in Spain. And if that happened, the Republicans would have the full support of Britain, America, and all other European forces against him. It might just work, thought 'C'.

"Rebecca - brilliant. It might just be the way into Franco that we need - well done. If it works out, I'll treat you and your boyfriend to dinner at Claridge's. Now, let's get your father on the phone."

Rebecca went back to her desk to put a call through to her father in Hong Kong. She smiled as she gave the telephone operator the number to call. It was good to show that she had brains as well as long legs - bloody men!

Talbot Bashall, Rebecca's father, worked for the Foreign Office. He was currently in Hong Kong attached to the prison service there. He was also, as were many members of the FO, an MI5 agent. 'C' knew that he really ought to go through Hollis, but time was of the essence and there wasn't a moment to be lost. He could tell Roger later.

Dick White didn't go into detail but asked if Talbot was still in touch with Smiling Albert. Talbot told him that in fact, he'd recently met up with the old soldier at a reception in Wiesbaden in Germany. He said that he was half the man he'd translated for in 1948. Bored out of his mind and spent most of his time fishing in the Rhine.

'C' stressed that what he was about to tell Talbot was Top Secret. He outlined the situation in Ireland and explained what they were considering asking Kesselring to do. Talbot thought that Kesselring would jump at the idea and he confirmed what Rebecca had said about Kesselring being violently anti-Nazi and felt he would be very receptive.

It was arranged that Talbot would call the Field Marshall and invite him for a weekend sea fishing trip off the Isle of Wight. When 'C' put the phone down he called Roger Hollis and updated him. He apologised for contacting Talbot before speaking to him, but it had been important to strike while the iron was hot. He said that if Kesselring was against helping his old enemy, Britain, he could easily have a tragic accident and fall overboard on the fishing trip, so keeping Rat Trap plans tightly secure.

However, everything went to plan. Kesselring not only enjoyed the weekend fishing, but his enthusiasm for striking a blow against Otto Skorzeny and the other perverted remnants of the Third Reich was more than Hollis and 'C' could have expected. Kesselring was aboard the team. Over a dinner of fresh grilled mackerel, the two intelligence chiefs had explained that they were up against the clock and that the Nazi *Blitzkrieg* might erupt at any time.

The following day, *Generalfeldmarschall* Kesselring flew to Spain and arranged to visit 'El Caudillo', Franco, at his Palacio Real de El Pardo a few kilometres outside Madrid. And by Friday, he was back in London. He told 'C' that it had really been quite easy. He'd simply explained to Franco the stark choice he had. Remain dictator of Spain and find a way to scupper the Nazi armada, or face bloodshed and total annihilation. Franco was awaiting further instructions from MI6.

CHAPTER 37

Captain Lavelle had no idea how long he had
been held captive. He'd lost consciousness after
being beaten up by the men at Portglenone, but
he'd thought it nothing compared to the prac-
tical interrogation exercise at Hereford. Now,
he was locked in a small cell like room. It had
nothing more than two bunk beds and a bucket,
which he had used. Through the small barred
window, he could hear the noise of vehicles,
marching, and every so often, voices shouting
- what he was hearing was German. He sat on
the side of his bunk, head in his hands feeling
faint from lack of food and water. Where was
he? Was he still at the monastery? Or was he at
that Nazi place Bob Deacon had told him about
when he arrived at London Airport?

The answer to his questions came when he
heard a key in the door and bolts being pulled
back. He could hardly believe his eyes. He
thought he must be dreaming. The person
who entered was immaculately dressed in the
uniform of a Nazi SS officer. He introduced
himself in stilted English as *Hauptsturmführer*

Wilhelm Boger. In a haughty Germanic tone, he informed Chris that he was his guest at the new Reich's headquarters in the Republic of Ireland. He said that he was in charge of the interrogation of prisoners, an art he had perfected at Auschwitz when he had had plenty of Yiddish scum to practice on. The mention of the death camp sparked Chris' memory. He had seen Boger's name on the list of those wanted for war crimes when he had been serving in West Germany. "You stupid Britishers think our War is over," he sneered. "Well, I have good news. The Reich is rising again. But, for you, not such good news. I doubt you live long enough to see our glory, you *Klumpen Scheiße,* lump of shit".

Chris tried hard to show bravado and laugh, but after the beating he'd been given at the monastery, his speech was slurred. "Piss off you fucking relic. Tell your stories to the leprechauns," he tried to speak in as strong a voice he could muster - although scarcely loud enough for Boger to hear. But he did manage to summon up just enough strength to seize his bucket and to throw its contents at the bastard Nazi. Boger screamed with anger and leapt back to avoid Chris' fecal matter. The attempt had been brave, but in such a weak state, it had only smeared the Nazi's jackboot, sufficient however to wipe the arrogance off Boger's face - and enough at least to give Chris some satisfaction. It didn't last long. Boger's clenched fist hit him full in the face and he once more passed out.

"Hiendrix! Get in here, *sehr schnell*, "yelled Boger. One of his assistants, a giant of a man strode into the room and stood stiffly to attention. "*Jawohl herr oberst*"

"Quickly, take my boots and clean them. Then when you come back, we will take this Britisher into the interrogation room. I'm looking forward to breaking this scum – as slowly and as painfully as I can".

Twenty or so minutes later, Chris was coming round. He could see that he had been moved from his cell into a large domed room with the Nazi was leaning over him. "Ah so! we have *ein harter Mann,* a hard man here, ja? Unbreakable ja? But I think not. Soon, like all my other cases you will tell me what I want to know. You will plead to die, and eventually, I will be kind and concede to your wish. However, first, let me introduce you to the menu of torture I'm about to inflict on your mind and your body." Boger enjoyed creating terror in his victims.

He detailed to the young British Captain what he called the Boger interrogation method. He showed Chris the device suspended from the

ceiling, like a trapeze artist's bar in a circus.
"This," he said pointing at the bar, "is what
earned me my 'Tiger of Auschwitz' reputation.
You will be stripped naked and bent over it,
your wrists tied to your ankles. Then Hiendrix
will push you off and swing you round like *ein
Karussell.* You call it a merry go round - ja?"
Again, Chris tried to show contempt with a
chuckle, but it emerged as nothing more than a
cackle. Boger ignored him and continued. "As
you go round, I will ask the questions. If I don't
like your answers, Klaus here, my other assist-
ant will punish you with this whip to loosen
your tongue." Klaus showed Chris his instru-
ment of torture. A nine-inch-long handle with
a dozen or more thin chains connected to it.
Each chain was about 2 feet long and had what
looked like barbs at their ends. Inwardly, Chris
shuddered. His body was already weak. He
felt half dead, suffering from lack of food and
water. However, he managed to mutter a reply
through his swollen lips, forcing yet another
feeble yet defiant retort. "Cleaned your boots
then have you, you medieval dinosaur. I've
seen worse bondage techniques on a night out
in Hamburg's Reeperbahn."

"Boger smiled, he knew the Reeperbahn well
from his masochistic youth - he liked defiant
victims. It made an interrogation more chal-

lenging, he thought.   Hiendrix and Klaus tore off the remnants of the monk's white habit from their victim and then with surprising care placed Chris over the trapeze bar, tying his hands and ankles tightly together.   Giving it a push, the carousel started to swing around the room, Boger asked him who had sent him to the monastery.   Chris started to sing 'Rule Britannia'.   That was not what Boger wanted to hear, it irritated him.   This time, he bawled his question.   Chris kept singing, stopped only when the first blow from the whip tore into his buttocks.   His singing turned into agonised screams.

The questioning and the flaying went on until Chris passed out.   Boger stopped the carousel and Hiendrix threw an ice-cold bucket of water over their victim.   Chris slowly recovered consciousness.   Again and again Boger shrieked at him asking who he was working for.   It took time for Chris to gather a reply.   "Bugger you, I had worse beatings at school," adding defiantly, "when do I get that cup of tea?"

Boger couldn't help but smirk.   The braver they are, the more he enjoyed breaking them.   And this candidate could be one of the best.   He was about to start the 'whirligig' again when Hertha Bothe burst into the interrogation room.   She was momentarily shocked by the blood torn body hanging from the ceiling. It took a moment for her to remember she was a Nazi 'she devil'. She forced a leering smile. "Herr Boger, I apologise for disturbing your excellent work, but the Colonel needs you urgently in the house."

Boger could hardly contain his exasperation at being disturbed. Torture to him was like sexual foreplay and he was working up to a big climax here. But *Obergruppenfuhrer* Skorzeny was to be obeyed. Reluctantly, he stood back. "Thank you, Fraulein Bothe." Turning to his men, he told them to take the prisoner down and put him back in his cell. "We'll deal with him later. Rub salt into his wounds - that will teach the *schweinhund* piece of shit to be disrespectful about my interrogation techniques." He gave one last evil smirk at his victim.

Boger left and the two guards, watched by Fraulein Bothe, untied Chris and between them carried him out of the interrogation room to his cell. He was barely conscious; his buttocks were on fire. As much as he fought the pain and tried to remain silent, he couldn't help letting out a long tortuous scream as the white-hot agony of salt sank into his open wounds. Once again, relief came as he fell into unconsciousness.

Gillian had previously heard Otto's conversa-

tion with the IRA leader when Finbar had told
him about the arms dump disaster at Portglenone. From her GOLD meetings in London,
she remembered the discussion about how
important its destruction was to Operation Rat
Trap. So that's the brave hero who carried out
the attack single-handed, she thought. Behind
her fixed Fraulein Bothe smile, she was resolute
and coldly determined to find a way to help him
escape - or even just protect him from further
physical torture - even if it cost her her own
life. I'll get you out of this somehow and I will
kill that *putain de salaud* Boger before all this is
over, she vowed.

Now back in the main house, Gillian stood
outside the drawing room eavesdropping on
what Otto had to say to his assembled Shamrock team.

"I have heard from 'Axel' in London. He tells me
the British are aware of our plans. How much
they actually know, Axel's contact couldn't find
out. The destruction of our explosives store at
the monastery could be the start of their efforts
to counter our offensive. We have the man
responsible for that under the care of *Hauptsturmführer* Boger." He looked inquiringly at
Boger, who was still sweating from the strenu-
ous business of interrogating the prisoner. He

confirmed with a nod.

"He will talk, be assured of that, even the hardest of my victims break, it's only a matter of time."

"Time is what we don't have," replied Skorzeny angrily. "Get back there now, and find out what he knows, then exterminate *das Schwein.*"

As soon as Gillian heard that Boger was about to leave the meeting, she stepped back from her eavesdropping at the door and sat on the chair in the hallway next to the phone looking down at the knitting she had in her hands. If she was going to save the prisoner from a certain and horrific death, she had to act now. Boger barely glanced at her as he rushed past on his way back to the prisoner. Nor did he notice the slight prick as the needle like dart from Gillian's knitting needle penetrated the back of his uniform. He opened Martinstown's main door and ran. In the ten seconds it took for the poison to work, he'd reached the door of the interrogation centre. He staggered, clutched desperately at the door frame and collapsed on the ground, writhing in fatal agony.

Gillian was back in the kitchen when one of the guards barged through the front door and burst into the Shamrock meeting. "*Entschuldigung*

Oberst, Chef, Herr Boger ist draußen zusammenge-brochen - Colonel Sir, Herr Boger has collapsed outside."

Gillian heard the uproar as the meeting erupted. Doctor Mengele and Otto rushed past the guard followed by others from the meeting. They saw the body of Boger lying contorted on the ground. At first, they thought he'd been shot, but there was no wound or blood on the ground. Mengele saw the purple colour of his face and bulging eyes. It was an obvious seizure, perhaps a heart attack, but there was no doubt he was dead.

Gillian came and stood by the front door, watching the spectacle of Nazis gathered around Boger's body. Memories of her harsh time as an inmate at Ravensbrück camp flooded back into her mind. She felt sick but elated at the same time. Peter Fleming, you're a bloody genius, she thought, your dart was an instant success. Such a shame though - Boger should have had the slow and painful death he deserved - like so many of his victims. At least, she'd postponed further torture of the prisoner. She briefly thought of throwing her knitting wool bomb into the crowd around Boger's body. But she dismissed the idea. She didn't know how effective it would be. Plus, it would certainly blow her cover and any chance of helping Boger's victim.

Standing over his chief torturer's body, Otto spoke in a cold and calm way. "Wilhelm could have died from natural causes, but with this and the death of my Dorothea, I'm not so sure. Two deaths are too much of a coincidence, I suspect we have a spy in our midst." His penetrating eyes searched around the gathered circle of his *Kriegsrat,* war council and camp guards hoping to see guilt in one of them. "So all of you, take extra care, watch out for anything or anyone suspicious. We must launch our *Blitzkrieg* immediately."

There were grunts of acknowledgement from his shocked audience.

"You" he turned to one of the guards. "Take the body of *Hauptsturmführer* Boger into his workshop." Then to Mengele, he added. "Josef, after we finish our meeting, find out for me how he died." His cruel and scarred face slowly swept round his silent audience again looking for the assassin. "If it's murder, I will hang the *Schweinhund* killer on meat hooks and leave him to the crows as I did with the vermin who tried to assassinate our Fuhrer. Now we finish our meeting. After that, we will telex Spain and tell them Shamrock is imminent. They must be prepared to launch as soon as I give my order. We will now decide on the precise timing of our attack and inform the IRA.

The Shamrock meeting reconvened. It was too dangerous for Gillian to listen. 'C' had told her that both the telex and telephone lines out of Martinstown were tapped and so the Irish and British intelligence services should know the Nazi's change of plans and set Rat Trap in motion. There was no time to be lost. First thing was to put the prisoner out of his misery. She quietly crossed the hall and walked out of the main house to the cells of Boger's workshop. There was just one guard on the door. When she told him that the Colonel had asked her to check on the prisoner, he stood back and let her enter.

The excruciating pain of salt in his wounds had almost receded. Chris was hardly conscious. He saw the face of a woman looking down at him. Probably some vindictive turd come to goad and gloat, he thought, and prepared himself mentally for more pain. But her voice was gentle and she spoke in a whisper. He didn't need to know anything more than she was on his side. She just told him that she was a friend. She knew the pain of salt in his wounds was horrendous but said it would keep infection at bay. "I've no time to explain now, but things here are about to erupt and these scumbag Nazis will be erased from the planet. You should be free within the next 48 hours. In the meantime, would you like a pill to knock you out?"

Chris, hardly able to raise his head, managed a grunted affirmative.

Gillian undid the heel of her shoe and took out several pills, each a different colour. The blue one was a knockout for 24hours, the red one gave oblivion for between two or three days and the black one, coated with rubber was the cyanide pill. She was keeping that one for herself, just in case. She selected the red pill and put the rest back in the tiny compartment.

"When you come round, it should be all over and you will probably be in hospital being looked after properly." She eased his mouth open and gently placed the pill on his tongue. The pain was becoming so unbearable that even if she was a Nazi, what had he got to lose. If the pill was poison, death would be a welcome relief from his raw suffering. Even if the pill was a truth drug, Scopolamine or whatever, he'd not much to tell anyway. So, what the hell he reasoned, and swallowed.

CHAPTER 38

When Fraulein Bothe, Gillian, returned to the house, Otto was in the hallway on the phone. As she made her way to the kitchen, she heard him talking in Spanish, *"La Operación Shamrock debía lanzarse a las cinco en punto del lunes por la mañana, es decir, dentro de tres días."* She only had a smattering of the language, but understood the mention of Shamrock, 'three days' and 'five o'clock'. It was enough to set alarm bells ringing. Could Skorzeny be changing his attack schedule? The phone line was probably tapped by the Irish security services or MI6, but could she rely on that? Whatever, she decided, it was too important to leave to chance. She had to make sure and pass on what she thought she heard. The only way was to use the phone, but could she call again without being detected? Perhaps she could use Peter's ball of wool bomb and assassinate Skorzeny. That would bugger his bloody *Blitzkrieg*. In the end, she decided to wait and catch him together with as many of his cohorts as possible.

Otto came into the kitchen. His whole aura had

changed. The adrenalin fueled excitement of being able to get back to his first love, war, was like a drug. His tone to her now took on an aggressive edge - that of a commander about to go into battle. "Fraulein Bothe." No more 'Hertha'. "Take this message immediately to the radio room and tell them to broadcast it to all farm unit commanders. They will be here tomorrow afternoon at 3.00pm, so prepare the conference room and food for them. It will be my final briefing before we attack. And Frau Bothe, I want you to take Wilhelm's place and see what you can squeeze out of the Britisher prisoner." He smirked, making his scar disfigured face look even more fanatical. "With your camp guard experience at Ravensbrück-Stutthof camp, you should enjoy that. Heil Hitler!"

"*Jawohl Herr Oberst,* Heil Hitler." Gillian, acting her part, stood stiffly to attention, arm raised in salute. She took the handwritten message from Skorzeny and rushed out to obey his command. A quick glance at the order to his commanders confirmed what she had overheard. The time for launching the Nazi attack was there, set in concrete. The note instructed them to be at Martinstown for a final briefing at 3.00pm tomorrow. If there wasn't a line tap, perhaps the Allies were aware that the Nazis were using ex *Wehrmacht Funkgerät* radios and were monitoring transmissions. But that was a long shot - she would have to carry out her own plan. The ideal time to catch all the Nazi rats was when the commanders from the farms were being briefed together in the dining room.

But Gillian need not have worried. Not only was there a wiretap on the Martinstown telephones, but the Nazi telex messages in and out were being decoded and their radio traffic monitored.

After delivering the message to the communications orderly, Gillian walked briskly over to the interrogation centre. The guard didn't even bother to greet her. He simply grunted a *'hallo'* as he opened the door. Inside, she walked down the short dark corridor to the cell door. Still ajar as she had left it. Obviously, nobody had been in to check on the prisoner. Chris appeared white, lifeless and hardly breathing. Anyone giving him a casual glance would think him dead or in a coma, useless for interrogation.   And, by the time you come round young man, she thought, you'll be free. The bunk on the other side of the cell had been empty on her last visit. Now she saw it was occupied by Wilhelm Boger's body, his face a frozen mask, grotesquely swollen and distorted, with his eyes bursting out of their sockets. The stench of open bowels filled the space. She thought of all the thousands of innocent people he'd tortured and murdered - If there is an afterlife, may you burn in the eternal fires of hell, *cul plus gros.*

CHAPTER 39

Chink and Sean MacEoin, sitting in Chink's study at Bellamont, had spent an hour-long secure conference telephone call with Field Marshal Sir Richard Hull, 'C', Roger Hollis, and Kesselring. The wiretap had revealed that Otto knew the date for his attack on May 20 had been blown. His *Blitzkrieg* had now been rushed forward to Monday, in just 48 hours' time. Operation Rat Trap was hardly more than an agreed coalition of military forces. On the positive side, Portglenone had been neutralised and the IRA were no longer an issue, but no strategy or implementation tactics had been agreed. They had all been caught unawares - what was the way forward?

It was Kesselring who had stated the obvious. Whilst he said he would be delighted to help in any way he could, it was obvious to him that Chink's military genius was unparalleled and he should be invited to take charge. Everyone else should provide whatever resources he needed. Sean backed the *Feldmarschall's* suggestion. He stressed that Chink understood Skorzeny better than anyone else, and he knew the layout of the enemy HQ at Martinstown. Agreement to the suggestion had been unanimous, echoing down the telephone lines. Chink had reluctantly accepted the nomination.

When the conference call ended, Chink and Sean both sat back, momentarily stunned by the task ahead. There was no time to be lost, they had only a matter of hours. Operation Rat Trap was still valid, but could they put everything in place and squeeze it into the short timescale they had?

"So," the Irish General turned to Chink, "where do we go from here?"

Whiskey always had a part to play to help focus the mind and so Chink went to his drinks cupboard, took out a bottle of Bushmills and two glasses, and poured them both a generous measure. Then he opened the top drawer of his desk and took out a large roll of paper which he spread out. . It was the rough layout of Martinstown he'd drawn for the Ninja Katsumi Akanari. It showed the house, the buildings, the drive and the lane leading to the estate.

"Sean, you said at our meeting with de Valera, we need to crush the snake's head. Well, that's exactly what we must to do – strike first and destroy Martinstown." He switched on his Anglepoise lamp to give a clearer view over the diagram. "This large building over here" he said pointing to the schematic, "is where the Nazi rats have their weapons and vehicles stored. Otto told me they had a fortified ammunition arsenal beneath it. And here," he put his finger on another small building, "is their communications centre." Chink went on to explain his immediate thoughts. He asked Sean what troops were stationed at the Curragh military base. Sean told him there were about 400 men, a 3 inch Stokes mortar platoon, some Irish Rangers, he wasn't sure how many, and a squadron of Vickers Mark VIII armoured cars.

" It's vital that we are able to keep in close contact with everyone Sean. What short range communications kit have you got? "

"We're still using the old valve Motorola SCR536 handie-talkies - good enough for 'D' Day, so I'm sure they will be fine - and we've got dozens of them."

"Perfect." Chink mulled over his whiskey for some minutes, then spoke. "Surprise is the key to our success. Otto's men will be nervous. They've just had their *Blitzkrieg* brought forward a full month. They will be buzzing around trying hard to make sure they have everything ready. And right now, Skorzeny will think he has the initiative. He won't be expecting us to take the fight to him. So, this is how I see it working." He paused, taking another gulp from his glass.

Again, he pointed to the map. "I want you to put the mortar platoon split between here and here in the field 700 yards away from the main buildings. They will have a clear view of their targets, the weapons and arms store, the communications centre and will have some protection from enemy fire by the slope of the land there. There are two places they should avoid, the main house because our undercover agent is in there, and this place here," Chink pointed to a small building near to the house, "that's the bastards' interrogation centre - our man who destroyed the arms dump at Portglenone is in there, hopefully still alive."

Chink continued. "We know Skorzeny has called a meeting of his Nazi farm commanders for 1800hrs on Sunday. As soon as they've all arrived for their final briefing, a couple of your men should silently neutralise the guard at the entrance to the drive up to Martinstown. Then barricade both ends of the lane to block the enemy's escape routes. A couple of the armoured cars could be used for that. And for all the other roads around and behind the farm, put up temporary road blocks. How does that sound to you, Sean?"

Chink's mind was back in North Africa before the decisive battle at El Alamain. This, he thought, would not be on the same scale, but the key to success was surprise.

"That's all very well as far as it goes, Chink, but what then? Do we go in with the infantry? Sure, it could be a bloodbath. Those nasties have their Spandau machine guns and will be mowing our men down like cutting hay before they get to the buildings."

"No, not if it works out the way I think it will, there'll be minimum loss of life, on our side anyway. When the Nazi farm commanders leave their briefing, which could be any time after 1830hrs or thereabouts, they will drive out and be stopped by the barricades. They won't have time to reverse back into the shelter of Martinstown because your troops will swoop and overwhelm them. With luck, they should be so shaken and stunned by the unexpected ambush, they will surrender without a shot being fired - if they resist, your men shoot to kill. And, by the way, make sure their weapons have silencers fitted - it's vital we don't alert Skorzeny with small arms fire before the mortar attack."

Chink continued to discuss his strategy with Sean until they had settled the complete battle plan. They'd finally agreed that the mortar attack would commence once the farm commanders were captive. It would last for no more than 10 minutes, raining shells at a rate of twenty-five shells per minute on the enemy barracks and armoury. And as a precaution Chink also suggested that some of the infantry should be placed with the mortar platoon just in case any of the Nazi troops attempted to counter-attack.

After the mortar barrage, Chink would demand Skorzeny's surrender. "Is it the whiskey talking now? Do you think such a warrior like Otto is going to be walking out with his little white flag?" kidded the Irish General with a smile. "Let that be a surprise for you, Sean. It'll be a touch of the theatricals and I'm positive they will accept." Sean remained sceptical, but he knew his friend well enough to know that whatever Chink had in mind would be a corker of an idea.

"However, Sean," Chink continued, "no matter how much we think we have the detail covered, the best laid plans etc., We'll have to be on our toes and prepared for the unknown."

Chink saw his friend off, agreeing to meet at the Curragh base at lunch time the next day, the day they would trap the rats.

It was late evening and he knew he should try to get some sleep, but he had one piece of his plan to arrange. After which, he would update 'C'. He fixed his portable scrambler to his phone and called Peter Fleming.

"Peter. We are going in on the attack tomorrow evening and I urgently need your help." Chink went on to outline his idea. The MI6 boffin thought it brilliant and agreed to Chink's request. "If I start now, I should have everything put together by dawn tomorrow morning. I'll fly into Langford Lodge and drive over to you. Then we can all go together down to the rallying point."

After finalising exactly what he needed Peter to bring with him, Chink rang 'C'. He outlined the plan he and Sean had agreed and what he had asked Peter to supply. He also asked 'C' to coordinate the airborne attacks on the Nazi farms with Bob Deacon and the Irish Rangers. They should be in the air ready to drop at dusk Sunday evening, but wait for my signal. Timing is critical. And, if everything works out as I think it will, they may not indeed be needed.

CHAPTER 40

It was early Sunday evening just after 1800hrs and the last of the farm commanders had arrived, dressed like the others in his *SS* uniform. He greeted Gillian with a rigid 'Heil Hitler' salute. It physically hurt her to return it with the false enthusiasm her role demanded, but not for much longer, she thought. She showed him into the large dining room where Otto and the others were waiting. Gillian hadn't met any of them before, and it was her constant worry that one of these might have known the real Hertha Bothe. The worry was well-founded. As soon as everyone had arrived, Otto called a guard and told him to bring a crate of German beer for the meeting and told him to tell Fraulein Bothe in the kitchen they were now ready for food. Minutes later, Gillian entered the room with a large tray carrying plates of Alsacienne *flammkuchen* flatbread, *kuchen* cake, and sandwiches, and distributed them along the table.

She was about to leave the room when one of the farm commanders called her name. It was *Sturmbannfurer* Weiss, the Corkan Island farm commander. He was a typical Nazi, a short serious looking man with a small, mean mouth and Himmler style round wire-rimmed glasses. He looked more intellectual than the others and could have easily been taken for a librarian or a government official. But his cold blue eyes gave him away and she inwardly shuddered as he stared at her. Hard, cruel and utterly soulless.

"Fraulein Bothe?" Weiss rose repeating her name as if he was digging deep into his memory. "Did I hear our O*bergruppenfuhrer* correctly? You are Hertha Bothe - yes?"
"Ja, mein Herr" she replied nervously.
"You were an *aufseherin,* a camp guard, at Ravensbrück, am I not right?" He smiled like a cobra about to strike.
"*Ja, Herr Obers,*" there was a slight tremor in Gillian's voice.

"Sit down *Sturmbannfurer*, no time for small talk. We are all comrades here." Otto spoke tersely. Then to Gillian in a commanding tone. "Fraulein Bothe, leave the room and bring us coffee, quickly woman - *sehr schnell.*"

"*Jawohl Chef!*" Feeling relief at the chance to escape, she started quickly to leave, but froze when Weiss shrieked "*Halt!*" Ignoring Skorzeny, his drew his weapon, a luger pistol and pointed it at Gillian. "Ah so!" he paused, looking

at the startled faces around the table, then back
at Gillian. "Who have we here? – turn around
woman." Gillian slowly turned. Without taking his eyes of her, Weiss addressed Skorzeny,
his voice seething with venom.

"*Entschuldigung meine Obergruppenfuhrer*,
excuse me Colonel. This woman, this *Abschaum*
scum, is not the Fraulein Bothe I worked with.
This is an imposter. The Hertha Bothe I knew
was a tall, thin, blonde woman. We were close
friends at Ravensbrück, *Herr Oberst*. This fraud
is half a metre shorter. Has she shrunk? Has she
dyed her hair? I think not."

This was the moment Gillian had dreaded,
someone who had actually met the real Hertha
Bothe. Her cover was blown. If she had her
knitting with her, it would have been an ideal
time to use it, but she did the next best thing.
She made a dash for the door. If she could
reach the kitchen, she could still use her bomb.
She almost made it, but too late, Weiss fired.
She crashed to the ground, a paralysing pain
slammed through her thigh, lying screaming in
agony, unable to move.

Everyone, including Skorzeny, was stunned,
shocked by the scene in front of them. Then
pandemonium broke out, Gillian screaming,
everyone shouting and Otto, banging the table

in an attempt to restore order.

"*Um Himmels willen, halt die Klappe und setz dich* - For God's sake, silence!" he yelled, still hardly able to believe what had played out before his eyes. Quickly, the noise abated, everyone looked apprehensively at their leader, Gillian sobbing bitterly in the doorway.

"You Weiss, *Meine Gott,* well done man. Bring the *Ungeziefer* vermin here." Weiss and one of the other commanders wrenched Gillian to her feet and dragged her along the floor to the *Obersturmbannführer*. "*Das Weibsstück,* slut." He thwacked her face viciously with the back of his hand. He was incandescent with rage, but he knew he had to keep control of his emotions at such a critical moment. "So, bitch, whoever you are. What do we call you? Who are you working for?"

Summoning up as much strength and pride as she could she spat full into Skorzeny's face. Shocked, he wiped the spittle off his face with his sleeve and hit her again, this time with his fist. Her head shot back with the force of the blow. If it wasn't for the two holding her, she would have collapsed to the floor. She was hardly conscious, but she managed a sneer of defiance, "*du Hurensohn - you son of a whore.*"

Skorzeny ignored her slur. If his plans had any chance of success, he had to launch his Shamrock *Blitzkrieg* immediately. *"Meine Kommandeure,* my Commanders, we have been over our plans before, you know your orders. With this betrayal, we don't have time for more discussion or refinement. Check your watches gentlemen, it is now almost 1822hrs. Shamrock *Blitzkrieg* will launch at 0500hrs tomorrow morning. Now - you must leave and return to your posts to carry out your orders. Remember; strike fast, strike hard, be ruthless and be brutal - that way we will be victorious."

The farm commanders rose, and stood stiffly, heels clicking and raising their right arms in the Nazi salute. With one voice they roared *"Sieg Heil"*, and as they marched out to their waiting cars, Skorzeny called after Weiss, "One moment *Sturmbannfurer* Weiss." Weiss hurried back into the room.

"Jawohl Chef," ignoring Gillian, he stood stiffly to attention looking directly at Skorzeny.

"I can't thank you enough *Sturmbannfurer*. You are a true Aryan patriot and when we are victorious, you will be amply rewarded."

"D*anke mein kommandant."* Weiss once again

gave the Nazi salute and hurried out to his waiting car.

Skorzeny turned to Andrija Artuković, the Croation 'Butcher of the Balkans'. "You, Artuković," snarled Skorzeny, take this *Stück Scheiße* piece of shit into the kitchen and use your expertise on her. We can't waste time. We must know who she works for and what damage she might have caused before we launch our attack."

The brute of a man stood. Unlike the others, he had remained ice calm during the drama. He'd lived a life inflicting wholesale bloody slaughter on innocents and the anticipation of making Gillian talk brought a evil smile to his face. He stood, gave a courteous bow. "It will be my pleasure, Colonel." Then grabbing Gillian by her hair, he dragged her screaming with pain from the meeting room and into the kitchen. "And Artuković," Otto barked after him, "be quick."

"While Andrija interrogates that traitorous woman, we must make sure our mobile units and stormtroopers are ready and prepared for action. Fritz, go and tell the *Hauptscharführer*, Sergeant Major, Fischer that I want to inspect them and their weapons on the parade ground in full fighting kit."

"*Jawohl,*" Fritz Suhren hurried out and went in

search of   the Sergeant Major.

The Yugoslavian brute flung Gillian onto the table in the middle of kitchen, like meat onto a butcher's block, and looked around for instruments he could use to torture her. Three kitchen knives, a meat cleaver, string and a bucket.

"You heard the Colonel. Talk, you bitch! Be quick. Who are you and who sent you?" But Gillian's mind was paralysed by the devastating pain of her wound, made worse by his manhandling of her. She couldn't have answered even if she'd wanted to. No answer annoyed the impatient Yugoslav. "Bitch - talk" he snarled. "I'll soon loosen your tongue." With that, he tied a tourniquet with the string around her right wrist, raised the meat cleaver and with one blow severed her hand. Thankfully, Gillian was hardly conscious and was fast losing blood from the gaping hole in her side. She scarcely felt the sadistic assault of the monster. She was beyond pain. Through the curtain of her semi-consciousness, she could see the ogling face of her tormentor. She knew she was going to die slowly. She felt strangely at peace - was she back at the Natweiler extermination camp - her mind was deserting her. Again, he fired his questions at her. Still no answer. He tied another tourniquet, this time around her left wrist. With another vicious blow, her other hand hit the floor.

"Who sent you bitch?" He shouted again and again. But Gillian was slowly fading into a welcome unconsciousness and couldn't react. This angered the frustrated Artuković even more. It was critical he found out who this imposter was for the Colonel before she died.
Butchering her was obviously not working. He could tell she was resigned to dying. How could he break through to her mind before it was too late? Then he saw her knitting on the kitchen dresser. It gave him an idea. "Bitch, tell me who sent you or I will take each of your eyes out and skewer them onto your own knitting needles."

Gillian managed a scornful smile. *"visage de chatte* - you subhuman freak, do it, just do it." she hissed. She knew it would end her pain and suffering.

This infuriated Artuković, who swung the cleaver again, this time pinning her bleeding right arm to the table. It only brought a whimper from Gillian. She was past caring and knew she was about to die. He picked up the ball of knitting. Then, glowering over his victim, he grabbed her by the jaw and forcibly turned her head to look at him. The thought of what he was about to do brought a witch-like cackle from Gillian. He grasped both needles. *Au re-*

voir putain de salaud, you bastard, she thought as he pulled both needles free of the wool.

The huge explosion blew out the windows and the doors off their hinges. Artuković was obliterated. His corpse shredded amongst the wreckage of the kitchen and through the gap where the window had been onto the lawn outside. The table was demolished scattering Gillian's remains onto the floor. And in that split second before death engulfed her, she felt the peace and satisfaction of revenge.

CHAPTER 41

Skorzeny was just winding up his briefing next door, when the blast from the kitchen hit them. The solid walls of Martinstown held fast, but shards of window glass flew in all directions, pieces of ceiling showered down striking those below and the air was thick with a fog of white dust.

Shock fuelled mayhem filled the room, confused shrieks, choking, and spluttering. For a split second, Skorzeny himself was stunned by the explosion, but dusting himself down, he quickly took command, yelling "Schnell, raus, raus, get outside quickly."

They stumbled their way out of the room through the wrecked hallway. The front door had blown open and was hanging on a single hinge. Outside, Fritz Suhren and *Sturmscharführer* Fischer were marshalling the troops pouring out of their barracks on the other side of the parking area, bringing out their motor bike/sidecar machine-gun combinations – all distracted by the explosion that had shaken the house.

Apart from superficial cuts from the flying
bits of glass and ceiling plaster, Mors, Menten,
Mengele and Otto had escaped serious hurt.
As they dusted themselves down, Otto told
them that he was going back inside to see what
happened in the kitchen. In the meantime, he
instructed Mors to inspect the men. "When you
are satisfied with their readiness *Sturmbannführer*, tell Fischer to stand them down until
0400hrs when we prepare to launch the real
thing."

Not waiting for an answer, Otto went back into
the hallway and coughed his way through the
debris towards the opening that had once been
the kitchen. The place was a total wreck. A ceiling beam had fallen and blocked what had been
the door to the outside and there was a gaping
hole where the window had been. There was no
sign of the Yugoslav, only debris littered with
flesh and body parts and stark splashes of red
throughout the scene. Then he saw the mangled body of the Hertha Bothe imposter on the
floor amongst the rubble.

First, the death Frau Binz, then the destruction
of the arms dump at the Monastery, Boger's
killing, and now this, Skorzeny's mind was in
turmoil. It was Folens who had introduced the

bitch. "That *scheisse gesicht* shit face Folens," he roared. "That Belgian scum, that traitorous pig dog." For moments that seemed like hours, he stood looking at the wreckage, incandescent rage consuming his senses. Thoughts of what else Folens might have revealed to the enemy rankled in his mind. Who else was preparing to betray him?

But he was a professional soldier. He fought to control his emotions, finally replacing his anger with a cold determination. Nothing, but nothing, was going to stop his *Blitzkrieg*, he swore to himself.

As he picked his way back outside to the others, the communication clerk ran up to him. "*Herr Oberst, Sie ist ein Fernschreiben aus Spanien,*" a message from Spain. Otto seized the sheet of paper from his outstretched hand and focused his eyes - a terse message from Ramcke. '*Franco blocked all planes. Unable to launch offensive. Good luck - signed General der Fallschirmtruppe Ramcke.*' The news was a killer blow - a disaster. Instead of the 500 plus troops from Spain and the 2000 from Argentina still awaiting his signal to launch, he only had his SS Stormtroopers at Martinstown and the farms. There was the IRA and they would cause havoc in the North, but now the odds were piling high against him - the vision of a Fourth Reich was vanishing before his eyes.

CHAPTER 42

At that moment, all hell broke loose. Martins-town was under attack. The sound of rapid mortar fire shocked Skorzeny into action. He could hear the dull thump, thump of firing followed by rapid explosions as shells hit the outbuildings. He told Josef Mengele and Pieter Menten to get back into the house for shelter, then quickly ran over to join Mors, and Fritz Suhren, who were both sheltering behind one of the Mercedes limousines parked near the house. The mortar fire was coming from a field about seven hundred yards behind Martins-town.

They could see puffs of white smoke as shells were fired, but the attackers were hidden in a small hollow. After a quick discussion, Mors said he would take six of his men to neutralise the mortars. But as Mors was running over to the barracks, there was an almighty explosion which threw him and those around him off their feet. The mortar fire had penetrated the Nazi arsenal. Mors slowly stood up, staggered a few steps, then fell and lay motionless. From

around the destroyed buildings, men were
emerging, many wounded, some staggering,
some hardly able to walk, all visibly shattered
by the eruption.

From behind the Mercedes, Skorzeny and
Suhren had been protected from the worst of
the blast. Seeing Mors was either unconscious
or dead, Skorzeny told Fritz Suhren to take over
the counter attack on the mortars. He had
no sooner gone to round up some men, when
the mortar fire stopped as suddenly as it had
started. An eerie silence ensued, broken only
by the cries of the wounded, his once glorious
SS Wehrmacht. Skorzeny's exhilaration for
forthcoming action drained away. It was catastrophic. But they would fight on, he knew no
such word as 'surrender'.

The farms would now be preparing to play their
parts in the Shamrock *Blitzkrieg*; the Corkan
Island Fallschirmjäger paratroopers would be
sitting in their troop carrier planes ready to
take off and seize Dublin airport.

Martinstown should be buzzing with men,
preparing to move off to seize the Irish capital,
not this rabble he saw in front of him. As
he stood surveying the scene, he saw his SS
Sergeant Major Fischer, his uniform in tatters,
left arm bloody and hanging limply. He was
moving around trying to muster survivors into

some semblance of order. Skorzeny screamed at him. *"Sturmscharführer!"* Fischer limped over as quickly as he could and stood to attention in front of his commander. Skorzeny ignored the fact that he needed medical attention. "We will strike immediately. Get your assault troops mounted and ready to leave."

Skorzeny watched him as he hobbled away to carry out his orders, rounding up the motor-bike crews with their Spandau machine guns mounted on their sidecars. It was a slow process. Eventually, Fischer returned to face him, but even in the short time he'd been gone to carry out his orders, his demeanour had flagged. He still managed to stand ramrod straight, but the expression on his blanched face not only showed the pain and suffering from his shattered arm, but there were signs of panic and alarm in his eyes.

"So, *Sturmscharführer*, how many of our motor-cycle crew are ready for action?"

Skorzeny didn't like the answer he got. Fischer told him that of the thirty-six motorbike com-binations, only eleven had survived the mortar attack and even then, there weren't enough riders and gunners. Fischer had been in Ireland for six years. He now saw that Skorzeny's prom-ised wealth and a new Reich was no more than a pipe dream. He'd had enough.

"*Entschuldigung Herr Oberst*," his voice now with the tone of defeat, "We want no more of this. Your men are broken. Let us lay down our arms and go back to our Irish homes." Skorzeny's build-up of frustration and anger focused on Fischer. "You, you... *Schweinhund und Feigling,* traitorous dog." Without a second thought, he drew his pistol and shot him at point blank range. The look of surprise on Fischer's face was reflected by the horror and dismay of his men as he collapsed in front of them. He would never again see his wife and children and the home he had built in Galway.

It was as if the shot that killed Fischer was a signal to the enemy. "Skorzeny - Colonel Otto Skorzeny" an unseen voice bellowed out of the dusk. "We, the Army of Ireland, call on you to surrender. You are surrounded by our tanks and special forces. Tell your troops to throw down their arms, walk out and they will not be harmed. If not, you will all be annihilated." The message was repeated in German.

Suddenly, the roar of tanks revving their engines, drowning the cries and moans of the wounded SS soldiers. Again, the voice. "Twenty minutes to make your decision," interrupted this time by the deafening explosions of another salvo of mortar shells impacting the wreckage of the arsenal. "Next time, you, your house and your men will be the target. We captured your farm commanders as they left your compound, and we will be eliminating the farm compounds before the night's out. It is now up to you - surrender or die." For Skorzeny, it was a nightmare. Surrender was unthinkable.

Then another voice, one this time he knew, came over the loudspeaker. It was Finbar Kelly, Chief of the IRA. "You deranged arseshite Skorzeny. You didn't just want to help our cause, you had other ideas didn't you. I was told of your fecking plans by our President, Mr de Valera himself. You and your Nazi shites can rot in hell for all we care and if you don't all bloody surrender, we'll be sending you there."

Then another voice blared out. "Otto my friend, the game's up. Tell your men to lay down their arms." Skorzeny could hardly believe it. It was the traitor, Albert Folens. Hearing him sent Otto into an even greater rage. Folens continued. "I made my home here in Ireland and I don't want to see that destroyed. You are delusional, utterly mad. Give up now or you and all your men will be destroyed together with your nightmare of a dream."

By now, his once crack SS troops were starting

to lay down their arms and the motorbike riders with their sidecar machine gun passengers were dismounting. Josef Mengele came up and put his arm around his friend. "It looks like all the cards are stacked against us, Otto. We've lost all our support. It's just us now. The odds are overwhelming."

Then a final voice. *"Obersturmbannführer Skorzeny. Das ist Generalfeldmarschall Kesselring."* Speaking in German so that all the troops could understand, the old German military leader, Kesselring continued. "I command you all to lay down your arms and proceed down the drive with hands behind their heads. The President of the Irish Republic has given me his word that you will all be treated with leniency, given either Irish citizenship or a safe trip to South America." He paused. "Unfortunately for you, Skorzeny and your fellow criminals, you will be taken into custody and put on trial for your crimes. *Sie haben nur vierzig Minuten*, you have ten minutes."

The noise of tanks and other vehicles revving their engines and moving into position plus a background of orders being shouted was all too much for the dejected Nazi troops. A trickle became a stream of the able-bodied helping their wounded comrades down the drive into the hands of the Irish army.

CHAPTER 43

Otto Skorzeny, Mengele and Menten stood at
the front door of Martinstown house watching
the Shamrock *Blitzkrieg* dream melt away. The
years of planning in Argentina all crumbling
into utter failure. But now was not the time for
emotions, he knew he had to accept the battle
was lost - a battle yes, not the end of the Reich.

He had no intention of ceding to the enemy,
his own bullet would be better, but he had
other plans. The three Nazis went back into the
house. They needed to escape. Before that they
had to destroy whatever confidential material,
they couldn't take with them. Entering the
dining room, they overturned the table and
were about to pile it with anything that would
burn, when Otto noticed a small metal box
taped to its underside. He recognised it for
what it was – a microphone transmitter, a spy
bug.

He could now see how all along, he had been
outwitted. The IRA, that phoney bloody ex
British General, that slimy government minister, Charles Haughey and that traitorous
pig, *verräterisches Schwein* Folens, they had all
been against him. Why hadn't he seen their

treachery long ago – perhaps it was all the good living. He had gone soft, blind to the scheming of others. He could only blame himself. He could rant and rave as much as he liked, but his focus now had to be on escape. Once they were safe, he could spend as much time as he liked having a post-mortem. So, they heaped chairs, curtains, rugs and pictures on top of the up-turned table.

Otto took a small holdall from the safe and gave it to Mengele. "Guard that with your life Herr doktor. That's to fund our escape. There's over a million dollars in mixed currencies."

"With respect Otto, no amount of money is going to save us. We are surrounded. Our troops are defeated and our farm commanders are already prisoners. You heard Kesselring. We have no choice. Escape is not an option"

"*Gotteh himmel,*" Otto cursed, "I thought better of you Josef, go on then, *abhauen*, run away. Join that SS rabble and surrender if you like, I won't stop you – you too Menten."

Terror-stricken, Pieter Menten looked at Mengele. He could see that Josef felt the same way he did. They were both wanted men for their war crimes. Surrender would mean certain death. "You know we can't surrender Colonel. If you have a plan, tell us."

"What do you mean 'if', you cretin. Do you think I'm a suicidal dog?" Otto was in two minds to shoot both men there and then. They were just passengers. His escape plan would work better alone. But he dismissed the idea. Despite his streak of ruthlessness and brutality, he was a man of honour. They were all Nazis. Josef was an old friend; Menten on the other hand had used the Reich for his own gain. He already had a large estate in Waterford, bought with Ratlines money. Once they were away from Martinstown, Otto could dump him. "Of course, I have a plan *Dummkopf*. I will explain all to you both later, but now we must be quick. First, I want you both to fetch three corpses from outside and bring them in here – any bodies will do. They are going to be our decoys"

They were both mystified, but there was no other choice, they had to trust Otto. Wasn't he the man who against all odds had led the daring rescue of the Italian Fascist dictator Benito Mussolini from the Gran Sasso distalia? And if the *Obersturmbannführer* had a plan, who were they to argue? They hurried outside to find the bodies and bring them back into the house. While they were gone, Otto took all the remaining papers out of the safe. He paused for a moment, looking at his Shamrock *blitzkrieg* plan, then shrugging and flung it onto the growing heap.

Menten and Mengele returned dragging the first corpse, an SS *Korporal,* as Otto was shutting the safe. They watched mesmerised as in a flurry of bottle openings, he drained the contents of the drink's cabinet onto the heap. "Don't just stand there. Go, hurry, *schnell*, we have little time. Throw that body on the pile and get out there and fetch the others."

They went out again and returned with a second corpse, then out again for the third. This time, they chose the Skorzeny's crack SS troops, now a shambles of shell shocked and walking wounded, were slowly making their way down the drive to surrender, when some saw Menten and Mengele, they hurled cat calls, threats and obscenities at the two men, but they ignored them, and this time dragged the body of *Sturmscharführer* Fischer into the house, throwing him alongside the other bodies on their funeral pyre.

"Excellent," said Skorzeny glowering. "The perfect end for our spineless *Sturmscharführer* eh!" Otto couldn't help but chuckle. "We put our hats in a pile away from the fire, so that whoever finds the charred remains will assume the bodies belong to us." With that, he took out his cigar lighter, lent forward and with one click torched the pyre. There was a whoosh as the alcohol caught and they watched as the flames took hold and flared around the bodies.

"Now, to get away. Follow me. We are going down into the wine cellar." Otto saw confusion on their faces, but they followed him into the hall. The cellar door had suffered damage, but Otto pushed it out of the way and led them down old stone steps into Martinstown cellar. It was small, no more than ten feet square. Dark and dank. Fortunately, the electricity still worked and as Otto switched on the light, they could see the left and right walls had shelves, with boxes of tinned foods, sacks and household supplies. On the wall facing them was a floor to ceiling wine rack with Otto's prized collection of vintage wines.

"First we must get out of our uniforms." Otto said, and took some of the sacks off the shelving and emptied the contents onto the cellar floor. "These are some of the civilian clothes our SS *unter Offizieren* were wearing when they first arrived at Martinstown. Find trousers, shirts, coats and hats to fit yourselves. No matter what we look like for now, we will be buying clothes later when we are safe. Shoes on the bottom shelf."

Rushing now, they changed, putting their

discarded uniforms into one of the empty sacks. Then taking a flashlight from one of the shelves, Otto shone it onto the top right-hand bottle in the rack. "Now for our secret escape route." He pulled the bottle out, reached in and pressed a button hidden at the back of the empty space. And as he did so, the centre of the rack swung open. A fog of dust billowed out from the opening that faced them, a cavern, no more than five feet high, three feet wide.

CHAPTER 44

Earlier, Chink and Sean watched as the mortar barrage hit Martinstown and seen the massive explosion as the arsenal was hit. "Radio the mortar platoon to stop firing," Sean told his second in command. Then to Chink, "time to try out your crazy boffin's idea."

"Well, you'll find out just how crazy he is," Chink replied, "His ideas may be 'off-the-wall', but from my experience, they never fail." With that, he ran over to Peter, who was immersed in a tangle of wires and plugs and told him to start his theatricals.

"Won't be a moment," Peter Fleming answered without looking up, "just making some final adjustments." He quickly finished his tinkering, stood up and turned to a console of switches he had lashed together, beneath which was a Grundig tape recorder. On it was a tape he had previously recorded of British Army tank manoeuvres outside Hamlin in West Germany.

"OK, ready. Bring on the performers. Sean,

the IRA Chief, Albert Folens, and Kesselring, who were still finalising their words stepped up to the microphone Peter had set up. "Right, get ready. On my cue, you go first Sean, then Finbar, then Albert and finally you sir, *Generalfeldmarschall*. Take it slowly and speak up because you will have the sound of tanks in the background."

He started the tape recorder, and the monster speakers blasted out the sound of Centurion tanks, their officers shouting to each other over the roar of their engines.

On cue, as soon as the mortar fire stopped, Peter, like the conductor of an orchestra, introduced the speeches, one after the other over the sound of the armour in the background. When they finished, they waited for the reaction from Skorzeny and his men. They hadn't long to wait.

A string of SS soldiers started to emerge from the driveway of Martinstown, bedraggled and defeated, with those that could, helping the wounded. Irish soldiers armed to the teeth, marshalled them along the barbed-wire lined lane, past the captured black Mercedes of Skorzeny's farm commanders, through a gateway and into a secure enclosure. The prisoners looked in vain for all the tanks they'd heard,

but apart from three armoured cars, there were
only the soldiers. They saw the farm commanders too, prominently on display, securely
bound.

A mixed team of military police and garda
were beginning to interrogate the prisoners.
Those who had previously settled in Ireland
were given the option to go home to their Irish
families on probation, otherwise, it was deportation. Those with Irish families who chose
to stay, were told they would have to report
to their local garda station every month for at
least two years. One missed visit, they were
told, and it was deportation.

An officer amongst the prisoners was de-
nounced by one of those who had chosen to
stay in Ireland. It was Fritz Suhren. Ignoring
Skorzeny's order to attack the enemy mortars,
he had realised the game was up and decided
get out, but not before trying to hide his identity by swopping his jacket with one of the dead
SS men. Chink, who had been watching the
line of prisoners, had been quick to recognise
Suhren. Despite his protests, he was immediately dragged out of the line of prisoners and
handcuffed.

Chink told Sean that Suhren was one of
Skorzeny's inner sanctum. He had been Com-

mandant of Ravensbrück concentration camp and was an escaped war criminal. There was a rope waiting for him in Munich. They both agreed to put him into one of the trucks under armed guard. As and when the Nazis had been routed, they would send him plus any others they captured to Mountjoy Prison in Dublin for onward transit to face their just desserts.

"Well, Peter, whoever would think that you could win a battle with a tape recorder," said Sean , putting a friendly arm around MI5's genius. Sure, that must have been the first-time stereo gear has ever been used in a military environment. Just bloody amazin'."

Peter grinned. "It was brilliant, quite right." He briefly enjoyed the accolade. "But you are praising the wrong man. It was Chink's idea. I just had to scramble like mad to put it all together."

Sean went over to Chink who was watching out for more of Otto's henchmen trying to evade detection, and thinking that perhaps the man himself might try a disguise. Sean congratulated him on his brilliantly thought up charade. "As I was sayin' to Peter, that was awesome. It sounded like bloody 'D' day all over again. Will you be looking at those Nazi rats no - wonderin' where the hell all our tanks are."

Chink merely nodded an acknowledgement.

"We have the initiative, but a cornered rat can be a deadly threat. Otto and some of his men are still in there. And once we've cleaned up here, we've got to decide how we deal with the farms."

"Well, the dribble of prisoners is drying up and I'm thinking it's time to send in a task force of my Rangers to neutralise any remaining SS fanatics, dispose of any booby traps and flush out that Skorzeny fella' and his friends. "

"Perfect, Sean, Chink replied, "and could you ask your boys to check any remaining out buildings for Chris Lavelle, our man they captured in Portglenone. With any luck, he may still alive".

"Will do." Sean said, and called over to an Irish Ranger Corporal standing nearby, keeping an eye on the surrendered. "McNally, go and find Captain Butler and bring him over here at the double!"

"Sah!", the young corporal saluted smartly and ran off.

The Captain came as quickly as he could. Sean showed him a copy of the map drawn by the Ninja Katsumi. "Butler, we don't know if there are any more Nazi bastards in there, but if there are, they will be fanatics, holed-up and ready to give you and your men a hot reception. Clean the buggers out. Watch out for booby traps and trip wires, and if this building here," he said pointing to the Nazi interrogation centre, "is still standing, one of our men may still be alive in there."

"And here," Chink chipped in, with his finger pointing to Martinstown house, "that's where we think the Nazi SS Colonel, Otto Skorzeny is holed up. Take care, we want him alive. Take the armoured cars with you." Sean continued. "If you meet any resistance, their fire power could prove useful!"

"With respect sir, looking at the layout of the area, the armoured cars will present too much of a target for the enemy; we'll have more flexibility if we take our Heckler and Koch assault rifles and a couple of rocket propelled grenade launchers."

"OK Captain, it's your call. Good luck. And radio in when it's safe for us to send in the medics."

Butler saluted, turned and dashed off to round up his team. Sean, Peter and Chink now had time to discuss how to deal with the farms. Sean said, "There are Anglo-Irish planes in the air ready to bomb the farms then drop our paras to finish them off. They just await the order."

However, Chink wasn't sure it was the right approach. "We've managed so far with minimum casualties on our side, and I want to keep it that way - and save the lives of as many of the enemy too. Most of them have been led up Otto's garden path with promises and, like most of these prisoners here, they just want to go back to their homes. Bombing raids are a last resort. Why don't we tell our planes to return to base and take leaflets to drop instead offering them the chance to surrender? Then your...."

"With respect Chink," Sean interrupted him in mid-flow. "I'm thinkin' you're going soft in your old age. A leaflet drop would take hours if not days to prepare and we could still have a fight on our hands at the end of it".

The two generals threw ideas at each other, each one being discarded for one reason or another. After some 20 minutes, they had almost reached a stalemate when Peter, who had been quietly standing by listening, broke in. "I do find you chaps so unimaginative." They looked at him, surprised and disconcerted by his interruption. "Think out of your tiny military boxes for a change. You have the answer to the farms under your noses. All the farm camp commanders are under lock and key. You have their staff cars. Their men at the farms have no idea what is happening here and are waiting for their leaders to return."

"Yes?   So. What are you suggesting?" Sean, slightly annoyed by the intrusion, looked baffled, still not seeing what Peter was driving at.

"It's so bleeding obvious, you clowns. You give the commanders an ultimatum. They tell their men the planned insurrection is dead in the water; *Sturmbannführer* Skorzeny has been defeated; his *Blitzkrieg* is no more; support troops from Spain or South America are non-existent - the Nazi bubble is burst; They lay down their weapons and go free."

"I'm not so sure they can just evaporate back into their previous lives, we'll have to see about that, but what's the other side of your proposed ultimatum," said Chink.

"Or, you shoot them right here and now for leading an insurrection"

"We'd never do that, no matter what," Sean was aghast.

"Yes, but they can't be sure of that. After what these commanders have seen here, I'm sure they will be only too pleased to comply and I'm sure their troops will too. We've been moni-

toring their telex connections, so the first thing
we do is send telexes from the commanders to
their farms ordering their men to stand down.
Secondly, we know their radio frequencies
and so we can follow up the telexes by their
commanders radioing them to say Skorzeny
has capitulated and that they will be returning
shortly. Then finally, we send each one of the
commanders back to their farms in their Mercedes chariots and with a personal Irish Ranger
escort to enforce their surrender".

Sean and Chink looked at each, amazed. "It's
audacious but, Christ almighty, bloody right."
They chimed.

"Simple, easy and quick to implement, said
Sean, "I'll get right on to it," and he went off to
issue the necessary instructions. "You really
are a bloody genius Peter," Chink slapped him
on the back. "You've probably just saved a great
many lives".

-

The three Nazis heard the sounds and felt the
shock waves of the shells exploding above
them plus muffled small arms fire. Being an ex-
Nazi policeman, Menten was used to being the
hunter, not the hunted - used to inflicting pain
on others, but no experience of the stress and

strain of combat conditions. He was near to panic.

But the noise of battle pumped adrenaline into Skorzeny. Coughing and choking with the dust that now filled the cellar, *"Schnell*, no time to lose," he shouted, stepping forward and shining the torch into the hole exposed by the secret wine rack door. They could now see stone steps leading into a black abyss. "Inside! We have run out of options; once we are in, I will close the door."

"But what's down there? I don't want to be buried alive. Where does it go?" Menten was shaking with fear – traumatised.

"You gutless cretin," Otto drew his Luger and aimed it at him. He had never liked the Gestapo and was of two minds to shoot him. Menten backed away, cowering in the opposite corner of the cellar, a broken snivelling wreck.

"Leave him Otto", Josef grasped Skorzeny's arm, "leave him to be caught by that Irish rabble. A bullet is too good for *der Schweinehund.*"

Mengele was right - quicker on their own, thought Otto. and Menten would probably end up at the end of rope anyway for his war crimes. He holstered his gun and whispered to Josef.

"That Dutch bastard will tell the enemy how we escaped, in fact, I hope he does. I'll set a booby trap for anyone chasing us. It will seal the entrance and with any luck kill *das Arschloch*."

Otto handed the torch to Josef and told him to lead the way. Unlike Menten, Josef had complete faith in his friend, having known him for more than twenty years. But he was puzzled. How big was this cavern? What would happen to them when the entrance was sealed? Nevertheless, he picked up the briefcase, and with the torch illuminating the way, started down the steps followed by his *Obersturmbannführer*, who grabbed a handle and heaved the door shut behind the them. Menten was still too traumatised to even notice.

The air was thick with dust, disturbed by the explosions above. Once Otto had armed the boobytrap, they started making their way along what Josef realised was a passageway. He was bursting with more questions – how long was this tunnel? where were they going? what was the plan? But again, he said nothing, relying on the leadership of Skorzeny. The height of the tunnel was such that they had to bend low. For Skorzeny, It was like walking through a fog. Even with the torch, visibility was no more than two metres. Cobwebs, lumps of rubble from its roof and the thick choking dust, made the going gruelling. At one stage a large piece of roof had collapsed leaving only just enough room for them to squeeze through. After that, the going became easier and they were able to move along faster. The sounds of gunfire quickly faded until the only sounds were their crunching boots, and laboured breathing echoing around them. After what seemed like hours, but actually no more than 30 minutes, the passageway ended with another flight of steps. "Stand aside my friend, give me the torch." Otto squeezed past Josef and, with him following, hurried up to the top, grabbed a handle and hauled back a floor to ceiling sliding door. As they gasped in the fresh air, the torch light revealed a battered old truck loaded with what looked like a pile of rubbish. "That", pronounced Otto, "is the means of our escape."

CHAPTER 45

All firing had ceased when Sean's mobile radio squawked. "Butler here sir. All enemy resistance extinguished. Clear to send in medics. Dead bodies all over the place. None of our men wounded, but enemy casualties around 40, some very severe. Went into house. Found remains of a fire with three charred bodies. Looks like a suicide pact. Heard noises in cellar. Threw down stun grenade. Went down and took one prisoner – can't make any sense of his blathering –some foreign language - over."

"Sure that's a fine job Captain, well done. Secure the site. Will send in blood wagons and medics. Any news ref our man – over."

"Interrogation centre in ruins. Found one Nazi there, dead; and a civilian, unconsciousness and severely wounded. Might be your man – over."

Sean looked at Chink. "If it's that young British officer, we'll tell the medics to give him priority. Do you think the bodies in the house are Skorzeny and his friends? Should we be goin' in to check?"

"Not now Sean, the urgent priority is sorting out these farm commanders. We can check the bodies later; they won't be going anywhere soon. However, their prisoner might know something. It might even be Skorzeny. Tell Butler to bring him here.

Ten minutes later, just as Sean and Chink were off to give their ultimatum to the farm commanders, Butler and two of his rangers arrived half carrying, half dragging the individual they'd found in the cellar. His clothes, face and hair were covered in filth and brick dust; half unconscious from the effects of the stun grenade.

Sean and Chink looked at the bedraggled heap Infront of them. It couldn't be Skorzeny, Chink thought, the man was too short; it could be anyone. Chink stepped closer and roughly wiped the prisoner's face with his handkerchief. Then he recognised him. It was that ex-SS Nazi criminal, Pieter Menten. One of the evil bunch who'd been at the Martinstown meeting Chink attended. Yet another who'd been given sanctuary in Ireland. MI6 feedback had detailed the bloody atrocities Menten inflicted on the Poles – thousands murdered in and around Cracow. And Chink was sure that wasn't his only crime against humanity.

"Well, well, Pieter Menten." Menten's head lifted on hearing his name. His face a mix of fear and confusion as he stared at Chink. "I don't know if you've met this scumbag before Sean," Chink said, still keeping his eyes on Menten, "he's one of Skorzeny's close friends; another Nazi war criminal, who sneaked into Ireland. Dutch if my memory serves me right. We should send him straight back to face the music in Holland; I do know he's wanted for war crimes there and in Poland."

Chink's words seemed to jolt Menten out of his trance like state. Still slumped on the floor in front of them, he mumbled weakly, "no, no. Please no. Don't send me back. Skorzeny's no friend of mine. I hate the man." His voice gathered strength as he went on. "He black-mailed me into helping him. He lent me money, money to buy my Waterford estate and threatened to…"

But Chink cut him off. "That's rot, plain bloody rot, Menten. I was at the meeting with you and Otto. You seemed very pally with him then. Just tell us where Otto is and we may think kindly towards you."

"I can show you; I can show you, but please,

please, promise not to send me back to Holland. He's hiding in a cave behind the wine rack in the cellar of the house. I saw him go in there with Mengele."

"We saw the wine rack." Butler confirmed, "it was wall to wall bottles before our stun grenade popped a few corks."

"Thank you, Captain," said Sean, "Go back and see if you can find anything behind the racking. We'll join you and take a look for ourselves once we've sorted out these farm fellers. Where's Kesselring? I'd like him with us too".

"Last time I saw him, he was with me watching the line of prisoners, looking for more fanatics like Fritz Suhren", replied Chink. "I'll go and find him and have a word with Folens too. He could have a word with the estate agent he used to find Martinstown for Skorzeny and ask him if there was mention of a cave somewhere in the cellar".

Folens was only too eager to help. Although late into the evening, he said he would get hold of the agent and tell him that the head of the Irish army needed to know if there was anything on the plans of Martinstown that showed a cave.

As Folens departed to find a military landline,

Chink found Kesselring and together caught up
with the others. The farm commanders were
sitting, handcuffed with their ankles bound
to the legs of their chairs, and surrounded by
heavily armed Rangers. From where they sat,
they could see the last of the slow-moving line
of Skorzeny's men making their way into the
barbed wire enclosure, crushed and no longer
the crack troops of 24 hours earlier - stunned
and dejected by the dramatic turn of events.

"Would you like to be putting our proposition
to this lot, or would you like me to?" asked Sean.

"You do it Sean," Chink replied, "And perhaps
you *Feldmarschall*, could translate, to reinforce
the message." Kesselring nodded. It took little
time explaining the options facing the commanders, they either complied or would be shot
there and then. All but one were eager to agree.
They'd seen the dream of a new Reich evaporate
in front of their eyes. That was all but Martin
Weiss. Defiance burned in his eyes. "We do
what you demand, and then what? You shoot
us anyway."

Sean was about to assure him that the Irish
weren't ruthless maniacs like the Nazis, when
one of the other commanders interrupted him.
"Weiss is not like us," "he's Gestapo. We are
professional soldiers, he's a sadist, a wanted war

criminal."

"Shut your face, *fotze gesicht*" Weiss snarled at the speaker.

"Jew hunter! You judge the Irish by your own standards, you scum *Abschaum der Welt*" another snapped back.

"Quiet! silence!" Sean ordered, "There'll be time enough for recriminations, we'll be interrogating you all later. Right now, you'll be getting on the radio to your troops at the farms and ordering them to lay down their arm, the *blitzkrieg* is over. You tell them you will be returning soon with an Irish army escort to explain the situation in more detail. You'll have *Feldmarschall* Kesselring with you while you broadcast, so you better stick to the script, eh *Feldmarschall* ." Kesselring nodded.

As they went, Weiss mumbled, "I never said I wouldn't comply" his arrogance evaporating.

While the farm commanders were broadcasting to their farms, Sean and Chink talked through the best strategy for dealing with the soldiers at the farms. "We're going to find a mixed bunch at the farm, some Irish, some British, Germans, French and others - all bloody fascists. Perhaps the simplest and quickest solution would be to obliterate them all - bomb the hell out of them," Chink's suggestion was tongue in cheek. "And I'm sure the RAF would be happy to help too"

"You can't be serious Chink. If we start bombing along the border, particularly if the RAF gets involved, the whole world will think civil war has erupted all over again."

"I was being flippant Sean, but what else can we do? We're telling them to lay down their arms and wait for us like naughty boys until we pick them up. If I was one of them, I wouldn't wait - I'd scarper."

They both sat facing each other mulling over the problem. Sean broke the silence. "You are probably right Chink, I'd do the same if I was in one of the farms, and a few will slip through the net, but our President, de Valera himself, has told us to keep as low a profile as possible, and so far, we've done that. Our shindig here would have come as no surprise to the locals, they're used to the explosions and gunfire with the army exercises on the Curragh, but it wouldn't be the same with the farms. I see no alternative but to send our lads to bring them in, farm by farm. So, we've got to keep it that way"

They continued to discuss the options. From Otto's Shamrock *Blitzkrieg* document, they knew how many men were at each farm. The most were at the Corkan island farm; seventy-eight there and around forty at each of the other farms. A total of almost 300 men.

"I'll get Captain Butler back here to organise bringing them in from the farms for interrogation," said Sean. "We've plenty of trucks over at the Curragh training depot for him to use.

"I'll stay out of it Sean, it's your party, but I would suggest a demolition specialist goes with your men to destroy whatever guns and armaments they find. We don't want them falling into the hands of the IRA do we."

"You can be sure nothing will be going to the IRA Chink, but from what I've seen and from what you have told me, we might be able to use some of Skorzeny's military hardware and ammunition for ourselves - or even sell some to the Brits. "He added with the smile.

When Butler came back from Martinstown, Sean briefed him on what to expect at the farms. He told him that the surrendering SS soldiers had been ordered to stack all their weapons in piles and when their Nazi commanders arrived with their Irish escorts, they should be assembled, standing together in whatever open space they had available. He said that once the escort

officers were satisfied that all the Nazis were dis-
armed and accounted for, they should put them
on the empty trucks they'd arrived with and
brought under guard to Martinstown for interrogation. And as a final word, Sean told Butler to
tell his officers that they had his blessing to take
what action they thought necessary if they met
any resistance.

It took Captain Butler a little under four hours
to organise the transport and men, and have
them assembled ready to leave. He'd managed
to find sixteen troop carriers, some from the
Curragh and some from Cathar barracks in Dublin. He'd organised them into five groups, four
with three carriers and one with four carriers
for the extra prisoners from the Corkan Island
farm. Each group had twenty-five Irish Rangers
commanded by a subaltern, who would go in
the Nazi farm commander's Mercedes with two
of the Rangers, the rest in the lead carrier.

The convoys set off to their allocated farms,
and to make sure there was no trouble with
Martin Weiss at his Dundalk farm, Kesselring
went with him.   The fight to crush the Nazi
threat was virtually over, but there was still the
question of Skorzeny and his henchman Josef
Mengele. Where were they? They had tried to
fool everyone with the charade of a funeral pyre

in the dining room, but Pieter Menten had exposed that for what it was.

If what Menten had said was true, Otto was hiding in a cave behind the wine rack. In the meantime, Folens had been able to get hold of the estate agent, a Mr. O'Toole, on the field telephone. Disgruntled at first, O'Toole had become keen to assist when Folens told him the Irish military needed his help urgently on a national security matter. They wanted to know the layout of Martinstown house and whether there was a secret room or cave off the cellar. Naturally, the agent wanted to know why, but security was security and he didn't pry.

After a lot of blarney about having a great memory and what a charming man indeed the German colonel was, O'Toole hadn't been able to recall anything on the plans about a cave. But he'd told Folens what he'd told Skorzeny; that the original owner of Martinstown, Augustus FitzGerald, the 3rd Duke of Leinster, Master of the Grand Lodge of Ireland, had built his own Freemasonry Lodge on the perimeter of the estate with its own private road for fellow masonic visitors. And indeed, there were tales, just tales he'd insisted, about how the Duke had built a secret underground passage from the house to the Lodge so that he could attend all the private ceremonies in his fine regalia without having to parade himself in front of all the hoi polloi.

O'Toole was in full flood, but Folens had heard enough. As they were mulling over their next move, Chink and Sean were interrupted by an excited Folens. "O'Toole, the agent. He says rumour has it there's a tunnel from the cellar to a building on the edge of the estate. He said it was built years ago. A masonic lodge, he said." Chink and Sean looked at each other. "Did O'Toole tell Skorzeny about this - er - rumour?" Sean asked. "

"He says he did," said Folens. He remembered talking about it and how Skorzeny had become quite animated, deriding the masonic movement. But I think I know the old lodge building he was talking about -I believe it is now a dilapidated barn about a mile to the West. If the tunnel exists, Skorzeny would have found it and ..."

"Menten told us he saw Skorzeny and Mengele enter some cave or void through a door in the wine rack" said Chink cutting Folens to silence. "OK. Let's assume the tunnel exists. Trying to follow them through that route will not only take time, but knowing Otto, he would have set traps for whoever follows along the way. We should keep our guards at the cellar entrance and hare over to the other end with a few of your men Sean. If we're quick, we might just catch the buggers. You lead the way Folens." They ran out and commandeered two jeeps, Chink, Folens and Sean in the lead one, followed by the second with four fully armed Rangers. They drove as fast as they could over the fields towards the derelict building pointed out by Folens. As they skidded to a stop, the Rangers leapt from their jeep and ran towards the open barn doors.   The inside looked anything but derelict. They saw an open doorway, which they assumed was the other end of the tunnel, but apart from an old work bench and storage shelve, the place was empty. Then, glistening in the headlights of the jeeps, they saw fresh tyre tracks leading from the barn along a muddy track away from the estate. "Sod it all, we've missed the buggers." Chink exclaimed .

"Don't you be worrying ol' friend. I've got barriers set up on all the exits out of Martinstown, including this track. My men will have stopped them", said Sean.

Saying that, they leapt back into their jeeps and sped down the track and onto a lane to the road block. A temporary red and white bar spread across the road with a large round stop sign in the middle. A corporal and one of the guards were leaning against it and three other soldiers were seated at a table in a tent playing cards.

There was an instant transformation when they realised who their visitors were. The corporal quickly marched over to Sean, stood stiffly to attention and saluted. " Sir!"

"We're chasing the feckin ringleader of these Nazis. They're on the run," answered Sean, "anyone through here recently?"

"No sir, it's been quiet as the grave here it has. Mind you sir, we've been watching the fireworks over at the farm, a fine display if I may say so sir. Is it all over now?"

"We certainly hope so corporal. We just need to catch the bastard behind the uprising. Your orders were to block anyone coming down this lane - are you quite sure nobody's come down here? "

"Well sir, yes and no," the corporal looked embarrassed and lost for words. "Ah sir," he stuttered - actually, when I ses nobody, that's one hundred percent true, but not quite accurate if you're countin' feckin' tinkers. Not so long ago, we did have a couple of them filthy feckers in one of them old beat-up trucks they have, pass by. You could see they'd been up to no good with all the junk they'd thieved in the back. Sure, I'd 'ave copped them sir, but we didn't want them cloggin' up the road with all their shite, so we sent them packin' pretty quick, we did sir."

"Chink and Sean looked at each other. They both knew for certain that the 'fecking tinkers', as the Corporal called them, must have been Skorzeny and Mengele. The corporal and his men had unwittingly let the king rats through the road block.

Sean fumed. He told the corporal that he and his men had been duped. They had let the ringleaders of the coup escape. They would be dealt with later, charged with disobeying orders. Meanwhile, Skorzeny and Mengele could be anywhere - the tunnel, truck, the tinker disguise showed Skorzeny had a prepared escape route. They would be well on their way back to some safe haven. The only option was to put out an immediate alert to the Garda, the British police, RUC and Interpol.

The Nazi Shamrock *blitzkrieg* had been well and truly squashed - no longer a threat to Ireland or indeed Europe. But while people like Skorzeny and his other Nazi extremists existed, insurrections, coups, and revolutions would continue to reek havoc around the globe.

EPILOGUE

For Otto Skorzeny, the Shamrock *Blitzkrieg* was a lost campaign, not a defeat for the Nazi cause. After their escape from Martinstown, he and Mengele made their way to Corkan Island well before Sturmbannführer Weiss arrived with Kesselring and their Irish Ranger escort. They were met by confusion. The SS soldiers, obeying the orders they received from their commander, were dumping all their weapons in the farm yard.

The fugitives were ignored as they drove their truck to the airfield, where they took the Fieseler Fi 156 Storch and flew to the Spanish military base Zaragoza. After which, Mengele went to South America and Skorzeny to the Nazi community on the Costa Blanca in Spain. He and fellow fascist friends would continue their fight for national socialism for as long as they lived.

After a week-long vacation fishing on the loughs of Bellamont and swapping old war stories with his host, Chink, Feldmarschall Kesselring returned to Bad Nauheim in Germany to continue writing his memoirs.

Chink continued to work for the Irish government in an advisory capacity as he did for the IRA. He continued to be in touch with his old army friends in England and his work for MI6 went into even deeper cover. Owen remained at Bellamont as the family butler, handyman and friend. He too continued to work for MI5.

After novice monk Lynskey left Our Lady of Bethlehem Monastery he worked his way up the IRA organisation and became a member of their Army Council. He was disappeared during a violent internal IRA feud in Belfast in August 1972.

Dick White and Roger Hollis maintained their squabbling and distrust each other, but in a rare moment of togetherness, they told the Prime Minister about Profumo's affair with Christine Keeler. The ensuing public scandal dealt a fatal blow to Macmillan's premiership forcing him to step down in favour of Sir Alec Douglas-Home.

Throughout the years into the 1990s, lives continued to be lost on both sides of the bloody conflict as the IRA continued its war for a reunited Ireland. It finally ended in 1998 with the signing of The Good Friday Agreement.

Through this agreement, the desire for one Ireland was acknowledged by both the British and Irish Governments, but only with the consent of a majority of the people of Northern Ireland.

More information about Chink, Skorzeny, Peter Flemming and many of the other characters in this book, can be found through Wikipedia, YouTube, and searches on Google.

AUTHOR'S NOTES

I've written 'Rat Trap' to give myself some feeling of closure over the unexplained death of my brother. It happened over 60 years ago but I still feel sadness and frustration at not knowing what actually happened to him. Chris joined the army at 18 and became a demolition specialist, taking part in SAS missions in Northern Yemen, Malaya, and Borneo. Suddenly, with no warning, he threw away his army career, gave away all his worldly possessions, and became a Cistercian Monk. Nobody could understand why, but it was his life, and eventually, we all had to accept the new Brother Christopher.

Eighteen months after he joined Our Lady of Bethlehem Monastery in Ballymena, my parents received a call from the Novice Master. It was devastating news. He told them their son had taken his own life. He explained that Chris had become mentally sick. He had been taken across the border to St John of God hospital in Southern Ireland on the outskirts of Dublin for psychiatric treatment. He said that whilst there, Chris had taken an overdose of pills. He said that despite the frantic efforts of the hospital staff, he had passed away.

The news crucified my parents - utterly devastating us all, so shocking, so unbelievable.

I accompanied my parents to his funeral. We wanted to see his body and say our goodbyes for one last time. But the Novice Master from the Ballymena monastery, said Chris was in an awful mess and it was far better to remember him as the person he was. To this day, I remember his words - '*For sure, God bless his soul, our blessed Brother Christopher is now at peace in heaven with our Lord Jesus*'.

At the time, we were all too heartbroken and grief-stricken to argue or insist on seeing him. He was buried in Deans Grange Cemetery, Dún Laoghaire on the outskirts of Dublin. But the novice master's words sowed seeds of doubt in my mind.

What was the real reason why he didn't want us to see the body?

If Chris had only taken an overdose, why would his body be too terrible for us to see?

Had he really taken his own life. Then I found out about Joe Lynskey. Was he the only pro IRA monk or were there several?

If they had known my brother's background, a British Royal Engineers' demolition specialist, they might well have thought he was a spy. They then would have had no option but to interrogate then murder him. Perhaps that's the true reason why the Novice Master didn't want us to see his body.

The jury is out.

Made in the USA
Columbia, SC
19 February 2022

55981444R00293